THE WHITE SEA BIRD

DAVID BEATY

The White Sea Bird

WILLIAM MORROW AND COMPANY, INC.
New York 1980

Library of Congress Cataloging in Publication Data

Beaty, David.
    The white sea bird.

    1. World War, 1939-1945—Fiction.   I. Title.
PZ3.B38073Wh   1980   [PR6003.E264]   823'.9'14   79-25789
ISBN 0-688-03615-5

Printed in the United States of America

First U.S. Edition

1 2 3 4 5 6 7 8 9 10

For B, as always

All characters and incidents in this novel are
entirely fictitious

ONE

"THE *Groningen*? Impossible!"

The Intelligence Officer spoke with the curt clipped certainty that comes naturally after serving a lifetime in the Royal Navy. Lieutenant-Commander Brackenbury had seen action at Jutland and now had been recalled off the beach to play his part yet again—this time at the Coastal Command Station at Kilcreggan on the north-east tip of Scotland, briefing Liberator crews before they took off to attack ships and U-boats off the Norwegian coast and de-briefing them on their return. A solitary dark-blue figure amongst all this light blue, he could be seen sipping pink gin on his own at Mess parties, focusing pale eyes on the beer-drinkers banging their tankards on the counter in time to rude Air Force ballads, with a look of tight-lipped disapproval.

That same look he now directed on Guy Strickland and the eight other members of his crew, sitting around his office in their flying clothes nursing hot mugs of cocoa after a thirteen-hour stopper patrol outside the fjords to the Arctic Circle.

"Why?"

The scar just below Strickland's left eye showed up white as it always did when he was angry. The gold flecks in his grey eyes glinted under the neons. What rank he was, indeed whether Army, Navy, Air Force or fox-hunting man was not possible to identify, for he wore a soldier's khaki battledress blouse over an immaculate white sweater, a cream silk scarf round his neck clipped with a silver hunting-pin, a hat with no badge on it, its crown black with oil, pushed to the back of his fair-haired head. One blue barathea leg sheathed in a brown leather riding boot was crossed over its twin.

"Because the *Groningen* was sighted at eleven o'clock this morning, Squadron-Leader Strickland." Brackenbury picked

1

up a ruler and pointed to a green lozenge shape in the centre of a large map of the Atlantic on the wall beside him. "*Here!*"

From his chair in the outside ring of the circle—furthest from the Intelligence Officer's table, nearest the door—Pilot Officer Peter Irvine dipped his nose deeper into his mug for the last sweet dregs of cocoa and let his mind bask in the warm prospect of bed. It was two in the morning, long past the time when he should be tucked up and asleep in Room Number 27. He had only just joined 507 Squadron after General Reconnaissance School and a Liberator conversion course at the Operational Training Unit, and as the youngest and greenest crew-member, it was unlikely that he would be called upon for his opinion in the argument that was developing between the Intelligence Officer and his aircraft captain.

Strickland got up from his seat, slowly walked over to the map, bent down and microscopically examined the lozenge that Brackenbury was still pointing at.

"What've you got there? A lime jujube?"

"HM submarine *Seawolf*."

"So *that's* what it is!" Strickland began winding up the heavy Omega astro-watch on his wrist. "Positive identification through a periscope is always difficult."

Peter Irvine put his empty mug down on the floor and lit a cigarette. Strickland had no need of his support. He was well able to look after himself—and everybody else for that matter. Irvine had been extremely glad to discover that he was flying as second pilot to an experienced captain who had already completed two operational tours and had the DSO and the DFC. Of the thirty-one members of his elementary flying training course, already six were missing and eleven were dead, including Pensford, the oldest and best of the lot of them, killed on his first operation when his captain ran through the hedge in a Whitley after landing at his home aerodrome.

"The *Groningen* was positively identified."

"Why didn't they torpedo her then?"

"Too far away," Brackenbury snapped back. "Come to that why didn't you drop your load?"

"What the hell good would depth charges be against the *Groningen*'s armour-plated sides?"

"But it *wasn't* the *Groningen*."

2

"It *was* the *Groningen* all right . . . tucked in under the cliff."

Lee, Garland, Quennell—all gone, with their operational score still in single figures. Rodway had collected twenty-nine before getting the chop and that was a useful contribution. Peter Irvine was twenty-two, three years out of Bradfield Grammar School. For some obscure reason—he had never been good at cricket, his top score in one innings was only twelve—he viewed the war like some gigantic cricket match where each operation was a run to your side. A century would be nice, but better still to remain *not out* till the end of play.

"Couldn't have been."

"I'm right . . . I *know* I'm right!"

Irvine had once named his History and English notebooks after warships—inking in their silhouettes on the cardboard covers—hoping that such a fleet would fight and win the Higher School Certificate for him. They hadn't done too badly, and three years in a bank afterwards had not dimmed his grateful memory of them. But they were British—the battleship *King George V*, the aircraft carrier *Ark Royal*, the cruiser *Marlborough*. His knowledge of German warships was small, and as for the *Groningen*, how the hell could anyone tell her from any other large merchantman?

"Pity you didn't get a photograph."

"Not a hope in that light. But I saw her cruiser stern quite clearly . . ."

A snub-nosed smudge, cobwebbed in trailing cloud, tucked in under the mountains at the far end of Falstand Fjord—that was all that Irvine had seen. The Liberator was bucking in heavy turbulence, and rain was singing in through the open side windows. Above the bleat of the engines, Strickland's voice had shouted out that one word, *Groningen*.

"Unless the *Groningen*'s speed is—" Brackenbury had seized a pair of large dividers and was using them like stilts across the Atlantic map from the lozenge shape to the serrated edges of North Norway "—325 knots, she couldn't have been at latitude 46 North, longitude 38 West at eleven this morning and in Falstand Fjord at three forty-five this afternoon."

"*Seawolf*'s got it wrong."

"Commander Crabbet? He knows the *Groningen* like—"

The back of his hand, wasn't that the expression? Irvine

3

inhaled deeply and closed his eyes. *Groningen. Groningen . . .* the bloody name was ringing in his ears like a carillon of bells. Wasn't it Mary Tudor who had *Calais* engraved on her heart? If this went on, *Groningen* would certainly be engraved on his heart when all he wanted was a bit of peace and quiet so he could go to sleep.

He stubbed out his cigarette and looked across at his three room-mates—the round-faced Navigator Wardle, the Radio Operator Railton, and Flight-Lieutenant Cargill, the Squadron Gunnery Leader—wondering if they, too, were itching for their beds. But they were leaning forward like greyhounds in the slips—now where had he heard those words before?—supporting the Skipper.

". . . *Groningen* . . ."

Irvine would have liked to have done the same. But this was only his third operational trip—Irvine 3 not out—and he was still too shy to open his mouth. As Flight-Commander in charge of Training, Strickland was either in his office or up on check flights. He had introduced himself to Irvine at the Mess bar, bought him half a pint of bitter, advised him he was replacing a man called Gooch who was "no good so we sent him back for further training", told him that he expected his second pilot to be able to do every job in the aircraft—navigate, man the wireless, work the Gee* and radar, bomb-aim, operate the turrets, fire the guns. As a result, Irvine had spent most of his waking hours working up on these crafts with the help of the rest of the crew. Cargill was Australian, Wardle was Canadian, Railton came from Birmingham. Of the four Sergeants, Jenks, the Engineer, was a cockney, Mackenzie was, naturally, a Scot, Oakroyd the Rear Gunner was broad Yorkshire, and O'Connor, their king-pin Radar Operator, was Irish. But they all shared one thing in common. As they instructed him in their jobs, each had told him, "You're lucky to be flying with Strickland."

". . . *Groningen* . . ."

Tick-*tock*, tick-*tock*. Groningen-*Groningen*.

He liked them all. They were friendly. They were gen men at their jobs. He was nervous that *he* was the least competent. On the first operation, he had been all thumbs. The second trip was a low-level night patrol in the Skagerrak, shadowed by a swarm

* Hyperbolic radio navigation system.

4

of German night-fighters clearly visible on the radar screen. They were safe—so long as they kept at fifty feet on the radio altimeter and so long as they managed to avoid crashing into the sea. Added to that, Strickland would not let him use the marvellous Minneapolis-Honeywell automatic pilot but made him hand fly the aircraft. Twice the Front Gunner had yelled that sea-water was practically coming in the turret, as the heavy Liberator wallowed up and down in the darkness, while Irvine struggled to keep her steady.

On this last operation, Strickland had again made him do the flying by hand, which was one of the reasons he was so shagged. Nobody had criticized. There was no gossiping on Strickland's crew. When you heard a microphone click on, you held your breath for something important—a contact on the radar, an Me 110 sighted by the rear turret, the Front Gunner reporting a German motor torpedo boat.

"... *Groningen* ..."

The name was familiar. Irvine had heard it first at General Reconnaissance School, along with *Scharnhorst*, *Gneisenau* and *Graf Spee*. A solitary loner, what in the First World War had been called a Q ship, on the surface apparently a two-funnelled ten-thousand-ton merchantman, but instead of cargo in her holds, she had six 5.9 inch guns hidden behind collapsible bulkheads, a Heinkel seaplane aft, a dozen torpedo tubes in her deck housing, a massive anti-aircraft armament of 75 millimetres, Oerlikons, cannon and multiple pom-poms and her speed was thirty knots. Carrying almost the punch of a cruiser, she was allowed a free hand by Admiral Dönitz, and specialized in slipping amongst Atlantic slow convoys under cover of mist and rain and darkness. Manoeuvring herself into position astern, she would discreetly pick off a couple of stragglers, then just as discreetly she would disappear. She was commanded by a veteran Merchant Marine officer called Captain Leitzen.

"If it wasn't the *Groningen*," Strickland asked, "what was it?"

A mirage made of ectoplasm, a ghost ship, a rock, a wreck, part of a mountain—all such possibilities clearly flitted through Brackenbury's mind, but all he said was, "That's something we should very much like to know."

Strickland flicked a speck of dust off the knife-edge crease of his trousers, got up, and said quite simply, "Then you shall."

The meaning of those three words did not immediately strike home, even to the crew, who had also got to their feet.

Brackenbury glanced up from finishing off his debriefing report to wish them goodnight.

"Oh, we're not off to bed."

Already halfway through the door, Irvine felt his heart lurch.

"Bar's closed, old boy," Brackenbury said. "No party tonight."

"We'll be having our own party." Suddenly Strickland was issuing short crisp orders. "Jenks, check Sugar's refuelled." Passing Irvine, he led the way out of the Intelligence Office into the Operations Room and said to the Controller on watch, "We're going back to Falstand Fjord."

"Why?"

"Spot of unfinished business."

"What?"

"I say I saw the *Groningen* in there. The Navy say I didn't."

"Couldn't it wait?"

"No, it can't."

"You're not serious?"

"Of course I am!"

"But you've only just come back! Who's next on the Mayfly?" The Controller peered down at 507 Battle Order. "Tallack. I'll call him out."

"No."

"For God's sake—"

"The Navy is asking to see the holes in the hands. Get hold of the SASO* for me, would you?" Then Strickland called through to the duty Meteorological Officer, "Tom, could you rustle up a new forecast? Arriving over Falstand at dawn." And to the WAAF clerk, "Ring the Mess, Dinah, for two big thermoses of coffee. Very black and very hot. And if they can whip up some sandwiches, we'd be obliged. *Not* corned beef." All at once he seemed conscious of Irvine's dismayed face. "You're in luck, Peter! Two operational trips in one night! And as a bonus, I'll let you do the take off."

Silence fell on the Operations Room. Methodically Wardle began drawing in his track to Falstand on the Mercator chart laid out on the table. The wireless operators and gunners stood

* Senior Air Staff Officer at Group.

6

quite still beside the wall, watching him. Irvine sat under the neon-lighted glare, trying to look busy but actually half asleep.

The red scrambler telephone suddenly shrilled. It was the SASO at Group.

"I'm sure myself it's the *Groningen*, sir. But the Navy swear blind it isn't." Now Strickland was speaking in that relaxed drawl as though it was the most natural thing in the world to take off again on a second operational trip an hour after landing from the first. "We've *got* to know straightaway one way or another. And the weather's too bad for PRU* to get anything. My crew, sir? Like me, they're raring to finish the job . . ."

Were they? Irvine was watching Wardle's face—tired, drawn, set—as carefully he pencilled in two arrowheads on the track he had drawn across the North Sea. Like Railton and Cargill and himself, he was sure, aching only for his little bed in whitepainted Room 27 in the west wing of the Officers' Mess. Yet none of them said anything. Neither did the Sergeants, still leaning against the huge maps on the walls, staring silently at the yellow taped squares of the submarine sanctuaries, the clusters of red pins which were the anti-aircraft gun batteries along the Norwegian coast, and the round white disc marking the position of the Me 109 fighter squadrons at Malstrom aerodrome, just south of Falstand Fjord.

Into the jaws of death, Irvine thought—now where had he heard *that* one? Not Shakespeare this time, but the Charge of the Light Brigade. Why did the cavalry go? Why, ninety years later, was Liberator S Sugar going?

Nobody would question why—but for what reason? If this had been some other crew, surely they would have protested? Garfield's, there would have been a near-mutiny. The only married captain, Flight-Lieutenant Mowbray, he wouldn't have dreamed of doing it. Even in the Wing-Commander's crew, there would have been grumbles, and they'd have hauled out the next crew on the Mayfly to go. Why then did nobody say anything to Strickland? Why didn't he himself get up—after all, he was second in command—and say simply: "Honestly, Skipper, we're all too tired."

His mouth had gone so suddenly dry, he doubted whether

* Photographic Reconnaissance Unit, usually equipped with Spitfires or Mosquitoes.

7

he'd be able to get the words out anyway. But what if he did? Wouldn't Strickland simply put Jenks, the Engineer, whom he had taught to do elementary flying, into the right-hand seat? And wouldn't he, Irvine, simply follow in the footsteps of Gooch, his predecessor, to that strange limboland where second pilots receive "more training"?

And nobody would question it, because it was Strickland. Strickland's decision, Strickland had said it was necessary.

Even now, with Strickland for a few minutes out of the centre of them, it was cold. There was a shiver under the crew's feet. Ever so slightly, their world shook. Yet as soon as he came over, walking slowly, hands in his pockets, nothing apparent of the *Gauleiter* about him, no orders, no bullshit, his grey eyes alert—the whole atmosphere warmed, the air became electric. The tiredness fell off. Only the excitement and the challenge remained.

"Ready, Jack?"

Wardle nodded, rolled up the chart and stowed his instruments back into his green canvas bag.

"Then let's go!"

Nobody seemed to mind now, though outside it was pouring with rain. The wheels of the lorry hissed round the perimeter track. Winkled out of a gloomy wet visibility by the hooded headlights, S Sugar materialized, crouched on her thick short oleo legs like a rhinoceros, the .5 guns in her front turret turned up into a sharp horn.

"Everything on there top line, Chiefie?" Strickland asked the Maintenance Sergeant.

"All set, sir."

Out of the fuselage through the open bomb-doors came armourers and fitters. The thick hoses were lifted off the wings as the filler caps on the petrol tanks were replaced. The bowsers moved away.

Humping their parachutes, dipping their heads to get under the bomb-doors, lifting their right feet to get onto the catwalk, in went the crew.

Irvine got in. He felt the Liberator lift up her nose as Oakroyd, pulling on his long leather gauntlets, went clumping down to the rear turret. Standing for a moment in the tiny steel cathedral of the bomb-bay, Irvine looked up at the duralumin pillars, the

8

arched silver ceiling. He could smell that well-known aircraft smell—metal, oil, rubber, the sweet scent of petrol, and the curious brass reek of belted ammunition. Guns everywhere: two .5s in the nose, two in the top turret, two on the beam, two in the tail. He was reassured to see the long canisters of depth charges stacked one on top of the other. If Strickland had been bent on attack, the load would have been changed to bombs. The trip was just as Strickland said: simply a reconnaissance to identify for certain that mysterious smudge in Falstand Fjord.

"Got the camera, Peter?"

Strickland was coming up behind him.

The RAF photo-reconnaissance camera looked like a cross between an Aldis lamp and a small searchlight: big, cumbersome, heavy and uncomfortable to hold. At GR School, he had been sent off to do "reconnaissances" of the Isle of Man, photographing harbours and Chicken Rock lighthouse, coming back with blurs or blanks mostly, but glad to be back at all, because the Bothas in which they flew had a terrible habit of disappearing into the Irish Sea.

"It's in the Navigator's position, sir."

"Give it a good check over. And keep it cocked by your seat."

"Will do, sir."

He squeezed forward into the Navigator's compartment behind the front turret. Already Wardle was tucked up snugly, his chart spread out on the table, his angle-poise lamp on, his black bubble-sextant sitting on top of his astro-navigation tables. Irvine collected the camera, lugging it up with his parachute onto the flight deck, past O'Connor staring through the rubber visor at the radar, past Railton sitting at the Marconi, its green eye twinkling as he tuned. He parked his parachute into the seat well, put the camera on the floor, pulled his seat forward, strapped himself up, and began the second pilot's checks.

The familiar nature of his checks—winding on and off full rudder and elevator trim, adjusting the throttle nut, checking the magneto switches were off and the turbo-superchargers out, calling up the crew one by one in their places on the intercom—fitted snugly over him like a warm overcoat. By the time Strickland had settled in his seat and strapped himself in Irvine

9

could say calmly, "All checks complete! Ready for starting engines, sir!"

"Then start Number Three!"

"Energizing Three!"

The starboard inner propeller creaked round like a hurdy-gurdy and burst into life. Number Four chimed in, followed by Number Two and finally the port outer, Number One. A real symphony of noise had started. S Sugar began rocking gently on her oleo legs, dancing against the chocks.

"Cleared to taxi, sir."

"Then taxi! *You're* doing the take-off!"

"Yes, sir." He opened up his side window, waved his right arm to and fro. "Chocks away!" Then he stood on the foot-brakes, unlocking them.

Nodding her nose, brakes squealing like stuck pigs, S Sugar ambled round the perimeter track towards Runway 09. Ahead of him, Irvine saw the two .5s moving left and right and up and down as Cargill tested the hydraulic operation of the front turret. A fully loaded night Liberator take-off was quite a dicey business, and most captains allowed their Front Gunners—as being the most vulnerable if they crashed—to come up on the flight deck and stand behind the Engineer. Not Strickland. All posts manned at all times. Just after take-off, there might be a German night-fighter waiting.

The twin parallel lines of the flarepath came swivelling round to meet them, the butter-coloured lights muzzy in the wet darkness. Irvine lined her up in the centre, put on the brakes, called for the Before Take-off Check.

"Revolutions?"

"Fully fine."

"Superchargers?"

"In."

"Mixture?"

"Rich."

"Controls?"

"Free."

"Flaps?"

"Up."

Now Irvine put his left hand on the four throttle levers. Excitement had taken over from all other feelings, concentrating his mind on this one single difficult operation. He had never before done a fully laden night take-off, and he could feel his heart hammering.

He moved the throttles fully forward. The roar of the four Pratt and Whitney Twin Wasps deafened him. Every plate in S Sugar began shivering as though in a palsy.

He released the brakes. As the Liberator began moving, the Engineer grabbed the four throttles and held them hard against the stops.

Sixty-five thousand pounds of metal, petrol, ammunition and men lumbered forward into the night. Infinitely slowly, the runway lights slipped past them. Infinitely slowly, the needle moved round the dial of the airspeed indicator.

"Seventy-five knots!"

Strickland was reminding him to lift the nosewheel off the ground. He moved the stick back too far—his first mistake. He felt Strickland correct on his own set of controls.

They were running out of runway lights now. Four, three, two—

The wheels began banging heavily up and down on the oleo legs, as though trying to jump but failing. There was no life there, nothing but a kind of metallic flabbiness. S Sugar seemed stuck to the ground.

And here came the threshold lights like a horizontal red sword across the runway to cut them to ribbons! And beyond no white lights, no yellow lights, no red lights—nothing but darkness.

He pulled back with all his might.

Groaning, gasping, shaking, S Sugar inched off the ground into the night.

"Gear up!"

Wallowing in the wet air, the aircraft began sluggishly climbing. Surreptitiously Irvine wiped the sweat off his forehead. The Liberator take-off was notorious, but until you had done one at full load, you had no idea that you had actually to wrench her out of the womb of Mother Earth and up.

"Superchargers out!"

Wardle came up onto the flight deck and laid a chit on the throttle box: *Course 077*. He seemed quite unconcerned. Nobody said *good take-off* or *bad take-off*. Everybody seemed to take it

11

as normal and for granted. The needle on the radio altimeter had moved full travel to 400 feet, and the Kollsmann was inching upwards.

Breathing a sigh of relief, he stretched forward to line up the indices on the Minneapolis-Honeywell automatic pilot.

"No, you don't!" said Strickland. "You need all the instrument flying practice you can get! Take her up to 500 feet and stay there!"

Irvine also needed all his concentration. The green bar of the artificial horizon wavered. The needle between the compass lubberlines wandered. Up and down went the altimeter—above, below, but rarely steady on 500 exactly.

Matters were made worse by the gunners testing their guns. Sudden white tracer flashes in front momentarily blinded him. He heard chatter all round him. The flight deck reeked with the fumes of cordite.

"Front turret . . .OK."

"Rear turret . . . OK."

"Top turret . . . OK."

"Beam guns . . . OK."

Gradually, Irvine steadied the Liberator up. Gradually he balanced the aircraft *exactly* on 077, *exactly* on 500 feet. All his tiredness had gone. So had any fears of flak, of fighters, of mountains, of the *Groningen*. His whole being was bound up in the minute movements of his hands and feet on the control column and the rudders. He was chained to the altimeter and the gyro compass. The numbers 500 and 077 were his only laws, as quietly now, her engines at cruising revolutions murmuring like sewing-machines, S Sugar slipped through the night towards Falstand Fjord.

The minutes changed to hours. Still Strickland did not suggest relieving him. Total silence on the intercom till Wardle called up with a new ETA. "07.15."

"We're early?"

"Yes, sir. Tail-wind. Clearing, too. I saw Betelgeuse just now."

"Dawn is?"

"07.20."

"Just right!"

Now Irvine could see a pale straight streak underlining the horizon ahead—first light. And almost simultaneously O'Connor reported from the radar, "Norwegian coast at forty miles, sir!"

It was then that Strickland relieved him, simply putting up his thumb and saying "Got to get under the radar", and, pushing the stick forward, levelled off just above the sea, the radio altimeter flickering around thirty feet.

The horizon now was *above* their wings. Irvine could actually smell the salt scent of sea-water.

"Can you see Falstand Fjord, Radar?"

"Yes, sir. Three degrees to port."

Suddenly the horizon ahead became a zig-zag black silhouette peaked with silver—the Norwegian mountains. Underneath, the sea turned from dirty black to a dark green flecked with white spume. High above, all the stars had gone out in a cloudless blaze of blue.

"Can you see a lighthouse, Skipper?" Wardle asked.

Strickland leaned forward till his forehead was practically touching the windscreen. "Yes."

"That's Aalstrom. At the entrance to Falstand Fjord."

"Thanks, Jack." He called out to the gunners. "See any fighters?"

"None."

"Good! O'Connor, leave the radar and man the top turret! Jenks, man the beam guns with Mackenzie. Irvine, give me full power when I ask, and hold it on. If we lose an engine, feather* it."

The sea gave way to grey rocks and seaweed. Over to starboard, Irvine could see a row of white wooden houses and fields glistening with recent rain. There was a road winding round the headland and long strings of telephone wires. Cows going through a gate, a man's face looking up from an open doorway.

"Now this is what we're going to do . . ."

It was Strickland's practice to give his crew a minute briefing before carrying out any operational manoeuvre, to make absolutely certain that they all knew exactly what he expected of them.

". . . *Groningen* is at the far end of the fjord, tucked up against the cliff face, torpedo nets all round her, tail sticking out. You can be damned certain that they'll have Oerlikons, pom-

* Stop the engine with the propeller blades turned sharp into the slipstream to avoid drag.

13

poms and 88s all round her, as well as her own ack-ack armament. I'm going to hug the south shore, getting as close to the ship as I can so as to position Irvine exactly right for his photographs. Get the camera set up."

Reluctantly Irvine picked up the bulky camera from the floor. His minute knowledge of photography told him that in this light, if the sun remained below the mountains, he would need the widest aperture he could get. This he set. As for exposure, they'd be travelling fast so he guessed 1/500th of a second. Then he opened up his side window and propped the camera on the metal sill.

"All set, sir."

He did not feel as confident as his voice sounded. His heart had started hammering again. He was glad of the cold wind from the open window that fanned his hot face.

They were into the fjord now, the sea glassy calm, the air still grey but rapidly lightening. Inches below them, blades of grass, a sandy beach. Inches to starboard a sheer granite rock face.

". . . when they start shooting, I'll drop the depth charges pilot-release. You never know, the splashes might give us some cover. And it'll make us lighter. Then I'll scarper to the left in a split-arse turn out."

The land had flattened here. S Sugar screamed just above a road. Two cars had stopped. A helmeted grey-green figure holding a sub-machine gun began firing.

"They've seen us, Skipper! They're shooting!"

"Then shoot back! Irvine, full power!"

The engine noise surged upwards at the same time as the .5s began chattering. Now ahead of them all at once were great grey puffs of smoke from heavy ack-ack mixing with red and green and white tinsel necklaces lazily stringing across the water.

"Talk about Guy Fawkes night . . ."

But Irvine hardly saw it. He was staring ahead, holding tightly to the camera, all tensed up for the first sight of the ship.

Round a headland now, skidding up on one wing, all plates vibrating, wings practically flapping, trailing silver tracer from all her guns, S Sugar roared onwards. There was a thick curtain of ack-ack now. Guns on the mountain sides were firing down on her.

A 4.5 exploded under her port wing, tilting it to the sky.

14

Irvine could hear cannon-shells tearing into the fabric. Inches above the muzzles of the 88s, S Sugar skimmed over a sandbagged gun emplacement.

"There she is, Skipper!"

There was a violent jerk as Strickland kicked her round to starboard. Ahead Irvine could only see mist and smoke and the flashes of guns. He screwed up his eyes, trying to make out the shape of a ship. But all he could see was a huddle of houses ringed with garlands of flak.

"Railton, open the bomb-doors," Strickland was saying when suddenly, from a gap in the hills to the south-east, stretching out a long straight beam like a searchlight—the sun over the oily water.

Now the greyness and the smoke were shot through with an electric brilliance. Now everything was highlighted—the small wharf, a long warehouse, a railway line with a tiny engine, a lorry park, a line of small boats, and then high above everything else the straight grey and green camouflaged metal cliff of the ship, the two stocky funnels, a thin, tall single mast, the sharp bow tucked deep into the small harbour, the rounded cruiser stern projecting into the fjord.

"*Groningen!*"

Just that one word, spoken softly by Strickland. And then everything seemed to erupt at once. Flak like a multi-coloured bead curtain had come down over the ship. Puffs of heavy ack-ack as thick as clouds in front of them now. A 4.5 shell exploded above them in a blinding flash that sent hot metal rain tinkling down on the fuselage. The starboard inner engine was hit and the windmilling propeller started screaming its head off. With his left hand Irvine punched the red feathering button as Strickland leaned forward and pressed the pilot release for the depth charges.

In that pandemonium, with the aircraft bucking and sliding, deafened by noise, blinded by the continuous magnesium flashes of fire, Irvine still gripped the camera, still had it pointing at the blur of speed and smoke and tracer and houses and ship and harbour that was flashing past the open starboard window.

In desperation, he pressed the shutter trigger down. He heard the click, would have pressed again—but it was too late. Strickland had turned the Liberator up on the port wing in his

15

promised screaming turn to the left. As they straightened up again, Irvine had a momentary glimpse of the fjord: the sea a sheet of grey glass, and behind, cupped in the mountains, shot through with the colours of early morning, a black broth where the Germans—too late—had set off a smoke-screen.

Houses, harbour, flak, ship—all had vanished. Ahead now was a rapidly approaching mountainside which Strickland shaved before diving down to the water again and heading out west towards the entrance to Falstand Fjord.

Suddenly everything was quiet. The enemy firing from the coast had ceased. The starboard inner had been feathered. The aircraft guns had gone silent.

Nose up, right wing low, the Liberator was wallowing crabwise, hunting, yawing, and sliding. The speed was down to 110 knots. Strickland was fiddling with the throttles and the rev switches, trying to get her into flying shape. There were shreds of metal sticking out of the starboard wing. A cannon-shell had scarred the perspex windscreen.

"Come on, you old cow!" Sweat was pouring off Strickland's face, his concentration all on flying, but still speaking softly, almost affectionately. As he edged S Sugar out of the fjord, on past Aalstrom lighthouse, he settled the power settings, managed to get the speed up, picked up his microphone and simply said, "Course for home, Jack."

There was no answer.

"Jack, are you receiving me?"

Still nothing.

"Gunners, look out for fighters!"

Again, there was no answer.

"Gunners, are you receiving me?"

And when again there was nothing, he said suddenly to Irvine, "What's happened to the Engineer?"

"I don't know, sir."

"Checking the damage, I expect." Strickland picked up his microphone again, "Is *anybody* receiving me?"

As the Liberator went wallowing westwards, both pilots listened.

Just silence.

Finally Strickland said, "Intercom's gone. You better check all positions."

16

"Can you hold her, sir?"

"I can."

But the flying was still needing all his attention, Irvine noticed, as he unstrapped himself and pushed back his seat. Getting out onto the flight deck, he stretched himself, looked over towards the mid-upper turret under which O'Connor's legs were protruding.

Then he walked over to the radio cubbyhole and said to Railton, "Can you do anything about the intercom?"

The green tuning light winked viscously at him. The heavy helmeted head did not move. At first he thought Railton was receiving, hesitated to disturb him. He bent his head lower so as to catch his eye.

There was no face there. Nothing except a great, wet, red round plate held together by the tight leather helmet. Horrified, he moved away, impulsively reached forward to the mid-upper turret to tell O'Connor, pulled at his legs.

Soundlessly, the air-gunner's body fell out of the turret and crumpled up on the flight deck floor like a broken doll. Peering up into the turret, he saw the broken perspex and the twisted metal snakes of shattered guns.

Irvine froze. There was no feeling in his limbs. His eyes would not focus. Colours were draining away. Shapes were dissolving. Only a hazy blur of red remained.

He swayed. Grasping a stanchion, he stood gasping for breath. Then, suddenly galvanized, he swung himself down off the flight deck and squeezed forward into the navigation compartment.

Wardle was bent over his chart, his hand holding a pencil.

"Jack—"

He put his hand on the white sweater. A light touch, but Wardle seemed to flinch away. The next moment, the Navigator simply keeled over, lay in a heap round his seat.

"*Jack!*"

Irvine bent down, put his arms round his shoulders, trying to pull him up. The adjustable chart-lamp pencilled a thin beam on the small round hole in the middle of the Navigator's forehead.

Now his whole mind was blurred. Numb, shocked, auto-

17

matically he got up in a panic, not knowing what he was doing, not seeing what was in front of his eyes.

He fumbled with the door release on the front turret. Opening it at last, he called "Cargill!" into the cramped round perspex-and-metal womb.

The wind answered him, shrieking into his ears. The whole front of the turret had been shot away. No guns remained. Only Cargill, huddled up like a withered foetus, stared into the icy slipstream with wide-open eyes.

Struggling against the pressure, Irvine shut and locked the turret doors. He ran now, anything to get away from this morgue in the nose of the Liberator! Holes, holes everywhere! Patterns of cannon-shells over the radio racks. Jagged tears in the bomb-bay lit up blue and yellow with early morning light. Broken pipes, twisted stanchions, pieces of red and yellow wiring hanging down like hair, the catwalk turned into a zig-zag.

As he struggled aft through a maze of mangled metal, he was calling out "Oakroyd! Mackenzie! Jenks!", forcing his way up through the entrance to the beam gun position, fighting down a parachute that had become released and was billowing up and down in the draughts that were coming in through the riddled skin, the cords catching his legs.

The beam guns—they were still manned. The two .5s on their mountings, their barrels pointing through the rectangular open positions, Jenks and Mackenzie were still standing, propped up by the fuselage—no sign of a wound on them. Both dead from blast.

Railton, Wardle, O'Connor, Cargill, Jenks and Mackenzie—what terrifying roll-call was this where nobody answered? Or am I dead, he thought, and they are living? This can't be what happens in life—it's a dream, a nightmare! Any moment now and I'll wake up in Room 27 and make a dash to the dining room so as not to miss breakfast.

"Oakroyd!"

He was shouting at the top of his voice now—above the noise of the engines, above the whistling of the wind through the cannon holes in the skin, yelling for an answering human voice.

"Len! *Len!*"

Len Oakroyd would be all right—he always was. He'd be watching there in the rear turret, guarding the tail. First tour on Blenheims, second tour on Beauforts—both killers—now half-way through his third tour.

As Irvine scrambled over the bulkheads, sure enough he saw that the cannon holes in the fuselage became fewer. This part of the Liberator anyway was reasonably intact. He bent his head, crouched down, opened the rear turret doors.

Nobody there—that was his first reaction. Len must have vacated it, now they were well clear of the Norwegian coast. Not being able to get through on the intercom, the Yorkshireman would have gone up to the flight deck while he had been up forward.

And then he saw two long brown bloodstained gauntlets on the barrels of both guns, as though the hands inside had clung onto them for support while the rest of the body was sucked out through the gaping hole in the floor of the turret.

Irvine stayed there—half in the turret, half out—staring down at the sea racing past five hundred feet below. All his strength had been drained out of him. He felt sick and desperately tired. He just wanted to curl up and die himself, as the Liberator's tail thrashed this way and that in the uneven air, and the slipstream whistled through her lacerated skin.

When at last he managed to get himself upright, hanging on to each stanchion, shakily he made his way forward.

As he clambered up on the flight deck, Strickland turned his head momentarily away from his flying to watch him. Perhaps he saw it all in Irvine's eyes or the blood on his face, for he said nothing.

Neither did Irvine. As he climbed back into his seat, he could not trust himself to speak. And, anyway, there was no need, for he was sure that Strickland knew.

After a little while, Strickland asked quite gently, "Would you like to fly her?"

He nodded his head, reached for the stick, put his legs on the rudder pedals. The touch of the controls brought relief. The familiar instruments, the steady artificial horizon, the altimeter now registering 1000 feet, the airspeed indicator on 130 knots demanded his concentration.

But he could not forget. He could feel himself trembling. He saw the gyro swirl to the left, the compass needle wander away from the lubberlines. Off course, off speed, off height, he overcorrected as he jerked the Liberator back.

He knew he was flying the Liberator roughly. But Strickland said nothing, let him go on struggling, limping back across the North Sea on three engines, bucking a strong west wind till they picked up their beacon on the radio compass and steered towards it.

And after an eternity, he saw the pale estuary, the fishing village of Kilcreggan, the purple heather-covered moors bathed in sunlight behind and then the white sticking plaster of the aerodrome runways.

Strickland took over then, circled above the hangars and the Tower as Irvine pumped the wheels down on the emergency system. All radios were dead, but Control had got the message from the feathered engine, and a fire engine and an ambulance came out on the grass beside the hedge on the duty runway, followed S Sugar down as Strickland flared out from a high approach, levelled off, touched down softly, turned onto the perimeter track and returned to Dispersal.

"Finished with the engines!"

Silence descended as Irvine switched off, broken by the blipping of the blood wagon and the clang of the fire engine. Then Strickland leaned over and said, "Don't forget the camera!"

Irvine was in an immediate panic till he saw it there on the floor on the right-hand side of his seat where he'd left it. He stretched out his hand and picked it up.

"Give it to me."

He handed it over.

Carefully Strickland examined it. "You only took one!"

He could feel himself flushing. "All I had time for."

Strickland simply said, "One will be enough."

One photograph—seven dead men. That was the tally. And would there be a photograph at all? If there wasn't, what had been achieved? They would be back where they started— Strickland saying it was the *Groningen*, Brackenbury saying it wasn't. Back where they were eight hours ago—with seven men dead.

Strickland unstrapped himself, bent down to release the lock, pushed the seat back, slowly got out, stretched himself, pulled his parachute out of the bucket of the seat, and carrying it by its straps over his right shoulder and hugging the camera, precious as a baby, close against his chest, he made his way aft, jumped off the flight deck onto the cakewalk, stepped down onto the concrete of Dispersal, ducked under the open bomb-bay doors and disappeared.

Like a sleep-walker, Irvine followed him. Warm air scented with new-mown grass filled his lungs.

Just the two of them, humping their parachutes. No one else.

The ground crew ringing the aircraft watched them. The same WAAF driver who had brought them stared out from the same Commer truck.

"You've had a rough trip, sir," the Maintenance Sergeant said.

"But a successful one, Flight." Strickland remained unperturbed. He shouted out to the ambulance driver, "Ring the MO and tell him to bring all his medical orderlies." He turned back to the Flight-Sergeant. "Nobody is to go inside the aircraft till Doc Flint gives the OK."

"No, sir."

"Pike!" Strickland had caught sight of the lurking photographic corporal. "There's a film in here!" He held up the camera. "I want enlarged prints straightaway!"

"Yes, sir."

He continued onto the Commer, followed by Irvine, his parachute bumping against the back of his legs. He opened the side door and said to the WAAF driver, "Room up front for two small ones?"

Speechless, she nodded. Seconds later, all three of them squeezed up front together, she started up, let in the clutch, and moved sedately round the perimeter track back to Operations.

Only the news of their arrival had preceded them. Nine cups of cocoa, piping hot, were waiting in the Intelligence Office. Lieutenant-Commander Brackenbury looked up from his desk as the two of them came in.

"It *was* the *Groningen*," Strickland said. "This time we've got a photograph."

That was all. Seconds after they arrived, the two of them were out of Intelligence, out of the neon-lighted Operations Room,

21

back in the Commer and off to 507 Squadron Headquarters.

As they came to a stop outside, Strickland said unexpectedly, "No need for you to come in. I'll put your helmet and parachute back in your locker."

"No, sir. I'll—"

But Strickland had already opened the side door and pulled both parachutes out. "I've got to see the Wingco." He slammed the door shut. "Off you go and get some shut-eye!"

The driver said nothing at all during the short journey to the Mess. Which was a good thing, because Irvine could not have answered her.

It was not he who was riding in this Commer beside the plump WAAF. It was not he who got out at the Mess, walked up the stone steps, pushed open the glass door, walked along the deserted corridor with its familiar red and blue carpet, up the steps to Room 27. It was not he who drew the curtains against the daylight, flung off all his clothes, huddled up cold and naked inside the clean sheets of the bed in the corner.

Somebody not himself provided for the mattress this dead-weight of flesh. His real self was still suspended somewhere over the North Sea, half way to whatever place Railton, Jenks, Wardle and the others had gone. This other being lay as still as stone, eyes closed, but could not sleep.

A vast panorama, colourful and loud, was being played continually before his eyes: the red, white and green of tracer bullets, the grey puffs of 88mm shells, the sound of the engines, the high screech as Number Three propeller raced its head off, the sight of Railton's missing face, O'Connor and Wardle crumpled on the floor, Cargill's corpse, that nightmare passage down the fuselage to be welcomed by the bloodstained gauntlets spread wide in the empty rear turret.

He opened his eyes to get away from the bright colours exploding in his head and the deafening sounds in his ears. Sunlight streaming through the crack in the curtains brought up into a high varnish the polished brown linoleum, whitened to marble the three empty beds on their japanned black iron legs. The standard RAF coverlets now were like carved tomb-stones—one to the right, one to the left, the third on the other side of the room by the basin. The sheets of all four beds had been turned down invitingly by Mavis, their pretty WAAF batwoman. Three sheets still remained turned down. Wardle, Railton, Cargill gone—he had gone too. That photograph would be a total dud. He remembered taking Brownie snaps of the family at Dudley Castle—skew-whiff, dark, out of focus, sometimes blank. He had made a fearful mess of the exposure, he was sure of that. The shutter speed was wrong.

This was it. He would never be any use now. The thought of going off on a trip again sent him trembling. He began throwing his arms around in a paroxysm of hopelessness, his eyes twitching with tiredness yet wide awake.

He began wondering what they would do with him—Irvine 4, retired hurt.

No doubt he would be examined by the doctors, passed to a Board, declared LMF—Lack of Moral Fibre—be demoted from his officer rank down to aircrafthand. The RAF spent a lot of time and money on its air crew, and it cut its losses quickly if there was clearly to be no dividend. If he wasn't going to make it, he would go.

Where?

Something would have to be done with him. Whatever was left of him would have to be retrieved from floating above the North Sea, hammered back into a human frame, legs and arms serviced into moving, brain wound up again, heart set ticking, skin polished up and then pushed back into the War Effort again for some less demanding work.

A jazzing kaleidoscope burst in his mind—changing patterns, circling, dazzling, glittering, clouding. Somehow or other, all that noise and colour must have hypnotized him into unconsciousness, because the next thing he remembered was opening his eyes and now it was evening.

Sitting on his bed in the half light was Strickland.

He felt his heart lurch. He had both expected this and hoped it would never come.

"Sorry if I woke you."

Nothing given away in the tone of voice. Strickland's face was turned away from the window in heavy shadow.

"I thought you might like to see this."

Now for the crunch—the empty print passed over for him to see the total blackness of his future.

Here it came, the standard RAF five-by-five-inch print—and

23

sure enough, it was dark all right! As it was passed across to him in slow motion, he could see nothing but glossy black blankness.

"Take a look."

He had it in his own hands now. Black, yes black—but greying towards the centre into what suddenly he realized was camouflage paint.

It was an enlargement—a blow-up for a purpose.

And now the purpose became evident. For underneath the paint could just be made out in heavy German Script letters

Groningen

Hamburg

He looked up and saw the huge smile spread right across Strickland's face.

"Not just a picture of the two funnels. Or of the cruiser stern. But the name! The actual name!" The smile was still right across his face. "Good *boy*! The Group Captain is very impressed. So are—" the smile widened, "the Navy." He paused. "So am I."

He appeared to be waiting for Irvine to say something. When he still kept silent, Strickland said, "I'd already realized I'd got a first-class pilot as my second dickey.* But I hadn't realized I'd also got an ace photographer! With all that joshing and all that flak, just one photograph but you didn't make a mistake!" He leaned forward, tapped Irvine lightly on his shoulder. "I knew I could trust you!"

"Oh I don't know." He could feel his cheeks burning. "Luck—"

"Come off it! That wasn't luck! Coolness and skill! What the captain of an aircraft needs!" Strickland paused. "You know we're making up a new crew?"

"I'd heard."

"Of which you're the captain."

He couldn't believe his ears, so he said nothing.

"That's right."

Irvine still kept silent.

"What's happened to you? You look as though you've seen a ghost!"

"It's just that—well, you know . . ."

* Second pilot.

24

"Yes, I know!" Strickland looked down at his wrist. "Have you any idea what time it is?"

"No."

"Six-fifteen! You'll miss dinner if you're not careful!" Strickland got off the bed, still smiling. "And that command! Aren't you coming down to the bar to wet it?"

TWO

ASSISTANT SECTION OFFICER JONES finished her bread and butter pudding, pushed back her chair, got up, walked across the polished wood floor of the dining room, opened the glass swing doors and crossed the corridor into the ante-room.

The Mess was quiet tonight. Almost deserted. A few ground-staff officers were relaxing after the day's work in leather armchairs, silently reading the newspapers. One of them looked up and watched her go over to the coffee urn on the white-clothed table.

"Hello, Emma."

She turned. "Hello, John."

Flight-Lieutenant Wilkinson was the Station Equipment Officer and her boss. He was a happily married man but that did not preclude his admiring a dainty little figure and a nice line in legs, even, he had himself noted, wearing the hideous grey stockings and the black leather beetle-crushers in which the WAAF caused its ladies to be hosed and shod. Miss Jones also had on her personal inventory dark brown shiny hair cut into a knave of hearts and blue eyes the colour of some flowers of whose name he hadn't the faintest idea but which grew in profusion between the runways in north-east Scotland's surprisingly benign autumn.

"Be a poppet and bring an old man a coffee, too."

She smiled at him over her shoulder and nodded. The silky hair swung and caught the light. He enjoyed watching her hair. Sometimes in the office, seeing her head earnestly bent over a pile of indent forms, he would be tempted to reach out his hand and touch it. But never in the two weeks since she'd arrived had he ever done so. He was forty and fatherly. And he had a photo of his wife and fifteen-year-old daughter on his desk to

26

prove it. Emma Jones was just six years his daughter's senior. Which, if nothing else, proved that a hell of a lot could happen in six years.

He watched her as she came across the red-and-blue-patterned standard-issue carpet towards him, holding a coffee cup carefully in each hand. She had an endearing habit of sticking the tip of her little pink tongue out whenever she was doing something with concentrated care.

He was aware that one or two of the other officers watched him from behind their papers, slyly and with envy. There were a couple at least who would have given if not their vital right arms at least their home leave for the duration to have Miss Jones as their assistant.

He got up and took the cups from her and set them on the round table. There was an empty chair beside him. He pulled it nearer the fire.

"Not that there's much bloody heat coming out of it. The wood's wet and so's the wind."

She nodded. She could hear the wind howling outside as she sat down in the chair he waved her towards. It pushed great billows of smoke down the chimney and hissed and sucked on the glowing logs, so that they crackled like gunfire.

She wondered if it looked something like that over a battle area. Smoke. A red-hot glow, little intermittent sparks. Is that what it had looked like to those seven men? Seven boys really. She had sat next to one of them at lunch yesterday. He'd asked her if she'd like to walk to the local for a drink one evening. He'd got a second helping of sago pudding and he'd sweet-hearted the WAAF waitress into putting a dab of raspberry jam on it.

Now his effects were in the returned (deceased) end of the clothing store. She'd helped check them this morning, his battledress oily and sodden in blood. The aircraft had been running with it, the flight mechs said. It was a miracle the two pilots had got it back.

Determinedly, Miss Jones reached out for her coffee cup and lifted it to her lips. She drained the small cup in a couple of gulps, and looked at her watch.

"Too quiet for you, is it, Emma?"

She shook her head. Her hair glistened again. Beautiful! He

27

reminded himself to ask her as many questions as possible where the answer would be no. And immediately dubbed himself a saucy fellow.

"No. But there's a Bob Hope film on at the camp cinema." She hadn't been aware that she wanted to see it till then. But somehow, suddenly, the need to laugh, to be taken out of herself was as imperative as hunger.

"The film's rotten," Wilkinson said. "Anyway the reel always breaks or the projector does. And it's draughty as hell in there."

She hesitated.

"It'll brighten up here later on. There'll be quite a thrash. Always is when . . ."

"When?" She turned those blue eyes (what the hell was the name of that flower?) onto his face.

He drew in a deep breath. He didn't know quite how to put it. When some of the lads have got the chop, when there are a few empty chairs, when we're having a jug to launch old so-and-so. While he was pondering a suitable euphemism, she guessed. Black lashes hid the disconcerting eyes.

"You'll get a drink or three."

She shot him a sad sideways smile. "I think I'd prefer Bob Hope."

"Ops stations get a bit of getting used to." He sounded apologetic. "You're still a bit . . ."

"What?"

"Well, green. In the nicest possible way of course." He jerked his head towards the three WAAF officers sitting in the far corner. "In no time at all you'll be like them." He paused. "No, on second thoughts, delete that last. Perish the bloody thought! Stay as sweet as you are, Miss Jones."

She stood up.

As she did so, the glass ante-room doors were flung open and, making his usual Garrick entrance, in came Strickland. As usual, he was improperly dressed. He was wearing his white polo-necked sweater and his brown leather riding boots. As usual, nobody said anything. Tonight, he was shadowed by a stocky Pilot Officer with brown hair and a manner as uncertain as Strickland's reeked of confidence.

Strickland was not Flight-Lieutenant Wilkinson's favourite fruit. Press-on types rarely endeared themselves to overworked

28

Equipment Officers, harried by the perennial lack of spares. It was therefore with surprise, irritation and some consternation that he noticed the booted feet change course and make for his direction. Then he saw that Strickland's eyes were fixed not on his own hang-dog countenance, but on Miss Jones, still standing unhurriedly putting her barathea bag over her shoulder, about to go.

Strickland's opening remark to her was typical. "You don't *have* to stand when I come in." He gave her a dazzling smile to show it was all in good fun. "But it helps."

"I didn't. I was just leaving."

Strickland changed his tactics. "Oh, no! Please don't! Just because Wilkinson's bored you rigid."

"He hasn't."

"You've been talking shop, I bet. How the hell to get spares for S Sugar."

"Not so." Wilkinson smiled—relieved, despite himself, that Strickland appeared to be in such a good mood.

"Then you should have been!" Strickland's smile withered. "Or is it all buttoned up?"

Wilkinson decided that least said was soonest mended. The bloody thing was a write-off anyway. The idea of getting enough spares to mend that colander was lunatic. Spares were as scarce as hen's teeth and an aircraft like S Sugar to cannibalize would be very welcome. So he murmured vaguely that Hart, the Engineering Officer, and he had been "on it all day".

"Well, let's hope *it* works," Strickland said sharply. "And talking of It, you're too young, Peter, to know what It means. But meet Emma Jones! Who has It in abundance! I expect you already know Wilkinson, don't you? The lads call him weigh-out Wilkinson. Used to be a weighing scales salesman. Isn't that so, Wilkinson?"

It was—and no shame in that. But somehow Wilkinson felt it was unkind to mention it. Somehow it cut him down to unglamorous size in a way Strickland was most marvellously equipped to do.

The young man flushed and shook his head. "No, I don't think we've met."

"Never tried to get a new battledress before yours was

showing your backside? No? When you do, that's when he shows you the way out!"

The young man smiled politely.

"But Miss Jones, as you can see, is a different kettle of fish."

"You won't get a new battledress out of her, either," Wilkinson said, with assumed sternness. He hated the way Strickland had accompanied his last remark with a frank head-to-toe appraisal of Emma, which he could see by her heightened colour she found embarrassing.

Strickland laughed out loud. "It's not a new battledress I want. Not from Miss Jones! Hell, no! Battledress indeed, Wilkinson! Miss Jones has more to offer. Even my beloved Squadron Commander was heard to comment . . . well, never mind. Where is Vance, by the way? Seen him anywhere?"

Wilkinson shook his head.

"Been in for dinner?"

"Haven't a clue."

"Ah well, not to worry! He'll be studying the Air Force List* as usual. I just wanted to tell him that Peter here's on a command course."

The young pilot went scarlet.

"Congratulations," Wilkinson said, thinking Christ, they got younger and greener: you'd think they'd manage to stop blushing before they got their commands. But Emma Jones eyed him with obvious sympathy. Birds of a feather. Little kids hardly out of the kindergarten.

"Peter was with me on S Sugar."

The sole survivor of your crew, Wilkinson thought, but all he said aloud was "So I gathered." He glanced sideways at Miss Jones. The sympathy in those incredibly blue eyes had deepened.

"So come on! Into the bar, the pair of you! We've got to wet his command. Quick march!"

"Sorry, sir." Wilkinson looked at his watch. "I'm due in the Guard Room. Orderly Officer." He smiled as regretfully as he could. "Duty calls."

"Far be it from me to stand between you and your duty."

* List of all officers with ranks and dates of their seniority, required reading for all interested in promotion. The next rank up from Wing-Commander was Group-Captain, normally an administrative position.

30

Strickland didn't look in the slightest regretful. "That leaves Emma. She can't be engaged too. That wouldn't do at all. Would it, Peter?"

"No." Irvine spoke with the sudden loudness of the very shy. "Do come."

"There, the captain himself requests it! You'll bring him luck, I shouldn't wonder. Launch him like a ship."

Wilkinson thought she might put up a token resistance but she didn't. Something had got through to her as he never could. What was it? Strickland's so-called charm? His sheer will power? Some unstoppable quality that in his heart of hearts even he recognized. And resented too. Was this the mythical quality the top brass called leadership? That certain something you were born with or weren't? And which senior officers were on the look-out for? Or was Strickland glamorous? Was he attractive to women? Sexy? His own wife thought he was. Or was Miss Jones motivated by sympathy for that nearly beardless boy, that young casualty in the making? Did she with the incomparable romantic gullibility of women nurse the idea she might actually bring him luck?

Whatever it was that had got her going, he watched them go with a jaundiced eye. Halfway to the door, Strickland put his hand under Miss Jones' elbow just to guide her across the terrain of the carpet. As he did so, he bent his head to hear some remark she made. Or was it to admire that shimmering hair? To catch a whiff of its freshly washed fragrance? Now he was smiling in reply to what Miss Jones had said. Nodding in flattering approval.

Maybe he should get *her* to tell Strickland tomorrow that S Sugar was a write-off, Category C, and that he'd just have to wait till they got a replacement aircraft. Now Strickland was opening the glass doors for her, bowing, waving her through, while the new captain, as if exhausted by his endorsement of the invitation to her, followed them in silence, heavy-footed as a sleep-walker.

Standing against the wall at the far end of the counter, only half listening to what Wisby was wittering on about, Flight-Lieutenant Andrew Flint watched the little procession come trooping through the door.

31

First the girl. Then the boy. Finally the white-sweatered Squadron-Leader.

The metal snakes twisted round the rods in the lapels of his jacket identified Flint as a Medical Officer. Now in his mid-thirties he was a good deal older than most of the other officers. Already grey-haired, he had brown eyes of a peculiarly soft brightness. Though none of them realized it, these aircrew were his permanent patients. He would have called himself a hard-headed practical doctor who always did things for a reason. And he had come into the bar this evening, not to drink the neat malt whisky he now held in his right hand, but to take the temperature of squadron morale after S Sugar's bloody escapade.

It was low. Flint could actually *feel* the atmosphere of the crowded bar on his skin, jagged and sharp-edged. Half an hour ago, somebody had dropped a mug onto the radiator where it had smashed into myriads of glass fragments. There they still lay on the linoleum, the drips of beer glittering orange under the wall light like symbols of caution. Every now and then, somebody inadvertently trod on them, making a crunching sound that set your teeth on edge.

"What the hell did Strickland think he was doing?"

"Wanted to rub Brackenbury's nose in it, that's why!"

"Shouldn't he have waited for the PRU, Mossie?"

"Seven lives for a fucking photograph."

Why had Strickland done it? Was it just bravado? Was it that a leader had always to be right? Or was it just pique at being contradicted? Mind you, Flint thought, if he *had* got away with it unscathed that would have been another accolade to the growing legend of Guy Strickland.

Who was he anyway, and where did he come from? Apart from his medical history Flint knew few facts about the Squadron-Leader. The only child of a Company Secretary, six years at a minor public school, half way through an engineering course at a London Institute when the war came and he joined the RAF. And since then, a dangerous tour on Blenheims, ship-busting from Malta. A short rest instructing and then another tour on a torpedo-carrying Beaufort squadron of which he and his crew had been the sole survivors. Somewhere along the line he had collected that scar under his left eye and the

32

DSO and the DFC, what for nobody seemed to know and of which Strickland never spoke—but coming from that war record perfectly understandable.

Had Strickland's apparent invulnerability gone to his head? Did he really believe that the Germans would never shoot him down, which was certainly what the squadron believed?

Until tonight, of course. Tonight it looked almost as though they were going to shoot him down themselves.

". . . bloody waste . . ."

". . . the AOC* should have stopped him."

"Nuttall? Never! Strickland's got him in his pocket."

Flint had never before heard criticism of Strickland. The conversation in the bar so far this evening—except for Wisby's offering—had been nothing else but. And these were senior captains—sensible types and very experienced. The dark-haired Mason had been vociferously anti. Even Carter, a press-on South African noted for recklessness, had declared it "bloody stupid".

"Bloody stupid?" Edward Mowbray, as the only married captain, lived out with his wife Madeleine in Kilcreggan village. "Bloody criminal."

It was at this moment that the little party—Strickland, Irvine, Assistant Section Officer Jones—had entered the crowded bar.

Framed in the lintel, they stopped in their tracks.

There was an immediate silence. Faces turned towards the door in a unanimous expression of hostility. Nobody made way for them. Nobody gave any sign of even recognizing them.

Had Strickland heard Mowbray's remark, Flint wondered. He's made a mistake, he must realize that. What's he going to do now?

Slowly the Squadron-Leader closed the door. Standing with his legs apart, arms folded, his eyes travelled round the silent room.

Softly he said, "Trust you lot to be as drunk as skunks, you bastards!"

He smiled—benignly, forgivingly. Then assuredly: "Doc . . . what's your medicine?" And before Flint could answer, "Barman . . . a Glenfyddich for the doctor!"

Unerringly Strickland had chosen the one person in the room

* Air Officer Commanding.

33

whom he knew at that difficult moment he could rely on. Flint did not want another malt whisky. Nor did he want to show his support for Strickland. But because he was the pivot on which squadron morale rested, he could not say no. He picked up the dram. "Cheers!"

"Tommy?"

Dacres—quiet, pipe-smoking, regular Air Force ex-Halton boy, risen from the ranks, the last person to question a senior officer—"Thanks." He pushed the empty pint mug across the counter. "Bitter."

"Ken?"

"Bitter."

He was calling the roll in a weird ceremonial vote. Now he turned to the little group of elders—Carter, Linton and Ames. "Tim?"

"Bitter."

"Rory?"

"Bitter."

He went round the room in descending order of reliable seniority. And now, except for one, he was down to the tiddlers, the second pilots whose future commands hung on his appro-bation. There was a chorus of "Bitter, sir . . . thank you, sir . . . bitter, sir . . . bitter."

Then finally he came to Mowbray, "And what about you, Edward?" And before the married pilot could answer, "But you'll be wanting to get back home . . . and who can blame you?"

Pulled by the apron strings to the wee wifey waiting.

Mowbray just nodded.

"Give the beautiful Madeleine the squadron salaams, eh?"

"I'll do that."

Mowbray finished his beer, got off his stool, waved goodnight. Confidently Strickland led the way forward towards his empty seat at the counter. Like the waters of the Red Sea for Moses, the crush of humanity parted to let the three of them through, the occupiers of the bar stools shifted their shoulders.

"Farquhar, didn't they ever teach you manners at Eton? Get off your bottom and give your seat to the lady!" Strickland was already there—in the centre of the counter. He had already won. He lifted Emma Jones off her feet, parked her on the now vacant stool, ordered her a gin and orange, and two more pints of bitter for himself and Irvine.

He never mentioned the *Groningen*. He never mentioned those six whose remains were now lying in Sick Quarters' mortuary and the seventh who lay in the sea—though the whole of this evening, Flint knew, would in some strange primeval way be dedicated to them. He was far too clever to try a full frontal approach. He was taking them off centre all round the houses but to exactly the same destination.

"This is a celebration, for God's sake! A toast! Will you raise your glasses to 507's new captain! To Peter Irvine's command!"

Buying Irvine off, Flint thought. Getting his silence and his support by giving him a command.

Initially there was hesitation. Then one by one, some of them slowly, they lifted up their glasses to their lips. One by one, they began to drink.

"Come on now! Bottoms up!"

Having established his base at the centre of the bar, now Strickland was moving around the groups, beer mug in his right hand, his left hand hard behind his back in a kind of self-induced half-nelson, working on them all. To guard his rear he had his man Irvine, now talking to the pretty WAAF officer.

Flint could just hear the boy taking the first few halting steps towards better acquaintance, the words coming intermittently over Wisby's left shoulder: *where before coming to Kilcreggan?* . . . *dull places, Maintenance Units* . . . *how d'you like* . . . in direct contrast with what Wisby was going on about, which was about his imminent leave. Two round eyes, glassy and un-blinking as those of a fish, hypnotized the doctor away from Strickland and onto the problem of transport to the station at Blairculloch on Tuesday, there to catch a train to his uncle's estate in Banffshire.

The *Groningen*, the seven dead men, S Sugar, not even Strickland, Flint realized, were at all relevant to Wisby. He was escaping. He was all-right-Jack.

". . . and after my leave I'll be going on rest. Of course you won't know, Doc, but they've told me I've only got to do five more trips . . ."

They—the extraordinary amorphism all aircrew showed about *they*! As though *they* were some gods in the sky, giving them their parts to play, their present and their future! Grizzling because *they* have put me on air-to-air gunnery—*they* being Strickland. *They* are sending me to patrol the Baltic—Air Vice-Marshal Nuttall commanding 35 Group. Now *they* have told Wisby he had only to do five more trips . . .

In that instance, *they* was Flint. Copies of all intelligence reports were sent to him at Sick Quarters. He kept his own record of everyone on the squadron, every trip they did, the bad ones and the good ones. He had told Strickland that after forty-five undistinguished sorties, including three in the last fortnight when he had returned early on his own initiative, twice for weather, and once for imaginary engine trouble, Wisby had only five more trips left in him.

". . . fortnight's shooting, Doc. My uncle . . ."

Coming over Wisby's shoulder, the young WAAF officer's voice now. Hesitant, shy: "You're on Squadron-Leader Strickland's crew?"

"Was."

The medicine was working. The second dickey, like Alice, was growing taller and taller.

"I heard about that trip of yours. It must have been—"

She would have got the story filtered down by hearsay. She hadn't been inside the Liberator. Nobody had, except Flint and his two medical orderlies, scraping all the bits together, hacking away to get Cargill's body out of the front turret.

The growing boy interrupted her. "Just one of those things."

Already he was becoming a man, practically as big as a captain.

The rearguard was holding. In the front line, from the pilots who had so recently been uneasily questioning came the clink of beer mugs, even some sporadic laughter. Unruffled ease oozed out of Strickland like oil over troubled waters. The three other WAAF officers came in, and immediately he had equipped them with double gins and orange—that was his standard drink for all females—surrounded them with four men each and left them feeling like princesses.

". . . particularly fine shot, my uncle. He bagged . . ."

It was becoming noisier. The air was blue with cigarette smoke. From all sides of the bar, Flint could hear snatches of conversations.

36

". . . forty-six inches boost and twenty-six hundred revs . . ."
". . . whipped out the turbos too soon . . ."
". . . thought she was stuck to the ground, I tell you . . ."
". . . a beaut of a landing! Like a cat pissing on glass!"
The hangar doors had been opened. Unease and uncertainty began floating away. Strickland was talking now about tactics, the best way to avoid flak, praising the Liberator, its strength, its fire power, its Pratt and Whitney engines. "Best aircraft in the business. We're bloody lucky . . ."
". . . the speed of a pheasant, my uncle says . . ."
It was extraordinary how Strickland was doing it. Stage-manager, director, producer, he had allocated the parts, fixed the action, and had begun rehearsing their performances. Now it was as though, Flint thought, they were all in some play of Strickland's devising, complete with plot that had a beginning, a middle, and there in the distance some hazy indistinct end. The temperature of the squadron, the doctor noted on his morale thermometer, was rising rapidly.

More and more people were coming into the bar. Voices became loud and cheerful. Faces turned red and began sweating. The air was an electric medley of different voices and accents—Canadian, Australian, Yorkshire, Scots, South African. Under a slur of beer, words became sharper. "When's old man Vance going to take himself off on an operation?"

"Can't tear himself away from the bumpff, old boy."

"Where *is* our beloved Wing-Commander anyway? Go and find him, Rory! Drag him away from the Air Force List! Tell him it's *his* round!"

"You're wrong, there, Charles," Strickland called across the room. "It's mine! Peter, fill 'em up!"

Rearguard safe, the right-hand man was coming round with a jug. The young WAAF officer was deserted, thrown to the tiddlers, the equally young second pilots who welcomed her with open arms and more gins, while Irvine joined his peers, the captains.

The jagged pieces of the early evening had all been filed smooth. A male bonhomie descended. The hierarchy had been restored. Each man was back in his place, each pat with his lines, each with his role, subordinate to the leading man. Peace had been restored, and with it a raucous good humour led by Strickland calling out "They're not sending us any more beer!"

"Boo!" they all yelled happily back at him.

"They're sending champagne instead!" the Squadron-Leader ring-master went on.

"Hurrah!"

"They're stopping bacon and eggs in the Aircrew Mess!"

"Boo!"

"They're giving us steak instead!"

"Hurrah!"

"They're taking away the WAAFs!"

"Boo!"

"They're sending us Windmill chorus-girls instead!"

"Hurrah!"

Now it was past midnight. Knowing what was in store, most of the ground officers began slipping away. So did the WAAF Flight-Officer and her minions, the riding mistress of an Adjutant and the pale-haired Cypher Queen.

". . . the bells of Hell go ting-a-ling-a-ling
For you but not for me."

Crackers, the old Gas Officer, wearing the Pip, Squeak and Wilfrid* ribbons of the last war, had gone over to the baby grand piano in the corner, weighted down by empty beer mugs, had opened it up, run his fingers over the keys, lovingly, his white-haired head on one side, had started singing, his bloodshot eyes far away. "Tickling the ivories" he called it, as his long bony fingers switched from the infantry to the RFC songs of the First World War, the ones that identified the singers with the gay intrepid knights of the air, laughing at death:

". . . here's a toast to the dead already.
Hurrah for the next man to die!"

Then imperceptibly time moved on. The notes changed. The mood altered from a loud bravado to an aching loneliness, to the wistful laments of the RAF who policed the Middle Eastern deserts between the wars. The heat, the boredom.

"Shaibah Blues, I've got those Shai . . . ai . . . bah Blues. I'm fed up, and I'm fucked up, and I'm bluuue . . ."

And the dangers, the faltering engines, the unspeakable

* The rainbow collection of World War I medal ribbons—the Mons Star, the 1914–15 Star and the British War Medal named after a strip cartoon in the *Daily Mirror* in which the hero was a rabbit (Wilfrid) and his two playmates were Pip and Squeak.

cruelties from the hands of the Arabs that awaited down below.
"... no balls at all, no balls at all.
If your engines cut out, you'll have no balls at all ..."
And naturally coming out of it all, the yearning for the troopship home, the Bibby liner SS *Somersetshire*.
"Shire, shire, *Somersetshire*,
The Skipper looks on her with pride ..."
The sing-song had started. The psalms were about to be sung for the dead. And the little WAAF officer, surrounded by second pilots, another gin and orange in her hand, was oblivious of it, not knowing what it meant, didn't hear the music change or the soft male chorus from all round the bar.
"Goodnight, ladies! Goodnight, ladies!"
The singing grew louder. They began banging their beer mugs on the counter.
"Goodnight, ladies!"
And then louder still, 507 Squadron's anthem.
"An airman told me before he died,
I do not think the bastard lied.
He had a girl—"
The second pilots had gone silent. Sensing something, the young WAAF officer looked up.
"Emma." It was Squadron Leader Strickland, the man who had brought her in, looking down at her, smiling and singing. "It's time to say goodnight!"
"Goodnight, ladies!" he sang, and they all sang with him "Goodnight, ladies!"
He bent down, and to the accompaniment of cheers and claps and the chattering of beer mugs, he kissed her full on the lips.
Seeing the flush rise to her face and her total bewilderment of what to do, Flint began pushing his way towards her.
But she had realized before he reached her. Suddenly she was aware she was the only girl in the room. She was being dismissed, as Mowbray earlier had been dismissed. Her cheeks now were scarlet, but she didn't lose her head. She didn't down her gin and scuttle to the door. As the singing reached a crescendo, she finished her drink, put down the empty glass on the counter, and then, head held high, walked slowly to the door.
Just before she went out, she turned and faced them all.
"Goodnight." Imperceptibly she paused. "*Gentlemen!*"

39

THREE

"Egg for breakfast!" Madeleine Mowbray called up to her husband, "Don't be too long, Edward. I'm scrambling it."

She whipped up the precious egg with milk, then slipped some bread under the grill. Lifting the tubby brown teapot, she set it on its stand on the tablecloth with the cups and plates and the knife and fork.

Then she straightened, listening for some sound of stirring in the bedroom immediately above. She was a strikingly handsome, well-built woman who moved with surprising lightness and grace and who, in repose, radiated a calm which alas she knew to be illusory. Her eyes compounded the illusion. They were hazel, very clear and steady, very feminine and yet not flirtatious. She had light brown hair cut at the back in a shingle, and arranged round her face in thick, shiny, freshly washed waves.

"Coming, darling. Scrambling for the scrambled!"

At the sound of her husband's forcedly jolly voice, a sad indulgent smile curved up the corners of her sculpted lips.

"It's just about ready," she said, staring out of the window of this fisherman's cottage across the small inlet to Kilcreggan aerodrome on the other side. It was where her eyes were constantly drawn. Either there or the grey skies above it, watching and waiting for the white shapes of the returning Liberators to materialize out of the east. So often that now she had become interested in the other denizens of the sky. She had begun to know the birds like she knew the aircraft. It was both an interest and an alibi. She wasn't watching the sky for Edward's return, she was trying to spot the remnants of that flock of grey-legged geese which had alighted on the inlet two days ago, or the one-legged guillemot who fed regularly at her bird table.

40

The bird table was a large, chipped white bowl, hung in an old feed net from the branch of the solitary tree in the garden, a stunted sycamore. One day Edward was going to build a proper bird table. Just as one day when the war was over, he would let them start a family.

"Edward," she called, pouring the egg mixture into the hot pan, lifting the toast out mechanically, her eyes still fixed on Kilcreggan. The red-brick Officers' Mess, like a Queen Anne mansion, the two hangars, twentieth-century cathedrals, metallic, heartless, dark Satanic mills, the big warehouses of the Stores buildings, the bungalow of Station Headquarters with its matchstick pole and its miniscule RAF flag were all too familiar to hold her attention for long. She was looking at a Liberator on the nearest hard standing, just above the rocks on the other side of the water. On its white side, flanking 507 Squadron's DF and on the other side of the red, white and blue roundel was the letter S.

She stirred the scrambled egg. She turned down the gas and began to butter the toast.

"Edward! It'll be spoiled!"

There were three things strange about that Liberator. First, it had stayed there all yesterday while its other sisters had been flying. Secondly, a large collection of vans had collected round it around lunch time, after which it had been totally deserted. Thirdly, most of the front turret was missing, so was a portion of the tailplane and the inner starboard engine. There were so many holes in the fuselage that it resembled a giant colander.

Carefully she cut off the crusts from the toast and set them aside for the birds.

"Edward!"

Her husband never discussed operations with her, but she found out more than he knew. She knew every aircraft that he flew, would watch it take off, would wait by the window all day for its return. All night sometimes, slipping into bed just before the transport brought him safely home, pretending to be asleep when he came tip-toeing up the stairs, only opening her eyes when she heard the soft sounds of his undressing, asking drowsily, "What sort of trip did you have, darling?"

"Average."

Always the same question, always the same reply, as though

it was a magic incantation between them that kept away evil. One more trip completed. One more milestone to the end of his second tour and his second rest. Then no more chance of running into the sort of trouble S had clearly run into on what might have been its last trip.

It didn't look as though it could ever fly again. She knew American spares were very difficult to get. They had to come by ship, and the U-boats kept torpedoing the ships. She hoped S Sugar was what they called a write-off. The squadron strength would then be down from twelve to eleven aircraft. And since the American Air Force and Bomber Command grabbed every Liberator they could lay their hands on, with luck it would stay that way. And that meant one-twelfth less flying, one-twelfth fewer operations, one-twelfth longer to have Edward safe on the ground.

"Edward!"

"Just putting a little perfume behind my ears."

Edward had not flown it, she knew that. His aircraft was L London, and if that wasn't available O Orange. S was Squadron-Leader Strickland's aircraft. S for Strickland, that's how she remembered it.

Strickland was the king of the squadron. Strickland ruled over all—507's Wing-Commander and the Group-Captain commanding the Station were nonentities. Strickland made out the Mayfly with which her life was ruled. *Mayfly* . . . an innocent enough word and totally logical, giving notice to five crews that they *may fly*, 1, 2, 3, 4, 5 in the order named. But for her it was altogether too reminiscent of the pretty insect with its life of one summer's day. She heard the loose board creak on the landing.

She poured the scrambled egg on the toast.

"Darling! It's on the table!"

On his first tour, Edward had been on radar Whitleys. He had a rooted objection to bombing cities, which was why he had opted for Coastal Command. Safer than bombers, he had told her, but in fact the Merlins at low altitude used to fail regularly and the Whitleys would flop far too far out into the Atlantic ever to be rescued. For his rest, he was instructing in the Cotswolds on Hudsons and that she liked. There had been just one ugly episode, when Bomber Command had demanded two hundred and fifty Coastal captains and their aircraft for one thousand-bomber raid on Cologne, including Edward. "Just to get into four figures," he had told her. "Sending the boys off with no high-level bombing experience in clapped-out OTU* aircraft!" He had refused to go and had got the others to refuse to go, too. Court-martial proceedings were being contemplated, when the Navy (who controlled Coastal Command) had another of its frequent tiffs with Bomber Command and withdrew all two hundred and fifty, thus saving everyone's bacon. The thousand was made up from other sources. The raid took place. As Edward had predicted, the majority of the RAF casualties were raw inexperienced crews.

"Edward!"

Footsteps on the stairs now. In he came, kissed the back of her neck, sat himself down, said "Mm . . . darling, that looks good." He picked up his knife and fork, then laid them down and said, "What about you?"

"I just want toast."

"There was just the one egg? That was the ration?"

She didn't answer.

"Well, if you think I'm going to hog it all," he picked up his knife again and carefully carved the egg on toast in two, "you're very much mistaken!"

"Edward . . . eat it while it's hot!"

He pushed away her hands and slipped half onto her plate. "I'm not starting eating till you do."

"I'd *rather* have toast."

"Eat!"

"I'm slimming."

"I don't like my women skinny. Eat."

Conceding defeat, she ate. So did he. When he passed his cup for a second cup of tea, he said casually, "Oh by the way, I won't be in to lunch."

Fearfully she asked, "You're not on the Mayfly?"

He smiled and shook his head. "A massive training programme's started, that's all."

"One of Strickland's ideas?"

He nodded. "But I'll be on the ground today."

"What's this massive training programme in aid of?"

* Operational Training Unit.

43

He shrugged his shoulders. "Oh, nothing much. Brushing up on anti-shipping operations, that's all. New tactics." He drank down his tea, put the empty cup on the saucer and stood up. "Got to go now, darling. Look after yourself."

"Look after *yourself*." She put her arms round his neck and kissed him. "Will you be *flying* on training tomorrow?"

He opened the front door and began wheeling his rusty bicycle outside. She scooped up the crusts of toast and a lump of bread and followed him.

"Edward, will you?"

"Doubt it, darling." He got on the bike and began pedalling down the garden path. "We're a bit short of aircraft."

She nodded, trying not to let her pleasure show.

"Strickland got himself in a spot of bother the other day. S Sugar's a write-off."

She waited till he was out of sight, before walking round to the sycamore with a light and joyful step. Crumbling the scraps into the chipped bowl, she watched the sky joyfully as the white sea-birds came sailing in.

S Sugar appeared on that day's Q Form.

The Q Form was the squadron aircraft unserviceability state, one of a load of bumpff that regularly came into Flint's office, together with Daily Routine Orders and Squadron Orders, Notices, Amendments and Air Council missives. It did not basically concern him, apart from realizing that losing his own aircraft would be a blow to Strickland personally. He thought no more about it, and was in the process of depositing it in his Out tray, from which it would be filed by his corporal, never to be looked at again, when there was a knock on his door, and in came Flying Officer Wisby, pink-faced and waving a small square piece of white paper that Flint immediately recognized.

"I say, Doc . . . this is a bit much!"

"What's the trouble?"

"The Wingco won't sign my leave form!"

Reprieved were all his uncle's pheasants. Wisby himself had been jolted back into the firing line.

"Why not?"

"It's Strickland's intensive training programme. All leave

cancelled, the Wingco says, until the *Groningen* business is sorted out."

"What does that mean?"

"That's what I asked him."

"What did he say?"

"Nothing, Doc. Very hush-hush, I gathered. Strickland, he said, would be telling us something later."

Not only was Wisby clearly disappointed. He was in an acute nervous state.

"It's not only me, Doc. It's my crew as well."

"I see that."

"They persuaded me to come and see you."

He doubted that, but did not question it. "I'll see what I can do."

"Thanks, Doc." Wisby immediately brightened. "Thanks very much."

"I warn you, I may not be able to do anything."

"Oh, you'll be able to fix it, Doc!"

He doubted that, too. Things were becoming altogether too psychologically complicated. Something further of Strickland's strategy was emerging. His error over the *Groningen* was going to be interpreted as a victory, as are most calamities by astute leaders. If he'd had the chance, medals would have come showering down from heaven on the dead crew of his, but DFCs or DFMs—the only applicable decorations in the circumstances —could not be recommended posthumously. So his guess was that 507, by means of an intensive training programme and all leave cancelled, were going to be transformed into a *corps d'élite*, a Band of Brothers, all dedicated to rid the world for ever of this troublesome ship.

He rang Strickland in his office.

"Yes, Doc?"

"Wisby's just been in to see me."

"Anything the matter with him?"

"He's not ill, if that's what you mean."

"Good."

"He's just a bit upset about having his leave cancelled."

"Nothing to do with me, Doc. AOC's orders."

Knowing Air Vice-Marshal Nuttall of 55 Group and knowing that Strickland was his favourite blue-eyed boy, Flint very much doubted that. But all he said was, "It isn't a good thing psychologically, interfering with leave."

"I wouldn't know about those things, Doc. But surely giving the boys a goal to strive for, a pole to reach—"

"Both poles have already been reached years ago."

"A star then. A star to reach. *Per ardua ad astra*. Hell, Doc, you know what I mean!"

"If Wisby doesn't go on leave, I may have to ground him."

"*Ground* him? What for?"

"Fatigue."

"Fatigue? *Fatigue*? He hasn't flown for the last ten days!"

"I still may have to ground him."

"You mean, send him to the Aircrew Refresher School at Sheffield?"

This establishment with its typically euphemistic name was designed to put a bit of pep back into aircrew who, while not exactly refusing to fly on operations, were showing marked reluctance to stick their necks out at the enemy further than a tortoise. There was a lot of PT and parades and marching and heartiness and everything was done at the double. The spartan quarters, the messing and the restrictions on coming in and going out were in complete contrast to the average RAF Officers' and Sergeants' Mess and the total freedom (provided only that they carried out their flying operations) allowed all aircrew.

"No, I don't. I mean I'll diagnose fatigue."

"You mean, if Wisby doesn't go on leave, you'll give him a rest on medical grounds."

"That's what I mean."

"Because of fatigue?"

"Because of fatigue."

"Fatigue appears a pretty complicated medical condition."

"It is."

"Can't say I grasped it all, not having the benefit of a medical education, Doc . . . but I do see the position. I'll have a word with the Wingco. See if a special case can be made of Wisby."

Which being interpreted, Flint thought, is that nothing will be done on the leave front but the Wingco (it was after all about the only thing he was good for) would carry the can.

46

"And now if you'll excuse me, Doc, there's been some cock-up over S Sugar I'll have to see to."

He would be upset at losing for ever his personal aircraft. The same way as crews stuck together, pilots had a fierce loyalty for their own aircraft, particularly if it had brought them back on a wing and a prayer. Strickland could do nothing about the burials of his seven crew, but clearly he was damned if he was going to have S Sugar buried with them.

"I'm just off to see Wilkinson now. Bye, Doc."

When he had put the receiver down, Flint nearly picked it up again to warn the Equipment Officer. But that was not his business. In his own particular neck of the woods, he'd already come out into the open with Strickland rather more than he liked. He had a feeling that the *Groningen* affair was growing, and he had no wish to be involved in it further than he had to be. In any case, there was no need, because both Wilkinson and Hart, the Engineering Officer, were expecting a full frontal attack and were at that moment waiting in the Equipment Office, sitting on the left of Emma Jones' desk, keeping a watch out for the Squadron Leader's green-and-brown-camouflaged Hillman van.

"Here he is."

They watched him park the van and start to walk up the path towards the door. He was no stranger to the route—he was always coming to Equipment for material for his good ideas.

In he came through the door, nodded to the two men, said "Hello, Emma," to the girl.

"Hello, sir."

"You're looking very pretty this morning." And then without any more ado, "What's this nonsense about S?"

Wilkinson said, "I'm afraid we've had to write her off, sir."

"Over my dead body!"

"S Sugar," said Hart, "needs two new engines, a port tail-plane, front and rear turrets, six stanchions, two mainwheel tyres, most of a starboard wing, new bomb-doors, a new hydraulic reservoir, main rudder control rods, numerous plates, twelve—"

"There's such things as spares."

"And we've been spending most of yesterday trying to locate them," said Wilkinson.

47

"Where?"

"Every MU* in the country."

"You haven't been tough enough, Wilkinson."

"Look, sir, you know what the position is on spares for American aircraft."

"You could have got them if you'd used your savvy."

"Sir . . . the MUs haven't got them! If S Sugar had been a British aircraft, I'd have contacted the factories, but—"

"So what do you propose to do?"

"Well, sir," said the Engineering Officer soothingly, "Sugar will be very useful. We need her to provide spares we can't get otherwise."

"You mean you're going to cannibalize her?"

"Well, sir, she is our only source—"

"I'm not having her innards eaten up for other people's aircraft!"

"Sir, there's no alternative!"

"Look, we need every damned aircraft we've got! With this big training programme on, I've no intention of losing her."

"Sir, she's as near a total wreck as ever I've seen!"

"She still managed to fly five hundred miles home without much difficulty."

"Sir, the MUs—"

"You're too nice, Wilkinson. You've got to be rude to these characters. Ring 'em up and tell 'em you'll go over their heads to Maintenance Command."

"I have done."

"And what was the result?"

"A hollow laugh. Maintenance Command haven't any Liberator spares either."

"*Somebody* must have some."

"Only the Americans." Two small round spots had appeared on Wilkinson's normally pale cheeks. "You seem to think we can make gold out of straw! We haven't got a Griselda locked up in Stores weaving Liberator spares, sir!"

"But there you're wrong, Wilkinson."

Strickland turned his head round and looked meaningfully at the girl, who had kept her eyes down on her desk as she checked

* Maintenance Unit.

48

through a consignment note, while the argument around her became more heated.

"You've got Emma."

"What d'you mean?"

"No psychology, that's your trouble, Wilkinson! No ideas! Surely you know that a pretty face sells everything?"

"We've got nothing to sell."

"It also *obtains* everything! Haven't you heard that an American Navy B-24* Squadron has just arrived at Machrannoch?"

"No."

"Christ, even old Brackenbury knew that! The Sixty-sixth."

"I still don't see the connection."

"Emma, man! Emma's the connection!"

Wilkinson said stiffly, "Sir?"

"Ring up the Stores Officer at Machrannoch. Give a big warm welcome to the Sixty-sixth. Tell him you're sending one of your staff to make the connection. To see if we can be of any assistance. To show them the ropes."

"Sir, I really don't think—"

"That's your trouble, Wilkinson, you don't! No ideas! No imagination! Our new crew—Irvine's boys—begins ground school today. As a start to their flying programme, I'll lay on a cross-country to Machrannoch. Griselda Jones can go along with them. You'd love that, wouldn't you, Emma?"

* The official American designation of the Liberator.

49

FOUR

OVER the snow-covered mountains of Sutherland, the Liberator wallowed. The port wing dropped. Two thousand feet below, the salmon-filled Naver zig-zagged a glittering invitation as the aircraft slowly descended to the left. Then up came the wing as F Freddie resumed a straight and level course south-west along the long valley to Machrannoch.

"She's doing very well, isn't she?"

Standing between the two front seats, Irvine's beanpole of a second pilot, Flight-Sergeant Henty, nodded his head towards the girl in the co-pilot's position flying the aeroplane, and gave her an encouraging smile.

Irvine grunted out an unwilling affirmative. He had heard the news that he was taking the WAAF Equipment Officer on a training cross-country with mixed feelings. Emma Jones had seemed a nice enough girl when he had talked to her in the bar, and she had turned up wearing a smart new battledress and her brown hair neatly turned over the peak of an immaculate cap. But this was the first time he had flown with his new crew and he had his hands full enough without acting as chauffeur to a girl.

Strickland had not even told him the names of his crew, perhaps because he thought (quite unnecessarily, for Irvine would not have dared to do so) that if he actually knew them, he might object. All he had said was, "Your crew is waiting at Number 2 hangar, Peter. Now remember, you're the captain. Start how you mean to go on."

A thick drizzle had started as he set off from 507 to HQ. Rounding the corner of the perimeter track, through the glassy air he had seen them standing just inside the huge open doors, a bundle of bods dominated by what appeared to be an ancient barrage balloon.

50

This plump apparition he immediately recognized, and his heart went down to his boots. For the last month, it had been hanging around the Officers' Mess, scrupulously avoided by everyone, including Irvine. But one evening he had been caught like an aeroplane in its mooring rope, brought down, forced to listen to a difficult-to-understand soliloquy about the waste of an experienced air-gunner, twenty-five years in the Polish Air Force, so long lying uncrewed up in the aircrew pool.

"Flight-Lieutenant Vladimir Moscovich." Crystallized in minute water drops, the barrage balloon had come floating towards him. "At your service, Captain!"

Irvine hadn't known what else to do, so he had shaken hands. He had shaken hands with the others too—all Sergeants. The tall Henty, his second pilot, was clearly anxious to please. His Navigator was a rather elderly schoolmaster called Garth. Two tough-looking Australian Wireless Operator/Air Gunners in dark blue uniforms both had hard handshakes—Brett and Jarman. A white-faced, red-nosed man, Trembath, was his Wireless Operator/Radar. Craik was his Engineer, a waif with big gob-stopper eyes and a Birmingham accent. The most cheerful of the lot was a pink-faced Radio Operator with black hair carefully sleeked and parted called Miggs, who had immediately endeared himself to Irvine by giving him a big smile and saying in a tone of utter confidence, "Looks like a cracking good crew we've got here, Skipper!"

Apart from naming their names, none of the others had said anything. Leading them off to the Intelligence Office for a briefing from Brackenbury, hearing their footsteps behind him splashing in the puddles on the tarmac, Irvine had all of a sudden been assailed by the burden and loneliness of command.

The only reason that he had this command, he knew perfectly well, was that nightmare trip and the lucky photograph of the *Groningen*. He was grateful to Strickland for his faith in him—a faith that was not shared by other members of 507 Squadron. The other co-pilots, most of whom had been sitting in the right-hand seat for nearly a year, had been far from pleased by his quick promotion. They made it clear that nowhere near did he have sufficient operational experience to be a Liberator captain. Only one friend did he have amongst them—Bertie Maltravers, an aristocratic young gentleman two years younger than himself, scion of a family with vast estates in Dorset, who had joined the RAF straight from Harrow. He was second pilot to Guilonard, an ex-KLM captain who had lost all his family in the Stuka raid on Rotterdam, now in the Dutch Naval Air Service. Maltravers was not in the least jealous. In fact, he actually congratulated him. Irvine knew only too well his own inexperience—Irvine 4, not out. The trouble was he suspected that his new crew knew it too.

Irvine also recognized the awkwardness and unsureness of his multi-national crew. That had shown perfectly clearly in their few days' ground-training together: gunnery practice, Intelligence briefings, a compass swing, dinghy and escape drill, radio and navigation exercises, radar, astro and armament instruction, attack tactics on ships and U-boats. Apart from the Australians, who were inseparable, he had a feeling that all the others were too individual and too different to form an efficient and inter-related crew. As for Mosco, he was almost old enough to be his grandfather, and acted more like the captain of the crew than Irvine himself. Only Miggs, the man with the permanent smile, had by his eternal optimism managed to inject into Irvine a few cubic centimetres of confidence.

"Killing two birds with one stone," Strickland had said to him as the reason for this communication-cum-flying training exercise. "Your Wops will be able to get some radio practice in. Put them on the radar, watching the lochs and the rivers, and see if they learn to pick up other aircraft. Try getting some W/T bearings. And see how your Navigator shapes up on Dead Reckoning navigation."

So far, none of them had shaped up particularly well. The appearance of the girl had meant that they had treated the whole thing as a social occasion rather than a training trip. Instead of practising on radio and radar, they put themselves out to entertain the lady. Miggs had sat her down at the Marconi, put her hand on the key, taught her to transmit their call sign to Control. Instead of practising himself, Trembath had explained the relentless illuminated line that swept round the radar screen every five seconds, bringing up a muzzy portrait of the lines of Loch Shin and the wriggling of the river Naver. She had been up in the mid-upper turret, swapped places with Jarman and been shown how to move the guns up and down and swivel the front

52

turret. Garth had explained the mysteries of wind drift that changed a course into a track, and had got her lying prone in the perspex-bottomed nose, manipulating the low-level bombsight. Even Craik had been heard to expound on throttle and rpm settings in his broad Birmingham accent. Finally, there had been a call of "Give her a go, Skipper!" and reluctantly Irvine had agreed to her being installed in the co-pilot's seat, flying the aircraft.

The only person on board who had not been pleased was Moscovich who, after an initial assault of foreign charm had not succeeded in luring her out of the sharp end, had retreated to the rear turret and was now sitting in high dudgeon as the tail swung erratically this way and that.

As a training exercise, it was not a success. There was far too much brilliant sunshine. Lines of white-coned mountain peaks unmistakably pointed the way, and as an additional aid to direction the forty-mile-long Loch Inver arrowheaded their destination. Miss Jones drew in a deep breath of enthusiastic awe at the beauty of the view, at the same time sending the Liberator into a heavy yaw to starboard.

Mercifully, Machrannoch's long runway showed up clear as crystal fifty miles away.

"Cleared for a straight-in on 27," said the clipped American voice from the Tower.

As his final share of the entertainment, Irvine allowed Miss Jones to stay in the right-hand seat for the landing. Instructed by Henty, she put down the lever first for the wheels, then the flaps. He kept his own hands on the throttles, reduced the power to fifteen inches, came down in quite a nice descent at 500 feet a minute, then rounded out just right and came down very sweetly.

"Nice landing, sir," said Flight-Sergeant Henty.

He was pleased to do such a good landing on the first trip with his crew. Taxiing confidently and quickly, he swung the Liberator round the perimeter track.

Over by the white Control Tower, a man wearing olive-green drab and what looked like a huge-brimmed baseball cap was waving two bats at him. He taxied up, switched off, and they all crawled out of the belly through the open bomb doors.

A tall US Navy Lieutenant was waiting to greet them.

"The name's Greaves. Ba-a-a-b Greaves." He held his hand out to the girl. "You're Miss Jones. We've spoken on the telephone."

She introduced his crew, Irvine thought, like a Queen presenting her chauffeur and bodyguard to a foreign dignitary. This would be the Equipment Officer, the chap out of whom it was hoped to squeeze—in Strickland's words—"a few bits and pieces for poor old Sugar".

The American looked at his watch. "Twelve after one. What d'you say to lunch? The Mess is just on the other side of the hangar there."

"That would be fine."

Now the American began actually apologizing for the absence of the CO in the welcoming committee. "A U-boat pack has been sighted on the surface at 20 West." He had grey wrinkly eyes, but spoke in a dry crackling drawl. "So they've been sending the boys off all morning. The Captain hasn't even seen a U-boat yet, so naturally he was the first to go. He's seen one now all right. We got an attack message an hour ago."

And now I've seen my first American, Irvine thought—in the flesh, that is, not in a film. But my God, they all behave as though they *are* in a film. The American flag was fluttering at the top of the mast outside a superior Nissen hut, obviously of American construction, that was clearly the Station Head-quarters. A tractor driven by the spitting image of Harpo Marx, curly hair waving wildly in the wind, passed them pulling trolleys filled with a layer of 250-pound depth charges. From the balcony outside the Control Room, the twin of Robert Taylor put binoculars to his eyes to watch a Liberator lumbering off to the west. Even this Equipment Officer, leading the way with Miss Jones, walked in a gangling loose-shouldered lope that was a cross between Gregory Peck and James Stewart.

Irvine followed with Henty. The other Sergeants made an untidy bunch in their centre. Mosco, still sulking, brought up the rear.

"Here we are!"

It was quite unlike an RAF Nissen hut, which usually resembled half a tin can. This one had a greeny tinge to it, and in comparison was a cavern of comfort. Far more paper hung by clips on the wall. A big hand-painted poster announced a dance that night. The chairs were not so comfortable though. No deep, leather-covered, standard issue RAF armchairs. These were more utilitarian. Five men were playing crap, crooning to the dice and snapping their fingers. A big letter rack, bulging with mail. No WAAF orderlies in neat blue overalls, just a barman straight out of a Western, cigar and all, at the other side of the counter.

"I expect you're thirsty."

Five men looking like Deputy Marshals made way for them at the bar. Eleven ice-cold Coca-Colas dropped down one after the other like a stick of depth charges onto the counter. Two men in heavy fur-lined jackets wearing hats with brims bent almost double downwards ("Hats on in the Mess!" whispered Henty) gave a wolf whistle at Assistant Section Officer Jones and called out "Nice goin', Ba-a-a-ab!"

The American talked to Miss Jones. Irvine and crew drank their drinks. Their glasses empty, cigarettes extinguished, no red-carpeted dining room with the soft sound of WAAF waitresses' feet, but a noisy Mess hall with long tables and an endless counter at which they queued with metal trays with appropriate holes.

"The chow line," explained the American as they began moving forward towards steamy, shining aluminium bins where white-overalled cooks were busy with huge spoons. Instead of two frugal sausages and some grey mashed potato, followed by rice pudding—steaks as big as your hand, or turkey if you wanted it, and french fried potatoes and tomatoes, followed by a mountain of different coloured ice-cream laid in dollops, one on top of the other.

They all sat together at one long table, Lieutenant Greaves and Miss Jones at one end, Mosco and the little Engineer at the other. The Sergeants immediately began tucking in without saying anything.

"Operating American aircraft as we do, Lieutenant Greaves—"

"Call me Ba-a-a-b, sweetheart."

"—Bob, our problem is—"

"You got a problem, sweetheart?"

"Yes, Bob, it's—"

"You got a first name, too?"

The conversation was largely concentrated on the Lieutenant

55

and Miss Jones. Miss Jones was explaining RAF shortages and economics, saying that the daily expenditure on food was one shilling and five pence per day per person. His laughing disbelief gave credence to the picture they were all making, Irvine thought, watching his crew with their noses inches away from their plates, of some rich and kindly uncle taking out Nicholas Nickleby and his friends for a treat from Dotheboys Hall.

"Anyone want seconds?"

All the Sergeants did. The American waved them up for a further assault at the counter and the shining steel bins. The rate he was going, Irvine's waif of an Engineer looked as though he'd go up for a third time. Meanwhile a bond of mutual sympathy, of shared similar experiences, appeared to have sprung up between the Lieutenant and Miss Jones. They had begun their own private language of Equipment technicalities. Stores reference numbers, parts, the difficulties of obtaining spares, their furious efforts with their own Maintenance Units to keep their aircraft flying, interspersed with their own life stories.

". . . Yorkshire. Highcliffe. My father's the doctor there . . ."

". . . computerized stock taking. Des Moines University, which was where I was lecturing. Mathematics, yes. I'd hoped to go flying, but as you see," he tapped his spectacles. "These."

"At University . . . London . . . English."

"Form 654 . . . no believe it or not, *sixteen* copies. That's right. Six-figure code reference numbers . . ."

"The RAF system is based on that of Selfridge's, the big store in Oxford Street."

"One brother in the Army. And a younger sister still at school."

"We go in for big families down Wyoming."

The two of them got up.

"Emma and I," said the American Lieutenant—they had advanced a lifetime in a lunch, American film-fashion—"are just going along to my office now. Go through the spares situation. See what we've got." A vague gesture with his right hand. "Get the paperwork sorted out. If you boys wouldn't mind waiting." Pointing to a hutted building on the other side of the road. "There's the Club over there. Magazines. Daily papers. A juke box."

56

Inside, it would have been comfortable except for the fact that the carpet had been rolled up in preparation for that night's dance. Some chairs—again not particularly comfortable, but at least they had cushions—lined up along the walls. Mosco's only comment was where did they get the women for a dance, stuck out miles away like this. He had only seen one American woman officer in the Mess. Irvine picked up the *Mirror*, turned to the cartoon to see what Jane had been up to, finding with some disappointment that she had just finished having a bath, and was coming out of the bathroom fully clothed.

The time ticked by. He kept looking at his watch. It was nearly four o'clock, and no sign of Miss Jones. He began to be fidgety, going over to the window and staring up at the sky. The forecast at Kilcreggan had warned of a warm front towards evening. Already the sky was darkening. He didn't want bad weather, what with the high hill beside the west-to-east runway. Scotch drizzle and fog he had heard about, but so far never met. The only blind landing system was QNH* or Babs† and he didn't want to trust his new crew to bring him down "in anger" —on an actual as apart from a practice bad weather let-down.

Four fifty-five. The light was draining out of the sky. Low stratus began rolling in, mute evidence that the front was closing in fast. He dug his hands deep into his pockets and stamped his feet impatiently.

"When are we going then, Skipper?"

He shrugged his shoulders. He didn't know the layout of the camp, where to go, what to do. It was like being imprisoned, and he felt his anger mounting against the indignity of it all, particularly in the way that Miss Jones and the Lieutenant had disappeared. He was just thinking he had better try telephoning their Equipment Section, had gone over to an instrument stuck in the corner, when suddenly it rang.

He picked up the receiver. It was Emma Jones. She sounded excited, high almost. Sorry to have kept them hanging around, but there was no further need. They could go back to Kilcreggan.

"What about you?"

"I'll be staying."

* Descent through cloud.
† Blind Approach Beam System.

57

"What for?"

Vaguely: "Supervising."

"But you didn't bring any overnight things!"

"There's shops in the village. Only two miles away. Bob Greaves is running me over there. It's all right, I've rung Kilcreggan and spoken to Squadron-Leader Strickland. I'm to stay and you're to go. That's an order, he said. Anything I have to buy will be refunded. He'll sign my expense form. But apparently the weather's closing in, so Squadron-Leader Strickland's getting worried about *you*."

"I see."

"Thanks for the ride. I did enjoy it."

He put down the receiver and explained the position to his crew. The only comment came from Mosco. "So *that* is how they get their women for dances!"

The departure was less ceremonial than the arrival. Liberators were still taking off. Bomb trolleys were moving in the half darkness. Nobody seemed to have any time for them. Nobody saw them off. There weren't even any starter accs* available, and Irvine had to start the Pratt and Whitneys off the internal batteries.

The trip back, trying to beat the weather in, was more like Dick Turpin's dash to York with frothing steed, and all idea of training was abandoned, as at thirty-three inches Manifold Pressure, 2300 rpm, they struggled up to 155 knots, trying to race the bad weather into Kilcreggan.

They lost.

Thick, wet cloud enveloped them. Rain started pouring down, making an eerie electric fuzz over the windscreen. Cloud base at Kilcreggan was given at six hundred feet, visibility half a mile. Suddenly it had gone very cold. Irvine had only done four blind let-downs using the radio descent through cloud, all of them on the ground in the Link Trainer.

But tonight there was nothing else for it. He called over his shoulder to Trembath, "We'll be doing a QNH."

"You're not going to try Babs?"

Babs needed even more practice. Besides, it was often erratic.

"No."

"OK, Skipper."

Trembath seemed calm and confident enough, getting regular

* Accumulators.

58

bearings and courses to steer. Well to the east of the Station, out over the sea, Irvine began descending, the Liberator bumping, wings flapping, engines flapping.

Lower and lower—the altimeter reading 1000, 800, 600. Everyone conscious they were well below the level of the mountains. He tried the R/T, but the static was terrible.

"Course 266, Skipper."

"Turning onto 266. Gear down!"

"Runway should be dead ahead now."

He held his height, skimming just under the cloud base.

"Lights, Skipper!" Henty called out. "To port! *To port!*"

He saw the flarepath: a disembodied muzzy yellow line drowning in damp darkness. He lifted the right wing right up, trying to get round. But it was too late.

"Gear up! Forty inches!"

Henty pulled up the undercarriage lever at the same time as Craik pushed forward the throttles. F Freddie roared up into the night.

"Trembath . . . we'll have to try another one."

"Roger, Skipper."

Again he began tapping out on his key.

Strickland had always said keep everyone in your crew informed. Conscious of Moscovich, out on a limb far away from the rest, Irvine lifted up his microphone. "Are you all right, Rear Gunner?"

"I-am-all-right." The Polish voice sounded more guttural than ever on the intercom.

"It won't be long now, Mosco."

There was a pause. "Not understand."

"I said . . . not long now."

He was struggling in the rough air to get the Liberator back onto 266.

"What is not long?"

"It won't be long before we're down on the ground."

"Down in the ground?"

An updraught lifted the port wing. The engines hiccupped. "*On* the ground. Not long now and we'll be down *on* the ground."

"600 feet, Skipper."

"Levelling off. Gear down!"

"Gear down. Three green lights."

"Let me know when you see lights."

"How-do-you-mean-on-the-ground?"

"On the runway!"

"Not long now and we will be back on the runway?"

"Yes. *Yes!*"

A longer pause this time. Then: "Which runway? Where is this runway?"

"Lights, Skipper! Starboard! *Starboard!*"

Again it was too late. He could not get round. Up went the wheels. Steeply F Freddie began climbing.

Altogether it took him over an hour to get settled on a landing approach. By that time, the night was a glassy sheet of rain. Misjudging his approach, he brought F Freddie in far too fast and set her down with a bang.

There was a squeal of protest from the brakes as he jammed them on. F Freddie slithered to a stop inches away from the red boundary lights.

"Nice landing, sir," said Flight-Sergeant Henty loyally.

As they taxied to Dispersal up onto the flight deck came a horrible smell of burning rubber.

Irvine saw the gloomy faces of F's fitter and rigger—Heaton and Race—as they waved him into position with torches. Smoke was rising from the main wheels.

"Looks like a double tyre change," they told him. "The Equipment Officer'll go spare!"

Nobody said anything in the lorry that took them from Dispersal to the crew room and then to the Officers' Mess.

Trailing up the corridor, water was literally streaming from the Pole's battledress.

"Mosco, you're wet through!"

"It is the turret. It leaks."

For some reason, Irvine felt guilty about that too. "Sorry about that."

Moscovich took a large white handkerchief out of his pocket and began to wipe his wet grey face. Reaching the stairs in the east wing leading up to the room he shared with Garfield, he turned his head and looked back at Irvine with his grey-green hound-dog eyes. "One day I write a book about the RAF . . . a *fonny* book!"

*　*　*

After dropping the officers, the next point of call was the Sergeants' Mess.

"Here we are again! Happy as can be . . ."

Jumping over the tailboard of the lorry even before it stopped, Miggs landed with a thump and a laugh.

". . . all good pals and jolly good company!"

One after the other, the rest of Irvine's crew disembarked silently and went up the steps in through the blacked-out doors.

Miggs stayed behind. Waiting till the rest of the crew had disappeared, he sauntered up to the front, put his left foot on the running board and looked up at the shadowy WAAF behind the wheel.

"You are," he said authoritatively, "a beautiful driver."

From the darkness of the cab came a snort of derisive laughter followed by the grind of the self-starter turning.

"What's so funny about that?"

"First time I've ever heard *that* line."

The engine burst into life. The quivering of the running board rocked his knee.

"Beautiful I said, beautiful I mean." He put his right arm through the open window into the cab, and slid his fingers round the steering wheel. "I should know. A racing driver . . . that's what I was before joining this lark."

"Pull the other one!"

Out came the clutch. The lorry made a jerk forward.

"Hey, what's the hurry then?"

Miggs had got onto the running board. The lorry grizzled along the wet tarmac.

"Get off!" the WAAF shouted at him.

"Not on your nelly!"

"The SWO*'ll see you and then—"

He had put his head right into the cab, and finding her face gave the side of her mouth a quick kiss.

The lorry ground to a stop at the same time as a slap landed hard on his cheek. "Get off!"

"Hitting a non-commissioned officer . . . now where's the SWO?"

"I'll hit you again if you don't get off!"

* Station Warrant Officer.

61

Inches away from her face, she could see his eyes sparkling in the light reflected off the mist from the hooded headlamps.

"Deirdre Winter—you're a beautiful girl too!"

There was the slightest pause. "How did you know my name?"

"There's lots I know about *you*."

She gave an uncertain laugh. "All good, I hope?"

"The best."

"That shows you don't know anything about me at all!"

"Oh, but I do!" He put his face hard against hers. "For instance, your last station was Coningsby—"

"How did you know that?"

"And you've got a brother in the Army."

"Hey, what's this? Have you been—"

"And you're nineteen."

There was a gasp. "You—"

"I've been watching you. Ever since I've come to this Station, I've been watching you."

"Here, you're not an SP*, are you? I've done nothing. I tell you—"

"Interesting . . .*very* interesting." He pulled her forward and put his arms round her. "I know *lots* about you!"

"But *how*?"

"In the Secret Service . . . that's where I was, before joining this lark."

"You!" He had put his face against hers again and this time she made no effort to pull away. "You're a right one!"

"*You're* the right one, Deirdre Winter. You're a bit of all right, all right! First thing I ever found out."

"But why?"

"Because, because—"

"Because what?"

"I told you."

"You didn't!"

"Because—"

"Go *on*!"

"Because, Deirdre Winter, you're beautiful."

His mouth came hard against hers. His tongue had come out like a soft blunt probe and was forcing her lips apart. It had

* Service Police.

62

just managed to break through the portcullis, and big as a tidal wave had come flooding into her mouth when she pulled her head away.

"What's the matter now?"

"First time I've ever done it like this."

"Done what?"

"Snogging with a chap on the running board. Can't half look funny . . . you with your bum hanging out of the window."

"There are more comfortable places. One I know in particular."

"Where's that?"

"That staircase opposite the kitchen in the Sergeants' Mess. Up at the top, there's a little room—"

He felt her body stiffen in his arms.

"You know it, don't you?"

Her body was still hard and unrelaxed.

"I know you do!"

His face had come down again on hers. His tongue, demanding now, turned into a battering ram and forced its way through her lips. Taking its time, it began exploring the warm wet cave that it found itself in, slid along her even teeth, reached the roof of her mouth.

Then he pulled away. "Getting cramp." He began edging his body out of the cab. "So what time shall I be seeing you?"

"What d'you mean . . . what time?"

"What time d'you get off duty?"

"Nine."

He jumped off the running board. Looking up at her, he said. "In half an hour then . . . right?"

"I don't know about that."

"I'll tell you lots more. Lots more about what makes you tick. A psychologist, that's what I was, before joining this lark."

"You . . . *you!*"

"So that's all fixed then."

"Who says?"

"I say. And what *I* say goes."

"And who are you?"

"I am Squadron-Leader Strickland."

"Wish you was! All the girls think he's smashing."

"So you're a very lucky girl to get me."

"If you're Squadron-Leader Strickland, what's happened to your lovely fair hair then? Why are you wearing Sergeant's stripes?"

"Demoted this morning." Miggs lowered his voice. "Deirdre, I'm deserting. I'm running away *to you!*" In quite a different tone, he added, "Can't stay out here all night! Getting drenched! Bloody cold too! Wouldn't be surprised if it snows." He jumped off the running board. "See you in half an hour."

"But I don't know your name!"

"Strickland."

"Don't be silly!"

"I've never liked my name. Not my *real* name."

"What is it?"

"Well—" He paused. "It's Miggs."

"Miggs? Mm . . . yes, I see. Well, what's your *other* name?"

"I like that less."

"Tell me!"

"No."

"I bet I'd like it."

"You wouldn't."

"I'll find out."

"You won't be able to."

"I'll ask your crew."

"They don't know. Nobody knows."

"But what shall I call you?"

"Miggs."

"Oh, come on!"

He began moving away, blowing a kiss as he went. "See you soon."

As the lorry went rumbling past him, she shouted, "Now no nonsense, mind! No funny business, Miggs!"

"No funny business *promise*, Deirdre Winter!"

He ran all the way to the Sergeants' Mess. The rain was turning to sleet. Up at the bar, he found the rest of his crew.

"What's the matter with you lot then?" he demanded, turning to Craik. "Curly, you look as though you'd seen a ghost."

"We was holding a book on what our chances are of lasting till Christmas."

"If you're feeling that bad, Curly, why don't you go and see the Doc?"

"I mean the Skipper's flying," Craik said sepulchrally.

"What's the matter with the Skipper's flying?"

"Well, did *you* expect to get back on the ground tonight?" Trembath demanded. "All in one piece, I mean?"

"Nice chap, the Skipper," Henty said. Second pilots were always the most loyal and the least critical of the crew. They knew that, God willing, they might be soon in the left-hand seat and be receiving the same scrutiny and criticism.

"Oh, he's a nice chap . . . nobody's saying he isn't," Trembath went on. "But he's a kid. No experience. And he flies a Liberator like—"

"The Skipper flies OK," Henty said stubbornly. "There's nothing the matter with the Skipper's flying."

"Then why was it touch-and-go today?" Craik asked. "I mean it was only the weather he had to cope with today. What happens when he has to cope with the Jerries?" The Engineer's big eyes nearly bulged out of their sockets. "What happens when he has to cope with the weather *and* the Jerries?"

Garth took the pipe out of his mouth. Above the beaked nose, the eyes looked down on Craik and Trembath benevolently from the great height of a schoolmaster on two Third Formers. "Listening to you two, I was reminded particularly of *A Midsummer Night's Dream*."

"I'm not dreaming," Trembath said indignantly.

"Bottom and Co . . . the players, you remember. You two are so like Snout, the Tinker, and Starveling, the Tailor."

Leaning on the counter, the two Australian gunners, lean and lithe as greyhounds, glinting blue eyes in sunburned chiselled faces, listened good-humouredly to the pommies, drank up the weak, warm beer and pushed their glasses over to the barman for another. "Want one, Miggs?" they asked him.

"Not now, lads, thanks." To the barman he said "Four bottles of light ale. And you wouldn't have a quarter bottle of gin, by any chance?" He turned round to the others. "I'm very glad to be on Mr Irvine's crew."

"So am I," said Jim Henty. "All Mr Irvine needs is a bit of jollying along."

65

The bottles were passed across the counter. "That'll be eighteen and six."

"You drinking in your room?" Trembath asked disapprovingly.

Miggs indicated the smoky bar atmosphere. "Best place."

"Have they put anybody in Oakroyd's bed yet?"

Miggs shook his head. "Nor will do, if I can help it."

"Poor old Len Oakroyd!" said Garth. "Nice bod."

"What happened to that blonde of his?" Henty asked. "What was her name again?"

"Winter," supplied Brett, the taller Australian.

"Deirdre," said Jarman, the shorter one.

"Deirdre Winter," Craik said darkly. "Have you noticed?"

"Noticed what?" asked Garth.

"Every chap she goes out with gets the chop. She was Rackham's girl—and Rackham was killed when Marshall attacked that U-boat. Then she was Warrant-Officer Gaunt's girl—and he was shot down by night fighters. Then she was handed over to Oakroyd, and look what happened to him!"

"A real jinx," Trembath said.

"Delilah," said Craik.

"Lovely looking girl," observed Henty.

"Those sort always are," said Craik. "Hope for our sakes Moscovich doesn't get hold of her."

"He will, don't worry," Trembath said. "Those fat old Poles always get the girls."

"No need to worry," Jarman said. "Lynch on Wisby's crew's taken her over now."

Henty asked, "Where does she work?"

"MT.* She's a driver," said Brett.

"Wasn't our driver tonight a blonde?" asked Henty.

"Didn't notice," Trembath said. "Too bloody glad to be back on the ground to care."

"Me neither," said Craik. "Was she a blonde, Miggs?"

The Wireless Operator pocketed his change. "Never notice such things, Curly."

"You never notice anything else!"

"Me for a little shut-eye."

"Aren't you going to have any supper?"

* Motor Transport Section.

66

"Not hungry." Miggs picked up his bottles. " 'Night, chaps."

He waved his hand, walked out of the bar, down the passage and then up to his room. He knew she was there before he pressed down the switch. The light reflected off the bright golden hair: real chocolate-box blonde, blue eyes, nice figure, the lot.

She was standing by the window in the darkness.

"Well, where've you been then?"

He put down the bottles and came over and kissed her. "Sorry, love. Didn't expect you so soon."

"The Sarge let me off early."

He got out two glasses and a bottle of lime juice from his locker. He poured a gin and lime for her. Then he opened a beer for himself, and sat down on his bed.

"Come and sit on my knee."

In the darkness, she came over, carefully nursing the gin in both her hands, and perched herself precariously on his legs.

"Comfy?"

"Not very."

"You will be soon." He clinked his glass with hers. "Bottoms up!"

"Cheers."

There was a long silence. Then he said, "Len Oakroyd used to bring you here, didn't he?"

She said nothing.

"When he had the room to himself. Before I arrived. That's what he told me." Miggs paused. "He told me a lot about you. Said you were—"

"Said I was what?"

"A bit of all right."

She said suspiciously, "What did he mean by that?"

"Love . . . just that you were a real beauty." He paused. "And you are."

She drank her gin, looking at him over the rim of the glass.

"Come on, love!" He took hold of her right arm and draped it round his neck. "I'm not going to bite!"

He bent his head down and kissed her. The arm round his neck tightened.

67

"Drink up and have another one!"

The gin disappeared. The beer disappeared. Only the lime juice remained.

A flush had come up into her cheeks. He had his left arm round her waist. One by one, the buttons of her serge blouse became undone. He felt for her trouser zip.

Between kisses, she said accusingly, "You're an expert!"

"Look who's talking! Why d'you girls have to wear battle dress?" he demanded, pulling down the zip of her trousers.

"You promised no funny business, remember?"

"I remember."

"What's this then?"

"This is *serious* business."

She said nothing for so long that at first he thought she hadn't heard him.

Then suddenly she pushed him away and stood up. "Yep," she said, "Serious for some." She swayed slightly on her feet.

"And what does that mean, Deirdre?"

"It means, it means, it means . . . oh, Christ!" She began to cry. He had given her too much gin, that was certain. Big unreal tears ran down her cheeks. "It means you've no right to. It means I couldn't. Not here. Not now, don't you see? I couldn't, couldn't." She wrenched up her zip. "*Couldn't.*"

"All right then, love. All right," he said soothingly, taken aback by her sudden vehemence. "I get the message."

He began to do up her blouse buttons for her. All the time her eyes roamed his face anxiously.

"Don't you understand?" she asked.

"I *think* so."

"Not here, not so soon. Not this time."

"Time!" he repeated shaking his head. "Ah, sweetheart. Time."

He helped her into her greatcoat. Everything was the wrong way round. He should have been taking her clothes off, not putting them on. Damn the ghost of old Oakroyd!

"Come with me to the door, eh?" she said.

He followed her down the concrete steps along the brown linoleum corridor. No one saw them. As he opened the side door, a gust of cold wind and a handful of snow blew in. "The north wind doth blow," Miggs sighed, "and we shall have snow," he pulled a long, sad face, "And what shall the robin do then, poor thing?"

The snow continued all next day. The day after that it was worse. Operations continued, but there was no training flying—just lectures and Intelligence briefings. Irvine was disconsolately drinking coffee after lunch in the Mess ante-room, standing by the window, looking down the white carpet of the Mess drive to the main road, when he saw an RAF trailer lorry, the type known as *Queen Mary* because they were so long, coming in through the Station gates.

Seasonally sprinkled with glittering snow, it was packed higher than Father Christmas' sledge. A Liberator wing, tailplanes, wheels, tyres, two Pratt and Whitney engines, plates, gun turrets, Hamilton propellers.

And there in front beside the driver, looking out of the window from under the peak of a WAAF officer's cap, was the pink and white face of Assistant Section Officer Jones.

FIVE

Softly from over the mountains, the flakes fell like white feathers moulting off the sky, melting into slush almost as soon as they touched the ground. Then that weekend the wind veered east, solidifying the grey-green grass in front of Station Headquarters into crisp crystals, and turning the wet runways into skating rinks of ice.

All Operations were scrubbed for twelve days running.

Strickland was not so concerned as might have been thought. Intelligence Reports confirmed by PRU photographs indicated that the *Groningen* was stuck by the iced-up shallow entrance to Falstand Fjord. In his efforts for new ideas, Strickland had flown down to the Telecommunications Research Establishment at Malvern to see if he could pick up some new secret devices before Bomber Command laid their mitts on them, returning with a radar device called a Blind Bombsight which was designed to hit ships in fog or pitch darkness. The idea behind it was altogether too hush-hush to be broadcast, but as a special favour Strickland let on to Irvine that the principle was that you picked your target and centred it on the radar at five miles, locking on a strobe. That course was maintained for two and a half miles, at the end of which the target would have drifted. Double that drift was then applied in a new course during which, as it grew very close, the target would be swamped as always by sea-returns. But the bombsight had timed the entire run, and released the bombs automatically.

While the spares that Emma Jones had collected from Machrannoch were being fitted to S Sugar, now dominating the main hangar, the Blind Bombsight was fitted to Z Zebra. Strickland and his new crew—the three officers, Tarrant, Yates and Wheeler, had taken over the three empty beds in Room 27 from their predecessors—were on strictly secret exercises with the cruiser *Marlborough*, provided from Scapa Flow. Little white practice bombs filled with hydrochloric acid were released by the Blind Bombsight. A hit could be recognized by a most impressive white plume of smoke. Strickland reported "very interesting" results. A story began circulating, perhaps generated by the Navy, that the BB (Strickland's code name for Security reasons) was missing by miles—but then all inventions and "good ideas" take time to develop.

The intensive training programme nevertheless went on—if not in the air, then on the ground. Leave was still cancelled. The only snow-plough was out all day and half the night, airmen shovelling the stuff in big heaps to the sides in order to keep the runways clear. Muffled up in balaclavas, the flight mechs doing the Daily Inspections on the Flight Dispersals slapped their arms across their bodies, trying to keep warm. In the Officers' Mess ante-room, the rustlings of newspaper pages being turned over and the slow drip-drips of coffee from the urn were drowned by sniffs and coughs and sneezes.

Worst of all was Mosco. Ashen-faced, watery-eyed, with a blue woollen scarf wrapped round his neck, he sent a Triple Grandsire peal of coughing echoing round the Mess every few minutes. Garfield, who shared a room with him, buttonholed Irvine as he came out of breakfast a fortnight before Christmas, and complained bitterly that he hadn't had a wink of sleep for three nights running.

"Tough," Irvine said.

"Is that all you're going to say?"

"Remember the poor chap's ill."

"Then he's got no bloody right spreading his germs all over the place."

"Why don't you suggest he goes and sees the Doc?"

"I have done."

"Well, then?"

"He pretends he doesn't understand. You know what he's like."

"Then we'll just have to wait till his cough gets better."

"No fear! That's a real graveyard hack he's got. I'm damned if he's going to give it to me."

"What the hell can I do about it?"

71

"You're his captain. He's your responsibility."

He tackled Mosco next morning, as the Pole struggled gallantly into his greatcoat in the cloakroom and then bent down to put galoshes over his shoes.

"I shouldn't come to Flights if I were you, Mosco. Tuck up by the radiator in the ante-room. I'll explain to Strickland."

Moscovich regarded him stonily. "What do you mean?"

"Your cough, Mosco."

"It is because I became so wet," he said reproachfully, "on the flight back from Machrannoch."

Irvine countered with "Why didn't you go and see the Doc?"

Moscovich shrugged his shoulders.

"Well, anyway, go and see him now!"

"No."

The sight of Mosco struggling doggedly through the snow, pausing every few minutes to cough his heart out, was, however, eventually perceived through Sick Quarters' window by Flint himself. Immediately, the Pole was hauled in, protesting. At lunch time that same day, the doctor told Irvine that he had examined Moscovich and packed him off to the local hospital in the hills above Kilcreggan.

"Is there something the matter with his lungs, Doc?"

"Not that I could see. But they've got the X-ray equipment. They'll be able to tell better."

"Do you think he'll come back?"

"What on earth d'you mean? He's not *that* bad!"

"I meant for flying duties, Doc." Irvine said hopefully, "Bit old, isn't he?"

"Don't worry about Mosco! He's as tough as old boots!"

All the same, he reported to Strickland that he was a Rear Gunner short, Mosco having been sent to a "sanatorium" (making it sound serious, like TB) for indefinite observation. He was given a red-haired boy with freckles and a big melon smile from the pool as replacement. Barlow was still in his teens, very quick and slightly in awe of Irvine. No longer would there be "No understand" or Jehovah-like judgments on the Intercom from the rear turret. No longer would there be those silent sulks on practice cross-countries. They did more ditching drill exercises in O Orange and with Mosco absent got their speed abandoning the aircraft and into the dinghies down to nineteen

72

seconds. Three days before Christmas, the weather cleared sufficiently for training to be resumed, and in air-to-air firing practice on a drogue towed by a Henley over the snow-covered Sutherland hills, Barlow distinguished himself by getting ninety-six hits with the twin .5s.

In the preparations for Christmas, Mosco sank to the bottom of Irvine's conscious mind. The Mess WAAFs went out and cut holly from the trees behind the firing range. There was a recce for mistletoe, which was spotted hanging in abundance in the woods east of the perimeter track. The NAAFI was cleaned out of what streamers and baubles they'd managed to get in and anything that glittered in Stores mysteriously disappeared, to reappear again in Messes and Sections transforming into Christmas tree decorations. A posse of Sergeants, ground staff and aircrew armed with spades climbed the snowy mountain side to liberate the Forestry Commission's biggest and best-shaped pine trees.

One of these found its way to the entrance hall of the Officers' Mess where, just after lunch on Christmas Eve, the WAAF officers began to decorate it.

"I meant to tell you earlier, Emma." Flight Officer Wendy Beauchamp watched Assistant Section Officer Jones climbing up the step-ladder. "You're going to have a room-mate."

The Flight Officer made her voice sound cheerful and congratulatory, the way she always did when she was imparting less than welcome news. And, as always, it didn't work. Emma Jones glanced down at her over her shoulder, frowning. Her rather pretty mouth simply formed the one syllable, "Oh." And then, the frown deepening, "Who?"

"I was hoping to give the gel a room on her own," Flight Officer Beauchamp went on, handing Emma a somewhat aged silver fairy from the padre's Christmas decorations box. "They do ask that these gels should have rooms on their own. But space in the Mess is so tight. The men have to share so why not us gels?"

Emma Jones said nothing as she stretched up to hook the fairy's rather tattered skirt over the topmost branch. Her own skirt was pulled high. A couple of Flying Officers whistled.

"Don't try too hard, Emma dear." Flight Officer Beauchamp spoke irritably. Her pendulous cheeks coloured a dusky red.

She strove to interpose her bulk between the foolish gel and her audience. "Look, dear, drape some of this rather nice tinsel over there. Lower down. *Much* lower down. And this lovely gypsy ball. That's better. Now what was I saying?"

"About this girl. When is she coming?"

"Tomorrow night. Rather appropriate don't you think?" Obviously Emma Jones did not. "What's her name?"

"Sylvia Talbot."

"I didn't know we'd had anyone posted in."

"We haven't dear. Not us as us." Flight Officer Beauchamp stood on tiptoe to whisper. "She's an Ensa girl."

Emma raised her brows. "That'll please the boys," she murmured.

The Ensa girls had the reputation of being very fast. Emma Jones had never met one so she had no way of judging if the reputation was justified. They held the rank of officer, but they were not subjected to the same discipline. So that probably accounted for their reputation.

Flight Officer Beauchamp nodded. "At least she won't be one of *my* brood. She's supposed to be splendid. Apparently Squadron-Leader Strickland was very keen to have a real professional. To run the cinema properly. Bring in the good entertainers."

"Let's hope he's got what he wants," Emma Jones smiled wryly. "He usually does."

In line with the other aircrew, Irvine watched such preparations indulgently. There was nothing much to do except play cards in the Flight Office, though he did conscientiously go along to Intelligence and read up the latest reports. The Germans were reported as developing a new sort of breathing device called a schnorkel—to all intents and purposes an exhaust pipe—so that the U-boats could stay underwater indefinitely using their diesels instead of having to come up to the surface at night to recharge the batteries for their electric motors and thus make themselves targets for radar-equipped aircraft and warships. There was nothing much about the *Groningen* except that she was still ice-bound in Falstand Fjord.

So that it looked as though her crew, too, would be singing *Stille Nacht, heilige Nacht* while they waited for the thaw. On

74

Christmas Eve, his sergeants had asked him along to their Mess and he had drunk beer with them till well after midnight. None of them—least of all Barlow, who desperately wanted to stay with a crew and not be thrown back in the pool—even mentioned Mosco.

Irvine woke up on Christmas Day with that slight fuzziness in his head he always got after drinking too much beer—not exactly a hang-over but a kind of hazy heaviness over his forehead and a slightly sticky feel to his tongue. He missed breakfast, and it was well past ten by the time he had shaved and started dressing.

He was just shouldering his way into his uniform jacket when he heard that weird mish-mashing sound of marching feet. Going over to the window, he stared out at the parade ground on the other side of the road beyond the laurel shrubbery bounding the Mess.

Christmas parade—trust Group-Captain Pym to start the day off on the right foot with God! It had started to snow again, too, the flakes whirring around like white of egg in a mixer against the uncooked yolk of a pale yellow sun.

A slight smile curled up his lips as he watched the squadron's ground-crew wilting along like so many pieces of oily-blue blotting paper. Station Headquarters staff—a full turn out there, of course. And all the ground officers who weren't on duty. The WAAFs were the smartest of the lot as usual. Here they came now, swinging along behind Old Mother Beauchamp, the Flight Officer, in fours—heads up, shoulders right back, arms moving like pistons.

Right at the rear was a solitary figure marching all on its own behind the rear rank. He watched Emma Jones right wheel along with the others, halt, come smartly to attention.

"*Parade*," the Station Warrant Officer's voice came through to Irvine strangely muffled, "left turn!"

She had her back to him now. It was a nice back with trim slender legs. Pity about that WAAF officer's greatcoat—turned them all into dumpy blue teddy-bears, none the less cuddly for that, mind.

Now it was Padre Binks' turn, pale blue eyes blinking behind half-moon spectacles, standing there in his ecclesiasticals with stole swinging in the wind.

75

A halting hymn started, so faint and feeble that Irvine had difficulty recognizing it as *Noël, Noël*. He looked down on it all from his place of vantage, slightly superior, faintly amused. Not for the likes of him was this sort of nonsense. Such antics were for ordinary mortals. For aircrew there were no parades, no fatigues, no rules, no laws, no censure, no punishments. Nothing but a heady licence and liberty—so long, of course, as whenever they were told to, out they went to attack the *Groningen*.

They were running up the flag now. It was practically over. He took one last look at the back view of Assistant Section Officer Jones, and then sauntered downstairs to the empty ante-room to get hold of the *Daily Mirror* and see if Jane was back in her bath before the ground-wallahs returned to grab it.

The day stretched before him, empty and delightful. Nothing to do, not even attendance at Flights. All morning to lounge around, and the Mess dance this evening. The only chore he had to do was to help serve Christmas dinner at the airmen's Mess—the traditional RAF annual reversal of roles—and anyway that could be fun.

"Better be on our way soon."

Irvine looked over the top of the *Daily Mirror*, recognized the ginger curls of Farquhar.

"What time have we got to be there?"

"Twelve, Strickland said." Farquhar raised himself out of his armchair. "Coming to jug up?"

On the way to the bar, they passed the notice-board next to the letter-rack. Squadron Orders consisted simply of the Mayfly:

25th December
1. Flying Officer Wisby and crew.
2. Flying Officer Garfield and crew.
3. Flight-Lieutenant Mason and crew.
4. Flying Officer Ames and crew.
5. Flight-Lieutenant Carter and crew.

Some wit had added in red ink. 6. *Father Christmas*. Jerningham, in Farquhar's opinion: 'About his standard".

There was only time for a quick pint of bitter, and then they joined the other officers in a self-conscious group down to the airmen's Mess.

76

The fun had already started. As they came through the door, a yellow streamer whizzed like solidified flak just in front of them. The airmen were getting rid of what Jerningham described as "compulsory church-paradeitus". This diagnosis was confirmed when the Group Captain's appearance produced a resounding raspberry. Things quietened down when Strickland turned up (in snow-stained overalls for he had been working all morning in the cold with the erks* on S Sugar's starboard inner), and as soon as the turkey arrived and proved to be real white meat, breast and lots of stuffing, the noise settled down to the clatter of knives and forks and the chomping of jaws.

Irvine queued up at the kitchen counter, decorously collecting a plate of turkey and all the trimmings in each hand, not attempting to emulate Jerningham, who had plates balanced up both arms.

"Any more for beer?" Strickland raised a white enamelled jug high in the air, as Irvine deposited his two plates in front of the nearest airmen and went back to queue at the kitchen counter.

They were already pulling the crackers and putting on the fancy hats. Across the haze of tobacco smoke, as he collected his second two plates, he glimpsed the Queen Bee WAAF, her of the fixed smile and the cottage-loaf body, wearing a golden paper crown as though it was a chaplet of thorns. Ignoring the pleas and outstretched arms of hungry airmen, he hurried his two plates over to the other side of the dining room, where at three long tables the airwomen sat all huddled together on benches like broody blue hens, joining Jerningham, Garfield, Ames, Mason, in fact pretty well all 507 Squadron. Service was so good that he stood there with his two plates, uncertain if he had any customers when suddenly he heard, "Sir . . . sir!", and looking across saw the round smiling moon-face of Mavis stretching out her arms to him.

"Happy Christmas, Mavis!" He leaned across to give her the plate when he realized that one was already in the process of being deposited in front of the girl by Assistant Section Officer Jones, which now the girl promptly picked up and handed back to her, accepting instead the plate offered by him

* Airmen.

with a saucy smile followed by a smacking big kiss and a "Happy Christmas yourself, darling!"

Assistant Section Officer Jones having got rid of her plates on two less choosy and more quiescent WAAFs, they went back up again to the serving counter together.

They stood in the queue in silence. Feeling the need to say something, Irvine volunteered, "She's my batwoman."

"Oh?"

"Had a bit too much."

"Probably."

Four plates of plum-pudding—two each—parted them. This time, Irvine avoided the WAAF tables like the plague. In doing so, he had the misfortune to trip over an airman's leg sticking out from one of the benches, and deposited himself and his custard-covered load onto the laps of two corporal clerks from the Orderly Room in their Best Blue. Handkerchiefs were produced, and there were unseasonal murmurings about drunken officers.

Worse, Strickland had seen the accident and came over.

"You all right?"

"Fine!" He was cleaning himself up with his own none-too-clean handkerchief. "Slipped, that's all."

"I've been meaning to ask you. How's Mosco?"

"Mosco?"

"Your Rear Gunner. He's in dock, isn't he?"

"Oh yes . . . yes. Kilcreggan sanatorium."

"How is he?"

"He's all right." Fatally, he paused. "I think."

"You *think*?" Now it was Strickland's turn to pause. "Haven't you been to see him?"

It had not even dawned on Irvine that he should go and see Mosco. He didn't want to see Mosco, and he was pretty sure that Mosco didn't want to see him.

"Not yet."

"Not *yet*? But it's Christmas! And the poor bugger's sick and far from home! Christ, man, you're his *captain*! The least you can do is to take him along a bottle!"

Irvine was aware that in the passage of a very few minutes he had somehow slipped from being Strickland's boy-wonder captain to a clumsy heartless oaf with no idea of leadership.

The Squadron Leader's eagle eye had probably perceived the Mavis episode, too. He mumbled something about going to see him.

"You'll go and see him this afternoon. Get a bottle of his favourite medicine from the Bar Officer. Garfield, isn't it? And you can take my van. There's a lot more to being a captain than flying an aeroplane. Just as there's a lot more to being an officer than wearing barathea . . ."

Irvine felt about two inches tall.

". . . and here we are gossiping like a couple of old washerwomen while Race, Knapp, Heaton—" he knew the names of all the 507 maintenance crews—"still haven't had their mincepies . . ."

Glad tidings of comfort and joy, comfort and joy came carolling over the Tannoy, but by this time there wasn't much of either left in Irvine's heart. After serving the airmen's dinner, the officers had walked back for their own meal, Strickland leading the way, deep in conversation with Assistant Section Officer Jones, Irvine bringing up the rear.

Two further problems awaited him on his arrival inside the Mess. As he was going into the bar, Garfield had called across to him that the hospital had rung up about Mosco. At first he had thought, *Christ, he's gone and kicked the bucket and on Christmas Day too*, and had immediately been ashamed that he had felt no suitable sorrow. On further enlightenment, he had discovered that the message had simply been that Mosco wanted two clean pairs of his silk pyjamas, his dressing gown, six handkerchiefs and his library.

"What does he mean . . . his *library*?" Garfield demanded.

"Presumably his books."

"But he's only got *one* book, and by the looks of it, he's read it a dozen times already!"

"Well, bung it into a case with his other things. I'm off to see the old chap this afternoon."

"Tell him not to hurry back," said Garfield ungraciously.

"Oh, and one other thing! In your official capacity as Bar Officer—"

He stopped. Looking back on the day's happenings, they had all in their own way been lessons in leadership. How to behave, how to gain respect, how to be a captain. "What about a Guinness after all our efforts serving the airmen, Nigel?"

"Not for me."

"A whisky then?"

"There isn't any."

"But I can see a couple of Johnny Walkers." He pointed. "Up on that shelf!"

"We're saving those for the dance."

"Oh." He felt suddenly flat, but determinedly he pressed on. "But you'll be able to spare one of them for Mosco, surely?"

"*What?*"

"I thought I'd take along a bottle of whisky for him this afternoon."

"*A bottle of whisky?* D'you realize what our ration is? Four! Four bottles of whisky *a month*! For three hundred officers!"

"But it's Christmas!" Unconsciously Irvine was quoting Strickland word-perfect. "And the poor bugger's sick and far from home!"

"It wouldn't make any difference if he was drowning in mid-Atlantic."

"Christ, man, it's *Christmas*! Haven't you got feelings? Mosco's come all this way to fight on our side. A gentleman. And a bloody marvellous shot! What's more, he happens to be my Rear Gunner. I'm his captain and I tell you this, Garfield—"

"I'll let you have a bottle of vodka."

"But he doesn't drink vodka."

"They all drink vodka."

"That's the Russians. Mosco hates the Russians."

"Gin, then. You can have a bottle of gin."

"Mosco hates gin."

"Well, that's just too bad, isn't it?" Garfield began turning away. "I don't know about you, but I'm going in for my turkey before it all goes."

Desperately Irvine grabbed hold of the man's arm. Even as he played his last card, he knew that it was a borrowed one. No force of his personality, no strength of his character, no wit, no guile, no threat, no trick, nothing of his doing or devising would budge Garfield. Except: "Strickland told me to take him a bottle."

80

That stopped the man dead in his tracks all right.

"Strickland?"

"And he's lending me his van to get there."

"Oh well in that case—" He could actually see the cogs turning over behind Garfield's eyes, sorting out this powerful new development. "Tell you what. It's Christmas. And the poor bugger's sick and far from home. I'll give you a *half* bottle of whisky. How's that? And I'll pop it into his case with the rest of his stuff straightaway." He held out his hand. "That'll be twelve shillings."

Irvine paid across the money, and then went into the dining room without after all having a Guinness. He had lost his thirst, and the papery turkey breast and cold gravy failed to tickle his appetite. Better get this thing over and done with as soon as possible, he thought, bolting his food.

As he went out, he saw Strickland sitting with Assistant Section Officer Jones, and diffidently he went over and asked for the keys of his van.

"Catch!"

The Squadron Leader threw them over to him. He put out his hands, but too late, and they trickled through his fingers.

"Butterfingers!"

He felt his cheeks burning as he bent down to pick them off the floor.

"Tell Mosco from me . . . happy Christmas and get well soon."

"Will, sir."

"And don't bend my van!"

"Won't, sir."

At least Garfield had had the decency to have Mosco's bag packed and ready for him in the Mess Office. He took it out to the car park, found Strickland's van, and set off gingerly along the slushy road, out through the main gate, round the inlet, through Kilcreggan village and up the mountain towards the hospital.

Light flurries of snow were falling. As the van climbed, he could see in the driving mirror that behind him the sea was glassy calm. The air he breathed was that exhilarating ice-cold stuff as though it was vaporized mountain stream water. He began to feel better. Driving any sort of car was a rare luxury, and being on his own and on an errand of mercy gave him a sensation both of enjoying himself and of being virtuous. He had never in his life before visited the sick, and he began to imagine Mosco's surprise at seeing him and the pleasure he'd have from the gift of the whisky.

The hospital stood on a jutting promontory of cliff, six hundred feet up, surrounded by heather and dead bracken— a granite-built Victorian pile staring bleakly eastwards across the North Sea to Norway. The paper garlands, the coloured lights on the Christmas tree, the holly and the ivy could not quite take away the antiseptic coldness of the white-painted walls.

"Flight-Lieutenant Moscovich?" The VAD behind the desk pointed to the left. "Down there. Number six."

The corridor smelled of ether-meth and warm floor polish. He paused outside the door of room six to gather himself together and think of a few choice cheerful phrases.

Then he knocked. Mosco's voice through the wood, hoarse but perfectly audible, bade him come in.

He turned the bright brass doorknob and pushed. The scene now in front of his eyes took him completely by surprise.

No invalid this, huddled under the bedclothes. Framed by the big window, propped up high with half a dozen pillows, Mosco in scarlet pyjamas with gold dragon facings resembled some potentate extraordinary on his throne. The turned-back sheet decorated his mandarin belly like an immaculate white cummerbund. His arms lay by his sides, not loosely or untidily, but like two dignified Grand Viziers waiting quietly beside him to carry out immediately his least bidding. The bed-table beside him was a harvest festival of grapes, bananas, oranges, nuts, chocolates and bottles. And on his left side, his right side, and down at the bottom by his coverleted feet sat three young girls of the most exceptional prettiness.

Irvine stood uncertainly in the open doorway while the four faces inspected him silently.

"Merry Christmas, Mosco!" He held up the case. "I've brought your stuff."

From the huge grey face, the hound-dog eyes regarded him mysteriously. Bloodshot, bags bulging underneath them like pelicans' paunches, they conveyed neither pleasure nor welcome

82

nor even recognition. The nose down which they looked was straight as a spear, the two deep-cut lines on either side of it forming an arrowhead pointing to the rectangular forehead rimmed by the carefully brushed black hair.

The slug-coloured lips eventually opened. "So." Both Grand Viziers raised themselves to beckon him forward.

Still dazed, Irvine approached the bed. This couldn't be a Scottish hospital. By mistake, he had stumbled into Aladdin's cave, flown backwards in time on a magic carpet from the Arabian Nights, cracked his way through the looking-glass, an alien intruder into some fairy tale.

"Well, how's things, Mosco?"

"What you mean . . . how's *things*?"

"Just . . . how are you feeling?"

"A little better . . . *now*."

"Yes, I can see that." He aimed a rather foolish smile at the three girls, which clearly missed. The blonde at the foot of the bed was tucking in the blankets, the dark-haired girl now close beside him had her eyes on the book spread on her tartan-skirted lap from which she had clearly been reading aloud before he had interrupted. The girl opposite picked through a stem of grapes, searching for the most succulent.

The Pole made no effort to introduce him. It was as though these three girls were extensions of his Grand Vizier arms and as unnecessary to identify.

"The chaps have sent you a Christmas present, Mosco." Irvine tried to pump some Christian spirit into his voice. "Hope you're allowed to drink!"

"Oh yes." The voice sounded as though it came from a long, long way away. Irvine put the case down on the floor, flicked open the catches and produced the half bottle.

The grey-green eyes regarded it silently.

"It's Scotch, Mosco!"

"Black Label?"

Irvine shook his head. "Sorry. Just the ordinary stuff, I'm afraid."

"Ah well." The two Grand Viziers disposed of it towards the row of full-size bottles on the bed-table. Mosco inclined his head. "Thank you. I am grateful. It is kind." The courtesies were accompanied with a little nod, Chinese-style, till they were turned off abruptly with: "And what have you and your crew been up to?"

"Oh this and that, Mosco." There being no other chair in the room, Irvine had propped himself up uncomfortably against the wall. "This and that."

"Have you done your first operation against the enemy yet?"

"No." He tried another bit of joviality. "We're waiting for you to get well, Mosco. Wouldn't dream of going off without you."

The girl opposite had extracted the biggest and juiciest fruit off the grape stem and popped it into Mosco's mouth. The grey cheeks inflated in and out as he sucked it.

"And how is my friend Squadron-Leader Strickland?"

"Fine . . . fine!"

"Has he sunk the *Groningen*?"

"No, not yet, Mosco."

"Has anybody sunk anything?"

"No."

"Any attacks?"

"No."

"Any sightings?"

Irvine shook his head. "Things have been pretty quiet."

Moscovich sniffed.

"Winter. Bad weather. You know how it is, Mosco. Jerry hasn't been very active either. Even the *Groningen*'s ice-bound."

"So nobody's done anything!" Moscovich gave a massive sigh. "Sitting . . . just sitting! Is zis a war? When will they open a Polish Front? When will they seize the Oder-Neisse Line? What is the Army doing? What is the Navy doing? What is 507 Squadron doing? What is *any* squadron doing? I tell you zis." He nodded towards the girls. "I tell them, too. They know how I feel. They understand. Do you know what I tell them? I tell them . . . one day, I write a book about the RAF . . . a *fonny* book!" He paused. "You have my library?"

"I don't know about *library*, Mosco." Irvine ferreted around amongst the vests and pyjamas, eventually producing the thick volume. As he passed it over, he caught sight of the title—*Encyclopaedia of Sex*. "This was all Garfield could find."

The left-hand Grand Vizier rose to receive it. "Ah, my

84

library." Moscovich laid it down open in front of him as though the sheet was a lectern. "I have been missing it."

Irvine saw that both open pages were heavily marked in pencil with weird-looking words. "Surely they have books here, Mosco?"

"Oh yes . . . yes. Novels . . . nonsense." He reached over to the side table for a pair of black-rimmed spectacles. Adjusting them on the bridge of his nose, sonorously he read out the one word, "*Język*".

"*Język*," chorused the three girls back at him.

"No! *No!* How many more times do I have to tell you. Not so guttural. *Język*."

"*Język*," echoed the girls back at him.

"Good, good! And that means?"

Competing to be first, they all replied together. "Tongue."

"*Chlopiec*."

"*Chlopiec*."

"Ch . . . ch . . . mouth wide open."

Three scarlet mouths gaped like three wide-open beaks in a bird's nest.

"*Chlopiec*."

"Good! Very good! I am pleased with you. And *Chlopiec* means?"

"Boy."

"*Od lat chlopięcych*."

"Since I was a boy."

"Good! And *kobieta* means?"

"Woman."

"And *Czlowiek*?"

"Man."

The lesson proceeded as though Irvine wasn't there at all. He moved away from the wall, waiting in vain to catch Mosco's attention so that he could make his departure. But Mosco simply kept on turning the pages, mouthing deep unintelligible words and receiving back, sweeter and higher, the trio of unintelligible responses. The lesson would have gone on for the rest of the afternoon, had not the blonde at the foot of the bed suddenly interrupted in plain English, "Vladimir . . . it is time for your medicine."

There then followed a good-humoured scuffle as to who

would administer it. "It's my turn!" said the brunette. "No, mine!" contradicted the redhead. "Vladimir, Vladimir!" from the foot of the bed the blonde pleaded, reaching for a bottle of pink fluid on the glass shelf above the washbasin. "*You* choose. *You* tell us."

"It is Deborah's turn," pronounced Moscowski and opened his mouth to receive the teaspoon from the blonde's dainty fingers.

Irvine took advantage of the interruption hurriedly to say his adieux. Medicine swallowed, Mosco nodded, said solemnly, "Thank you."

"That's all right, Mosco. Get well soon!"

Just as he opened the door, he looked back. The lesson had been resumed. Mosco was reading very slowly the Polish words above their English equivalent in the *Encyclopaedia of Sex*, and the girls were solemnly repeating them back to him. The whole scene looked Eastern, with the Buddha-like figure so still and so solemn, and the three Scots lassies entranced before him— not geisha girls exactly because that implied frivolity and relaxation, while here everything was so serious, more like acolytes at a temple, or favourite pupils learning from their master.

"*Małżeństwo.*"

"*Małżeństwo,*" came trilling sweetly back.

Very quietly, Irvine closed the door, shutting away the scene and the voices. The VAD had vanished from the desk in the hall. He went through the glass doors back into the mountain air, climbed into Strickland's van and started off back to the airfield.

The snow was thicker now and settling. Through the darkening late afternoon, the hooded headlights illuminated the white speckling on the brown heather. By the time he reached Kilcreggan village, the road was an unbroken carpet of snow and the tyres were sliding on the turns. Driving up to the Mess, he thought, was like coming up to an Alpine ski lodge in a sleigh. The blackout had not yet been put up and, through the windows, he could see the coloured paper streamers in the lighted rooms, the Christmas tree in the hall.

Inside, already there was an air of excitement. The dining room had been cleared for dancing. Erks were setting up long tables in the lounge for the buffet and WAAFs were covering them with white cloths. Irvine grabbed a spam sandwich and queued up at the urn that had been set up in the Ladies' Room.

The Ladies' Room was quite different from the bar next door. There was no sign of aeroplanes, no sign of battles, no bar stools, no big leather sofas like the ante-room. Landscape prints of Constables, bright Van Goghs, Degas, ballet-dancers in their tutus hung on the cream-painted walls. Chintz curtains were drawn across the windows, and there were chrysanthemums in vases and small roses in china bowls arranged tastefully on the tables in front of small flower-patterned armchairs.

Irvine collected his tea and was walking away from the urn when he saw Strickland and went over to hand back the van keys. The Squadron-Leader asked him about Mosco, but perfunctorily, as though his mind had moved away onto more important things.

Irvine managed to get one of the flowered cretonne armchairs by the radiators. He had a second cup of tea and then a third. There was no hurry. Time now was his own. Airmen's dinner served, Mosco wrapped up—the rest of Christmas belonged to him and he intended to enjoy it.

He began to turn over in his mind the girls who would be coming to the dance. The Group-Captain's young wife, of course, and those of the other living-out ground officers. Mowbray's wife. With luck, he'd get a dance with Madeleine. Some of the village maidens—those, he thought wryly, that hadn't been scooped up by Mosco. No airwomen of course—not allowed. The WAAF officers naturally. He wondered whether he would be able to manage a dance with Assistant Section Officer Jones, or whether Strickland would monopolize her.

He ambled off to get hold of a bathroom before they were all bagged. Room 27 was blessedly empty. None of the new occupants—again officers in Strickland's crew—were around. On his bed lay his Best Blue with all the brass buttons gleaming. Good old Mavis, he thought. I should really have given her a Christmas present. Or, at the very least, a card.

He undressed, padded off down the corridor in his dressing gown. There was still lots of hot water. Luxuriantly he lay back in his bath, half suffocated in comforting warm steam, taking no notice when people started banging on the door, shouting, "For Christ's sake, hurry up!"

A more polite knock was at that moment sounding out on Emma Jones' door at the other side of the Mess. In came one of the Mess ACHs* carrying two large pigskin suitcases. He was followed by a tall thin girl swathed in a fur coat with a small black and khaki Ensa forage cap perched on her auburn hair. Her cap, her hair, her coat, even her mascaraed eyelashes were speckled in snow. Her face was thin and hauntingly beautiful, in a Marlene Dietrich way. She looked theatrical, certainly. Fragile and frivolous.

"Hello, Sylvia." Emma stood up. "Welcome. Merry Christmas. You look like a snow fairy. Come on in and get warm." She waved her hand towards the glowing stove. "I'll see if I can get you some coffee. Or shall we go to the bar for a drink?"

"Neither, thank you." Miss Talbot had a husky voice. A little theatrical like her appearance but beautifully modulated and pleasing. "I'm dying for a hot bath." She slid herself out of her fur coat, disclosing the neat khaki Ensa uniform underneath. "D'you run to hot water? Everyone said it was the back of beyond up here."

"We do. And it is. The back of beyond." Emma smiled. "We're lucky, the bathroom's next door. I'll run it for you."

"Don't bother." She heaved one of her bags onto a chair and opened it. She took out a large matching beauty box and a sensible blue woollen dressing gown. "Mind if I undress in here? Then we can chat."

"Of course not. I always do."

The Ensa girl shuddered. "Now you know my name," she went on, unbuttoning her jacket, then bending to unfasten her shoes. "God, my feet are frozen! And I know *yours*. The chap in the whatsitsname office told me. Emma Jones, nice and easy to remember. He said you were a sweetie."

"Nice of him."

"He said you were young and pretty. Quite right. Came from Yorkshire. I'm from the Big City. I'm twenty-six. Unmarried

* Aircrafthands.

88

but teetered on the brink many times. Never met the right man. That comes from dealing in too many films. You begin to believe them. True love. That rot. My father owns a clutch, and I do mean clutch, of cinemas. I'm a failed actress, you could say. He found me a job in his organization. Dear Daddy! Hence my entry into Ensa."

On Sylvia Talbot's return from her lengthy bath, Emma Jones found out a good deal more. She was an only child. She'd been to a naice school at Broadstairs. Hated it. To drama school. Loved it. Had a few minor parts, tried her hand as a model. Was devastated by it.

"God, you've no idea what they expect." She brooded on those expectations for a while before continuing, "Then after that into one of Daddy's cinemas as assistant manageress. Actually I'm not at all bad. At the managing side, I mean. I'm an organization woman at heart. I got some first-class shows going. It's my niche. My métier. Oh, and I'm still a virgin. How about you?"

Actually Emma's single embarrassed yes was all the conversation she contributed till the Ensa girl had dried herself in the heat from the stove, carefully powdered her slender body and then slipped into her warm blue dressing gown.

"So it's Christmas Eve in the workhouse," the girl settled herself down and sighed.

"Yes."

"The jolliest night of the year?"

"It is really. Very jolly. There's a dance on." She looked at her watch. "We should start getting ready."

"I saw all the decorations. Can we get all dressed up in our glad rags?"

"You can. I can't."

"I could lend you a dress."

"Oh, no. Not allowed. Uniform only for me."

"Oh, what a damned shame. Look," the large clear eyes under the thinly plucked brows looked genuinely regretful, "If you'd rather I didn't dress up, I won't either."

"Of course you will!" Emma smiled. "You'll be a sight for sore eyes. A treat for the boys."

Just on seven, the two girls emerged—Emma Jones in uniform, the Ensa girl in tight-fitting silver lamé. Peter Irvine

89

saw them coming down the corridor and, after being introduced to Sylvia Talbot, escorted them into the bar.

Already there was a fair amount of noise. The Canadians were tanking up in the far corner. Irvine pushed his way to the counter.

"What are you drinking, Sylvia . . . Emma?"

They both asked for gin and tonic.

Eventually he caught the barman's eye and ordered three gins and tonic—one for himself. "Large ones. With ice."

"That'll be three and sixpence, sir."

"Well, cheers!" Smiling, the three of them clinked glasses. "Happy Christmas!"

He put his glass down. "What sort of Christmas have you had so far?"

The Ensa girl made a face about the icy journey.

"Oh very nice," Emma said.

"Like me, I suppose, keeping up morale?"

She said nothing.

"I've been visiting one of my crew in hospital." It seemed necessary to explain to her what he meant. Us officers—the duties we have to perform. But both girls seemed strangely unmoved by his Christmas charity. He gulped down his drink. "What about another one?"

"We haven't even started the one you've bought us."

"Go on!" He pushed his own empty glass across the counter. "The gin'll be running out in a minute."

Suddenly a voice behind him said, "Steady on, old chap!"

He turned his head to find Mason standing behind him, holding up a large glass of orange juice and tapping it virtuously.

Irvine demanded indignantly, "What d'you mean?"

"Haven't you seen tomorrow's Mayfly?"

"It's the same as today's!"

"Not quite."

"It must be the same! Nobody's flown."

"Why don't you take a look for yourself?"

Irvine felt a sudden wave of panic rush up his throat. Abruptly he turned back to the girls. "Excuse me," he said thickly. "Be back in a moment."

Through the now crowded bar, he dashed for the door.

Outside in the hall, half a dozen 507 characters were standing

90

by the notice-board, one of which was Garfield. He pushed his way to the front and read:

26th December.

1. Flying Officer Wisby and crew.
2. Flying Officer Garfield and crew.
3. Flight-Lieutenant Mason and crew.
4. Flying Officer Ames and crew.
5. Flight-Lieutenant Carter and crew.
6. Pilot Officer Irvine and crew.

"Six!" Irvine demanded. "Why *six*?"

"Haven't you heard?" Garfield replied. "The PRU photographs show ice-breakers are making a channel at the fjord entrance. Strickland reckons the *Groningen*'s going to make a dash for it."

"Well, what are we supposed to do about it?"

"That I wouldn't know, old chap."

In the dining room, the Station band had started up with a waltz. Not of course that anybody would dance till the boys had tanked up. But the music sent a lilting lift, the sound of trumpets and drums against the shriller violins. It was sufficiently stirring to send Irvine back to the bar thinking of the night before Waterloo, to give him sufficient bravura to smile and say lightly to Emma Jones and Sylvia Talbot as he put his hand over his gin, "No drinking for me. I'm off in the morning."

Such panache quickly disappeared. Though Emma looked at him expectantly, he could think of nothing else to say. Round and round in his mind was going the question: what the hell do they expect six Liberators to do against the *Groningen*? In any case, both girls were quickly engaged by Jerningham and Irvine was left on his own with his untouched glass of gin.

He stayed in the bar for another half hour, exchanging odd remarks with people. Then he went off to the lounge, and had a plate of pork and salad from the buffet. Before he went off to bed, he looked into the dining room where dancing had now started.

A slow foxtrot—*I'm Dreaming of a White Christmas*. Well, they've got that all right. So have I.

He left them to it, and went up to bed. Room 27 was totally empty. In fact, there didn't seem to be anyone in this whole wing of the Mess but him.

He put on his thickest pyjamas and a pullover, and slipped between the icy sheets. Shivering, he thought of the comfort of a hot water bottle, but that, he told himself sturdily, was altogether too sissy and anyway it was far too much trouble. And Mavis would have a fit! Next thing, he'd be wanting a teddy-bear!

He closed his eyes. Sleep—that's what he had to do. Sleep now! Immediately! It was absolutely imperative that before his first operation he should have a good night's sleep. Tomorrow he would have to be alert, on the ball, fresh as a daisy, quick as lightning, otherwise the enemy—

He closed his eyes tighter. They seemed to be revolving inside their sockets, transformed into those glass marbles veined with colours, red, black, green, blue, yellow snakes, each one of them a different wriggling thought. One thought—the red one— was about his crew and he wondered how they were feeling. Pretty panic-stricken, he reckoned. Then this red thread began grappling with the blue thread that disclosed itself as Assistant Section Officer Jones, and those two became entangled with the green thread which was a weaving Liberator lit up by multi-coloured flak bursts that led on to the black thread which was the holocaust of S Sugar . . .

In spite of the little nest of warmth in which he now lay curled, again he began shivering, but this time his teeth had started chattering too, making a weird kind of clicking noise that sounded like a clock gone haywire.

Sleep, he said to himself over and over again, you've *got* to go to sleep. But ten minutes later, he was still wide awake, those coloured veins inside his closed eyelids still weaving and waving. Another couple of minutes, and I'll be off and away, sound asleep, he thought. Just a hundred and twenty seconds—one, two, three, four . . .

Half an hour later, he threw back the bed-clothes and, jumping out onto the cold linoleum, paddled down to the bathroom. He sat on the lavatory seat with his pyjama trousers round his ankles and his head propped up by his arms, elbows resting on his knees.

You have *got* to go to sleep, he said to himself sternly. You have *got* to take a hold of yourself! You have *got* to be a man! You owe it to your crew! You owe it to Strickland!

Back in his room, he was horrified to find from his watch on the side table that it was three o'clock in the morning. And not a wink of sleep! Yet he felt absolutely fagged out. He had hardly the energy to climb back into bed. His mouth felt dry, yet he wasn't thirsty. In fact, if he drank anything, he knew he'd be sick.

Through the window leaked the soft sound of music. The three other occupants of Room 27 would be enjoying themselves. And Strickland—he would be drinking, talking, laughing, dancing, leading—

Yes, leading! Peter Irvine knew in his own heart that he was not a leader. If only he had those qualities of unblinking courage, tremendous drive, of that presence that envelops everyone in a cloak of total confidence! If only he was a leader, he would not be lying here like this, counting sheep, all having terribly human faces, all jumping to the command of a shadowy shepherd who had a face terribly like Strickland's, leaping one after the other over a gate—one, two, three, four, five, six . . .

Meanwhile, the Sergeants' Mess Christmas dance was already in full swing. Miggs and Deirdre Winter were cheek to cheek in the centre of the floor when Henty came up through the other dancers and tapped the Wireless Operator on the back.

"Go away!" Miggs said over his shoulder. "This isn't an excuse-me!"

It was all arranged. Tonight was the night. All evening he had been plying her with gin, holding her hand and whispering sweet nothings that led to, "What've you got me for Christmas, Deirdre?" and finally out in the open to, "You'll come up to my room after the dance?" She hadn't said yes and she hadn't said no. But as she was now, pliant in his arms, every now and again brushing her lips against his cheek, there was no need to ask for an answer.

"Miggs . . . break it up!"

There had been considerable opposition amongst the crew to his romance with Deirdre Winter. Curly Craik had been particularly vociferous—superstitious bastard! As if curses and jinxes and gremlins had anything to do with getting the chop! You were born lucky or you weren't, that's all there was to it. Having survived one tour of operations, Miggs considered that he certainly was. And as for Peter Irvine, to survive that wreck S Sugar (for Miggs had inspected that ruin on the south side of Dispersal) when seven men didn't proved that his captain (and thank Christ for it!) had the luck of Squadron-Leader Strickland.

"Push off, Henty! She's my girl!"

Increasing his rate of twirling, Miggs waltzed her off pursued by Henty. The crew could be trying to split them, to say cool it, sending the second pilot as an emissary.

"Miggs, we're off on ops tomorrow."

That stopped the pirouetting. Miggs dropped Deirdre like a red-hot coal.

"Can't be."

"We are. Go and look at the Mayfly."

Miggs knew it was true from the look on Henty's face.

"When are we off?"

"Any time, Ops said." Like all good second pilots, Henty was the sheepdog of the crew, rounding them up, passing on orders, seeing they were obeyed. "Best get to bed."

Miggs was too old a hand at operational flying to think he could burn the candle at both ends. As Henty moved away looking for the others, he smiled ruefully at Deirdre Winter.

"You heard that, love?"

"What does it mean?"

"Shut-eye."

"Not *now*?"

"*Now*. Me for the solitary couch tonight." He bent down and kissed her. Softly into her ear he whispered, "You'll have to give me my Christmas present tomorrow!"

As Miggs and Deirdre Winter reluctantly parted, a quarter of a mile away in the dining-cum-ballroom at the Officers' Mess, Sylvia Talbot and her silver lamé were receiving the warm approval of the entire male population of the Mess in general, and rather surprisingly of Strickland himself in particular.

Decorously moving round clasped in the arms of Flying Officer Jerningham, Emma Jones saw Sylvia and Strickland dancing cheek to cheek. Strickland's hand rested on the tight fitting silver lamé, a half inch below the bare skin of her flawless back.

"He's an expert at the light fantastic," Jerningham remarked.

"As with everything," Emma said drily.

"You're right there. Not like me."

Emma decided Jerningham's remark had somehow been an apology for his own modest performance as a dancer. "Anyway, she's very good. Sylvia," she said. "Much better than I am."

He didn't deny it. He was lost in admiration for the Squadron-Leader. His eyes followed them round the room as they swept along in perfect unison.

"Bloody good formation, sir," someone called out. But Strickland and his partner seemed lost to the world, indeed to be moving in some more exalted, more shimmering, more sophisticated yet still very physical plane. Everyone kept well back from them so that they could show off their paces.

The silver lamé dress had a pretty fish's tail train. Sylvia held it up with a loop over her little finger. It gave a tantalizing glimpse of high-heeled silver kid slippers and a finely turned pair of ankles. The auburn hair was brushed free in a long pageboy to below her bare shoulders. It shimmered in the spotlight. Once or twice as they danced, Strickland bent down and brushed it with his lips. Now they were doing some intricate little side turn, their feet never faltering, their bodies turning together.

"They must have radar," Jerningham said, not looking where he was going, stumbling.

When the music stopped. Strickland kept hold of Sylvia's hand for the next one.

"They make a good couple, don't they?" Jerningham said, conducting Emma back to her chair. "The best looking pair in the room."

He only noticed her ironically raised eyebrows when it was too late. She was claimed by Flint for the waltz he said she was saving him.

Traditionally, the lights were lowered to an underwater gloaming. Emma saw the silver lamé floating round dreamily in and out. But when the lights went up there was no sign of Sylvia or Strickland. Nor did they appear again until just before midnight. They executed a fast few turns of a quickstep. Then came the chimes of midnight and shrieks of Merry Christmas. Strickland and Sylvia were kissing centre stage right under the mistletoe. Then they were gone again. The Prince and Princess Charming, leaving the rest to kiss and revel through the kitchen and through the hall, kissing everyone that came in sight.

Sylvia's neat bed remained intact and virginal until three o'clock on Christmas morning, when Emma heard her struggling with the zip on her silver lamé dress.

"D'you want any help?" Emma asked.

"Oh, God. Yes, please. Did I wake you? Sorry."

She came over and sat on Emma's bed.

"No, I hadn't been in long." Emma put out her hand and pulled down the zip.

"Wizard, wasn't it? Dreamy. Delicious."

Emma yawned pointedly. "I'm glad you enjoyed it. Merry Christmas."

"Merry Christmas to you. I'll let you get back to sleep."

Emma heard her cleaning her face, climbing into bed, then exclaiming about its hardness, turning and twisting herself into a comfortable position.

Just as Emma was about to doze off again, Sylvia asked of her sleepily, "I can't think of a better Christmas present, can you?"

But she didn't specify what, nor did she appear to expect an answer.

SIX

MAVIS called Irvine at six-thirty with a cup of tea—which he left untouched on his table.

He arrived at Ops white-faced and practically sleep-walking to find his crew in much the same condition. Even the ginger-haired Barlow, Mosco's replacement, had had much of the bounce taken out of him and murmured something about a straight swap with the Pole in his hospital bed. The other five crews didn't look too happy either, and Wisby could be heard binding away that what he should be doing right at this moment was shooting at his uncle's pheasants, not at German warships.

Strickland changed all that, of course. He took over the briefing and made the trip sound like a ride on the roller-coaster at Blackpool fun-fair. It was known through Norwegian Intelligence that the *Groningen* was going to make a dash for it at noon. An ice-breaker had cleared the frozen water at the fjord entrance and out through the still ice-bound coastal waters to the open sea. The Liberators' job was going to be really quite simple. This passage through the ice would show up on their radar like a river. The weather was going to be cold mist; if they kept right down on the deck, they wouldn't be spotted either visually or on the radar, and certainly they would be safe from fighters. All they had to do was to locate the passage made by the ice-breakers and drop their load into it.

"You mean on the *Groningen*, sir?" Ames had asked apprehensively.

"No, I don't mean that at all." Strickland's big reassuring smile warmed the chilly Operations Room like the rays of the sun. "The *Groningen* won't be there. And I don't want you to go

97

anywhere near the ice-breaker. You shouldn't get any opposition at all."

"But, sir, I don't understand—"

"Your load is a new type of mine, Rory. Each Liberator carries eight of them. The *Groningen* will have to follow the ice-cut. Provided you lob your mines into it, one of them at least is bound to get her."

There was an immediate sigh of relief. Everyone had been expecting a low-level bombing attack right into the bristling muzzles of the *Groningen*'s guns. Only Wisby made any objection, "But, sir, we've never dropped any mines before . . ."

That was soon explained. Find the ice passage. Follow it at fifty feet. Drop, and, there being no wind, they'd be bound to fall into the crack. All nice and ready and waiting for the *Groningen* to come along . . .

Irvine had been allocated O Orange, known as the oldest and the slowest cow in the squadron. As he climbed under the open bomb-doors and up onto the cakewalk, he had seen instead of the accustomed cylinders of depth charges the eight round mines bristling with nipples. The only ones he'd ever seen before were on seaside promenades, harmless humpty-dumpties with small mouths into which you dropped pennies for the relief of ship-wrecked sailors. In comparison, those in Orange's bombbay looked as though they'd be set off any second by his own hammering heart.

He started up. All four engines turning, chocks away, he was the last in line, following Wisby in J Jig. As the six Liberators, nodding noses to nodding tails, brakes squealing, made their way through the icy mist like a herd of white elephants to the head of Runway 09, all Irvine's attention was riveted on preventing his wheels slipping off the narrow perimeter track and bogging down in the snow and mud.

He was aware only of sudden roars of sound, one after the other. One, two, three, four, five—

The stage was empty. Wisby could just be seen disappearing to the east into thick cloud. Irvine wheeled O Orange round, put on the brakes, and completed the Before Take-off checks.

It was then that Jarman in the front turret called on the intercom, "Look, Skipper! At the end of the runway! Over on the left!"

The green from the Tower had then rocketed up. So all Irvine had been conscious of was Craik, his Engineer, putting all four throttles fully forward and holding them there as he released the brakes.

But then as O Orange began slowly pounding its way down the runway, Jarman again called out, "It's WAAFs!" and Brett in the mid-upper turret shouted "Girls, Skipper!"

In the corner of his left eye, Irvine became conscious of a small blur of blue against the snow that began slowly to change into a kaleidoscope of blonde, brunette and redhead. Seeing them there waving and cheering all at once made him feel ten feet tall, like David going out against Goliath. And even old O Orange, similarly inspired to show the girls what she could do, gathered up her withering metal muscles for that sudden leap into space . . .

"There's Deirdre Winter!"

The words came out in that flat Birmingham accent of Craik, his Engineer. Fractionally, Irvine turned his head and saw the blonde hair, the chocolate-box face—the only girl there he recognized.

Oakroyd's girl friend, and before that Gaunt's. Unlucky Deirdre—the girl with the reputation of spelling death to aircrew. The rumour had reached him, propelled by Craik, that Miggs was consorting with this Delilah. His momentary exuberance flubbered away like air from a pricked balloon. O Orange became afflicted with an ague as the red boundary lights approached, and when just after unstick he pulled further back on the control column, thumped her wheels back firmly on the ground again, overrunning the tarmac beyond the threshold into soft slushy snow, with Irvine fighting all the time to get her airborne.

Finally, gasping, wheezing, shaking, rattling, O Orange shook herself free from the ground and inched up into the mist.

"Gear up!"

Craik pulled up the lever. Then he wiped the sweat off his small pinched face, and said in that horrible Birmingham accent, "Deirdre Winter nearly got us that time, Skipper!"

They went straight into cloud and stayed there for the next two hours. Hardly anybody said anything, not even Miggs.

99

Every now and then, Garth, his Navigator, would bring up a change of course written on a chit (Strickland would never allow navigational changes to be spoken over the intercom—too easily misinterpreted) and clip it to the board on the throttle box.

There was still nothing to be seen on the radar. And certainly nothing to be seen out of the windscreen except mist—and mist so fine, so icy, so opaque, like nothing Irvine had ever seen before. More like a breath spun on a spinning wheel and wrapped round the aircraft. Or ectoplasm, eerie, unearthly grey, sending drops like tears down the perspex, muffling the sound of the engines, making the smudgy navigation light on the Liberator's port wing (the furthest Irvine could see) look like a pink pill dissolving in water.

"What's the new ETA?" he asked Garth.

"Twelve thirty, Skipper. Another fifteen minutes."

"Still falling behind?"

"Seem to be. Difficult to be sure in this stuff."

"Isn't there anything on the radar *yet*?"

Trembath's voice answered uncertainly. "Nothing, sir."

"What the hell's happened to the coast of Norway?"

I am not really superstitious, Irvine said to himself. I do not really believe that Deirdre Winter has a strange mysterious power. It's just that I can't help seeing that face photographed on the grey mist all round me. It's just that it takes me back to those two bloodstained gauntlets in the rear turret of S Sugar.

"What's happened to our airspeed, Skipper?" Garth's voice, normally placid, over the intercom now suddenly sounded edgy. "No wonder we're falling behind!"

He looked down at the airspeed indicator, and was immediately appalled. 115 knots, and the needle still falling!

"What's wrong with the power?" he shouted to Craik.

Those gob-stopper eyes popped out from the tiny face even further. "Wrong, Skipper?"

"Wrong! Yes, wrong! We've lost twenty-five knots!"

The Engineer's bird-like hands began creeping over the throttles and the rpm switches.

"Power's all right, Skipper. Thirty inches Manifold Pressure. Twenty-one hundred revs."

"It can't be all right! Christ, man, we've lost an engine!"

100

More scrabbling round the cockpit. Then in a tone of injured Birmingham innocence: "We haven't lost an engine, sir."

"We must have done!"

"If we'd lost an engine, sir," said the Birmingham accent slowly, "the cylinder head temperature would have fallen."

Irvine turned his head and looked at the four of them—all reading 200° Centigrade.

"Well, what the hell's the matter then? She's wallowing like an old cow!"

"You've got the nose too high up, sir."

"I've got the nose up, Craik, because if I didn't we'd lose what little height we've got." He put the nose down to demonstrate. "Look!"

Sure enough, the altimeter needle left 500 feet, slipped back to 400, 300 . . .

"The radio altimeter's registering now! For God's sake man, give me more power!"

The Engineer moved the throttles up to thirty-five inches.

"More revs! More revs!"

Craik touched the switches. The engines went out of synchronization, began making a juddering discordant chorus.

"I'm still losing airspeed!"

"O Orange is slow, sir."

"Slow? She's practically stalling!"

"The power's there, sir."

"Then what the hell is it? And don't tell me it's gremlins!"

"I think it's ice, sir."

"Ice? Where's ice? I can't see any ice!"

"Over there, sir!"

The Engineer pointed to the port wing. A thin white piping of opaque rime lay across the leading edge.

"*That?* But that's nothing!"

"Shall we try the boots, sir?"

"Certainly you can *try* them."

Irvine knew nothing about ice. Flying so low, Coastal Command pilots did not expect ice, and anyway few people had any clear ideas of what it did to certain aerodynamic shapes like the finely chiselled Davis wing of the Liberator.

Now the rubber edging on the leading edge began inflating and deflating, cracking up the surface of the rime.

101

The ice began flaking off like dandruff. Very gradually, the speed increased.

With a relieved sigh, Irvine watched the needle on the indicator creep up the dial. But now the thin mist had darkened. Instead of being white outside, first it had become grey, then black. And instead of droning along steadily through wet white cottonwool, O Orange began banging around, hunting and yawing in heavy turbulence. It was as though Deirdre Winter, thwarted with rime ice, had now played another card—the ace of storms.

"It's got warmer, Skipper," Garth warned him. "The air temperature gauge is shooting upwards."

It had become darker, too—pitch dark. O Orange rolled uneasily from side to side. Snow came out of the blackness ahead, great white flying insects whirling towards the windscreen and crushing themselves to death on the perspex. Snow settled all round them, a white mask over the windows, relieved by a trickle of alcohol that Craik had turned on.

And now ice in all its white grandeur came down on them. Not just the thin opaque rime, but the heavy clear stuff. The snow disappeared. The windscreen had become three times as thick. The wing was a skating rink. The propellers, trying to thrash themselves free, aided by alcohol, threw great gobbets of ice like cannon-balls crashing against the metal sides of the Liberator.

The sound was like nothing Irvine had ever heard. The crashing of a thousand cymbals. A barrage of heavy guns firing directly on them. He shouted to Craik to put the boots back on again, but the Engineer could not hear him. It was as though they were all trapped inside a percussion band.

He leaned across Henty and put the boots on himself, but even as he did so, he realized it was useless. There was two inches of ice on the leading edge now, as clear as diamond, a solid jagged-edged seam.

"Look at your speed, Skipper!" An agonized shout over the intercom from Garth.

He looked. 95 knots—and still going down. Henty was flying the thing as though nothing was the matter—thick as they come, he thought, just sitting there, slowly being sucked under. He snatched the controls, felt how soggy they were, all life drained out of them. The aircraft was simply becoming an

102

iceberg, maintained in the sky by Pratt and Whitney engines.

And now *they* were being affected. He saw the Manifold Pressure dropping back on the dials—35, 30, 25 . . .

Ice was choking the air intakes to the carburettors, literally suffocating them. They were losing height. The airspeed was only three knots above stalling.

"It's an inversion, Skipper!" Garth on the intercom again. "We're flying under an inversion!"

That meant that instead of colder air above, there was a warm belt that was pouring rain down to freeze on top of them.

"Sir, we've *got* to climb!"

"Hot air!" Irvine called out to Craik.

The small white face came close to his ear again. The gob-stopper eyes were practically falling down his cheeks. "We're in hot air, sir."

"Then give me power! Take-off power! All the power we've got!"

Craik pushed the throttles hard against the stops, and held the rpm switches forward. Now the propellers began screaming their heads off, sending a fusillade of ice pellets against the fuselage.

The port wing dropped. As he lifted it, Irvine felt how droopy and drowsy it had become. He pushed the nose down, trying to build up the speed. All the time, he kept his eyes glued on the artificial horizon, the altimeter and the airspeed indicator—the only signposts he had that he was right side up and still alive in this black, tossing, visionless world, this limboland between earth and hell. Delicately he tried to coax a little more airspeed out of O Orange. He tried to give it artificial respiration, the kiss of life . . .

"Skipper—"

The small mouth of his Engineer brushed his right ear again. That horrible Birmingham accent shouted hoarsely, "We've 'ad it! Deirdre Winter—"

He brushed the man aside. What a load of claptrap, he told himself determinedly. He could feel the power of the engines now. Life was beginning to flow back into O Orange. The needle on the altimeter was climbing upwards—slowly at first, then faster, the engines still at take-off power. Higher and higher now, up into the warmer air—2000, 3000, 5000, 7000 . . .

"Norwegian coast twenty miles ahead, Skipper!"

He had in fact almost forgotten the operation, could hardly remember the *Groningen*. In that paroxysm of trying simply to keep alive, all other thoughts had gone. Now they were safe enough, through the worst of the storm, actually flying at eleven thousand feet—the highest he had ever been in his life— in and out of the tops of cloud with a pale wintry sun every now and then breaking the yolk of an egg on the starboard windows.

"They'll have picked us up on their radar, Skipper!"

He did not need Trembath to tell him that. He was aware that he had not gone about the operation according to Strickland's briefing. But it had been that or getting the chop. And at least O Orange was still flying. They were alive.

And now they had to carry out the operation.

He began wondering how he was going to do it. They were quite safe up here, well above even the highest of the Norwegian mountains. But how to get down, and then how to find Falstand Fjord and the cut in the ice made by the ice-breaker?

"Can you recognize anywhere on the coastline, Radar?"

Miggs' voice back at him, "Not really, Skipper."

"Navigator, can you tell me our position?"

"Not within twenty miles, Skipper."

Irvine handed over to Henty and went down to the nose to talk to Garth. It was not reassuring. No radio beacons appeared to be operating. The sun was too intermittent and too low for a decent sun shot. The only hope was to wait for a while and try to map-read on the radar.

That was far from easy as there was considerable interference even on minimum range. Ten miles before the coastline, Garth and Trembath took turns to stare into the round face of the radar with its revolving wand and its splodges of green leprosy and try to decide where they were.

"Looks like Aalstrom, that point there, Skipper."

"More like Brna to me."

It could be either, Irvine thought. "Well, where is Falstand d'you reckon?"

Garth pointed to an inlet north, Trembath to an inlet south.

"That spur of land and those tiny islands look more like it to me," Irvine said. "We'll have to descend now anyway. Let's aim there, and with a bit of luck I might be able to recognize something. If not, we'll go along the coast northwards till we can get a pin-point."

Going back into the left-hand seat, he drew back the throttles, and still in hot air, pushed the nose sharply down. At three thousand feet a minute, O Orange slipped through the cloud towards the sea.

Ice again began forming, but not so seriously. At five hundred feet, they broke cloud with the Radar calling the coastline with Irvine's spur on it dead ahead at three miles.

In fact, it was five miles. The iced-up sea had been showing up as coastline, completely distorting any idea of where they might be. They flew just above the white ice, every now and then seeing through the mist grey rocks or the beginnings of mountains.

Flying north, edged right in, they saw no road, no houses, no trees. Just snow and ice and rocks. Irvine had been sure he would recognize the entrance to Falstand Fjord—Aalstrom lighthouse, that road on the right where all the flak posts were—but after three-quarters of an hour's flying, he could see nothing familiar. And though the whole crew at their various stations were trying to map-read and pick up a pinpoint, nobody managed to recognize anything.

Irvine turned the Liberator right round. "Now we'll try south."

Still searching, still flying low, they followed the coastline south, looking for the pathway cut by the ice-breakers or the lighthouse at Aalstrom, or a village they could recognize or a promontory they could identify.

They flew over a village Garth thought was Lagsno. Irvine circled and explored, but decided it wasn't. Half an hour later, he thought he saw the lighthouse at Aalstrom, but it was a thin rock covered in snow. Twenty minutes further on, though there was no pathway cut through the ice, Irvine was sure he recognized the road to the wharf lined by telephone poles.

"Here we are!" he called through the intercom. "The entrance to Falstand Fjord. We'll go on up inside and see what's happening."

Nothing—that's what was happening. Nothing moving. No

people. No animals. A house or two half smothered in snow. No flak. No opposition.

Irvine went up to just underneath the cloud—three hundred feet. All the time, he kept looking out for something familiar, even a gun position.

But he could identify nothing. Everything looked totally different. He could have been flying over the North Pole for all the signs of life that were visible.

And now the visibility began to drop. Instead of a couple of miles, it went down to a mile, then less than half a mile.

Still the Liberator flew up the fjord, mist dewing its windscreen. The cloud base began lowering—two hundred feet, a hundred feet. Already the early dusk was falling.

We should have reached the wharf by now, Irvine was thinking. This can't be Falstand Fjord. I'd better turn round—

Suddenly he was in thick cloud. Pushing the nose down, he struggled back into visibility.

But now he was flying just above the snow, and he could hardly see anything. He was in a cave that was closing down on him. If he didn't look out, he'd be trapped.

A ridge loomed up out of the mist. Just in time, he snatched the right wing up. Rocks to the right now, tall ones, looming up into the cloud. He began edging past them to the left.

"We'll turn—"

Too late! A sheer cliff blocked their way. A mountain face, massive, half ice, half granite loomed ahead, trailing grey tendrils of cloud.

Frantically he turned the aircraft vertically up on its port wing.

"Full throttle!"

He could feel O Orange juddering under him, just about to stall as he kicked on full left rudder. He could actually see the moss and lichen on the rock face, the snow-filled crevices and the starboard wing inches away from the cliff face.

Then the whole aircraft was falling, falling further, slipping towards the gloomy fjord. He wrenched it straight, and seeing nothing but mist, headed back the way he had come.

Any moment, we'll hit something, he thought. I can't see ten yards. I can just make out water down below. Should I make a belly landing? But what about the mines? Christ, if we touch anything, we really *are* going to go up . . .

He flew on blind. Every second flying this way, he told himself, meant that much nearer better visibility and safety. A hill came up suddenly, but a shallow one and he skirted round it.

And then suddenly, he saw telegraph poles—the road he thought he'd recognized, and coming right down on it raced back towards the open sea.

It was a very quiet trip home. Apart from the Navigator's comings and goings on the flight deck with course changes, nobody moved. Irvine took the aircraft up to really cold air at seven thousand feet, and this time they had no trouble with ice.

It was pitch dark when they landed back at Kilcreggan. The groundcrew were extremely disappointed to find the mines still in the aircraft. Theirs was the fifth aircraft, the Armament Officer told them, to come back with all their mines. "Let's hope Flying Officer Wisby has been more successful."

Squadron-Leader Strickland was awaiting them at Operations. "Well, Peter . . . and how did it go?"

How did it go? What can you say? What can you tell anybody? That we're lucky to be alive? That I've learned a lot? That I'm ten years older?

Irvine simply said, "We didn't drop our mines." And then: "I'm sorry."

Strickland didn't want to hear any more. He didn't want to hear about ice or the weather or the cliff face or anything. He simply turned on his heel and said, "Old Wisby will have dropped them. Trust him to get it right!"

Brackenbury's Intelligence debriefing was short. Rather shyly Irvine looked round his crew, expecting them hotly to elaborate on this hell ride which they had just experienced. But they just sat there, drinking their cocoa, letting him do all the talking.

". . . bit of trouble with aircraft icing . . . visibility the other side was poor . . . the ice round the coastline made pinpointing very difficult . . . we searched for the entrance to Falstand Fjord, but couldn't find it . . . so we came home . . ."

That was that. That was his crew's experience during the last nine hours. At any rate, none of them dissented from it. Looking at them affectionately now, even at Craik, he thought to himself being crewed up is like a big marriage. They're tied to me. I'm tied to them. For better, for worse, for richer, for poorer—except that death won't part us because we'll all be in it together.

They were just starting supper when he got to the Mess. So he went in for sausage and fried egg, followed by prunes and custard. Assistant Section Officer Jones was sitting at his table. He didn't feel like talking to anybody, so he didn't say anything. He didn't even nod to her, though, now it was over, romantically he wondered if she'd been one of those out there waving, and that perhaps *her* influence had managed to keep him safe.

Though he was tired, he couldn't rest. He couldn't keep still. He wandered from the ante-room into the bar, out again, in again. He talked to some of the other captains who'd been on the operation. They had all experienced much the same weather as he had done—though not with the hair-raising appendages.

Round about eleven, still in the bar, he heard J Jig was missing, and half an hour later, Strickland announced, "Old Wisby's gone! But remember, chaps . . . that's the way he'd have wanted to go!"

He expressed total confidence that Wisby alone had found the cut in the ice, dropped his mines "and written *finis* to the *Groningen*".

Good show, Irvine thought, as he finally pushed off to Room 27 and bed. Bloody good effort! Wouldn't have thought old Wisby had it in him. Saved us all a hell of a lot of trouble.

He undressed and had a bath. His room-mates had still not come up from the bar by the time he tucked himself back in bed. It seemed a little warmer than the last time he crept into it.

He closed his eyes. Just before he went immediately off to sleep, he saw in his mind's eye a gigantic scoreboard such as they use at county cricket grounds.

And on it in big block capitals was written: IRVINE 5 NOT OUT.

"Miggs gives up that bloody floozy or else—"

Up at the bar of the Sergeants' Mess, Curly Craik was discussing with Trembath their first operational trip. It was not quite clear who was the real culprit for the crew's misfortunes—Irvine or Deirdre Winter.

"Going up a fucking fjord blind!" said Trembath.

"Turned us all into a bleeding icicle!"

"What about that mountain then . . . right in front of us? Christ Almighty!"

Once they had had a couple of days on the ground to recover, the rest of the crew took their adventures philosophically. They had swapped their experiences with other crews and come to the conclusion that they'd all had much the same sort of hell. Miggs reiterated again that their safe return indicated how lucky they were.

He had not so much luck with his room. A Regular Air Force Warrant-Officer captain had been put in with him. No Christmas present after all awaited him on Boxing Day. Warrant-Officer Price was on his second tour and was known both as a good pilot and a strict disciplinarian. As soon as Miggs saw Price kneel down by his bed and pray, he knew there was no hope of a Box-and-Cox arrangement, no straight swap of your-night-my-night as far as girl friends in the room was concerned.

Not that it might ever be needed. In his absence from the dance, Deirdre Winter had become acquainted with Flight-Sergeant Hoyle who was the Navigator on Jerningham's crew. Hoyle had been particularly attentive, and a date with Deirdre Winter was difficult to arrange.

Eventually she agreed to go—not very enthusiastically—to Kilcreggan village with him on Saturday night. They got a lift in and spent the evening drinking at the *Kilcreggan Arms*.

The follow-up Miggs had all arranged.

But then things started to go wrong. They missed the Liberty bus back to camp because Miggs had insisted on one more beer. The walk back to the camp through the snowy woods in bright moonlight was romantic but very chilly. By the time they got to the Mess the bar was closed. Miggs had popped up to his room to see if by any chance Price had been called out on a trip, but there he was in his bed, gently snoring.

Miggs had anticipated this, and was not completely thrown. But there are on an RAF Station very few places for a courting couple to go. On an icy winter's night in Scotland even that small number is cut to near zero. This of course Miggs knew well enough and had made provision for. He had scouted the land. Done a recce for a suitable nesting place.

"I'm cold and I'm wet," Deirdre Winter informed him on the steps of the Sergeants' Mess.

"I'll soon warm you up, sweetheart."

"No thank you very much. I'm going back to my hut."

"Come and get a warm up first." He looked down at her, smiling. "Not the way you think, promise!" He took her hand. "Come along, love."

He took her over the crunching snow to the back of the Mess.

"Where are you taking me?"

"Wait and see."

He opened up a door.

A blessed warm draught of air came sweeping over them. There was a hot dusty smell. Three bright glowing rectangles sent a cosy glow over grey coke, black iron and red brick.

"The boiler house!" she said at first distastefully and then, as the heat began to soak into her, "It's nice and warm, Miggs!"

"Told you I'd get you warm." He shut the door softly behind them. There was no bolt on the inside. But you couldn't have everything.

"What about this then?" A wide wooden ledge stretched across the room opposite the boilers. "Seating accommodation as well. Shall we get the weight off our feet?"

She hesitated.

"All right." She perched herself on the edge, then after a moment, sat back, holding up first one snow-caked foot and then the other towards the glow.

"Your shoes are soaked," Miggs said.

"And whose fault is that, eh?"

"Mine." He knelt down solicitously and began to unlace them. "Take 'em off and dry your feet."

"That's all I *am* going to take off, mind," she said wriggling her toes in the warmth.

"Of course, sweetie."

Her grey lisle stockings gently steamed. She sighed with pleasure. He took off his greatcoat and sat down beside her. After a while he persuaded her to take off hers. He put his arm round her shoulders. They sat side by side staring at the glowing rectangles. He let his fingers slide down and undo the top button of her jacket. She covered the others with her hand.

"Deirdre, don't you trust me?"

"Half and half."

"Don't toast your toes too long or you'll get chilblains, sweetheart. Here give 'em me. I'll rub your toes for you." He swung her legs across him. But he didn't massage her feet for long. His hand crept up to her suspenders. She pushed his hand down a couple of times. He let it creep up again. This time she didn't shove it away. He played idly with her suspenders, then let his hand creep higher. Above the top of her stockings, he touched the bare smooth flesh below her knickers.

"Hey, what's this then, airwoman?" His fingers encountered soft silk panties, beautifully wide-legged. "Not wearing your black-outs?" He clicked his tongue. "I'll tell your Flight-Sergeant. Have you up on a charge. Lace-edged too. Naughty. Very naughty."

She giggled weakly and breathlessly. The giggle turned to a little whimper of alarm as his fingers explored inexorably further. She tried to push his hand away. He held both of hers in his left hand while his right hand did its work. Now he knew he had her. His fingers might have been round her throat. She wriggled and moaned. He leaned over and pushed her back with his free hand, till she was lying on the bench. The glow of the stove threw his black shadow on the ceiling. He heard heavy feet but far enough in the distance. He fastened his mouth over hers. Her lips were parted, protesting, but somehow moist and ready. He thrust his tongue into the warm cave of her mouth. He felt her shudder. It had to happen. It was going to happen.

"God," he thought desperately, fumbling at his flies, sweating a bit now with the heat of the stoves, "Let my luck hold! Give me enough time! Don't let anyone come bursting in!"

111

SEVEN

"TIME like an ever rolling stream . . ."

Madeleine Mowbray lifted up her head and sang the words fervently in a rich contralto up towards the corrugated iron roof of the Station Chapel. Standing in front of her was a row of WAAFs, with the young Assistant Section Officer who had been in such demand at the Christmas Mess dance—Jones, wasn't that her name? On her left was the Equipment Officer and the Station Engineer and Crackers, the old Gas Officer. In the row behind her was Peter Irvine, looking uncomfortable, and even more surprisingly, Squadron Leader Strickland—the only aircrew present.

"Bears all her sons away."

To the left of the simple altar on which were two vases of yellow chrysanthemums flanking the brass cross was a wheezing organ played by Wendy Beauchamp, the WAAF Flight Officer. Standing at the lectern, the white stole round his neck embroidered at each end with RAF insignia, Padre Binks looked over the top of his half-moon spectacles with his watery blue eyes at his minute congregation, a wide smile on his pale round face.

"They die forgotten as a dream
Dies at the opening day . . ."

Why was Binks smiling, Madeleine wondered. Was it because tomorrow was a New Year, traditionally full of hope and promise and with the first tremors—like spring buds—of peace? Was it because he had captured as audience no less a person than Squadron-Leader Strickland? Or was the smile simply the padre's stock-in-trade, passport to God's grace?

Or was it because he had divined why they were all here, and was smiling wryly at the workings of the human heart? Were

112

those WAAFs simply here on a detailed detachment on church parade? Had the Equipment Officer come to pray for Liberator spares? Was the Station Engineer sending up a plea to the Lord to keep the Pratt and Whitneys turning? And Squadron-Leader Strickland, had he come for God's help in making 507 the top squadron in Coastal Command? And that young boy, Irvine, was he here simply because—so Edward said—he did everything Strickland told him to do? Or was he following the pretty Assistant Section Officer?

". . . when two or three are gathered together, Thou wilt grant their requests . . ."

Her own request she didn't mind Binks, God, anyone or anything knowing. Now on her knees, her face cupped in her hands, softly whispering the words, she didn't mind if anybody heard. She was not after all asking for anything very much. Nothing at all for herself. And for Edward, at this moment asleep at home and safe after returning in the early hours of the morning from an uneventful Atlantic stooge patrol, not wealth, nor success, nor fame. She didn't care if he never attacked a U-boat or hit a German aircraft. She didn't want him to be a hero like Wisby, to whom she had spoken once or twice in the Mess and who now apparently had sunk the *Groningen*, the ship that had made such a mess of S Sugar and for which, according to Edward, he deserved not only every gong going but the heartfelt thanks of all 507 Squadron.

Madeleine Mowbray knew there was a lot of luck in this war game all the boys had been sucked into—more than baccarat, the horses or *chemin-de-fer*. Bend the flak away from him, God. Make clouds cover him up when German fighters come. *Keep Edward safe*.

The sermon now—predictably about the New Year and resolutions and integrity. Not only "to thine own self be true", for one could indeed be false and dangerous to many men if that alone was so—but true to God.

Not a good sermon. Nothing whatever to reassure her about Edward. A bit wet, Binks, but good-hearted in his watery way. And mercifully short.

Up on their feet now for the last hymn.

"Praise my soul the king of Heaven—"

Madeleine Mowbray sang it with all her heart, high above the

113

organ, high above everyone else. Just this one small request, which is easily in Your power to grant, and You shall have me and everything I have or will ever have . . . keep Edward safe.
"'. . . Alleluia! Alleluia!
Praise with us the God of grace.''
Praise God certainly. Praise God for skilful leaders like Strickland, praise for heroes like Wisby who planned and attacked and sank dangerous ships like the *Groningen* . . . before Edward managed to get anywhere near them.

The hero's halo lingered over Wisby's head well into the New Year. The weather over Norway remained appalling, so no PRU Spitfire could be sent to photograph what had been going on in Falstand Fjord. When finally a reconnaissance aircraft did get through, sure enough it showed the berth beside the wharf under the gigantic rock face as empty, the pathway cut through the ice still leading to the open sea, and no sign whatever of the *Groningen*.

"On the bottom," Strickland had said at Wisby's funeral sing-song, and now he repeated it again even more confidently, if that were possible. For nothing, not a sight, not a peep, not a whisper had been heard anywhere in the world of the armed merchant cruiser, and nobody could answer his question, "If she's not on the bottom, where is she?"

The intensive training programme had been eased over the holiday, and such operations as there were had been only convoy escorts and cross-over anti-submarine patrols between the Faroes and Iceland. Irvine's name remained off the operational Mayfly, but was never off the training programme—air-to-air and air-to-ground gunnery, low-level bombing, night radar exercises, even two cross-countries round the British Isles—"so as to give your Navigator some more experience" was how Strickland put it.

Irvine's crew grumbled to him, but he did not pass their grumbles on to the Squadron-Leader. What he did grumble about was his Rear Gunner—for Mosco, as huge and grey and watery as a cumulo-nimbus cloud, had discharged himself from Kilcreggan hospital, giving as his reason that he had heard Irvine's first trip had been what he called expressively in Polish a "fiasko", and he felt it his duty to give the green crew the weight of his experience when next they took off on operations.

"I don't think he's really fit, sir," Irvine said to Strickland.

The Squadron-Leader was now obsessed with a new scheme for sinking the *Groningen*. Having heard that six-pounder anti-tank guns had been fitted to Mosquitoes, he was determined to lay his hands on a couple. Griselda Jones had already been detailed to make forays into Army Ordnance establishments for the specific purpose of obtaining them for him.

Strickland looked up from a drawing he had made of how S Sugar's front turret need not after all be replaced. The two 57 millimetres would fire through the nose instead. He was also toying with the idea of rockets fired from rails under each wing.

"The Doc says he's all right."

"I didn't know you could discharge yourself from hospital."

"He was only there under observation."

"But Barlow has fitted into the crew so well—"

Strickland raised an eyebrow. "Has he?"

In the event, Barlow showed himself nothing loathe to leave. He welcomed Mosco's return with open arms, particularly as that Wednesday suddenly Irvine's name appeared at the top of the Mayfly, which coincided with a dance at the Sergeants' Mess that night.

Take-off was early—three o'clock in the afternoon. Irvine had not got up for breakfast, and lay comfortably in bed till lunch-time, drinking endless cups of tea that Mavis had brought him. He was not particularly worried. With the *Groningen* gone, this trip could be nothing more than a stooge patrol, and the weather was noticeably better. He began wondering if Assistant Section Officer Jones would be waving him off.

Around twelve he washed, shaved, got himself into his battledress, and carrying his fur flying jacket under his arm clumped downstairs in his flying boots. Mosco was waiting in the hall, and together through the melting snow they walked over to Operations where the rest of his crew had already arrived.

As soon as he got in, Irvine's eyes went to the white tapes pinned on the big wall map. Just a cross-over patrol off Iceland.

Strickland was in Intelligence during briefing, waiting to go off on another blind-bombing exercise with the cruiser *Marlborough*. Irvine was just listening to the met man droning

115

on about a warm front and a ridge of high pressure when suddenly Brackenbury came in from talking on the red scrambler telephone to Group.

"I'm very sorry to interrupt." The Navy were past-masters at being courteous and superior at the same time. "But there's been a signal from the submarine *Seawolf*."

"Another one?" Strickland asked.

"As a result of which," Brackenbury went on, "Pilot-Officer Irvine's patrol is likely to be changed."

"What does Commander Crabbet say *this* time?"

"He's sighted the *Groningen*."

"*Again?*"

"Again."

"Where this time?"

"65 North, 05 East. Course 250°. Speed 19 knots."

There was no doubt at all of the satisfaction in the naval officer's voice. A silence fell in the Intelligence Room. Everyone was looking at Strickland, waiting for him to say something. Echoes of those two words of Brackenbury's uttered nearly two months ago began ringing in Irvine's ears—"The *Groningen*? Impossible!"

But this time neither Strickland nor Brackenbury said them. The Squadron-Leader simply lifted his eyebrows and commented, "He was wrong before."

"So you think he's wrong again?"

Strickland said nothing.

"The Admiralty are particularly concerned because of convoy PQ 39." Brackenbury tapped a collection of cardboard ship-shapes on its way to Murmansk.

"I can see they would be if the *Groningen*'s still afloat." Strickland paused. "*If*."

Nevertheless, he went out of the room to talk on the scrambler telephone to Group.

"In the circumstances," he said when he returned, "my idea ... and Air Vice Marshal Nuttall thinks it's a very good idea ... is that Irvine's patrol is changed to a square search at 65 North, 5 East."

Irvine's heart went down to the bottom of his boots.

"Weather's bad there," the met officer said.

Strickland took not the slightest notice. "I'll cancel my

116

training, and do a square search to the west. Who's next on the Mayfly . . . Mowbray? He can do a square search to the east. The rest of the squadron are to stand by with all our serviceable aircraft, bombed up with five-hundred-pounder armour-piercing."

For the next hour, Irvine and his crew stayed in Intelligence, making the necessary changes. Garth drew on his Mercator the tiny Chinese-box shapes, one inside the other, that made up the navigational mechanics of a square search. Mosco sat in the only armchair in the office, eyes closed, gently wheezing, while the rest of the crew, put out by the alteration of plan and disturbed by the news of the *Groningen*, began exchanging theories in low tones on what might have happened to Wisby.

In some strange way, it didn't matter if Wisby and his crew had disappeared "doing" the *Groningen*. That was understandable. An eye for an eye. A Liberator for an armed merchant-cruiser—and a very good swop too! Nine men for six hundred. Sixty thousand pounds of duralumin, petrol, bombs and bodies for ten thousand tons of high tensile steel. The aircrew's deaths were justified and sanctified—no matter how they went. But simply to vanish, to evaporate, inflicting no damage to the enemy at all, that was a totally different matter!

Sitting at the table, reading the latest Intelligence reports, Irvine could hear the murmurings of his crew. Fragments of their theories came across to him—"ice", "hit a mountain", "flew into the sea", "shot down by flak", "jumped by fighters", "blew up". It was all so ghostly, so other-worldly, for Wisby's crew to leave Kilcreggan one Boxing Day morning and simply fly off to eternity, leaving no trace, no message, nothing at all but the bits and pieces of their belongings still in their rooms. No wonder up came the gremlins, the mysteries, the warlocks and witches and the things that went bump in the night. Irvine wasn't in the least surprised when he heard a rustle beside him and, looking up, he saw Craik's gob-stopper eyes and heard that horrible Birmingham accent pronounce, "Lynch went out with Deirdre Winter."

"Who's Lynch?"

"Lynch *was* Mr Wisby's Rear Gunner, sir."

They moved off from Dispersal eventually at last light. The sun, breaking through the clouds just on the crack of the western horizon, had sent a pale pink benediction over the slushy snow. A light westerly wind smelling of the sea was blowing through Irvine's open side window as he taxied out to the head of the runway. Nobody else seemed to be moving. Nobody else seemed to be alive. The beginnings of sleep were seeping over the countryside, a last draught before darkness. A calmness everywhere, a reconciliation, a folding of feathers and a closing of eyes. Sitting there waiting for take-off clearance, Irvine was reminded of coming out of the school chapel after Sunday evening service, after singing *Now the day is over, night is drawing nigh, shadows of the evening steal across the sky* . . . and then he remembered the *Groningen*.

"Take-off check?"

"Take-off check complete!"

The green went up from the Tower.

"Give me full power on the engines!"

He released the brakes. Slowly, the Liberator moved.

He could see them there, despite the shadow. They came closer and closer, became focused and sharp, not so many as before, but unmistakably cheering, unmistakably waving their WAAF caps, and there unmistakably just before lift-off the blonde hair and the pink and white face, and beside him the Birmingham accent shouting "Sir!"

"I know! I know!" He laughed too loud and too long as he pulled back hard. "Deirdre Winter!"

Sweetly, the Liberator rose. Sweetly, she steadied herself in the quiet air. Sweetly, the wheels came up. Sweetly, the flaps came up. Sweetly, she turned on course, northbound to find the *Groningen*.

He glanced to the right. He thought he saw the glimmerings of sense on Craik's still astonished face, the hover of a smile round Henty's lips. Stamp on that sort of nonsense! Laugh it off! Put your fingers to your nose to all superstition! That's what Strickland would have done. That's what leadership was. At last he was beginning to be a captain . . .

"Rear Gunner . . . are you all right?"

"I-am-all-right-Kapitan."

"Front Gunner?"

"OK, sir."

"Mid-upper turret?"

118

"Ready, sir!"

"Then fire your guns!"

The sky was immediately filled with a chattering louder than any birds' dawn chorus, and the Liberator was suddenly scented with the sweet incense of cordite.

As they flew north, darkness fell fast. The cloud thinned, then disappeared completely. A full moon, pale as chalk, powdered the air and silvered the sea. Gradually inside the aircraft it grew colder—the Liberator heating was sometimes erratic. Just before reaching the search area, they had supper of hot, sweet coffee out of the thermos flasks and corned beef sandwiches brought round by Craik.

"Navigator . . . what visibility distance are you going to use?"

"Ten miles, Skipper."

"Make it five."

"But the *Groningen* should show up on the radar at twenty, sir!"

"Make it five. On no account must we miss her."

Irvine had hand-flown the aircraft to the patrol area himself. Now he handed over to Henty in thick cloud, saying, "Two hours on, two hours off suit you?"

"Suits me fine, Skipper."

Like Irvine had done only a few weeks before, now Henty began lining up the Minneapolis-Honeywell automatic pilot.

"No!" Like Strickland only a few weeks before, now Irvine put out a restraining hand. "Fly her yourself! You need all the blind-flying practice you can get!" Then, over the intercom, he told his crew, "We are now on patrol. Radar, everyone, keep your eyes skinned!"

Two minutes later: "Kapitan—"

"Yes, Rear Gunner?"

"What height are we flying?"

"A thousand."

"Make it four."

"We will fly at *one* thousand feet."

"Kapitan, the range of the radar will be much better higher!"

"And so will the ice," he said shortly.

There was the sound of heavy breathing on the intercom. Then Mosco's microphone clicked off. The disgruntled gloom that seeped up to the flight deck from the rear was as thick as the cloud outside.

Ten minutes later, "Kapitan—"

"What is it *this* time, Rear Gunner?"

"Number One."

"What is the matter with Number One?"

"Exhaust flame is very orange."

Irvine looked round at Craik and raised his eyebrows.

"Burning oil," the Engineer said. "Nothing we can do about it, Skipper."

"Thank you, Rear Gunner."

"I think I should tell you."

"Thank you, Mosco. Thank you very much. Thank you very very much indeed."

He caught Henty's eye, looked up at the dark perspex of the escape hatch above them and shook his head.

The hours went by. The legs of the square search lengthened. There was still nothing showing up on the radar. At midnight, he did a tour of his little kingdom.

First, he went to the front, opening up the turret doors, finding the Australian Brett having a crafty smoke in the darkness.

It was strictly forbidden. It was dangerous. What would Strickland have done?

He opened his mouth, checked himself, pretended not to notice the glowing red cigarette end, the reek of tobacco, simply said, "Not too cold, are you?"

"A bit, Skipper."

"Like to come out for a while? Sit in my seat?"

"Oh, yes please!"

So he changed places with Brett, and sat there half suffocated by cigarette smoke, swivelling the turret to and fro, moving the guns up and down, aiming at the stars.

What else could he have said? It was lonely stuck up at the front like this. Cold, too, and nothing really to do. Though in spite of the forecast the cloud was thinning and he could see the sea down there, there was not a hope of being able to make out a ship. As for an attacking fighter, they were too far away from land.

He stayed in the front turret for an hour, then went along to talk to Garth, busy working on his Course and Speed Calculator.

"Like a rest?" he asked.

He did two hours' navigation, drawing in the tracks of the ever-enlarging square Chinese box. Then he spent an hour on the radar, following the sweep of the green hand round and round, illuminating nothing. The radio he knew little about, but there were three Wireless Operators on the crew and they took turns. But he had a go on the mid-upper turret, before trailing down through the bomb-bay and the unmanned beam gun position to have a chat with Mosco in the tail.

He opened the turret doors. Mosco was bundled up inside, packed tight against the perspex.

"Not much room, eh, Mosco?"

"How you mean *much*, Kapitan?"

"Rather a squeeze."

The Pole must have taken this as a challenge to his ability because he elevated and lowered the two .5s in double quick time.

"Like to have a walk, Mosco?"

"A *walk*, Kapitan?"

"Up and down the fuselage. Stretch your legs."

"No. I am quite happy."

"Happy?"

"I sit here. I look at the stars. I think about Poland."

"What about Poland, Mosco?"

"It is a thousand miles," he nodded to the right, "*that* way."

"Homesick?"

"I do not hear, Kapitan."

He shouted, "*Homesick!*"

"I do not understand."

"You would like to go home?" Irvine yelled.

"Like to go home?"

"Never mind, Mosco. It won't be long now."

"We are going home?"

"*You* will be going home!"

"*I* will be going home? Why will you not be going home?"

The tail swung as Henty turned onto a new course.

"What I'm trying to say is . . . you will be going home to a free Poland!"

"Now?"

121

"No, of course not, Mosco."

"When?"

"After the war."

"How will I be going to a free Poland?"

"I don't know exactly, Mosco. We'll probably fly you back."

"Who will free Poland? Squadron-Leader Strickland? Mr Churchill?"

"You, Mosco." This is what Strickland would have done. Make them identify with the cause. "You're helping to free Poland on this trip. Protecting PQ 39. Making its route to Murmansk safe against the *Groningen*, so the Russians can liberate Poland."

"Liberate Poland? *Russia?*" Moscovich spat onto the perspex dome. "Liberate Poland! Who first will liberate Russia?"

Trust Moscovich to turn the thing into a political argument! No point going down those blind alleys. Irvine bit his lip and said nothing.

Now the Arctic sea below was the colour of milk.

"Lovely moon, Mosco. Makes you feel quite romantic."

"Ro-man-tic?"

"Women, Mosco."

"Women? *Now?*"

"Those were very nice girls you had up at the hospital."

"I *had* girls at the hospital? No! Never!"

"Those girls, Mosco—"

"I did not have any girl, Kapitan!"

"Those three girls—"

"Three girls now! I have *three* girls!"

"When I came up on Christmas day, you had . . . company."

"Company?"

"Friends."

"Friends?" The Pole shook his head. "Those were not friends. Those were my *students.*"

"Your students. That's what I mean, your three students."

"What do you mean . . . *my* three students?"

"Pretty. Your three students are very pretty."

"I do not notice such things." Moscovich gave a massive shrug to his shoulders. "They wish to learn Polish. I teach them Polish."

"Some day you must teach me Polish."

"You wish to learn Polish?"

122

"That's right, Mosco."

"Then you must join my class. But I warn you, Kapitan, you will be very far behind!"

Irvine looked at his watch. They had been on patrol now for six hours. "I'd better get back to the front." He tapped the Pole on the shoulder and put up his thumb. "Glad you're quite happy, Mosco."

Back on the flight deck, he began working out fuel figures with Craik, fixed a time with Garth to leave the patrol area. Then, mindful he had not kept to his two-hours-on-two-hours-off programme, he took over from Henty, and round the burgeoning square they went.

The weather had improved and the visibility was reasonable. But the Radar remained silent. Only Mosco in the rear turret every now and then called out "Kapitan!"

"Yes, Rear Gunner?"

"A ship! *A ship!*"

"Where?"

"Five miles south."

"Nothing on the radar."

They would go and have a look all the same. Nothing. Just slivers of cloud playing tricks on the moonlit sea.

"A shadow, Mosco. That's all."

"I thought . . . a ship. I thought . . . the *Groningen*."

"Pity it wasn't."

"I was . . . how you say, Kapitan?—keeping my eyes skinned."

"Quite right, Mosco. Absolutely right. Just in case."

What Irvine meant was just in case the armoured cruiser *isn't* sunk. But by the time the patrol was ended, he was certain that it had been.

So was Strickland. Neither he nor Mowbray had found any trace on the radar and the visibility in the moonlight on both their trips had been excellent. "Your Commander Crabbet," the Squadron-Leader declared to Brackenbury, "needs glasses!"

Two hours after debriefing, a signal arrived in Operations from the Admiralty. A straggler from PQ 39 carrying fuel oil and a deck cargo of tanks had been attacked and sunk. Radio conditions had been bad in static and only one word of a message it had sent could be deciphered.

Groningen.

EIGHT

ON stand-off, Irvine stayed in bed, read the newspapers in the ante-room, or drank the odd noggin in the bar. Now and then, he went over to the Sergeants' Mess and had a drink with his crew, but unlike some of the others (particularly the Canadians), he did not go about with them in a drove. Always something of a loner, he still had just Bertie Maltravers, the Dutchman Guilonard's second pilot, as a friend. On the rare occasions when it was fine and they happened to be on stand-off together, they walked round the sea edge on the road above the rocks and then took the short cut through the pine wood to Kilcreggan village.

On these excursions, Maltravers very rarely talked about flying. He certainly never talked about the *Groningen*. What he did talk about was girls—continuously and endlessly about girls.

He talked of girls at home, girls he'd met, girls he'd spoken to, girls he'd seen, girls in Kilcreggan, WAAFs on the Station. He was continually producing letters on violet note-paper, reading bits (rather dull bits, Irvine thought), passing the note-paper over with the instruction, "Smell!", and bidding him sniff deeply. From these exercises, Irvine had caught the faint whiff of faded scent, a sort of far-away smell of years gone by, pre-First World War. Indeed there was something far away and Edwardian about Bertie Maltravers, as though really he was some apparition from that earlier age. He talked of girls in that extravagant, poetical, flowery, worshipful, old-fashioned way—beings on a pedestal, belonging to some ethereal race having no connection whatever with the snails and puppydog tails that in his view constituted his and Irvine's make up.

Irvine was secretly impressed. The name, the huge Queen Anne house, the ancestry, the wealth, were in marked contrast to his own background, and he envied Bertie Maltravers as extremely sophisticated and very experienced, a womanizer of no little charm and attraction. For he was good-looking too—again in an old-fashioned way—a flop of brown hair hanging over dreaming grey eyes. These girls were just names with no story attached to them. Descriptions, yes, and all sorts of ideas and speculations. The letters were the same letters, produced again and again. The names were the same names, as evanescent as scent and just as elusive, as unknown as those in a telephone book, until coming into the Mess after one of their walks one evening early in the New Year, Maltravers had said suddenly, "But the real one is Emma."

At first Irvine did not know whom he meant.

"Emma!" Maltravers had become immediately irritable as though he was dealing with some wall-eyed moron. "Christ man, how could you miss her? That glorious dark hair! Those blue eyes. And the way she *looks* at you . . . at me, anyway—"

Irvine cottoned on to the fact that this object of Maltravers' adoration was Emma Jones. Since his own romance with Emma had progressed no further than the nodding and smiling stage, he had been more than a little taken aback. He listened morosely to further raptures, said nothing at all of his own feelings. They usually went to the bar for a pint, but that evening Irvine had stumped off to Room 27, where he lay on his bed reading a novel till it was time for supper.

Their lives had been ever since they met a strange Box-and-Cox affair. When Irvine was free, Maltravers would be out on patrol with Guilonard's crew or sleeping one off—and vice versa. While Irvine had been on training, they had seen more of each other, had both been looking forward to the Christmas dance, which in the event Irvine had celebrated over Norway on his fifth operation.

He heard all about it though. Maltravers saw to that. The evening appeared to have been a tremendous success for him. He had danced four times with Emma Jones—a waltz, two quicksteps and a tango—not to mention being in her group for the Dashing White Sergeant. He had also bought her two drinks and gone to fetch a sausage roll for her from the buffet.

"Did you fix up a date?"

Regretfully no, regretfully that had not been possible. One

125

never knew, did one, what with the intensive training programme as well as operations, when one would be on flying. And if there was one thing one hated, it was having to stand up a girl "simply because one was flying".

Irvine had thought that to be the acme of gentlemanliness. The picture it presented, the boredom, the nuisance, the irritants of practice bombing, cross-over patrols, sorties into the Skagerrak, enemy fighters, the *Groningen*, Strickland himself as being of the utmost insignificance beside the pleasure of a lady's company.

He had never in fact seen the two of them together. That was not surprising since with the return of the better weather, the squadron was flying more than ever. But he received a clear picture of what he would see from the odd times he met Bertie Maltravers in the bar, or went for the occasional walk in the pines. And that was one of twin souls, two turtle doves together, on the lacy front of a Valentine.

The actual doings were shrouded in mystery—or was it discretion? "One could never go far from the Station", "one finds the Mess so *public*", "one is being continually frustrated by quite unnecessary chores". Then the yawn, the foppish flick of the handkerchief pulled out of his uniform trouser pocket, followed by the sigh and the faraway yearning in the aristocratic grey eyes. Star-crossed lovers—no, war-crossed lovers: the man off to the enemy and the woman who waited.

Irvine saw Emma Jones now and again and gave her his permanent sheepish smile, receiving in return a nice smile back and "Hello, Peter". Once in the bar, he almost bought her a drink, but was forestalled by Strickland coming in and immediately buying her a gin and orange, his invariable medicine for females.

This pitiful little collection of words and smiles he never mentioned to Maltravers. For he was jealous, there was no doubt about that, jealous of Bertie's sophistication, ancestry, wealth, technique, control. Gauche in comparison, that's what he was! He reached the peak of his jealousy one night towards the end of January when he was alone in the ante-room just before he went to bed, and Bertie came in and presented him with the elbow of his right arm and commanded, "Smell!"

He smelled. A strangely acrid, rather too bitter-sweet, aroma filled his nostrils, which he gathered had come off Emma Jones' face (scent? face powder?) as it nestled in the crook of the Maltravers arm.

And then at the beginning of February, just after he'd got up from sleeping off an all-night operation in the Arctic circle and was having a quiet beer before going into lunch, watching Emma Jones up at the bar with four other officers, laughing and drinking the gin and orange that Strickland had bought her, in came Bertie Maltravers in battledress and flying boots, looked round the bar, recognized him and came over to where he was sitting alone by the window.

"Beer?" Irvine asked automatically.

Maltravers shook his head. "Flying." He perched himself on the small table beside the piano. "Ops."

Instead of his usual drawl, his voice sounded bright and brittle. He appeared agitated, swinging his legs under the table and out again, his hands clinging to the top as tightly as to a cliff-edge.

Irvine looked up and saw the look in his eyes. A strange look, flickering, uneasy, like the shimmering of moving water, above a fixed and dreadful smile.

"Anybody else going?"

"Just us. Every other aircraft is out. But the moment they're back, they're to be turned round and off again."

"Why?"

"Flap on."

Several times Irvine had seen Guilonard and his crew together in Operations. Twice as old as any of them, big and burly, with a cheerful face carved as though in cherry wood with brown-button eyes and a big mouth that was always laughing, the ex-KLM captain looked like a nutcracker souvenir from some Dutch seaside. Totally different from Mosco, experienced, genial, gentle, he always gave the impression of some kindly uncle surrounded by his young nephews. Maltravers never worried about flying—why should he, sitting beside a man with fifteen thousand hours? Colliding with a mountain, crashing on landing, not coping with low-level instrument flying—all such dangers with Guilonard were out of the question.

"Load's been changed to 500-pound armour-piercing."

127

"Oh?"

"Ship's been sighted."

"Oh?"

"Believed to be the *Groningen*."

Bertie had begun rocking himself to and fro on the table, his knuckles white with clinging to the top. Some kind of crooning, a weird humming perhaps of some song was coming out of his lips. And all the time, his eyes were roaming round the room, searching, flitting over the faces at the bar, Garfield's, Emma's, Strickland's as though appealing for someone to see him, to take notice of him, and then hopelessly coming back to Irvine sitting below him.

But why should anybody take any notice? It was just another trip. Something that happened five times a day. Something that had happened to Irvine less than twenty-four hours before.

Yet the eyes looking down seemed to be beseeching him to help.

Irvine offered, "Probably won't be the *Groningen*."

"Guilonard'll go straight in, whatever it is. Even if it's the *Tirpitz*."

Stop me, don't let me go, the grey eyes called out to him. Help me, *help me*!

Irvine tried again, "Probably won't find her."

"Guilonard'll find her, even if he has to use his last drop of petrol."

Do something, the dry cracked voice, the rocking body, the fixed smile called out to him silently. The eyes had left Irvine's face, moved to the faces at the bar to signal their message.

Strickland, Emma, Garfield, Mason—nobody heard it. Nobody seemed to know he was there, let alone what he was trying to communicate.

"Oh yes!" Unconsciously Maltravers was imitating Strickland. "Whatever the opposition, he'll attack. Flak, fighters . . . they won't mean a thing . . ."

The fixed smile had disappeared. The big eyes were still looking at him. You can't let us go, they were imploring. Why don't *you* go instead? Why doesn't Strickland go? Why doesn't the doc, for Flint had just come in and was standing up at the bar with the others, intervene and stop this relentless inevitable crazy progression?

128

Guilonard . . . that gentle smile, those brown sad eyes, those blunt skilled hands, what agonies they masked!

"This is what he's been waiting for! After Rotterdam he doesn't give a damn!" But *we* do, Maltravers' grey eyes tried to say, the eight Englishmen in his crew, we do. We have no private revenge to wreak. We are not Kamikaze pilots. Any ordinary war risk, yes—but he'll go in at nought feet in broad daylight, no cloud cover, nothing. We won't have a chance! In a Lib, not a chance! We won't even get anywhere near . . .

Rocking to and fro, the eyes as big as saucers now, rolling round the room, appealing against the death sentence. I'm young. I've done nothing wrong. I'm not in this war, not really. There's been some mistake in time. Some future crack I've slipped into ahead of my real life. *This* is the illusion: this world conflict, guns, aeroplanes, the *Groningen*. *My* world is the croquet lawn, the high starched collar, the soft sound of long dresses brushing pretty ankles, the church bells ringing, and the parlour-maid making anchovy toast for tea.

Nobody spoke. Nobody did anything. He's doomed, Irvine thought. That's why he came in here, to find me. But what can I do?

"You'll be all right." It was Irvine's final offering. He watched Bertie Maltravers turn the words over and over in his mind, as though perhaps they were gold and, finding they were valueless, simply sighed.

He looked over at the bunch at the counter. Why doesn't he go over and speak to her, Irvine wondered. Probably too shy with Strickland and the others around. Anyway, what could he say to her? What could she say to him?

And then a strange thing happened. In the middle of that male gathering up at the bar taking not a scrap of notice, as though suddenly she heard something, caught some signal of distress on some invisible wavelength, the girl turned her head, and, seeing Peter Irvine sitting over by the window, she smiled.

It was the usual smile she always gave him whenever she saw him in their awkward, faltering acquaintance. She had turned away as quickly as she had turned towards them. But suddenly he saw the echo of that smile on Maltravers' face.

Grey eyes still fixed upon her, smile still lingering round his lips, clearly Bertie Maltravers had interpreted that smile as exclusively for himself.

His mood changed completely. No longer was he sitting on the table, kicking his legs up and down, rocking himself to and fro. He was back in the pine woods—gesticulating, authoritative, talking about girls.

He looked at his watch, yawned, slipped gracefully off the table, said in that leisurely, bored, aristocratic drawl, "Ah well . . . time to get mobile."

He began to saunter across the bar. "Be seeing you, Peter."

"Be seeing you, Bertie."

Nobody else but Irvine saw him go. Just for a moment, before he closed the door, he let his eyes rest once more on Emma Jones' dark-haired head.

Then he was gone.

Irvine had a solitary lunch, snoozed all afternoon in the ante-room, went to bed early. But though he was tired, he could not sleep. He was one of the first into breakfast. Then he walked through the station, arriving in Operations at seven-thirty and saw what he expected to see chalked on the blackboard.

*ETD**	*ATD†*	*Aircraft*	*Captain*	*ETR‡*	*ATR§*	*Load*
13.30	13.30	X	Guilonard	02.45		10 × 500 lb

There had been no signal at all from X-Ray. He waited for another hour and a half, and still Guilonard had not returned. X-Ray and all her crew had simply disappeared.

Nothing more was ever heard. It was not even known for sure whether it was the *Groningen* that X-Ray attacked, but it was assumed by 507 Squadron to be so.

Two days after that strange last talk with Bertie Maltravers, Irvine sat next to Emma Jones at breakfast. He felt he should say something to her about her boyfriend, and, not knowing how to do it, went the roundabout way of mentioning that it was tough luck about Guilonard and his crew, particularly "Maltravers, a very good friend of mine."

"I'm sorry." She said it sweetly and sympathetically, and he had the impression that she thought he wanted comfort from *her*, not the other way round.

* Estimated Time of Departure.   ‡ Estimated Time of Return.
† Actual Time of Departure.   § Actual Time of Return.

"*Bertie* Maltravers, his second pilot."

She murmured something.

"A good chap. One of the best."

She screwed up her eyes as though she was trying to remember. "Bertie Maltravers?"

"Hair over his right eye. Dreamy sort of chap."

"I must have seen him . . ."

There was no reason why she should remember him. One young officer out of the three hundred in the Mess. One ghost escaped from Edwardian days, sitting in the right-hand seat of a Liberator as though on the Manor House lawn.

There was an awkward silence. He passed her the marmalade.

The little stories and dreams that poor old Bertie must have made up about her did not strike Irvine as sad. Everyone, he was beginning to realize, lived in an illusion anyway. What really pierced him was that she would never know, nor could anyone ever tell her, that Bertie Maltravers, of whose existence she was totally unconscious, had gone to certain death against the *Groningen* with the thought of her warming his old-fashioned heart.

NINE

"GRISELDA . . . what'll it be?"

Never once, during those freezing weeks of January and early February, did Strickland forget to call that out to Assistant Section Officer Jones whenever he saw her in the Mess bar. Patched up at last with American spares, S Sugar was flying better than ever and the Blind Bombsight had been transferred to her from Z Zebra. Rocket rails had been screwed into her wings, and, after a trip to Salisbury, true to her blue-eyed girl image, Griselda Jones had come up with two 57 millimetre anti-tank guns wheedled out of the Army, and the Engineering Officer was given the problem of fixing them both, complete with automatic loader and six-pounder ammunition, to fire forward through S Sugar's nose.

The intensive training programme continued. What was happening in Strickland's trials with the cruiser *Marlborough* remained a mystery. No one else was allowed to play with his new toys. Whenever he could find the time from his paperwork and his organization, Strickland would take off for further trials either on rocks in remote lochs or on the cruiser in the open sea, but how accurate the rockets, the 57 millimetres or the BB were and how many hits had been achieved were a closely guarded secret. The tradition of a Strickland crew was that it should be a crew apart, and this new one of his was now no exception. The three officers in Room 27 kept strictly silent.

Strickland still did more than his share of cross-over patrols and anti-submarine sweeps. On these exercises, the squadron was doing much the same as usual. Garfield had a U-boat sighting, but it dived before he could attack. Dacres machine-gunned a small naval trawler. Mason had a running battle with two Me 109s. Irvine did two more trips, totally uneventful, bringing his score to double figures.

Irvine tried to persuade himself that his crew were now beginning to settle down, that in reality they were a well-balanced lot. It was all like a see-saw with Mosco right out there at the far end (and by God he needed a lot of balancing) but bunched up forward to do it were the sober-sided Navigator Garth, the Wireless Operator Trembath, who had a good brain, the two tough Australian gunners, and Henty his second pilot, keen and anxious to please. Certainly there was the sepulchral Engineer Craik, purveyor of doom, but he was nicely matched by Miggs.

Miggs was older than the others and had done a lot of things before joining up. What sort of things was never quite clear, but Miggs had certainly seen the world and clearly liked what he had seen for he was always smiling. No matter what happened in the air, Miggs smiled. "It's nothing, Skipper" were three words always on his lips, closely pursued by "I'll fix it in a jiffy!"

The Marconi wouldn't work—then Miggs would have it in pieces on the W/T table. The radar was not picking things up clearly—Miggs had the leads out and was fiddling in its bowels. A turret jammed—Miggs was in there with a screwdriver. A .5 had a stoppage—Miggs had the breech-block out in a trice. The weather started closing in—Miggs blithely forecast it would clear. Mosco reported ME 110s at twelve o'clock high—Miggs said they were seagulls. Craik would point to the oil pressure dropping and report a master-rod going—Miggs would say it was the instrument.

The fact that Miggs was often incorrect, that the W/T remained in pieces till they landed, the weather did not clear, the oil pressure fell off the clock and the engine had to be hastily stopped and feathered was neither here nor there. Irvine had been given a comforting reassurance to hang on to, some hope on the horizon.

Irvine could have blessed him. If anything was wrong, he didn't want to know. There are few things worse on a dark night than watching the needle on an engine instrument twitch like a phosphorescent eyelid, nothing better than to hear Miggs' diagnosis, "It's the instrument." There are few things worse than a fire alarm bell going off on a peaceful Sunday afternoon high in the Arctic Circle, nothing better than to hear Miggs' confident call, "False alarm!" There are few things worse than ice piping the leading edge of the wings with white, great crystal gobs being slung off the propellers and clanging against the fuselage while the speed drops off on the airspeed indicator down and down towards stalling, nothing better than to hear Miggs call, "Soon be out of it, Skipper! Stuff's melting already!"

Mosco of course continued to be a trial.

"Ice, Kapitan, go up! Go up!", "Surely we are not leaving to return home so soon, Kapitan?", "Kapitan, the engines are out of synchronization", "Kapitan, tell the Navigator to throw out a flame float and I will take a drift sighting with my guns."

Eventually Irvine decided to tackle him head-on. Late one Saturday evening, when the ante-room was empty except for his Rear Gunner, who was sitting on the sofa and reading a book in Polish, Irvine sat down beside him and said, "Deserted tonight, eh Mosco?"

The Pole grunted.

"We've had some pretty good trips recently, eh Mosco?"

"Pretty good, Kapitan? We have seen nothing! Nothing but sea and cloud!"

"Don't worry! We'll see something some day!"

"That bloody ship you mean?" Moscovich snorted. "All this nonsense about the *Groningen*! I say to Squadron-Leader Strickland . . . I say to him when are we going to bomb Berlin?"

"All in good time."

"Time? Time is *good*? We wait and wait and—"

"The crew are shaping well."

Mosco's shoulders heaved up and down like a ship on a swell. "There is a lot to learn, Kapitan."

"Oh yes, yes! We all have a lot to learn . . . except," he added hastily, "you, of course, Mosco. But nevertheless, on a crew, there's only room for one captain."

"Another kapitan? Are we to have *another* kapitan?"

"No, Mosco. Only one captain."

"One kapitan, yes."

"And you know who that captain is?"

Mosco looked at him as though he had gone out of his mind. "You. You are the kapitan."

"That's what I want to remind you of."

"But I *know* you are the kapitan!"

"Just one captain. One person gives the orders," Irvine went on doggedly. "No back seat driving."

"Back seat?"

"The back seat of a car. An expression, Mosco."

"But it is not possible to drive a car from the back seat!"

"Exactly, Mosco. That's what I'm trying to say. Advice from the back seat, whether in a car or an aeroplane, is not wanted."

"Where in an aeroplane is the back seat?"

"The rear turret."

"The rear turret is now called the back seat?"

"What I'm trying to say, Mosco," Irvine said more sharply than he intended, "is that I can do without your instructions on how to fly the aircraft!"

The Pole said slowly, "You do not wish my advice?"

"No."

"Then I will say nothing." Moscovich closed his book with a decisive thud. "Nothing!"

"Of course if you see a German fighter, or a ship or a U-boat or something wrong, then naturally—"

"Nothing! I will say *nothing*!"

"Mosco," Irvine said desperately. "All I'm saying is . . . you do your job, I'll do mine."

"My job is to say nothing."

"Mosco, I didn't say that! What I mean is—"

"My kapitan orders me to say nothing." Moscovich heaved his huge bulk out of the chair. "So I say nothing." Stiffly he began to walk to the door.

Left to himself with no one in the ante-room, Irvine gave vent to his feelings by saying out loud, bowdlerizing Henry II and Thomas à Becket, "Oh, who will rid me of this turbulent Pole?"

On the next operational trip, true to his threat—Irvine was sure the Pole understood far better than he made out—Moscovich never said a word. Only a portentous silence, grey as gloom and just as infectious, permeated up to the flight deck from the rear turret.

It was an impossible crew situation. You couldn't go out on operations with this sort of atmosphere. Irvine conceded defeat

135

and said, "That talk we had, Mosco. I didn't mean you weren't to tell me what you see. You're a very valuable crew member."

Mosco regarded this as an apology, and accepted it graciously. Next trip, as soon as they were on patrol, there was a click of a microphone, a wheeze of heavy breathing, and Mosco's voice peremptorily over the intercom. "Higher, Kapitan, higher! We need to go higher . . ."

Darkness disorganized. Wind teased and bullied. Even before the engines were started on that fourteenth operation, he could feel the Liberator shudder as the wind punched the tail. Taxiing D Dog along to the runway, Irvine could hear it shrieking high above the mutter of the idling engines, pushing at the nose to get it off the taxi-track, then a real pommelling to get him limbered up just before the fully loaded night take-off.

And all the time the Liberator was quivering like a live bull under the darts and the spears of a matador. It was like being inside the bull, Irvine thought, as he opened up the engines to full power on the brakes and felt the vibration. A blind bull facing the darkness, till he stretched his hand over and switched on the landing lights.

Now two yellow eyes stared furiously out in front of him, picking out the cowed grass, the little runway lights. As he released the brakes, the wind rushed sideways on his tailplane, struggling to twist him off the flarepath. For Kilcreggan had only one main runway—the other was far too short for operations—and when the wind was from the north and at its strongest and coldest it meant a cross-wind take-off, a squealing of tyres on lift-off, and a desperate jab of the rudder to get D's nose straight when at last they were airborne.

They were on patrol up in the Arctic Circle where the *Groningen* was supposed to be lurking. Everybody was pretty quiet. The heating wasn't working well and, under his gloves, Irvine could feel his fingers stiff with cold.

Then twenty-five minutes after they reached the patrol area, just as Irvine was turning the fourth ninety-degree corner of the square search, he heard a click as a microphone was turned on followed by five seconds of heavy breathing. He knew who it was before the voice spoke, and his heart went down to the bottom of his flying boots.

136

"Rear Gunner to Kapitan!"

"Yes, Rear Gunner?"

"I smell . . . I smell—"

Oh Christ, what did he smell now?

"You smell all right, Mosco!" Miggs piped up from the radar. "And how!"

The microphone was switched off sharply. An offended silence hung over the aeroplane. Mosco had taken the huff.

Wild ideas of what the Pole might have smelled began coursing through Irvine's mind—cordite, smoke, poison gas, exhausts, cigarette smoke (from a crafty smoke), hydraulic fluid, oil, the Elsan which like Mosco was at the back of the aircraft. He had no desire whatever to find out, but he knew he would have to. He knew he would also have to coax Mosco back into the warmth of what the RAF called "the crew spirit" from his lonely ledge.

Whatever it was, the Pole was probably imagining it. Irritably he switched on his microphone. "What is it you smell, Rear Gunner?"

Like a crack of the whip back: "Petrol."

"No petrol anywhere near you, Mosco," he said to comfort himself.

"It is petrol. I smell *petrol*."

Up from the bottom of his flying boots, his heart jumped convulsively.

"You must be mistaken."

Coldly: "No mistake."

"There must be. You can't—"

"Not only smell, Kapitan. See."

"*See?*"

"On my turret."

"Raining petrol now, eh Mosco?" said Miggs.

Again the microphone was switched off. Then Craik said, "You know, Skipper, I can smell petrol now."

He *would*, Irvine thought. He drew in a deep breath, "Well, *I* can't." He turned to his second pilot. "Can you?"

In the cockpit everyone began breathing in and out like Health and Beauty exercises. Then from the top turret there was a sudden cry from Brett, "Christ, Skipper . . . *Christ*! It's petrol all right! Bloody great stream of it! Coming out of the starboard wing . . . right over the exhaust of Number Four engine!"

There was an immediate horrified silence.

"Gauges showing we're losing petrol, Craik?"

"No, sir." The gob-stopper eyes were popping out of their sockets. "But you know what they're like."

They were translucent tubes like big temperature gauges, notoriously inaccurate.

"Well," Irvine reluctantly unlocked his seat and pushed it back. "Better go and have a look, I s'pose."

Then he shuffled across the flight deck, swung himself down onto the catwalk of the bomb-bay and then up to the beam gun position.

It was open—rectangles cut out of the fuselage. The two single .5s swung on their mountings, ready for use but unmanned. Pushing the muzzle of the starboard one aside, Irvine stared out into the night.

Moonlight had painted the camouflaged wing a pale buttercup yellow. Not a cloud in the sky—a pastoral scene really, everything as still as a picture. The air smelled meadow-sweet.

Petrol.

He saw it, thick as his arm, a liquid cord of petrol streaming out of the filler cap over the starboard wing and shimmering greenly just above the yellow fang of Number Four's exhaust.

"Christ . . . !"

He said it out loud, staring out from the beam gun position. He felt his heart hammering. His knees seemed to have turned to water. At any moment that exhaust might lengthen, ignite the petrol and then—

He must think straight. There was no need to panic. The Liberator hadn't gone up yet. And if things stayed exactly the way they were, there was no reason why it should. But at what rate was the fuel coming out?

Irvine stood at the oblong opening, watching it. The open duralumin edge of the gun position sliced the slipstream in two with a high-pitched continuous whistle.

So this was life, he thought, atmosphere that wasn't yet fifteen parts of air to one part of petrol. Four inches lower, a bump, a wing dropping and the mixture in the crucible made

138

death. They flew through the cold Arctic night on the knife-edge of eternity.

He gazed at the green stream, twisting and gyrating above the yellow fire. It was all so very peaceful: the engines softly murmuring; the wings so steady; the sea below a field of wild buttercups.

Should he stay on patrol? Or should he go home?

The cold Arctic air blew over his hot face. He had been sent here to find the *Groningen*. The lives of British sailors depended on him completing the patrol and finding the armed merchant cruiser. But the lives of his crew also depended on him, and nobody could say that petrol pouring over hot exhaust gases wasn't dangerous, never mind the fact that he was losing it at the rate of an unknown number of gallons a minute.

He stood at the oblong opening, smelling the sweet scent of petrol, saying to himself my crew are my babies—even old Mosco, that big fat cuckoo in the nest. I am their brains. I am their heart. I am their lungs. Without me, they could not breathe. I am their guide. I am their touchstone. I am their faith. I must learn to be a captain. I must learn to be a leader.

Then he went slowly up to the flight deck. Getting back into his seat, over the intercom in a very matter-of-fact voice, he said, "You're quite right, Mosco. We *have* got a bit of a fuel leak out of the starboard wing tank."

He thought to himself wryly, that'll keep them from having a crafty smoke. Then he sent Craik up into the mid-upper turret to take a look at it with the Aldis lamp.

He had not expected his Engineer to come up with any remedy, so he was not surprised when he was informed that there was "nothing we can do, Skipper." Craik opened up his mouth again, and Irvine stopped him before he could speak, just in case he was going to repeat "We've 'ad it!", and said "We'll feather Number Four. At least that'll put the exhaust flame out."

"But it may catch fire from Number Three's exhaust!"

Irvine said, "We'll be all right." The cheerful confidence of his own voice surprised him.

"Shall I send a signal?" asked Trembath on the wireless.

"Christ, no! Might make a spark." He clambered into

his seat, moved it forward purposefully, called over his shoulder briskly, "Radar off! Lights off! Every damned thing off!"

"Are we going to continue patrol?" asked Trembath.

"For another fifteen minutes. If it doesn't get any better, we'll go home."

Fifteen minutes later to the second, Craik reported the fuel leak worse.

On the intercom Garth said, "Course to Kilcreggan 202°. ETA 06.32."

"Turning onto 202."

All the way back, it was as though the entire aeroplane held its breath. There wasn't even a peep from Mosco. When anyone moved, they went on tip-toe as though afraid of waking some fiery dragon.

It had begun to snow when they reached home—white polka dots on pitch black. The air on the flight deck was syrupy with the smell of petrol, and Irvine felt sick as though he'd eaten too many sweets. He came in with everything off—navigation lights, landing lights, the lot—and banged D Dog so hard on the runway that she enacted a convulsive trembling shudder that everyone in the aeroplane felt.

"Well, we've made it!" said Henty.

"Just," said Craik, pulling the cut-offs on the four engines.

As Irvine had feared, Strickland was in the Operations Room when they came in. He stood on the Controller's dais, legs wide apart and arms akimbo. "What's all this then?"

"Petrol leak."

"A *what*?"

"Petrol streaming out of the filler cap on the starboard wing." Irvine shoved his nose into the cocoa the WAAF brought him. "Wonder we made it home."

"Did you lose *all* your petrol then?"

"No."

"Well?"

"Wonder we didn't go up is what I meant."

"Up? Up? What d'you mean *up*? You were up already." Strickland was very far from pleased. "Coming back like a ghost, five hours early off patrol—no signal, quite unexpected. The rigger didn't screw the cap on tight enough."

140

"First thing I checked when we landed."

"Then it was a faulty filler cap." Strickland picked up the telephone. "Get me Stores! Emma, you've got filler caps? You haven't? Then get onto Machrannoch and get us some . . ."

"Deirdre Winter nearly got us that time!" In the lorry taking them back from the crew room after stowing their parachutes in their lockers, Curly Craik expressed his feelings to Irvine's Sergeants at large and Miggs in particular. "Another trip like that, and Christ, we've 'ad it!"

Miggs laughed. "Don't be so bloody silly!"

"Hell of a lot of things have been happening to us," the Australian Jarman said.

"Can't be all bloody coincidence," said his cobber, Brett.

"Work it out for yourself," Trembath said. "That training trip we couldn't get in. That first trip up the fjord . . . bloody nightmare! That op when we couldn't find the *Groningen*."

"Nor could anyone else," Garth pointed out. "Not even Strickland."

"Then last night we're within a millimetre of becoming a flaming torch," Trembath continued. "There's a curse on us, that's what I say. A jinx."

"Balls!" said Miggs.

"We got away with it because of the Skipper," said Henty.

"We're bloody lucky with our Skipper," said Miggs.

"Where we *are* unlucky," Craik persisted, "is having a Wop/AG with Deirdre Winter as his girl friend."

The lorry slowed by the steps of the Sergeants' Mess. Hopping over the tailboard, Miggs said equably, "You're just jealous, Curly."

Everyone trooped inside. Being nine o'clock in the morning, the place was deserted. The closed bar smelled of beer and tobacco smoke.

"Ta-ta for now." Miggs began walking down the corridor to the back. "Bit of shut-eye for me!"

He began whistling cheerfully as he went up the stairs. Warrant Officer Price would be bent over the latest gen in Intelligence. He'd have the place to himself. A good long zizz before supper, couple of drinks and then he'd try to contact Deirdre, if he could. A walk in the woods would be very, very nice, and if it was too bloody cold there was always the boiler house.

There was no difficulty contacting Deirdre Winter. She was sitting on his bed.

There was something about the way she sat there, bent right forward, her hands in her lap. The sight of her like that suddenly sent a shiver right through him.

Abruptly he stopped whistling. "'Ello, 'ello, 'ello," he said. "Look who's here!"

She looked up at him with no sign of recognition. He saw only a blank, shattered look on her face.

"What's the matter, sweetheart?"

When she said nothing, he went over and put his arm round her.

She pushed it away.

"Deirdre, darling—"

"Don't try that! It's too late for that!"

"Aren't you glad to see me back safe?"

"I don't care if I never see you again."

He sat down beside her. She shifted herself away from him towards the foot of the bed.

Silence.

Then she cried out suddenly, "I wish I'd never seen you! I wish I'd never set eyes on you!"

He leaned over and tried to kiss her.

"Don't touch me! You're all alike. After one thing. Like my Mum says . . ."

Her eyes filled with tears like two blue pools filling with spring rain.

He turned his head away, not being able to look at her. There was no need now to have an answer on what was the matter.

Getting up, he walked to the window and opened it up. Down there was green grass, the beginnings of buds on the trees, clean fresh air and beyond a limitless horizon over the sea. For two pins, he thought, I'd jump out and make a dash for it.

Miggs' background was London. An office boy in a clothing factory, he had lived with five brothers and three sisters in a back street near Victoria. His life had been dull, confined, and he had always been short of money. Suddenly the war had opened up a new vista, a limitless life in the air, a freedom and a

142

prestige as a Wop/AG that he would never ever have known if there had been peace. With luck he would have become a clerk. With luck he would have married a nice enough girl and, tied to her apron strings, and with kids all round him, he would have settled for a night out with the boys on Saturday, an occasional visit to the dogs at the greyhound stadium, and an annual week with the family, sitting on the beach at Brighton.

He shuddered.

"You're all right, Miggs." She was sniffing into her handkerchief. "It's all right for you."

"Deirdre, if you only knew what I was thinking."

A sudden ray of hope shot through her eyes.

He came back to the bed and sat down beside her. This time there was no resistance to his arm as it went around her.

"Miggs . . . I'm going to have a baby? Did you know?"

"I guessed."

"How?"

"From you coming here." He paused. "Look, duck, are you sure?"

"Yes."

He heaved a long, lugubrious sigh.

"You're not . . . angry?"

"No," he shook his head, "why should I be angry?"

He could feel her relaxing in his arms.

"So what'll we do, Miggs?"

"Well, of course—" He stopped. "Do you know what I was thinking?"

She shook her head.

"What I was thinking, Deirdre was . . . you deserve a much better man than me."

"Miggs. I don't. Honestly. I love you."

"Not really. You say this now."

"I do, I do! You're . . ."

She looked up at him expectantly. When he said nothing, she said hesitantly. "And you . . . me? Like you said in the boiler house?"

"Course, Deirdre. But it isn't fair."

"Fair?"

"Not to you, it isn't."

"Why not?"

143

"I've done one tour. The chances of finishing this tour . . . well," he put his thumb towards the floor and pulled down the corners of his mouth, "let's face it."

"How d'you mean?"

"I've got no future, Deirdre!"

"What about me?" The hope was dying out of her eyes.

"What about you?"

"What about me? What shall I do? Tell ma'am? Get me pregnancy discharge." She groaned. "Clause eleven. Everyone knows what that means. Then go home. To me Mum! You don't know me Mum."

"No, Deirdre." Nor ever intend to, he thought to himself.

She suddenly burst into a paroxysm of crying. "Oh, Miggs, Miggs! What'll I do? *What'll I do?*"

Gently he stroked her face. "We'll think up something."

"What is there to think up?"

"Hang on. You'll see. I won't let you down."

Her eyes brightened. "Are you going to marry me then, Miggs?"

"Deirdre, Deirdre, that would be letting you down. I couldn't do it to you. I'm not that much of a swine."

He saw suspicion blaze in her eyes. "*Aren't* you?"

He pretended not to hear the heavy emphasis. "Deirdre, sweetie, you've got to be brave."

"Brave. I like that. You're not brave. It's you that's scared."

"No. I'm not. It's just that I don't want to leave you a widow."

"You just want to leave me period. Me and It."

He scowled. "Anyway, how do I know *it's* mine?"

She drew in her breath. "You rotten filthy swine. Who else's could it be?"

He laughed. "Ha. Well. Since you ask. There's Rackham for a start. Gaunt. And Oakroyd—"

She hissed at him in a low, deadly voice. "I hate your bloody guts. You *know* it's yours. You'll never get away from that. You *know.*"

Something in her face got through. He believed her. He hadn't really disbelieved her. He stood up. "I take that back. I shouldn't have said it. Don't blow your bloody top. I've got an idea. Honest. Wait here." He pulled open the door. She heard his rapid footfall down the corridor then taking the stairs three

144

at a time. She was too numb and miserable to even speculate what he was up to.

He was back within minutes, his tunic bulging, a bright hopeful expression on his face.

"Look," he said smiling reassuringly. "I managed it. Shot a line. But I *got* it. Told you I wouldn't let you down." He unbuttoned his jacket and brought out half a bottle of gin. "This'll do the trick. So they tell me. Get into a real hot bath, Deirdre. Hot as you can bear. Drink as much of this mother's ruin as you can. Can't fail."

He held out the bottle to her. To his relief she held out her hand to take it. There was even the beginnings of a smile, or was it a different expression, an almost animal baring of the teeth?

He had no time to think which.

She grasped the outstretched bottle in her right hand, raised it in one swift motion above her head, and then hurled it with all her might against the pristine wall just above Warrant Officer Price's bed. It broke with a resounding bomb-like boom. Fragments went crashing everywhere. Gin spluttered and gurgled down the wall, soaked Price's top blanket, made a hideous stinking puddle on the clean floor.

Deirdre stepped forward and thrust the toes of her shoes in it, kicking the gin towards him and over him in an ecstasy of hatred. She advanced on him and he thought she was going to lay about him with a piece of glass, do him a bloody serious injury. She had that look.

But suddenly she turned. At the door, she said, "Don't you ever come near me again, you filthy murdering bastard!"

Then she ran out. He sat on the edge of the bed, listening to her furious footfall, wondering how the hell he was going to get the room clean before Price came back. He held his head in his hands. His hands shook. He felt bloody awful. Sick as if he'd drunk the bottleful. Sick as if he was having the bloody baby. Sick of Deirdre. Sick of himself. While loud and clear he said, "Deirdre Winter, you'll never get me now!"

TEN

THE leaking petrol tank incident toppled Irvine from his position as Strickland's blue-eyed boy. In fact, if he didn't watch out he was in danger of becoming the squadron kick-it.

The older squadron captains like Rory Ames and Ken Carter were now saying openly in the bar that Irvine was far too inexperienced to have been given a command. As for the odd fuel leak, everybody who'd flown Liberators for any length of time had them. There was no reason at all to come back early. The second pilots declared that after such an abortive operation, he should certainly be demoted and somebody else should be promoted in his place.

There had been only one dissenting voice. Edward Mowbray told him he was "a bloody fool not to have come home immediately he saw the fuel leak". He also went in and told Strickland that as far as he was concerned, he would not fly D Dog or any other fuel-leaking Liberator until petrol-tight fuel caps had been fitted. And as Mowbray was, after Strickland, by far the most experienced pilot on the squadron, that gave Irvine more than a crumb of comfort.

He had one person at least on his side. No, he had two. Walking back from Flights in the blackout, coming round the corner of Stores—hands in his pockets, as usual in a dream— he had collided with a sweet-smelling blue crombie overcoat, and putting out his arms only just in time, had managed to stop Assistant Section Officer Jones from keeling over onto the icy road.

"Sorry!"

"That's all right."

"I should have seen you."

"Difficult to see anything."

146

"At least I should have *smelled* you." And realizing by her laugh that this was perhaps not the thing to have said, he added, "A nice smell," and then as though he was an expert on the names of every perfume of Arabia asked, "What is it, by the way?"

"Coty."

"I like it."

"Every WAAF on the Station," she said gravely, "will be very glad you do."

"Oh?" he said, pleased. "Why?"

"Because it's all they have in the NAAFI, so that's what we all have to wear."

Deflated, he said, "I still like it." They continued along to the Mess in silence. "What is your favourite perfume?"

"Chanel Number Five."

"I shall remember that," he said, suddenly bold. And then remembering, again became deflated. "But I expect you can get that from the Americans."

She laughed again. "I haven't got around to asking for it. Still too busy on Liberator spares. Tank filler caps now." They walked up the steps of the Mess together. He opened the glass doors and pulled back the blackout. "It couldn't have been very nice . . . that petrol leak."

They walked into the hall together. "So you've heard about it?"

"Yes." He helped her off with her greatcoat. "I rang Machrannoch twice today."

"What do the—" well, it *was* their aircraft after all, "experts say? Can they give us replacements?"

"Wouldn't be any use, Bob says."

"Bob?" He remembered the tall lanky American Equipment Officer. "Oh yes!" He took off his own greatcoat, and hung both coats side by side on the pegs in the hall. "Why not?"

"Their boys have been having the same trouble. They don't like it, to use Bob's words, 'not one little bit'. Airflow over the top of the wing creates so much negative pressure that petrol is sucked from around the filler caps and is siphoned out of the tanks."

"My word!" He smiled at her. "Are you remustering to Engineering?"

147

"Bob's words. Not mine."

"Yes, of course." Slightly, he was disappointed. "Shall we see if there's any tea left?"

The ante-room was filled with 507 Squadron, but the atmosphere towards Irvine was distinctly chilly. There were only three cheese sandwiches and half a cup each of lukewarm tea left in the urn. While they were having it, sitting on the table, Mowbray came in and seeing what they were eating and drinking made a face, shuddered, said "Ugh!" and then suggested that they come along and see what Madeleine could rustle up for supper.

Probably feels sorry for me, Irvine thought, and the girl blocked it by saying, "She won't want two more just like that."

"So long as you take pot-luck, she'd be delighted."

"No transport," said Irvine.

"You can walk. And Emma can come on the crossbar of my bicycle."

Irvine turned to the girl. "What about it?"

"If you're sure, Edward? That would be nice."

Irvine slipped off the table and stood up. "Well, thanks very much . . ."

The three of them went into the hall. Irvine helped the girl back into her greatcoat. "And you'll need it." The wind blew in as the door opened. "Christ!"

"Don't worry, Peter!" Mowbray pulled his bicycle away from the wall and settled the girl on the crossbar. "I'll hold her tight, Peter."

"That's what I'm afraid of!"

"My arms'll keep her warm."

"Take care!" Irvine shouted as they wobbled off, the tiny front light dribbling a yellow stain on the snow.

"You OK?" Edward Mowbray asked. "Get ready to salute for us both when the guard opens the main gate. If I stop we might not get started again."

"Won't he . . .?"

"Not if you give him your stunning smile too!"

The guard saluted and smiled back.

"Told you!"

There was a tortuous few seconds during a turn onto the road to Kilcreggan village.

"I'm afraid my instrument flying isn't all it might be."

"We're still airborne."

"Just. But this sort of thing low down near the ground is best done by a wizard with the improbable name of Minneapolis-Honeywell."

"The automatic pilot."

"Ah, the gen lady!"

"I got a spare gyro unit from Bob this afternoon."

"That invaluable Yank! Do you think you could get a Minneapolis-Honeywell for this bicycle?"

They lurched at a bend and skidded round the corner. "You see, I need it! You can't fly bicycles and Liberators close to the ground at night!"

She laughed, but she felt an odd little shiver down her spine, as if something had been said too profound and sad for laughter.

"I'll see what I can do."

"You'll do it all right. Look at S Sugar! I gave her an airtest this afternoon. Whizzo! Good as new! Though *how* you do it remains a mystery."

"The Yanks are wildly generous."

"And you know how to winkle things out of them."

"Do I?"

"Some say you're Strickland's blue-eyed girl."

"Is that supposed to be a compliment?"

"From the people who say it, yes."

"I don't want to be anyone's blue-eyed girl."

"Don't blame you! Anyway Strickland's got a girl, hasn't he?"

"I'd say he'd got lots."

"I meant the Ensa girl."

"Sylvia? She shares a room with me."

"Nice?"

"Very."

"Maybe she'll soften him up a bit. Unless she too gets the bullet." He paused. "Like the character plodding behind us."

"Who?"

"The erstwhile Strickland boy."

"What does that mean?"

"That there's always a reckoning."

149

"That sounds ominous."

"Not meant to," he laughed. "Just too much S Sugar in my bloodstream."

She sighed, "And in mine."

Zig-zagging precariously, they reached the brow of the hill. "Ah, lights ahead! My good wife has as usual put the beacon at the window to guide the German bombers in!" And then as they came whistling down to the cottage, "Blackout, woman! Blackout! Don't you know there's a war on?" And when Madeleine opened the door and came out after they'd dismounted, he put his arms round her and kissed her and said, "Darling, Peter and Emma are coming to supper. Now isn't that nice?"

She looked genuinely, unaffectedly pleased, "Lovely!"

"I feel rather awful," Emma began. "Your rations . . ."

"What have we got on the menu, darling?"

"A fish."

"*A* fish? Just one? Was that all your seagull friends could catch you?"

"It wasn't the gulls. I bought it in Kilcreggan."

"It. Singular. Then for goodness sake, woman, either do a loaves and fishes act or let's have it before the footsoldier arrives. Emma, come on in!"

There was a peat fire burning in the grate of the tiny parlour. A blue-and-white check cloth was spread over the table, which was set for two. Madeleine was wearing a crimson woollen dress with a high neck. She moved quietly, putting out more knives and forks and plates.

"What is my husband like as a taxi-driver?"

"Expensive," Mowbray said immediately. "Which reminds me, you haven't paid the fare." He bent down and kissed Emma lightly on the forehead. "Mm . . . Coty! Right?"

"You're an expert."

"Shall we say I'm an experienced wine taster? Which reminds me," he called over his shoulder, "is there any of that cooking sherry left, darling?"

"Look and see. The bottle's in the cupboard."

"The last of the summer wine," Mowbray said as he poured out three glasses. "The blue-eyed boy is going to be disappointed. Ah, there he is! I can hear him stamping his poor

150

frozen feet." He went across and opened the door. "We were beginning to think you'd done a Captain Oates on us. And all the time," he stretched out his hand and took the bottles Irvine was carrying, "he'd stopped off at the pub and done a Good Samaritan!"

Beer and cider were poured out, Madeleine served the meal, and the conversation never wavered. They talked about Kilcreggan village, the loch, the cottage, Madeleine's photographs of the wild birds. Perhaps it was because the talk never wavered, Emma thought, that there was something uneasy about the atmosphere. She hardly knew either of them, though she had spoken to them both at Mess parties. But tonight somehow Edward Mowbray seemed different, altogether making too much the effort of mine jovial host after that rather strange conversation on the wobbling bicycle. Every now and then she saw Madeleine looking at him, puzzled, concerned.

"More cider, Emma? Madeleine darling? You two *are* being abstemious. You should have seen the pair of them at the Mess dance, Peter."

"I should have liked to have done."

"Shocking! Never off the dance floor once! In very high demand. I never even got a dance with Emma."

"Pity I missed it."

"Pity? Sheer carelessness! Fancy allowing yourself to get onto the Mayfly!"

"Edward is quite hopeless," Madeleine said to Irvine as though to explain him. "He never takes anything seriously."

"Unlike my darling wife with her birds. You'd think if she wasn't watching over them, the heavens would empty."

Madeleine smiled.

"She's got her eye on that piece of skin you've left, Peter. Make a good dinner for her favourite gull."

"Guillemot," Madeleine corrected, still beaming.

After the meal, Emma helped her clear away, scrape the plates and wash up, then cross the few yards of turf to put the bird scraps in the bowl. There was faint moonlight. Not the fullness yet of a bomber's moon, but to the south, a handful of searchlights fingered the sky.

Madeleine remarked on the moon, as they closed the blackout behind them. But not on the searchlights. Operations were

151

never mentioned throughout the evening—except once. Peter mentioned something about filler caps and petrol leaks, and in quite a different tone of voice, sharply Edward had said, "Hangar doors! Let's close the hangar doors!"

The guests left just before midnight. Edward insisted that they take his bicycle, "And don't forget," he shouted to Peter, "to get her fare!"

With Emma back on the crossbar, they began zig-zagging home again through the darkness.

"I'm not very good at this."

"You're doing very well."

"Mowbray's more experienced than me."

"He didn't drive so straight. He kept crying out for Minneapolis-Honeywell." They curved round the corner of the village. Suddenly she asked, "Is instrument flying very difficult?"

"It is when you're low down. My second operation was an eight-hour patrol at fifty feet in the Skagerrak. And Strickland wouldn't let me use the automatic pilot. God, I was tired! And above us all the time, there were German night-fighters just waiting—"

He broke off abruptly, aware he was shooting a line, "Hangar doors! Sorry about the hangar doors."

"Don't you think it strange that we *didn't* talk more about Kilcreggan and what it does tonight?"

"It's just that Edward doesn't want Madeleine to worry."

"Don't you think he's different at home?"

"I should imagine we all are."

"But tonight, he seemed worried. Is it about the filler caps?"

He was reluctant to talk shop. In any case, he still felt loyalty to Strickland. "Perhaps."

"Does Edward like Strickland?"

"They're not exactly buddies."

"He called us Strickland's blue-eyed boy and girl."

"I'm not. Not now. But he certainly thinks a lot about you."

"Only because of his spares."

The guard at the gate had changed, and they got a frown as they wobbled into the Station. They reached the Mess steps. He dismounted and she slid off the crossbar. Just before he pushed the door open, he said, "What did Edward mean . . . don't forget to get her fare?"

152

She leaned over and kissed him. "This."

"It's double after twelve."

He pulled her to him and held her tightly in his arms. He kissed her properly this time. Her lips were soft, responsive and delicious. Somehow they made him feel simultaneously expert and slightly shaken. "Coty. Still Coty. And don't let me ever catch you wearing Chanel Number Five!"

"What d'you think, Doc, about married operational aircrew living out with their wives?"

From the operational side of his own desk, Flint was conscious of Strickland's eyes intently upon him. They were having one of their usual weekly talks on squadron fitness and morale. Diplomatically he replied, "It all depends."

"On some operational Stations, they don't allow it."

"That's rather hard."

"I think it's sensible."

"That's because you're not married."

"Nor likely to be, Doc, while this war goes on."

"I don't think war and marriage are necessarily contradictory."

"That's because you're not a pilot."

Neat little dig there, Flint thought. What's he leading up to?

"Don't get me wrong, Doc. I'm not talking about sex."

"What are you talking about? Love?"

"I'm talking about flying."

"I gathered there was some connection."

"The things that affect it."

"Such as?"

"Well, you know as well as I do, Doc, that beer's a good thing. And sing-songs are a good thing. And taking a WAAF's knickers down under a hedge . . . hell, that's part of the perks! What the WAAFs are for!"

"You should pass this news on to Flight-Officer Beauchamp. She has other ideas."

"The British are so hypocritical, Doc! The Germans will have that sort of thing fixed up properly. A couple of Joy Maidens or whatever for shooting down a Liberator. A regiment of virgins for sinking the *King George V.*"

"Is this your new idea for sinking the *Groningen*?"

153

"You're a doctor, you know about these things. A little is a stimulus. A lot is . . . well—"

"What about a regiment?"

"That's afterwards, Doc. It doesn't matter a damn what they have *afterwards*. But too much *before* is fatal."

"You think so?"

"I *know* so."

"That's because you're not a doctor." He'd got it in at last. Strickland laughed. "Good crack, Doc! Always appreciate a good crack! But you know what I'm driving at."

"It's gradually beginning to seep through into my sluggish mind."

"It's been known for years. In the early 1930s there was every sort of fandeedangy going on at an RAF Station in Wessex. Mistresses in the Mess, wife-swapping, the lot! A Service scandal! And then the great Trenchard, Founder of the RAF, drove into the Station, and orders were given that all officers were to assemble in the Mess ante-room. And they said to each other . . . Christ, he's going to have the pants off us! They all stood up as he came into the room. He kept them standing there as he walked over to a table set up at the far end. There he picked up a carafe and filled a glass with water and drank it all very slowly as though to refresh himself for the long ordeal ahead. And then he simply looked up and said, 'Gentlemen, you cannot fuck and fly!'"

"Great man though he was, medically speaking he may have been mistaken."

"You know what he meant. Nobody can shag themselves silly and do a proper job."

"I can't see anybody up here who can possibly be in that happy position."

Strickland leaned across the desk. "Mowbray, Doc. Aren't you worried about Mowbray?"

"On the contrary, Edward Mowbray has that kind of relaxed attitude to life in difficult circumstances that I find very restful."

"Don't you think he looks washed-out?"

"I haven't noticed."

"In the Mess, he's always lounging around, eyes half-closed, practically asleep. Don't get me wrong. I have nothing against Edward."

154

"You could have fooled me there."

Strickland shrugged his shoulders. "We have the odd . . . arguments."

"Like this petrol cap business?"

"We differ . . . for technical reasons sometimes." He leaned over the desk. "Doesn't mean I've got anything against him. Nor Madeleine either. Lovely girl! Poor old Edward, no wonder he's asleep on his feet!"

"He looks all right to me."

"I'd suggest leave but he's not due. A course away from here, I thought."

"What sort of a course?"

"The Aircrew Refresher School."

"I've heard something about that."

"A good course, Doc. Three weeks doing everything at the double. Bed at nine o'clock. Up at six for two hours' PT. No beer. No women. He'd come back fighting fit!"

"What d'you expect me to do about it?"

"Give him a look-over."

"I'll certainly do that. If what you say is right, he may have something the matter with him."

"Such as this . . . fatigue you keep on talking about?"

"Such as fatigue."

"And if you find it, you'll recommend . . . a tonic?"

"If I find it, I'll recommend two weeks' extra leave."

"That really would put the fat into the fire!"

Flint leaned back in his chair. "Squadron-Leader Strickland, can I ask you a question?"

"Go ahead!"

"Why at this particular moment of time do you want to dispense with the services of your most experienced captain?"

"As I told you, Doc, he's tired. He needs to get away."

"I'll examine him straightaway."

Strickland gave a crooked little smile as he rose to go. "I'd be glad if you would, Doc."

Flint had recognized that war was not a single entity. Like schizophrenia and other forms of madness there were numerous variations and interpretations. Isolated fights went on under the blanket term of War. Feuds, personal antagonisms, revenge, scratching itches, need for thrills, because the others did it,

155

obsessions. General Montgomery staring at the photograph of Field Marshal Rommel in his caravan during the Desert campaign—was that a new psychological approach to chess? Painting swastikas and roundels for shot-down aircraft on the nose, was that a form of collecting? After this war, as with the last, would the antagonists meet and swap stories?

There was no doubt that up here could be diagnosed the private war of Strickland versus the *Groningen*. In the wartime RAF, age and rank were subordinate to panache and achievement. Those at the top knew they could not do what was wanted to win. They were too old to shoot down aeroplanes, sink ships or bomb cities. So youthful leaders like Strickland were given a power and independence that they would not have reached in peacetime if they had served till they were a hundred.

Flint realized that in effect he had been ordered to get rid of Mowbray. He saw him that afternoon, saying as an excuse he had instituted a regular check-over of all aircrew. As he expected, there was nothing whatever the matter with him. Certainly he was absolutely on the ball and very alert. Except, all the time he was talking to him, he got the idea that Mowbray was detached and uncharacteristically depressed.

"Feeling tired these days, Edward?"

"No."

"Anything on your mind?"

"Only this business you'll have heard about, Doc."

"What business is that? I've heard nothing."

"I was on the Mayfly for tonight, but I won't go. There's been some snag—"

"What's that?"

"—with petrol leaks." He paused. "I was due to go out in D Dog tonight."

"The aircraft Irvine had trouble with?"

"That's the one. If I take it, we'll go on with these petrol leaks till someone blows themselves up. A stop's got to be made somewhere."

"Sounds sensible."

"Strickland won't hear of it. You see—"

Mowbray paused and looked out of the window towards the football field where a match was in progress.

156

"Doc, have you noticed anything about Strickland since the S Sugar affair?"

"Noticed anything? Well, he's always been press-on."

"Press-on's fine. But where does press-on end and—"

"And?"

"Is there such a thing as too much press-on?"

"As an RAF doctor, I doubt if I'd be allowed to diagnose it."

Mowbray smiled wryly. "Particularly in circumstances where the *Groningen*'s involved."

"Don't tell me that wretched ship's turned up again!"

"That's what all the flap's about. Supposed to be somewhere in the North Sea. Five aircraft going off tonight to search. The Wingco's been shoe-horned into D Dog in my place as an example to the squadron."

Mowbray shouldered himself into his tunic and began doing up the buttons.

"Edward, how about two weeks' leave?"

The pilot turned to him, surprised. "I'm not due."

"*Extra* leave."

"Why? Is there something the matter with me?"

"Nothing at all."

"I don't understand."

"Get you out of the way until this *Groningen* enthusiasm of Strickland's dies down a bit."

Mowbray picked up his cap and began walking to the door. "Do you think it ever will?" And, before Flint could answer, added, "Thanks, Doc. Madeleine'll be pleased about the check. She had some bee in her bonnet about me. Nothing at all, of course. You know what women are."

And now he won't take leave, Flint thought, as the door closed behind Mowbray. So I shall have to think of something else. For when the Wingco and those four other crews return, whether they find the *Groningen* or not, Edward is going to be in trouble.

For the next hour, he sat there, concocting a water-tight scheme. In the event, it was unnecessary. At four in the morning, a white flash was noted by the Observer Corps forty miles east of Kilcreggan. On return home after an unsuccessful search, one of the other four Liberators on the operation reported an aircraft blowing up five miles south of him. D Dog did not return.

"It wouldn't be D Dog," Strickland said. "Probably a returning bomber bagged by a German night-fighter. Wouldn't be surprised if D Dog found the *Groningen* and was shot down on the attack. The Wingco may not have had much to give ... but when it came to the crunch, chaps, we must remember he gave it all!"

ELEVEN

Two days later, a signal arrived at Kilcreggan: SQUADRON-LEADER G STRICKLAND DSO DFC HAS BEEN APPOINTED TO COMMAND 507 SQUADRON WITH ACTING RANK OF WING-COMMANDER.

Nobody was at all surprised. At the party to wet his third thick stripe, they played High Cockalorum, choosing Rory Ames, who used to play rugger for Scotland, as anchorman. He knelt over by the bar wall, and, one after the other, the captains jumped on top of him, and then lay down flat to be jumped on themselves. Irvine bided his time till he was secured of a place near the top of the sandwich. Finally with a terrific scrambling leap up into the air, Strickland got up on top of the towering, sweating, panting, wavering, wriggling pyramid and held up his clenched hands in the boxer's victory wave, while those left still on the ground thumped their tankards and chanted, "The old sod! The dirty old sod! The bastard deserves to die!"

Altogether the party was a great success. It was a cheap evening too. Not only was Strickland's third stripe baptized that night but so was a pretty young thing called LACW Prendergast. One of the staff of the Electrical Officer had been a tailor in civvy street, and with his help a most ingenious device for obtaining free drinks had been manufactured. A kewpie doll made of plump pink celluloid had been dressed up in miniature WAAF uniform—beautifully cut tunic with tiny brightly polished buttons, neat little skirt coming down to the knees, grey lisle stockings, Oxford shoes, and a round squashy hat with shining black brim set saucily on a sea of frothy curls. She had been fixed very firmly that night in the men's lavatory where her big blue come-hither eyes with their long lashes followed every occupant's movements as he went about his business. Unseen however to any but the most observant were two wires leading from her and disappearing under the mirrors. These same wires could just be seen in the bar across the corridor behind an upended empty whisky bottle and leading to a small brass souvenir replica of the Lutine bell at Lloyd's.*

Whenever those come-hither eyes had succeeded in luring towards them any solitary occupant—for when others were present there was only jocular comment or admiration for workmanship—and invited him to satisfy a perfectly natural curiosity to find out whether LACW Prendergast was wearing her navy blue blackouts with elastic at waist and legs by lifting up her skirt, across in the bar the bell would sound and, as for the real thing, a hush would fall. Until with that extraordinary air of innocence and that high concentration on duty evident in the slight frown and brisk manner apparent since the Garden of Eden in all men trying to get away with a nibble at the apple, in would come the explorer from his labours. He would stop, look around, wonder why everyone was staring at him, go slightly pink, put his hand in his pocket, saunter up to the bar to be greeted with a concerted shout of "Drinks all round!" and a roar of laughter and sympathetic arms on his shoulders, and then after recovering from his surprise, he would be only too relieved to find that all he had to do to be saved was to shell out practically all he possessed as expiation for man's eternal original sin.

That night, it worked like a dream. Irvine never once had to pay for a drink. Though most of the squadron were in the know from the beginning, and others in the bar soon caught on or were told, one after the other in would come the innocents. The laughter was almost continuous, and none higher or more side-splitting than from the corner where Wendy Beauchamp and the pale-haired Cypher Queen could be seen bent double, holding out their glasses for another gin and orange.

Irvine woke up next day with a splitting headache and a mouth like the bottom of a bird-cage. He missed breakfast and was late for the captains' meeting that Strickland had called. It was held in the Wing-Commander's office, into which he had already moved. Old Wingco Vance had never really done much with the room above furnishing it with a copy of the Air Force

* Rung when a ship insured by Lloyd's is reported missing or wrecked.

List and a photograph of his wife. But already Strickland had effected a transformation. He must have had all the ACHs on the Station cleaning and polishing and painting. There were black wooden ship-recognition models hanging from the ceiling. Two new armchairs, a sofa, the whole place carpeted, curtains at the window, bookshelves lined with technical journals, three grey steel security cabinets, blown-up photographs of the *Groningen* from all angles pinned up everywhere.

Strickland himself, however, still dressed in his khaki battle-dress top, his white sweater, his cream silk scarf and his brown leather riding boots. He sat behind the desk silently watching them stream in, and Irvine was beginning to think the silence was going to go on for ever when suddenly the new Wing-Commander said, "Those of you with any education at all—"

Everyone laughed.

"—such as Edward . . ."

He looked across at Mowbray in what perhaps was a conciliatory way. Mowbray stared blankly back at him.

". . . will know that Nelson used to have regular meetings with his captains on board his flagship. Not that I'm Nelson or anything like him. But—"

Mowbray interrupted him with. "What about leaking petrol tanks?"

"That's all sorted out, Edward. The Americans have done tests and advise us to limit the filling of all wing tanks to three inches below the filler necks. That stops the siphoning. The beautiful Madeleine need worry no more. In fact, she should be pleased because it means shorter patrols."

"Good," Mowbray said.

"Glad you approve." Strickland paused. "But to get back to what I was saying before Edward interrupted . . . there *must* be a leader. However, he is simply the offshoot of a consensus of opinion amongst his most senior colleagues. So at these captains' meetings, I'll tell you the ideas in my mind. And then we discuss them. We toss the ball from one to the other. Everybody puts in their ideas, and we agree on an overall plan. Thus we formulate techniques, tactics, methods of attack . . ."

He looked at them as though he expected someone to say something, but nobody did.

"Now we haven't had much luck recently with our anti-

161

U-boat patrols. So from now on we're stopping them. We'll *always* carry 500-pound bombs. No more depth charges."

The anti-submarine bombs which Coastal Command inherited at the beginning of the Second World War were more dangerous to the aircraft that carried them than to the U-boats they were supposed to destroy. For the first year of the war, these were carried quite uselessly by aircraft, occasionally being dropped on a U-boat, after which there would result a fierce argument between the victorious pilot and the Admiralty, who not unnaturally would rarely allow a kill. A depth charge was then developed filled with sodium amatol, and provided it was dropped within a few feet, the enemy would be destroyed. Since U-boats had a habit of diving when attacked, the depth charges were designed to go off at depth, and bombs were not much good. By the same measure, depth charges were not effective against surface vessels as they were equipped with a fuse that was only activated by salt-water—thus a direct hit would not go off.

"Our effort will be anti-shipping."

The atmosphere inside the office suddenly went noticeably colder.

"—particularly against the *Groningen*."

Mowbray said, "Surely we should leave that sort of thing to the torpedo-carriers, Beauforts and—"

"They're mostly out in the Mediterranean and the Far East."

"Liberators aren't anti-shipping aircraft."

Strickland's eyes narrowed. "They are if you use your imagination, Edward. And that's exactly what I've been doing. I've already told you that my idea is to employ unusual and unexpected weapons and devices on the Liberator. The Blind Bombsight, for instance. We'll get that operational soon. We're going to have a searchlight, what's called a Leigh Light, fitted on our starboard wings for night attacks. Little Miss Griselda Goldilocks in Equipment has done wonders with the Americans, and it was she who got the 57 millimetres for Sugar's nose. I'm organizing torpedo-dropping training . . . we could carry four torpedoes in the bomb-bay. We're experimenting with rockets. I've even been trying to think up an idea from what may have happened to poor old Vance. There's even a lesson to be learned there." He raised his head. "Yes, Edward?"

"Aren't these the sort of things that should be done on the research units?"

"They *should* be, Edward. But they never are. My experience is that these particular characters . . . high-up officers and politicians come to that . . . look at Harris over night bombing, Eaker* over day-bombing, the Admiralty over battleships . . . get obsessed with their own particular baby and won't help anybody else with *their* particular baby."

"The *Groningen* being *our* particular baby?"

Strickland thought for a moment. "I would say yes to that, Edward. I would say yes, she is."

"I don't feel so fatherly towards her as you do, I'm afraid."

Nervously, in the far corner, a tittering started, quickly stifled.

"Fatherly is the last word I'd use about her, Edward," Strickland said softly. "Quite the reverse. 507 are going to be a crack RAF squadron, like 617, the Dambusters and 7 Squadron, the Pathfinders. 507 are going to be handed down in history as the squadron that sank the *Groningen* . . ."

"Come on, everybody! Stamp your feet! Get the bloody girl started!"

At Strickland's words, all the aircrew—sixty-three of them—sandwiched at the back of the five-tonner started stamping and banging and kicking the metal sides, making enough din to wake the dead.

A rumbling engine noise started as in the cab up front the WAAF driver got the message. There was a sudden grind of gears. Then the lorry began hiccoughing off.

"*Hurrah!*"

The whole thing had happened in a tearing hurry. The *Groningen* had been sighted moving up the Kattegat. This was Strickland's big chance and he wasn't going to miss it. Not only was a cheerleading WAAF contigent going to be present, but Padre Binks in his ecclesiasticals had been recruited to stand on the balcony of Flying Control and bless them on their way.

And we'll need it, Irvine thought, looking over the tailboard at the black figure with the white stole waving in the wind. The weather forecast over the Skagerrak was clear—not a cloud in

* General commanding the USAAF.

the sky. Every fighter in the area would have either been alerted or be up in the air waiting for them.

"My idea," Strickland had said at briefing, "and I think it's a very good idea—"

Watching the tarmac perimeter track unravel like a grey wake behind them, Irvine shuddered. It was one of Strickland's many maxims that in every misfortune was the germ of success. There was a lesson to be learned from the misfortune of the Wingco. Petrol could blow up other aircraft as well as your own.

Overload petrol tanks with quick release valves had been fitted to the rear of the bomb-bays. The load at the front was six 500-pound armour-piercing bombs.

"That'll make us two thousand pounds above our normal maximum weight, but don't worry . . . the old Lib'll do it all right! As usual, I'll go first."

The five-tonner began stopping, dropping nine men at each aircraft, and continuing round Dispersal. It dropped Irvine and crew last at F Freddie.

"Come on, chaps, pull your fingers out!"

Though he was to be the seventh out of seven to take off at one-minute intervals, Irvine had a horror of being late. None of the crew were stepping on it, but Mosco was being particularly slow. He'd got the straps for his parachute caught round his legs and was doing a lugubrious unravelling act with one leg up on the open bomb-bay cakewalk. Irvine put out a hand, unwound the straps and propelled the Pole up.

"Thank you, Kapitan."

"You'll be able to have a go at enough fighters today, Mosco! That'll please you!"

Mosco simply grunted and trailed off to the rear turret. Irvine jumped up onto the flight deck to find that Henty couldn't find the Check List. There was a hurried scramble round the cockpit that wasted valuable minutes. By the time Henty discovered he was sitting on it, the engines on all the other Liberators had been started.

"Start Number Three!"

Number Three whirred round a dozen times, coughed, spluttered and decided not to start. Irvine was still struggling with the thing, when over the R/T came Strickland's voice,

"OK chaps. I'm now moving to the head of the runway. Take up your appointed positions behind me."

Like a row of rhinoceroses sniffing the ground, six Liberators lumbered out of Dispersal. Irvine was supposed to be following Wilkes in V Victor, but the little procession had formed up on the perimeter track and had begun moving off without him.

"Come on! For God's sake, hurry up!"

He said it to no one in particular, perhaps to the engines themselves. Through his open side window, he saw that the tubby figure of Group-Captain Pym had joined the tall black and white clerical flagpole on the balcony outside Flying Control. Beyond the camouflaged hangar at the end of the runway against the grey-green winter grass was an irregular smudge of WAAF blue.

There was a kind of circus air about the whole thing, he thought, scampering off now with at last all the fans turning, trying to catch up Wilkes. Seven highly trained animals were about to go through their tricks at the crack of the circus-master's whip. A particularly difficult trick today and one never before practised, and he was going through his mind how he intended to let the Liberator ride on the ground till the very last inch of runway, when over the intercom came an earsplitting cacophony of whistles, yowls and crackles. "Eee ... yarroo ..."

"What the hell's that?"

"Coming from the rear turret, Skipper," Trembath said.

Henty looked up at the Liberator's metal roof. "Mosco's trying to say something."

As Irvine caught up with Wilkes in Victor, he saw Strickland move S Sugar onto the runway.

"Yarroo! Yow! Oi!"

A green Very light went up from the Tower. Like a horse working up speed for a jump, slowly at first, then faster and faster and faster, S Sugar went roaring away.

"Yow! Oi! Eeeee!"

"Mosco! *Mosco!*"

L took off. Then C and K. Nose nudging Victor's rear turret, Irvine began the Before Take-off Check and inched F closer to the head of the runway.

"Yarroo! Eee! Yow!" The shriek came singing into Irvine's ears like something out of sagas of Greyfriars Hall in the *Magnet*,

165

his favourite schoolboy reading. Billie Bunter, the fat owl of the Remove, was being severely dealt with by Mr Quelch. "Yow! Eee! Ya! Whoops! Eee!"

"It's water in his intercom, Skipper," Miggs said.

Irvine asked, "Why the hell doesn't he pull his plug out?" More than ever now, the scene resembled a circus. The five rhinoceroses which had butted their way into the air, by eating their wheels had been transformed into five fat swans and were circling the aerodrome in formation as V Victor began pounding off to join them.

"Yarroo! Yow!"

Irvine turned off the perimeter track onto the holding point. Wilkes was three-quarters of the way down the runway now, nosewheel just off the ground.

"Eeeee . . ."

All checks complete, Irvine waited for Wilkes to do his leap and leave the runway clear. He had his right hand on the throttle, only half watching Victor, but he had a sudden sense that it was taking a long time. The main wheels were still on the runway—

No! They were on the grass beyond! Why the hell didn't he pull her off?

"Yarroo! Yow!"

He saw everything suddenly in crystal detail, slowed down especially for him to remember for ever. V Victor was banging and bouncing now, rear turret soaring, right wing crumpling, fuselage twisting and slewing to starboard.

"Yarroo! Yow! Eee!"

The next second—smoke. A grey column all at once materializing like the genie of Aladdin's lamp, swaying a little in the wind. Then a sudden *flash* and the smoke turned into a black velvet cloak lined with shining yellow silk.

"Eeeee . . ."

Through his side window, he could smell the sweet scent of petrol burning. Christ, he thought, any second now she'll go up! He could see that others had anticipated the same. The balcony of Flying Control was empty. The smudge of WAAF blue at the end of the runway had dissolved. But above the aerodrome, the five fat swans still circled.

And then over the R/T, interspersed with the yowlings and

166

the shriekings of Mosco's intercom plug, suddenly Strickland's voice, "F Freddie, what are you waiting for?"

"Eee . . .yow!"

Irvine turned to his Engineer. "Go to the rear turret and pull that fat bastard's plug out!"

Craik scuttled off to the back. Round and round above them the five fat swans still flew gracefully. Irvine sat at the head of the runway, watching the black blob a mile further down it begin turning to yellow. Surely Strickland doesn't want me to take off over that? He must have seen what's happened! Any second now those bombs will be going off . . .

"F Freddie, we can't hang around up here for ever!"

"Eee . . . yarroo!"

He can't expect me to leap through the burning hoop! I'll bloody well go right through the centre of it! Instead of the blue smudge, now fire engines were there at the end of the runway, but even they were not getting too near . . .

In the middle of a *yarroo* on the intercom there was sudden silence. Craik came back and stood behind the throttle box, the gob-stopper eyes beseeching him. Nobody had said anything, but he could feel the fear.

"F Freddie . . . aren't you coming?"

Wisby, Guilonard, Wingco Vance, Wilkes—now it was his turn. His right hand was still on the throttles, but he did not push them forward. He tried to think it out dispassionately, trying to weigh up the different responsibilities that he carried. It was as though he was in a cleft stick: whatever he did would be wrong. The flames were higher than ever. The runway was thick with smoke. He couldn't go. But could he not go? Could he turn round now and taxi away and let those five circling Liberators set off against the *Groningen* on their own, leaving him on the ground in safety at Dispersal?

He pushed the throttles hard against the stops. He released the brakes. Slowly, into the smoke, the Liberator moved.

Once the decision was taken, in some strange way it was easier. As the aircraft gathered speed, there was no turning back. He was conscious of that yellow blur ahead of him like a target focussed on his mind. Every nerve in his body had become electric, every reaction immediate. At the tips of his fingers, he felt F Freddie become alive.

167

The smoke had thickened. It leaked into the cockpit now, stinging his eyes.

He eased back on the stick. Up came the nosewheel.

Here now was the threshold!

He still waited. He kept the stick where it was till, out of the corners of his eyes, he saw there was no more runway left.

Then he pulled. For all his worth, he pulled. F Freddie left the ground, lurched to the left, straightened, inched up into thick smoke.

"Gear up!"

He couldn't see at all. He was conscious only of a sudden blinding yellow. He began coughing as the smoke began pouring into his lungs.

The thick blanket cleared. Wisps of grey fled past the windscreen. He began climbing away into the clear.

And then suddenly it was as though there was an earthquake on board. The Liberator practically did a somersault.

"Bombs, Skipper!" Craik said hoarsely. "Victor's bombs!"

He could actually hear the sound of the explosions and the .5 ammunition going off, spluttering and spitting. The Liberator was thrown violently forward as blast caught the tail. It needed both him and Henty to pull the nose up and climb towards the formation.

"Good *boy*!" said Strickland.

Strickland was pleased with him. For some strange reason, as he tucked his port wing close behind Dacres' starboard tip, Irvine felt immensely gratified. He knew partly it was because he, who had fallen from favour, had now received a pat on the head from the circus-master. But it was also something more: he had been presented with a highly dangerous test of himself which he had not refused, a literally burning problem which he had solved. Gone from his mind now was any thought of Wilkes and his crew. Tough luck of course, but one of those things. Some people made it, some people didn't—that was the way Nature and Natural Selection worked.

He was one of the ones that had made it.

Irvine felt extraordinarily cheerful, proud in fact, as he looked at the five Liberators aligned with him over on his left, as they emerged from under the overcast and began shining in the bright sunshine.

Prickly with guns, they looked so invincible. So many eyes watching out to report danger to the others, so many arms to protect each other. And out there in front—as always—Strickland.

People could say what they liked about him, the Doc could make hints about his obsession with the *Groningen*—but he was brave. The world was much warmer for seeing him there, thinking up his ideas, yes—but always doing them first. He was the one who pressed on, who was always cheerful, who never gave up. He was the pace-maker, always turning his head to call encouragement to those behind him. He was your yardstick, he was what you could measure yourself against. Keep up with Strickland, and you were a *man*.

Droning side by side across the North Sea, the six aircraft began gently climbing to eight thousand feet. Watching the others through his open window, he thought how comfortably in the air a Liberator flies. Not all tensed up and head and shoulders pushing, a rugby forward in the scrum, like a Lancaster. Not crucified, arms outstretched, waiting for the nails of the flak like a Fortress. But lounging back on a sofa—fat body, thin limbs, ugly, strong, relaxed, not giving a damn for anyone or anything.

Not even the *Groningen*.

Up the ship came on their radar screens at twenty miles, then, a little further on, the little green darting sparks that were her fighter escort.

"There's her wash now, Skipper," Henty said, pointing ahead at the white cut across the grey silk sea. "She's going flat out by the looks of it!"

And, seconds later, Strickland's voice over the R/T. "She's got a 190 fighter escort . . . just as I hoped! They'll attack from behind and underneath to avoid our fire-power. They always do!"

On the trip across the North Sea, the intercom had remained almost totally silent. The eeeing and the yowing in the rear turret had been cured. His crew no doubt were relieved at getting safely airborne through fire and smoke, and somewhat awed by the thought of the *Groningen* ahead. Now she had actually made an appearance, they were simply interested in seeing what she looked like, everybody except Mosco coming up to the front and staring fascinated out at the sharp bow, the big forward superstructure and the two huge funnels, looking like a toy ship being buzzed by blue-bottles, peaceful, harmless, apparently unaware of them.

"Mosco," said Irvine over the intercom. "Would you like to come up and have a look at her?"

"And abandon my position, Kapitan?" The Pole sounded affronted, even more stuffy than usual. "I cannot leave my guns!"

"There's still bags of time before the 190s start attacking."

Irvine had intended to convey that easy insouciance, that bowls-before-Armadas attitude that is the image of all British leaders. Mosco made no comment. His silence implied continuing censure: my captain first has my intercom plug yanked out, then has me almost turned upside down on take-off, now he wants me to turn deserter in the face of the enemy.

"Battle stations, chaps! Tuck up very close together! Now this is what we're going to do . . ."

Oh, the easy insouciance of Strickland's voice, the cool, calm way he spoke from the centre of the formation! He might have been a guide on a conducted tour of the Skagerrak, pointing out things of interest, the coastline where the beautiful fighter stations were, the majestic merchant ship, the funny little aeroplanes.

". . . as soon as the fighters get in position behind us, open your bomb-doors. Station your Engineer in the bomb-bay beside the quick release valves on the tanks. From the mid-upper turret of Sugar, I will act as fire-controller. I'll give the word to dump the fuel. Meanwhile all aircraft carry on straight and level in very tight formation at eight thousand feet. My Navigator on Sugar's bombsight will give the word, and all bombs are to be dropped together . . . ah, good! Here are the 190s now! Wheeling round to attack . . ."

Irvine could see them—two, three, no *five* tubby little grey-green fighters leaving the ship and wheeling round behind them. Craik had already gone to the bomb-bay.

"Bomb-doors open!"

There was a whine in the hydraulic pipes as Craik pulled down the lever at Strickland's order. Irvine edged closer to Dacres in K King, keeping his mind concentrated totally on flying, as Strickland's second pilot turned the formation to starboard so as to position it for an attack from the ship's port beam to allow its maximum five-hundred-feet length to be spread directly below and in line with the formation.

Mosco's voice came up over the intercom just a little less lugubrious than usual. "Fighters forming up to attack, Kapitan."

"Thank you, Rear Gunner."

The formation was coming out of the turn. The *Groningen* was four miles away now, directly in front of them. Silhouetted against the sea, she was still holding her course, holding her fire, no doubt relying on her fighter escort and wary of opening up lest she hit them.

"Open fuel valves!"

The whole formation now was flying like one aeroplane, so close were they together in line abreast. Strickland's co-pilot was taking them all directly for the centre of the ship. And then suddenly over the intercom, Brett's voice from the mid-upper turret. "Christ . . . a 190 behind us, Skipper, just blown up! Coming up from behind us, straight into the dumped petrol! His exhaust must have set it alight. And now *another*! Over to port! Going down in flames!"

Strickland's plan was working. Though not a shot had been fired from the aircraft, two FW 190s had flown straight into the petrol vaporized air and had gone up in smoke.

"Another one!"

Now the gunners on the formation opened up. Irvine could hear the chattering of Mosco's and Brett's guns.

"Rear Gunner to Kapitan."

Trying to concentrate on the tight formation, Irvine cursed Mosco under his breath. They were only a couple of miles away from the release point now. "Just a moment, Mosco—"

Seeing the fate of her fighter escort, the *Groningen* must have decided to do something quickly. She began turning full speed towards the aircraft to lessen her target area, and now her big guns had opened up, making brown blobs come up like mushrooms on the blue air in front of them. And now a great mass of grey began issuing from her funnels as she began making a smoke-screen to hide under.

The formation banked, trying to keep the *Groningen* beam on for the attack. She was less than a mile away now, practically

171

hidden under her cloak of smoke. The flak was suddenly intense—red, green, and white tracer coming up in a thick coloured curtain. Out of the corner of his left eye, Irvine saw a huge yellow explosion—one of the Libs going up. He heard the rattle of shrapnel on his own wings.

"Bombs away!"

He felt the aircraft immediately lighten as, from the bomb-aimer's position forward, Garth pressed the tit. The flak followed them away from the ship as they made a slow turn right to port to get on a course of 270 towards home.

"Rear Gunner to Kapitan."

"Yes, Mosco?"

"I hit a 190."

"Good show! Did you see him crash?"

"No, Kapitan. I think perhaps I only damaged him."

"And the bombs? Did you see the bombs go off?"

"Yes, Kapitan."

"Did we get a hit?"

"I do not think so, Kapitan."

Over the R/T came Strickland's jubilant voice. "Terrific show, chaps! Can't be absolutely certain because of the smoke-screen, but I'm pretty sure we fairly clobbered her! And three 190s down! That idea of mine . . . it worked like a dream!"

The surviving 190s were still in the sky, but they did not follow the formation home. There were four Liberators left. The *Groningen*'s flak had accounted for Tallack in C Charlie and Jerningham in L London.

There had also been Wilkes in V Victor on take-off. Still for the *Groningen* and three 190s, it wasn't a bad tally.

"Pity about little Wilkie," Strickland said when they were back on the ground. "Too small really to be a pilot. Clearly his seat became unlatched on take off and went right back. He couldn't reach the controls with his arms and legs. Nice chap . . . but he suffered from duck's disease."

That same day, he rang the Equipment Officer. "Three Libs gone and a bit of damage to some of the others. We've *got* to get replacements! We've got to get more spares! We owe the Americans at Machrannoch some real British hospitality, Wilkinson. My idea is to give them one *hell* of a party . . ."

* * *

"Tradition, ceremony . . . squadron silver from the last war," said Group-Captain Pym. "That's what the Americans like."

Strickland nodded his head. "Exactly, sir. I'm sure you've got it right. We've got to impress them. Show we're solid, trustworthy allies. Not poor relations. Always borrowing Lib spares."

"No fear," called out the Engineer Officer, raising a laugh, "Or they'll begin to want them back!"

"No beginning about it," said the Equipment Officer soberly, mindful of the three Liberators on the Q Form, damaged in Strickland's "petrol defence" attack and awaiting spares. "They're wanting them back *now*. Loud and clear! And we've got nothing to give them."

"We're giving them a Dining-In night," Strickland pointed out. "That's the whole point of the exercise."

"I can't see the Yanks getting excited over that," said the Engineer Officer.

"Well," Strickland waved his hand, "we'll give them a special one. Entertainment afterwards. Maybe a cabaret. Get our Ensa girl cracking. Let her earn her rations."

"She's not done at all badly so far," said the Group-Captain. "That variety show for the other ranks. With John Mills, no less. I was most impressed."

"I knew I was right," said Strickland, "I'll have a word with her myself."

The ghost of a shared smile seemed momentarily to touch the lips of his elders but not betters. "Well, we'll leave that part of the op to you then, Guy," said the Group-Captain. "You'll speak to Miss Talbot, eh? I'll OK any transport that's necessary. And if the entertainers want to stay we'll bung them in officers' leave beds."

For the next few days, Sylvia Talbot was to be seen hurtling around the station in the Hillman van that had been put at her disposal. If not that, then she was on the telephone. The Officers' Mess echoed to the continual "Miss Talbot, phone call, number two box." And her excited "Darlings, oh, but please, sweetiepie, I know it's a short notice . . . but be a darling . . ."

Emma saw her only briefly, and that mainly at make-up time in the evening. It was a lengthy business, but requiring so much

173

concentration that not much information was passed. However Sylvia did convey that she was seeing Guy Strickland rather often. "More often, darling, than is good for me."

And the Friday before the Dining-In night, as she plucked the odd straggler out of her single hair eyebrows, "He's asked me to give tomorrow's do everything I've got. It's a labour of love, you could say."

But on the evening itself, she was nowhere to be seen. There was a note written in her flamboyant handwriting propped up on their shared dressing table, asking Emma to see the batwoman pressed her blue-green sequin gown carefully, underlined. And finishing, "Gone to meet the Ensa mob."

She was not back by dusk, when two B-24s with stars on their white sides arrived at Kilcreggan, crammed to the gills with American Navy fliers. Strickland was there to greet them, together with Wilkinson and the Engineer Officer.

"Come on! Hurry up!" The Engineer Officer called down the length of the corridor as Emma Jones came a little breathlessly to join them. "You're their real buddy."

"Sylvia isn't back yet," she whispered. "Hope she doesn't get held up."

"She won't. He's," a glance in Strickland's direction, "got her well trained."

Behind them, Doc Flint watched the Americans trooping in. With MT's usual miserliness, there had only been two dirty old lorries to fetch them from their aircraft, but they came in out of the cold laughing and joking, dusting themselves down, their eyes darting brightly and eagerly round the hall.

What did they expect to see, he wondered, paroled for the evening from their barren monastery of an aerodrome beside the salt waters of a Scottish loch?

Certainly not the shadowy husk of Group-Captain Pym. Certainly—for their eyes brightened—Pym's young blonde wife standing beside him.

The Mess had been given a special clean-up for their arrival. Chrysanthemums in the highly polished silver vases, LACW Prendergast removed temporarily from the Gentlemen's. As the Americans came sheepishly into the ante-room, the Station band under a perspiring Warrant Officer struck up with *Stars and Stripes for Ever* over in the far corner.

Sherry in small glasses was awaiting them on a white-clothed table.

Awkwardly 507 aircrew came over to talk to them. There are few things more off-putting than stone-cold-sober young British pilots trying to cover up their shyness as they chat to other nationals. They seized on the one topic of conversation they appeared to share—Liberators—and clung to it as to a life-raft, while the Americans sipped at their sherry as though at communion wine, their eyes roaming the room for some other sight than a phalanx of light-blue uniforms.

Wendy Beauchamp led her uniformed squad of WAAF officers in. Emma Jones was already preoccupied—too much so to Irvine's thinking. She had a peculiarly animated way of talking, looking up and smiling at the American Equipment Officer, who already had tight hold of her hand. Other Americans surrounded them—the only really animated group in the room.

The American Naval Captain was talking solemnly to Group-Captain Pym. His schoolgirl wife had three American pilots around her and was playing the lady of the manor. Madeleine Mowbray, a goddess in gold, was doing her best, and so was Edward beside her.

Dinner was announced by the Mess corporal. In they went, stately to begin with, Group-Captain Pym's wife on the arm of the American Captain, Strickland with Wendy Beauchamp, Emma Jones with Bob Greaves, Madeleine Mowbray with Group-Captain Pym, several other wives with several American officers all going up to the high table, a male shambles following to stand all cramped together at the long tables at either side of it—for more Americans had arrived than were expected.

The gavel struck silence from the high table. Padre Binks, eyes closed, hands tight together, said grace.

"For food and friends and fellowship we give Thee thanks, oh Lord!"

The typed menu was passed round. There was only one way, the Doc reflected, sitting by two very young Americans from New York who kept on calling him "Sir" as though he was their schoolmaster, of making a thing like this really successful and that was to have first-class food and drink.

Clear soup, probably half an Oxo cube. Rack of lamb—so that's what they called a piece of stringy neck swimming in

mashed potato and watery greens. Small glasses of *vin ordinaire*.
Trifle—shreds of rhubarb and apricot under a fat blubber of
yellow custard.

The meal dragged on. The Americans kept turning away from
the food and the conversation to look behind them. Nor could
you blame them, Flint thought. The WAAF waitresses in
spotless white overalls were the best part of the show.

The gavel again. "His Majesty the King!" proposed the
youngest RAF officer on the bottom of the lowest table.

"The President of the United States of America!"

Christ, speeches! Pym up on his feet, uttering clichés on
comradeship. A bewildered American captain, caught off guard
with this unexpected demand to speak, mumbled something
short and sweet.

Strickland was busy winding his watch and frowning. He
was not the only one discreetly squinting at the time. The
Yanks looked bored and embarrassed. Edward Mowbray had
closed his eyes. The atmosphere hung heavy, as diners cudgelled
their brains to keep up the faint hum of conversation and stop
it fading into intolerable silence.

Then a white-coated Mess Steward bent to whisper in
Strickland's ear. Strickland nodded several times, and, waving
him away, leaned across to Group-Captain Pym, who got to his
feet again.

"Ladies and gentlemen, fellow officers, we now have a small
entertainment for you."

Having sampled the liquor and the food and the dearth of
females, the Yanks were not inclined to expect much, if anything. They gave a modest handclap as a grey-bearded gentleman
in evening dress settled himself at the piano. They hardly
turned their heads as simultaneously he struck up and the doors
from the corridor burst open. But having once turned round,
their heads remained turned, their eyes widened, as in came a
troupe of high-kicking dancers. A dozen of them, in the briefest
of black pants and bras, with waving pink feathers on their
heads.

Not the usual run of provincial chorus girls. But real professionals, real Windmill stuff, matched in step and height and
looks. Beautiful mouth-watering girls.

The youngsters cheered and wolf-whistled. The older men

kept their mouths shut but their eyes twice as wide. Strickland clapped and waved a salute to the blue-green figure hovering outside in the corridor.

Sylvia appeared in person after the dancers had given two encores. She advanced to the middle of the floor. She looked stunningly beautiful and fragile—not unlike a mayfly herself, Doc Flint thought, in her blue-green gown. The spotlights glittered on the tightly fitting sequinned bodice. There were filmy trails from her shoulders, and from her waist flared a full skirt of the same diaphanous material. She announced the next item, a well-known baritone.

An anticlimax, Doc supposed at first. But no, it was sentiment and nostalgia beautifully rendered. Scottish songs, European, American songs. Hearth and homeland stuff, infinitely moving.

And then when the singer had reduced some of them to mild nostalgic tears, the lights were dimmed. In came a stripper. When the lights came on again, several of the more press-on types had acquired stockings and garters and the only male not stamping for an encore was Group-Captain Pym, sitting upright beside his wife.

But the stripper gave no encore. There was a comedian to get them to laugh off their tensions, and another high-kicking turn from the chorus girls. A skilful mixture. Just indeed what the doctor ordered.

The applause was thunderous. There was no doubt of the success of the show. Better still, the entertainers accompanied the officers into the Ladies' Room for coffee. They were friendly and pleasingly provocative, though they did not actually sit on their hosts' knees until Group-Captain Pym's pale face had disappeared to the ante-room, where civilian women were not allowed to penetrate.

There was only one fly in the spares-procuring ointment. The whisky ran out. Strickland was momentarily annoyed. But most of the Yanks and all the squadron remained in the Ladies' Room, into which the piano from the bar had been wheeled.

Crackers, the Gas Officer, obliged again. Smoochy stuff . . . *Thank you so much for that lovely week-end . . . These foolish things*. Everyone danced. Determinedly, Irvine managed to prise Emma Jones from Bob Greaves' side for a foxtrot. It was the one dance he could be sure of doing because it was just a plain walk. In any case, there wasn't the room for the fancy stuff, though Strickland and Sylvia were putting on quite a show.

"You can overdo this Yank solidarity stuff." Irvine frowned at Lieutenant Greaves as he released her. "But the next is mine."

She shook her head. "Not according to your Lord and Master."

"Who? Strickland?"

"Yes. Don't tell me you've got several." And then, her smile fading, "Talk of the devil . . . here he comes!"

Neatly and expertly steering Sylvia till they were side by side, Strickland bent down and whispered in Emma's ear, "Don't neglect our guests! And don't forget, Minneapolis-Honeywell automatic pilot spares, particularly main gyro units."

He gave her a sweet smile, patted her cheeks.

"And what were those sweet nothings he whispered in your ear?" Irvine asked her when Strickland had danced away.

"Much too tender to repeat," she frowned. "And your ears are too young."

He didn't see her again that evening. He had one dance with Madeleine Mowbray. Before midnight, the Ensa troupe retired dog-tired to bed, and just after midnight the Yanks went home. The sound of the B-24s, like Cinderella's footsteps, disappeared westwards.

Sylvia's bed remained all night unslept in. She appeared, still in the blue-green gown, just before seven. She said believe it or not, she'd stayed up drinking coffee with two of the chorus girls whom she'd known for donkey's years.

Emma was inclined to believe it not. No chorus girls, she decided, could light those eyes so brightly, no matter how many donkey's years.

TWELVE

EVERY time Edward Mowbray went off on an operational trip, he was reminded of the days when he went back to boarding-school at the beginning of term. As his mother used to do, all morning his wife would fuss about what he was wearing, whether he would be warm enough, urged him to rest, cooked him the best of whatever was in the house, slipped some ham sandwiches and her chocolate ration into his briefcase because she was sure the RAF rations were inadequate, kept on looking out of the window at the weather and then the clock to see how much time was left.

Finally, there was none. Like now. Outside, though the sun was shining it was cold.

"Bye, Edward. Take care."

His mother used simply to give him a hug and push him into a compartment with the other boys. Madeleine and he had their own particular parting, a sort of talisman act, two kisses on each cheek and a long one on the lips. Though Madeleine secretly wished that he would, he never carried a good luck charm. This secret ritual which they did at the doorway was his only concession to superstition.

"Back around four in the morning. Go to bed."

"Of course."

"Have a hot drink and a read. Help you to go to sleep."

"I will."

"Goodnight, sweet."

"Goodnight, love."

Then he simply got on his bicycle and wobbled off, turning his head at the corner to give her one last wave. It had been quite a pleasant day. There was a High over Scotland stretching out into the North Sea, and he had no particular apprehensions.

A daylight take-off was at three o'clock and on his own, which certainly meant simply a routine patrol. Nothing derring-do on some idea of Strickland's in company with the boys.

Since the bombing attack when the squadron had used his "petrol defence" against the FW 109s, there had been no sign of the *Groningen*. The Navy thought she was up in the Arctic. There was a rumour she was on her way to the China Seas. There had been one attack on a minesweeper by Warrant Officer Price. From his next trip, he had not returned. No signal, nothing. But the weather had been terrible, and it was suspected the killer was ice.

His aircraft was Q, one he had flown many times and possessing a remarkable turn of speed. Liberators were like women: some were fast and some were slow: some kept their noses high and some were shifty: some were real sluts and some were really naughty. Q lived up to her name: she was a real Queen, and he looked forward to flying her.

There was one snag. The Minneapolis-Honeywell automatic pilot was unserviceable. It needed a new gyro unit, Maintenance told him.

Mowbray felt his heart give a lurch—just a little one. They might have laid on a Skagerrak night patrol for him, and he knew his blind flying was his weakest point. Not that anyone could be expected to fly a Lib at fifty feet on a pitch-black night, but needs must when the devil drives . . .

On the credit side was that High. The weather should be good. He should be able to see the horizon at whatever height he flew.

All the same, he rang up Assistant Section Officer Jones. "Emma . . . this is Edward Mowbray. Do you remember me telling you that you can't fly Liberators or bicycles close to the ground at night?"

"Yes, I remember, Edward."

"Unfortunately I might be required to do that tonight. On a Lib, not a bicycle. My invaluable Minneapolis-Honeywell needs a new gyro unit. And it just happened to strike me that you said that you'd obtained a new one from that nice Bob Greaves."

"I'm sorry, Edward, but that went ages ago. Fitted to F Freddie."

"You wouldn't have another little one tucked away somewhere?"

180

"I'm sorry, Edward. I'll try to get one—"

"That'd be too late. Due off in three hours. Oh well." He paused. "Not to worry."

Aircrew Mess at twelve-thirty—bacon and eggs, hot stewy tea. Briefing at one-fifteen.

He saw straightaway as he entered Operations that it *was* a Skagerrak patrol. The tapes on the big wall map indicated their tracks, a cross-over between Denmark and Norway. The Intelligence briefing was short. Brackenbury pointed out the night-fighter airfields on either side of the Skagerrak, which Mowbray was only too well aware of. The Met Officer said the weather would be good to begin with, deteriorating later that night with the advent of a warm front.

Mowbray's heart sank.

It'll be all right, he said to himself. Like all introverts, he fought his battles in his mind before they happened. The reality, he had found, was usually either quite tame or non-existent. Half the battle was getting into the aircraft, he always said. Once you were on your way, all worries evaporated, and everything was a piece of cake.

Like this trip, for instance. He took off dead on time, climbed into a clear sky, began hand-flying the Liberator through clear calm air.

"Like to do the first two hours?" Mowbray asked Chisholm. "Hand-flying only, I'm afraid. George is U/S.*"

His second pilot simply put up his thumb and adjusted his seat up to the controls.

Mowbray pushed back his seat and lay back, staring at the darkening sky. He thought to himself . . . I catch a worry like I catch a cold. And in the end it turns out to be nothing . . .

They arrived on patrol while it was still daylight. It was Mowbray's turn to fly and he kept the Lib right down on the sea. Nothing seemed to be around. The weather still held.

"For your log-books, darkness fell at 17.01," said his Navigator over the intercom. "Check watches, please. Seventeen-oh-one-and-fifty-seconds-*now*!"

"Watch checks," said Mowbray and was echoed throughout the aircraft.

* The automatic pilot is unserviceable.

"We've got a tail-wind, Skipper." His Navigator's voice again.

"Which means we'll have a head-wind going home," put in his Engineer, who was highly conscious of fuel consumption.

"Don't worry so much, Charlie," said Mowbray, the worrier, in that slow, soft Cambridge drawl. "You're giving us the wind-up," and everybody laughed.

After his English Finals, Mowbray had taught in a minor public school, then got a job in an insurance office. He had thought of going into the Civil Service eventually. He would certainly never have gone anywhere near the RAF nor learned to fly but for the war. He was not, he knew, a born pilot, but he was a competent one. One of the advantages of being an introvert, he was always saying to Madeleine, was that you got a very fair assessment of yourself—of your strengths and weaknesses. And then all you had to do was to take jolly good care never to get into a position where such weakness showed or mattered. So it was with his flying. Though there were continued assessments of *Above Average* in his flying log-books, he was not fooled that they were a blanket commendation. Taking off, landing, most manoeuvres—fine! But he hated cross-wind approaches, so he avoided them, diverting to other aerodromes if necessary. And partly, he reckoned, because of some congenital slowness at keeping co-ordinated on three planes together for long periods, he was aware that his instrument flying could have been better, and that his Navigator's exasperation that the aircraft wasn't being kept steady while he was taking a star shot with the bubble sextant through the astro-dome was often justified.

"Time to turn, Skipper."

Strickland, of course, was marvellous at instrument flying. Mowbray knew that because he'd flown with him. So was all this feeling he had about the man nothing but jealousy?

"Turning."

He tried to put himself in Strickland's place. He tried to think like Strickland, feel like Strickland. If he had on an impulse gone and lost seven of his crew for a name-plate, what would happen to him? He knew he would be riddled with guilt, never able to forget them. What sort of defence mechanisms would he invent to stop himself going spare, going mad?

"East end of patrol now, Skipper. Turn back to 270."

People of course were different, and Strickland very much so. But since that S Sugar episode he'd done some odd things. All those "ideas" he had for sinking the *Groningen*, even his stone-wall refusal to see anything hazardous about leaking petrol caps, what was the driving force behind them? He would have very much liked to have discussed some of his ideas about Strickland with someone else, but the other pilots were younger and altogether too different from him, too struck on the man ever to understand. He could never really discuss it with Madeleine—she'd catch the worry from him and never have any peace when he was flying. He had tentatively had a go with the young WAAF Officer (and wasn't that really subterranean jealousy, to find Strickland's effect on her?) but she was really still a child. He'd mentioned it, too, to the Doc. Flint was a good type, but he didn't really give the impression of understanding. Mowbray had the Arts man's distrust for the scientist's understanding of human nature, and anyway Flint was part of the Establishment really, and it didn't do to talk to him about fears and worries lest he got the wrong idea—as indeed apparently he had done, offering him no answer to his tentative probings but only leave as an escape.

"West end now, Skipper. Turn back onto 090." His Navigator's voice hesitated. "Aren't we a bit high?"

The needle on the altimeter showed 600 feet.

"I'll go down," he said. "Radar, keep a good look out for contacts!"

Outside now it was totally black. Not the slightest line divided the sea from the sky. It was difficult to realize that the water was so close. Mowbray had pulled back his side window and stared down, but there was nothing. The wind brushed over his face, and he could smell the salt. The yellow exhausts flickered on the underside of the wing, turning the white to a ghostly copper.

He closed the window. Inside it was warm and snug. All the lights turned down on the flight deck. At least it was still calm. Not too difficult to fly. The radio altimeter read 200 feet.

"Can you keep a bit more steady, Skipper?" His Navigator's voice, just slightly irritable. "I'm trying to take a bearing."

The hours of the night went slowly by. Round about nine o'clock, during Chisholm's turn on the controls, Mowbray opened his brief-case, brought out Madeleine's ham sandwiches, passed one to Chisholm.

"Better than corned beef, sir!"

They sat side by side, munching, both keeping an eye on the radio altimeter. The Engineer came round with the big thermos, dishing out coffee into cardboard cups. Mowbray had just begun drinking when the Radar called out, "Contact! A big one! Thirty degrees port. Twenty miles."

"Turning."

"Still left, Skipper."

It took three minutes to complete the turn.

"Christ, three more blips above it! Aircraft, I think. I'm turning the scanner upwards."

"Keep an eye on them."

"Four blips, sir. No, *five*! She's got a night-fighter escort! This ship must be important!"

"At least she'll be chary of firing."

But there he was wrong. The next moment, the blackness around them had turned to bright yellow. In the backflash of heavy guns, he saw two funnels and a cruiser stern.

Mowbray pushed the throttles forward, put on full right bank at the same time pulling the stick hard back.

"I think she's the *Groningen*."

"She's the *Groningen* all right, sir," shouted the Front Gunner.

"Navigator, get a message with the sighting and our position. See the Radio sends it!"

"Right, sir."

"How far is the ship now?"

"Six miles port. Falling behind."

"And the fighters?"

"Just a moment, Skipper. I'll get the scanner up again." There was a pause. "One's coming towards us. No, two! *Three!*"

"Keep an eye on them."

He glanced down at the altimeter. 200 feet. At least he had the height to gather his thoughts, but he'd better think fast because he was a sitting duck for the fighters up here.

Outside it was still pitch black. A little rain was falling, speckling the windscreen. He steadied up the wings.

184

"Night-fighter dead behind us now, Skipper! One mile!"

I've got to go down, he thought. I've got to go right down to the sea. That's the only safe place.

As he was pushing the nose down, the Radio Operator tapped him on the arm. "They've got our message, sir. And I've got a reply."

"What is it?"

"Continue shadowing to the limit of your endurance."

He nodded silently. On the instrument panel ahead of him, the altimeter had begun to unwind fast—200, 150, 100.

"Fighter behind us! He's coming in! He's attacking!"

A white line of tracer underlined the starboard wing.

"There's another! And another! Lower! Lower! Skipper, get down!"

He pushed the stick still further forward. He said to Chisholm, "Keep your hands on the stick and watch me. If we get too low, pull back."

"*Lower!*"

More tracer—three lines this time. He heard the chattering of the Rear Gunner, then the Mid-upper Gunner starting firing. Their own red tracer began making patterns in front of them.

"Radar here . . . they're forming up again, Skipper. Two more have arrived."

And then suddenly from the front turret, "Look out! Pull back! The sea. *The sea!*"

He saw the radio altimeter flickering at 10 as he pulled back hard. Then the Front Gunner, "Christ, Skipper! We nearly had it that time!"

The altimeter needle climbed back to 200. And then high over the intercom from the rear turret, "Get down! *Lower!*" Three of them! Coming in from three o'clock. Turn starboard *now!*"

He pulled down right on the stick. But he had no idea if he turned. He had no idea whether he was upside down or sideways. It was a black vacuum the Liberator was flying in—wallowing, yawing, hunting.

"Get a message to base," he shouted to the Engineer. "Being attacked by night-fighters!"

"Get down, Skipper! *Down!*"

185

He pushed the stick forward. Like a roller-coaster, the Liberator began diving.

"Skipper, the sea! For Christ's sake, *the sea!*"

He caught a glimpse of the artificial horizon, crazily askew. He pulled the wing up, still felt the heavy aircraft slip.

He thought to himself . . . better get back. Better get home. But he had been ordered to stay out here. "You'd have been safe enough, right down on the deck," Strickland would have said.

Which was true. No German fighters would be crazy enough to fly this low in pitch darkness. Only Strickland and his disciples would try that sort of wall-of-death act in a heavy four-engined aircraft. Blind flying was his Achilles heel—at this height it was certainly beyond him.

The only hope was the Minneapolis-Honeywell. At least the elevators might work. Take some of the load off him. Sweat pouring down his face, he levelled the aircraft off at two hundred feet, slipped in the elevator lock, then the rudder.

A Broadway of lights winked angrily out at him. The nose lurched down. Up went the starboard wing.

"Totally U/S, Skipper," Chisholm shouted. "No good!"

And then high and frightened from the front turret, "Skipper, there's sea-water in the turret!"

In a daze, he pulled back. Up went the nose—too high! He could hear the propellers straining.

Momentarily he lifted his eyes from the instrument panel and stared at the night outside. Black! Nothing! No reference! No help! He could feel the aircraft slipping and sliding.

And from the rear turret, "Down, Skipper! They're coming in again! Four of them! *Five* of them!"

He pushed the nose down again. There was safety only in that tiny belt fifty feet above the sea into which the fighters dare not come. But with this sluggish wallowing Liberator, neither dared he. Q did not seem to be responding to the controls. She seemed to be slipping and sliding as though on ice. It was like suddenly losing the use of your arms and your legs—the aircraft was no longer an extension of him but a wayward puppet with the strings loose and broken.

"They're attacking from astern, Skipper. Down! Stay down on the sea!"

186

And from the front turret, "Up! Skipper, *up!* The sea . . ."

He was trapped. It was as though he was in the jaws of a shark. The sea was the mouth below, and above were the sharp teeth of the night-fighters.

"Turn port!"

He tried to turn. But it was as though he had lost all sense of direction.

"Get down! Skipper, *get down!*"

Again he pushed forward. The radio altimeter flickered. He could feel the aircraft falling.

"Skipper!" An agonized shout from the front turret. "We've touched! Water . . ."

He could feel the aircraft skidding sideways. Though he pulled back with all his might, he could not get the nose up further. He heard quite a soft sound. Then a crack like thunder. For one terrible moment, he saw the phosphorescent green of the instruments reflected in a white wave of water.

Then the sea crumpled the nose, crashed through the turret and the navigation compartment, and came flooding up over the flight deck.

Irvine came up to the surface reluctantly from a deep, long sleep. He had got back from his stooge patrol, just before the bar closed, to be greeted with the news that Mowbray had got the chop, and he'd tanked up so as to get a decent sleep.

Now, Mavis was shaking him by the shoulder. Her face hung over him. His heart lurched and then sank heavily. "Oh God," he thought, "they're sending me out again."

"Mr Irvine, sir," she shook him and smiled at the same time. Insensitive girl. Smiled, beamed, looked coy. He'd almost have liked to be a woman just to be as insensitive and unfeeling as that. "Sir. Mr Irvine. You're wanted on the corridor telephone."

"Tell him I'm dead. Or is it Wing-Commander Strickland?"

"No, Mr Irvine. No, sir. Not Wing-Commander Strickland." She held out his greatcoat invitingly to him. "And it isn't a *him*. It's a *her*." She giggled. "Miss Jones."

"Emma? Christ Almighty, Mavis!" He got out of bed. "Why didn't you say so?" He took the coat from his batwoman, let her help him into it, ignored the slippers she held out and opened the door. Then he went smacking his barefooted way down the corridor to the telephone halfway down on the wall.

He picked it up. "Irvine here."

There was a click from the Mess exchange as the line connected. He said heartily, "Hello there, Emma!"

He was unprepared for the muted tone of her voice, saying without preamble, "I've just heard about Edward."

He drew in his breath. "Edward? Oh, yes! Rotten luck!" What could he say? "Good type."

There was a silence from the other end, and he wasn't quite sure if she had heard him. He was just about to embark on a repeat of the rigmarole when she said, "What about Madeleine?"

"Madeleine? Madeleine? Yes, of course. I haven't a clue. She'll have relatives, I expect. Parents. And the padre will have been."

"I think we should go and see her."

"We? You and me?" His feelings were mixed and he was afraid that his voice reflected that mixture. He was pleased to be invited to go anywhere with Emma Jones. But to see a newly bereft widow, even one as nice as Madeleine, was about the least favourable date he could conceive.

"Yes. You and me."

"I'm not much good at that sort of thing, Emma. I didn't know Edward all that well." Irvine was going to add, he was just another pilot like me. But he didn't. He didn't want to be like Edward. Another pilot. Another casualty statistic.

"But we went to their home, Peter. And she seemed pleased to see us then."

"I suppose so." He thought quickly. "But how do we get there? We've no transport. It's a *hell* of a walk."

"We can go on the bike."

"*His?* Edward's?" He sounded shocked, he knew. Outraged.

"That one, yes. It was an issue one. It's been handed into Stores. With his other things. That's how I know."

Her tone more than anything else made him concede defeat. "Give me time to dress," he said. "I'll meet you outside Stores in half an hour." He tried to lighten the proceedings. "And I'm not taking you on the crossbar till we're clear of the Guard Room."

188

"Don't worry," her voice smiled faintly. "I won't get on it till we are."

He was going to greet her with some remark about not allowing the SP's to admire her knees, in order to keep the note of the outing something above mournful. But she was wearing her battledress. Though he preferred girls in skirts, the battledress was undoubtedly one of the more becoming parts of the uniform. The neatly fitting trousers showed off her shapely hips and the blouse top was tightly waisted round a very trim waist indeed. He felt a boor for noticing such things on a trip like this. But hell, life was short, God knew. And only God knew exactly how short for him.

So, instead, he gave her a warm smile, an exaggerated salute and said, striving for that lightness, "Has anyone told you you're a very pretty girl, Emma Jones?"

The light note came out wrongly, but somehow she made it all right. She gave a little shrug, a rather wistful smile and asked, "Are you telling me that, Peter Irvine?"

"Yes, I am." And that set the tone, the note—companionable, wistful, and a little tender. A mixture that was amazingly soothing to him as, without further immediate words, they walked briskly out of the main gates, with Peter wheeling the bike. Once beyond sight of the Guard Room, Emma arranged herself on the crossbar. And with something of a struggle, Peter managed to pedal like mad and get them both airborne and on course.

As he did on an operation, he went over in his mind what he'd do and say in the various eventualities. What if Madeleine was hysterical, what if she wouldn't open the door to them, what if she had a bevy of relatives with her or friends? What if she was silent? And, hopefully, what would he and Emma do if Madeleine was out shopping?

Perhaps similar thoughts were running through Emma's mind because she was silent, or perhaps she was too busy holding on to her cap against the rising wind from the west, and that caused by the considerable speed (downhill at least) of their going.

"The wind will be behind us on the way back," was about the only remark Emma made. But her silence was companionable, almost like that, he thought, of a married couple.

When they reached the thorn thicket, just before the cottage

189

gate, Emma said, "Let's park the bike here. It might upset Madeleine. It's only about fifty yards." She slid off the crossbar as he brought them to a halt.

"Can I have my fare please? Or wouldn't you like that?"

"I like to pay my way," she murmured softly, holding up her face. She returned his kiss with that same warm sweetness that both frightened him and made him feel ten feet tall. He held her hand all the way to the door. Then she withdrew it, perhaps not wanting Madeleine to see their dawning attachment, for that surely was what it was.

But she need not have worried. Even before they knocked on the door, he knew the cottage was empty. Its life had fled. The windows were shut. No smoke rose from the chimney.

After repeated echoing knocks, Irvine stepped onto the turf and peered in through the window. The place was neat and spotlessly clean, the rented furniture polished, the homely brown crockery put away. But it was deserted.

"She may be in the garden," Emma said. "Feeding the birds." She looked up at the wind-blown sky where small specks of gulls wheeled distantly.

Emma began to walk round the side of the cottage towards the sycamore tree. Irvine followed her. Suddenly she stopped in her tracks. In the neat patch of turf lay the only untidiness and disorder. The wind or the hungry gulls had dislodged the bowl. It lay in white fragments on the ground below. For a split second it looked to Irvine like the distant wreck of a Liberator. He hoped Emma Jones wouldn't think the same.

But all she said was, "She must have gone." Then she put her hand into his and added, "But thanks, Peter. I'm glad we came."

"Don't worry, chaps," Strickland said in the bar, in the ante-room, in his office—"we'll soon sink the bastard!"

Four aircraft had been lost in twelve days. There were many missing faces in the Mess. Madeleine Mowbray had gone home to her parents' house in Buckinghamshire. 507's mood was subdued. A success was badly needed.

But not even Strickland expected to get that success quite so quickly. His first Blind Bombsight operational trip was called

190

a Rover Patrol. That meant he could go anywhere he wanted, looking for targets.

He took off in that twilight zone—Last Light. The blackout was already drawn. In the offices, they were beginning to pack up their papers and put them in the Security cupboards. Sausage and tinned tomato was being prepared for the airmen's tea. The covers were put over the Liberators at Dispersal, tucking them in for the night. Over all the Station there was that hush that heralds the end of the day.

People looked around for things to do that evening. The film at the camp cinema was Greer Garson in *Mrs Miniver*. The new padre was organizing an amateur dramatic society in the Recreation Room. It was Domestic Evening for the WAAF, and they were going down to their huts to get down to their darning. In the Mess, the officers finished their dinner, had coffee in the ante-room, began drifting into the bar.

And then suddenly a whisper began getting around. Irvine heard it from Ames, who heard it from Dacres. Strickland had done something—that was all there was to it at first. But gradually it became plumped out into *Strickland's sunk a ship*. Still only a rumour, but as time went by it achieved shape—*it's the Groningen!*—colour and background—*off Copenhagen harbour in bloody awful weather*—and finally authenticity—*pukka gen! Brackenbury's received a signal!*

The whole Station was jubilant—nobody more than Irvine. As he said to the Doc, "Be able to get a bit of peace at last."

The party in the bar started immediately. It was in full swing when Strickland returned triumphant to cheers and shouts and songs. A signal of congratulation had come in from the Navy. A personal message from Air Vice-Marshal Nuttall.

Strickland was surrounded by senior captains, but Irvine managed to get more of the story from Tarrant, the most voluble of the three Strickland crew inhabitants in Room 27.

". . . black as the ace of spades . . . wind, fog, rain . . . been cruising up and down the Kattegat when the radar got a blip outside Copenhagen harbour. Strickland went and had a look at the radar and saw it was a big one so we might as well let the BB have a go on it. Went up to eight hundred feet slap into thick cloud. Centralized the blip at ten miles. At five miles doubled the drift and turned onto the new course. To be honest,

I wasn't expecting much. The BB had been slinging the practice bombs all over the place. In the *Marlborough*, the crew used to go freely about on deck as though we weren't there, so used had they become to the practice bombs falling nowhere near them. Anyway, up we came, rain streaming over us. And then suddenly, just as we were about half a mile away, the night got lighter, the cloud broke up a bit and there was a searchlight swinging around on the headland . . . and Christ, silhouetted against it two funnels, raked bow, cruiser stern . . . and Strickland, you know what a dab-hand at ship-recognition he is, shouted '*Groningen!*' so loudly I reckon the old BB must've heard it because for once it pulled its finger out and released on target. There was this terrific flash that lit up the rain. And then the Radar reported the blip had disappeared. Simply disappeared! Not a sign of it! We stayed there for an hour in nil visibility, but there was no blip. Then Strickland came right down to the water and swept the area to and fro . . . Christ, I was scared! . . . but we could find nothing. *Nothing!* The *Groningen* had gone!"

The party went on practically all night. "Good night ladies" was sung shortly after one. But neither Emma nor Sylvia could get to sleep for the noise in the bar and other things. The female attitude was different. Tending to be haunted by the faces and the personalities of Mowbray's aircrew, visions of more dead men's clothes and pathetic effects that would cram the returned clothing store tomorrow, Emma felt sombre and a little sick. Sylvia's mood on the other hand was high and brittle, as they both lay with their white counterpanes pulled high under their chins, staring up at the pink glow of the stove on the ceiling, listening to the raucous beery voices, the bumps, the breakages, the bouts of hilarity.

"At least it'll mean the heat will be off," Emma said. She was going to say, "Strickland's got what he wanted," but didn't. "They've got the *Groningen*. Thank God for that, I suppose."

"Amen." Sylvia gave a long sigh. "Guy can relax. He's been marvellous, hasn't he? It isn't often you can admire someone as well as . . ." She heaved a theatrical sigh, which said, Ask me.

"Love them?" Emma asked.

"God, yes. Head over . . . all that rubbish. Who'd have thought it?"

"And him?"

"Don't ask me that. Makes me superstitious, darling. Tempting providence. And Providence doesn't need much tempting. But . . . well . . . shall I say I don't reckon there's anyone else in the running . . . no one who's got . . ."

She broke off as some particular wild Red-Indian-like cries came nearer.

"High Cockalorum in the corridor," Emma explained.

"Oh. Didn't I hear Guy's voice?"

"Probably."

"Well, to continue . . . yes, sweetie, I think he is rather smitten. Physically *and* all the rest. He told me . . . oh, well never mind. But what *I* dread sometimes is that he might be the frightfully honourable type. The kind that doesn't want to get hitched up in wartime. *You* know. Likelihood of getting the chop and all that. Doesn't want to make the little woman a widow."

Emma said nothing. She could hear Strickland's voice above the rest yelling triumphantly at the top of the High Cockalorum pile.

"But now that beastly ship is sunk, he'll have more time for us. Sad, with all the casualties. I feel a bitch for even thinking it. But it's true. Just before we left the party he said, 'I'm wining and dining you tomorrow'. He didn't say it was going to be something special. But you know . . . somehow you can tell."

From downstairs at the far end of the long corridor there came the sound of beer glasses splintering against the wall, and the opening strains of "An airman told me before he died, I do not think the bastard lied . . ."

There were a lot of sore heads the next morning—including Irvine's. His relief that the *Groningen* had gone was almost as great as Strickland's triumph and he had drunk commensurately deep.

Sylvia Talbot's head spent most of the morning being shampooed, carefully set and then under the drier at the Camp hairdresser's.

Around two o'clock in the afternoon, a signal from the Admiralty came into Intelligence, and Brackenbury phoned Strickland. A message had been received on the radio from Danish partisans which said, *quantities of shaped and camouflaged*

193

wood being washed ashore off Copenhagen harbour indicate that a German dummy ship may have been attacked.

Sylvia Talbot returned from the wining and dining before nine-thirty. Though the Ensa girl pretended to be asleep, Emma was wakened in the night by the sound of her sobbing.

Two days later, Sylvia Talbot was immediately recalled by Ensa to London. "For a most frightfully important job, darling," she told Emma that morning.

She was gone when Emma went to their room that evening. Nothing of her remained.

Except in the wastepaper basket, the blue-green sheen of the discarded mayfly dress.

THIRTEEN

It was Tarrant, Strickland's new Navigator, a tall, very neat character who now occupied the centre bed in Room 27 and binded about the general untidiness of everybody else, who first brought Irvine's attention to it on the same night that Sylvia Talbot departed.

They were both undressing preparatory to an early bed and possible operations in the morning. The other occupants had not yet come up, and the two of them were talking in a desultory way of the flood of what Tarrant called "foreigners" that had recently been cramming the Mess to over-capacity. Anybody who was not actually English came under this category as far as Tarrant was concerned—a most extraordinary sort of Aryan philosophy which Irvine put down to a heritage of his public school and his Diplomatic Service ancestry.

"Some of them can't even speak the language," the Navigator said.

Irvine took off his shirt, bent over the washbasin, turned on the taps, and scooped warm water over his face.

"It's a great help in Strickland's crew to have everybody English."

Irvine dried his face and reached for his toothbrush in the glass under the mirror.

"You have rather a mixed crew, haven't you?"

Irvine squeezed a long white slug of toothpaste onto the bristles.

"Doesn't it make things rather difficult?"

"Doesn't worry me," Irvine said. "I'm pretty mixed myself, Scots, Irish, Canadian. My great-grandmother was an American."

"What I *really* mean," said Tarrant, slipping into his striped pyjamas, "is foreigners with a big F." Lovingly he folded his uniform and laid it on the chair beside his bed. "Central Europeans particularly."

Irvine scrubbed at his teeth and said nothing. Behind him, Tarrant carefully wound up his watch, put it on his bed table under the lamp and climbed into bed. "What riles me particularly," he said, propping himself up on his elbows, "is this lavatory seat business."

"What's that?"

"Haven't you noticed?"

Irvine put on his pyjama top, and turned his back on Tarrant —he had a partly Puritan-inherited, partly school-indoctrinated modesty—while he took off his trousers and put his legs one by one into his pyjama bottoms. "Noticed what?"

"Somebody's standing on the lavatory seats in the bogs."

"I haven't seen anything."

"Bloody great footmarks."

"Oh?"

"What I want to know is . . . who's the bugger who's doing it?"

"OK if I put the light out?"

"It's a filthy Central European habit, that's what it is!"

Irvine walked across to the switch by the door. "They'd probably think the same of us sitting down."

"And that's another thing! It's insulting! The character clearly thinks he'd catch some bloody disease from us!"

Irvine turned the switch up. Darkness fell over Room 27. " 'Night, Tarrant."

"I'll tell you this, Irvine . . . the bugger's got to be caught!"

There *was* an operation next day for both Irvine's and Strickland's crews—but only patrols off the north Norwegian fjords, and in thick rain and mist, neither crew saw a sausage, let alone the *Groningen*. But whether or not infected by Tarrant, Strickland's crew on return and back on the ground were filled to the exclusion of all else with one evangelical idea: to catch the bugger who was standing on the lavatory seats in the Officers' Mess bogs.

It was as though there was some infiltrator, a spy in the camp, some alien force even that had invaded and threatened them.

Flint had been brought into the business for his medical support on the risk to health of this extraordinary behaviour, but his suggestions of cleaning the seat or putting lavatory paper on it or going into the toilet next door were regarded as less than lukewarm. "The Doc is far too psychological," Tarrant told Irvine. "Not sufficiently hygienically orientated. Kept on talking about witch-hunts, and, of all things, the Captain of the *Groningen*! For Christ's sake, Doc, I said, I'm not saying it's *him*!"

But it was as though there was something just as unrealistic and other-worldly about the search for the real offender. Even Irvine became curious, even excited, every time he pushed open the door of the place. Perhaps one day he would see towering head and shoulders above the wooden partitions of the toilets—for they did not reach to the ceilings—some Brobdingnagian character, perhaps the giant at the top of Jack's beanstalk, materializing out of nothing, identified at last, caught in action red-handed.

For nobody who said they saw the footmarks could give any idea of when they might have been imprinted. One moment, there was nothing. The next moment, so they said, they were there. Swiftly, silently, the offender struck. No ears heard him. Only the eyes of LACW Prendergast, round and blue and celluloid, staring invitingly from the pretty little pink-and-white doll's face, appeared ever to have seen him—and she wasn't telling. And the Lutine bell made no sound.

Who could it be? How could the truth be discovered?

There had been other alarms of this sort, but none so baffling as this since the whisky disappeared too quickly on the night of the Dining-In night with the Americans.

What tell-tale bait could be offered? What inducement could be laid to come in and be discovered? The finger of suspicion seemed to point at so many people. There had been numbers of Czechs, French, Belgians, Dutch, Yugoslavs, Norwegians and Danes visiting Kilcreggan on training exercises or courses. Then there were numerous other nationals of the Allies amongst the regular inmates of the Mess. While a clean bill of health had been given by Tarrant to the English, he was not so sure of the Welsh, Irish and Scots, though these were hotly defended by the two other Strickland crew occupants of Room 27.

Irvine had never seen the footprints, so he kept quiet and expressed no opinion on who it might be. There were various "favourites". A visiting Frenchman was followed into the Gentlemen's every time he visited it, but with no result. A couple of Czech pilots next came under the microscope for a while. Then early one Thursday evening, when the bar was deserted and Irvine was buying a packet of cigarettes, Tarrant came up to him and said, "It's Mosco."

"What is?"

"*You* know . . ."

Irvine pocketed his change and opened the packet. "Like one?"

"No, thanks."

Irvine struck a match and lit his cigarette.

"Well," Tarrant said irritably, "what are you going to do about it?"

"What am *I* going to do about it?"

"Yes."

"Nothing to do with me."

"But it *is* to do with you."

"I don't see why." Irvine inhaled. "Anyway, I don't believe it *is* Mosco."

"We've got proof."

"What?"

"Garfield, his room-mate, got one of his shoes. It matches the latest print mark."

"But why *should* it be Mosco? Why suddenly *Mosco*?"

"Not a doubt."

"Well, *I* doubt it. If Mosco got up on a lavatory seat, he's so heavy, he'd bust the thing!"

"It *is* Mosco. And everybody wants to know what you're going to do about it."

"I'm going to do nothing."

"Oh yes you are!"

"Who says so?"

Tarrant played his trump card. "Strickland."

Irvine stubbed out his half-smoked cigarette into an ashtray.

"You're his captain, Strickland says. It's up to you."

Irvine considered the problem for the rest of that evening. After breakfast on Friday, he waited in the hall. When Mosco came down from his room, pulling on his raincoat, he said in a friendly fashion, "Walking up to Flights, Mosco?"

"Walk? I have to walk, Kapitan. I have no bicycle. I say to the Equipment Officer—"

"I haven't a bicycle either, Mosco. Let's walk up together."

Outside it was pouring. The Pole wound an enormous blue woollen muffler round his face. Side by side, they tramped through the rain in silence.

"Mosco, how are you feeling these days?"

"*Feeling*, Kapitan?"

"No recurrence?"

"Re-currence?"

"Of the old trouble. What you were in hospital with."

Over the top of the muffler, the baggy grey eyes regarded him suspiciously.

"Waterworks all right? No trouble with constipation?"

The Pole shrugged. "No understand."

"The seats in the lavatory, Mosco. They're not for standing."

"Who is standing?"

"You don't have any trouble going to the lavatory?"

"Who is in trouble? Me, Kapitan?"

"No, no, Mosco. It's just that Tarrant . . . you know, Strickland's Navigator . . ."

"Yes, yes. Ah, now I see! Pilot Officer Tarrant has been standing on the seats in the lavatory. He is in trouble." The blue woollen head nodded sympathetically. "Poor man! Does the Doctor know what is the matter with him?"

The rain had increased. It was making so much noise on the tarmac road that Moscovich would not have heard Irvine's reply, even if he had made one. They reached Flights, and Irvine opened the door and stood aside.

"After you, Kapitan."

"No, after you, Mosco."

Irvine did not mention the matter again. But a couple of days later, Strickland did say—not to him in particular but to a number of captains round the bar—"AOC's inspection next Monday, chaps. Hope he doesn't find anything to upset him in the bogs."

There is an old RAF saying that for AOC's inspections,

ACHs are put to work to whitewash the coal. Flint suspected that this was apocryphal, but he had been assured by several people that they had actually seen it done. Certainly for Air Vice-Marshal Nuttall's visit to RAF Station, Kilcreggan, it was *not* done—perhaps for the simple reason the coal had run out and it was freezing in the airmen's huts—but everything else was.

Bullshit, Flint thought as he watched the preparations, is a good diagnostic word that gets right to the heart of the matter, because bullshit is exactly what it is. The Station was literally scrubbed from top to toe. The Officers' Mess was repainted. Such squadron aircraft that were not required for operations were lined up on the hardstanding outside Flying Control, primped and polished and all guns gleaming. There was going to be a parade of all personnel, RAF and WAAF, at which, according to Strickland, there was going to be said "some pretty solemn things". And afterwards, there was going to be a Grand March Past.

The camouflaged Hillman flying the AOC's pennant on its bonnet arrived at Kilcreggan promptly at eleven o'clock, and the morning programme was a tour of inspection of the Station, finishing up at the bar of the Officers' Mess. The doctor had got himself a vantage point over by the far window, wanting to be as detached as possible from the proceedings. There he was joined by Peter Irvine and Emma Jones for half a pint of bitter, while they waited for the AOC's party to arrive.

Just after twelve-thirty, the door opened and half the officers on the Station appeared, forming an encircling bodyguard round quite a small man in the middle.

Air Vice-Marshal Nuttall had plump, pink, varnished cheeks, bright blue eyes under thick bushy eyebrows, and greying hair spread thinly over a big head. Wing-Commander Strickland was very much in attendance, with Flight-Officer Wendy Beauchamp a good second and Group-Captain Pym trailing.

The counter had been cleared so that the party would have free access to it. Everyone else was squeezed hard against the walls.

"What'll it be, sir?"

"Oh, beer, Guy. Always stick to beer."

"Wendy . . . need I ask?"

"You needn't, Wing-Commander."

200

"Group-Captain Pym?"

"Bitter, Strickland."

The drinks were downed. Introductions were made of trusty squadron types. Neither Flint nor Irvine were particularly surprised at not being called up, but Emma Jones was horrified when Flight-Officer Beauchamp came fussing around saying "Ah there you are! Come along now and meet Air Vice-Marshal Nuttall!"

There then followed a few minutes of Strickland's banter about "our Griselda, sir, makes Liberator spares from straw." A drink was provided for her while the dreadful spares situation was discussed, followed by the AOC asking her how she was getting along with the Army over the provision of the 57-millimetre guns.

"Quite well, sir. But now they're rather worried about what to do if they don't get them back."

"Oh, they'll get them back all right, never fear!"

The conversation then revolved about Strickland's ideas and how extremely fortunate it was to have so much imagination up here at Kilcreggan.

"You'll hurry up our Leigh Lights, won't you, sir?"

"Never fear!"

"And our parachute bombs?"

"Never fear!"

"And our torpedoes?"

"Guy, my dear fellow . . . you need never fear!" The AOC swivelled his blue gaze round the half circle. "You chaps," he said softly. "I envy you chaps!"

There were sheepish smiles and shifting of shoulders.

"You do a pretty good job on the ground, sir."

"On the ground, Strickland? I'm never on the ground! Always up there! Up with the boys!"

"We know we're always in your thoughts, sir."

"That's what they say at Group, Strickland. That's what they say when they see me far away. He's up there with the boys, they say. Always on my mind! Pictures . . . pictures of the boys! The boys! Always," he brought down his clenched fist on the bar counter in a paroxysm of protestation, "THE BOYS!"

"We know we're jolly lucky with our AOC, don't we, chaps?"

Everybody in the half circle except Emma nodded vigorously.

She was kept standing there during two more rounds of drinks while the AOC talked tactics against the *Groningen* with his boys. She was only relieved when the Air Vice-Marshal asked, "Just across the corridor is it, Guy?"

"That's where it is, sir."

Back she went to the window while out through the door went the AOC. She made a face at Peter Irvine when he asked her wasn't she slumming. The noise in the bar was so much they could hardly hear themselves speak, and Flint had to shout at her twice when he asked her whether she wanted another drink, when suddenly high above everything else and crystal clear rang the little Lutine bell.

And then there was immediate silence.

Alone and rubbing his hands, back briskly into the bar came Air Vice-Marshal Nuttall, took up his place in the centre of the half circle, lifted his tankard of beer.

Everybody kept their eyes away from him. Flint caught Irvine's eye and smiled. Then he looked across at Strickland.

What's going to happen now, he thought. Are they going to slap him on the shoulder and roll about the room laughing and demand he forks out for drinks all round? If they'd been Americans, that's what they'd have done. If they'd been French, they'd have kissed him on both cheeks with tears in their eyes. If they had been Russians, they would have shot either him or LACW Prendergast (probably both). But as they were English Cromwellians, what were they going to do?

It all depended on Strickland. They were watching Strickland for a lead.

"You're heel-tapping, sir. Drink up!"

"Guy, my dear fellow . . . I'll drink up, never fear!"

Nothing was going to be done. The incident would be assumed never to have happened. A chill descended on the bar. A strange odd chill. Cheeks their erstwhile cherubic pink, blue eyes innocently flashing, a couple more pints under his belt, certainly Air Vice-Marshall Nuttall never noticed.

They convoyed him to lunch shortly afterwards. Nobody on the squadron seemed to be saying anything. Never ones for bullshit, it was strange how obediently 507 aircrew in their Best Blue, buttons gleaming, formed up in fours and marched to

202

take their position on the parade ground. Doc Flint was already there, stuck n the centre of the SHQ contingent.

First there was a slow inspection of all ranks. Then solemnly was read out—this would be Strickland's idea, Flint thought, Give us this day, O Lord, since all else has failed to sink the *Groningen*, a bit of the old One-Two—what sounded exactly like a commination. It was supposed to be read out every three months, this he knew, but he had never heard it before. It would have been for Edward Mowbray if he'd been alive, and for him and for such as are not for us because they are certainly against us.

The Squadron-Leader Admin's sepulchral tones continued ". . . under the existing law, any person who shall maliciously and advisedly endeavour to seduce any person or persons in HM forces by sea, land or air from his or their duty and allegiance to His Majesty or to incite or stir up any such person or persons to commit any act of mutiny, or to make or endeavour to make any mutinous assembly, or to commit any traitorous or mutinous practices whatsoever, may, on being legally convicted of such offence, be sentenced to penal servitude for the term of the natural life of such person."

Don't you try saying *no* to Wing-Commander Strickland! Don't you try interfering with his good ideas for sinking the *Groningen*!

Now, from the dais, Air Vice-Marshal Nuttall spoke of the excellent show and the smart turnout and the fine work the Station was doing, all pulling together to bring the Hun to his knees. Beside him Padre Binks, white stole waving in the wind, said a few words of prayer.

And then it was the time of wheeling and dealing, with the Station Warrant Officer shouting, and feet stamping as, still in fours, one behind the other the formations moved off, with the Station band leading the way, playing the Air Force March for all it was worth.

RAF Regiment . . .

SHQ . . .

507 Squadron . . .

Ah, here came the WAAFS!

Heads up. Chests out. Backs straight. Blonde hair, brown

hair, red hair, black hair one inch off the collar. Legs lifting, arms swinging, polished shoes stepping.

"Eyes *left*!"

Pretty lipsticked faces turned like little moons towards him. Blue eyes, brown eyes, black eyes, green eyes regarded him standing there on the dais.

Right arm up in the salute, fingers just touching the golden laurel leaves round his cap.

Erect! Stiff as a poker! Rigid as a bar!

As all in tune and sweetly swaying, the skirts went marching by.

FOURTEEN

THE *Groningen* showed herself very much alive by appearing in the middle of PQ 47 off the Lofoten islands and sinking three merchantmen. British submarines, American cruisers, everybody was after her now, and Strickland nursed an oft-repeated fear that someone would sink her before they did. As some compensation, however, Leigh Light searchlights had arrived and were being fitted on the starboard wing of all 507 Liberators. And all the crews were now undergoing torpedo training.

It was extremely difficult dropping torpedoes accurately on a pitch black night against the wreck in the training area at Loch Nairn. Twice Irvine had near shaves in F Freddie against the side of the mountains. Results were not good, and Strickland was becoming impatient. In addition, Doc Flint had insisted on more leave for the crews and had sent two of the most experienced captains on rest.

Strickland was absolutely convinced, however, that the *Groningen* would eventually return to Falstand Fjord—"I know what's in that devil Leitzen's mind"—and there 507 would sink her.

However she was certainly not there now—daily PRU photographs proved that—and so 507 continued to search for her, now carrying their torpedoes.

Irvine had no particularly burning desire to find her. If she did happen to come along, well, that would be that and of course he would act. But he much preferred when it was Miggs' stint on the radar. Sure he would get a blip, but could be relied on to dismiss it as sea returns or a false echo. So when they were up on patrol in F Freddie at latitude 70 North 00 12 West at 03.30 on an icy, pitch-black night and Miggs on the radar reported a contact twenty miles away thirty degrees to port, Irvine's heart never missed a beat.

"Getting bigger, Skipper."

"Turning port."

"Five degrees more, Skipper . . . hold it . . . dead ahead now . . . fourteen miles."

Irvine went into the motions of carrying out the attack drill. He pushed the nose down. Cautiously F Freddie began to descend towards the sea.

The darkness was intense. Irvine kept his eyes on the radio altimeter, saw the needle begin twitching at 250 feet, and edged back on the stick.

"Nine miles . . . turn port, Skipper . . . still port."

"Turning."

"Central now."

A silence fell over the aeroplane.

"Front upper . . . all set?" Irvine asked.

"Ready and guns to fire!"

"Mid-upper?"

"Guns to fire, sir!"

"Seven miles . . . six miles . . ."

"Craik, open the bomb-doors and keep the lever fully open."

"Garth, man the Leigh Light controls!"

"Already manning them, sir!"

Clipped, efficient, everything beautifully carried out—calmly, quietly, confidently. Irvine concentrated his eyes on keeping the artificial horizon level. His flying was absolutely dead on and accurate.

"Skipper—"

"Yes, Radar?"

Here it was now—sea return, false echo? Mentally he began to prepare himself to clean up the aeroplane and climb.

"*Skipper*, it's—"

Miggs' voice had suddenly gone high—shrill and exalted.

"What is it, Radar?"

"Christ, Skipper—"

"What's the matter, Radar?" asked Irvine fearfully.

"It's the *Groningen*, Skipper!"

Liberator F Freddie lurched drunkenly to starboard.

"How d'you know, Miggs?" Irvine shouted at him. "How the hell d'you know?"

"Blips so bloody big! And exactly like they showed us on the training film!"

Oh Miggs, *Miggs*, Irvine thought. *Et tu*, Miggs! You know not what you do!

"Steady, Skipper, steady!"

"Trying to."

"Six miles . . . still port."

"Guns ready!"

"Leigh Light ready to focus."

Darkness—nothing but darkness. A few illuminated stars and stripes on the instrument board were doing a tipsy dance together.

"Port, Skipper, *port!*"

Irvine's heart had gone into his mouth. Sluggish, slow, the Liberator was wallowing in the uneven air.

"Hundred feet, sir." Henty warning him what the radio altimeter was reading.

"Four miles . . . still ten degrees port."

He overcorrected.

"Starboard now . . . *starboard*."

He tried to tip the Liberator up to the right.

"Still starboard."

"We're climbing, Skipper."

"Three miles . . . *still* starboard."

"We're diving, Skipper!"

Oh God, this darkness! To steady himself more than anything else, he said, "We'll put the Leigh Light on at two miles. As soon as it illuminates, gunners to open fire!"

"Front Gunner to Captain . . . the sea! Christ, the sea! It's practically in the turret!"

He pulled back.

"Port now . . . two and a half miles."

He turned the aircraft to the left.

"Two miles!"

He kept his eyes purposely down. Even so, there was a sudden bright white explosion. He heard the chatter of the .5s, smelled the cordite. Surely the *Groningen* would be firing back now?

"Christ, she's been camouflaged white!"

He lifted his head. Immediately his eyes exploded inside him. They were being burned out of their sockets. The whole world was on fire, everything was a blazing, shimmering wet white, punctuated by the blinding red tracer strings from the front and mid-upper turrets.

Two million candlepower was being mirrored straight back into his eyes by a solid sheet of high ice.

"We've 'ad it!" shrieked Craik.

Frantically Irvine pushed the throttles hard against the stops. The huge white phosphorescent horror loomed in front, above and around them. It was like diving into a white hell.

"Off!" he yelled. "Garth, switch that bloody thing off!"

The instruments had gone muzzy and out-of-focus. He was helpless, blind—the gunners shouting over the intercom, and the engines roaring out at full power from the wings.

With all his strength, he heaved the stick right back. He was aware of a pinnacle of white fire just ahead. He twisted the control column to the left and kicked on full rudder.

F Freddie practically slid on its belly along the side of a miniature glacier down to the sea.

All the light suddenly went off. The firing ceased. Irvine levelled the wings.

Nobody said anything for a full five minutes.

"*Jesus* . . ." From the front turret, the Australian Brett was uttering the benediction for all of them, "if that's an iceberg, give me the *Groningen* any old time!"

The cruiser *Marlborough*, unscathed and sceptical after her trial with the Blind Bombsight, good-humouredly agreed at the Admiralty's request to impersonate the *Groningen* for the Liberator torpedo trials. Strickland, Ames and Carter, the only three crews who had completed their torpedo ground school training, carried out exercises against her, dropping four practice torpedoes each. Bearing in mind the inexperience of two of the crews, the trials were reasonably successful.

Strickland had devised (and Hart, the Engineering Officer, had constructed) an ingenious dropping sight designed especially for the *Groningen*'s five-hundred-feet length. Deflection was incorporated by an adjustable speed control. Each aircraft was fitted with one, and four hits were achieved on the *Marlborough* at full speed—which was more than even Strickland expected.

There was only one snag. The Liberator was so big and turned so slowly that nobody had a hope of attacking the *Groningen* "neat" as Ames put it—meaning with no anti-flak escort—and getting away with it. After dropping the four torpedoes, the Lib captains had three choices: turning port, turning starboard, or continuing straight ahead. All three alternatives exposed that big fat belly and vulnerable underside to the attentions a few feet away of the myriad cannon and multiple pom-pom guns that the *Groningen* possessed. Since the German ship was now skulking in Arctic waters well out of range of flak-busting Mosquitoes and Beaufighters, the torpedo Liberators had either to provide their own flak-busting escort or carry out a Kamikaze operation for which even Strickland would have difficulty working up enthusiasm.

Strickland was carrying out trials of the two anti-tank guns now fitted to fire through the nose of S Sugar. Rockets had also been fitted on rails under her wings but there were snags. The 57 millimetres, complete with their automatic loader and six-pounder ammunition, weighed almost a ton each, making Sugar very nose-heavy. It was therefore at present very tricky to recover from a rocket-firing dive and some modifications were necessary both to the guns and the rocket rails.

Meanwhile Strickland decided to pursue his other idea of anti-personnel bombs.

These were fifteen-pound fragmentation bombs attached to parachutes, fused to go off just above the ground or on impact. Since on exploding they sprayed small pieces of shrapnel over a wide area, accurately dropped in sufficient numbers, they could be guaranteed to kill or wound most of the almost unguarded Oerlikon and light ack-ack gunners who were the real menace in the *Groningen* and put the survivors off their aim when the torpedo-carrying Liberators attacked shortly afterwards.

Strickland's idea was that six Liberators should carry three hundred anti-personnel bombs on special racks in the bomb-bay, and after ascertaining the wind and working out the drift, should drop a carpet of these parachute bombs from four thousand feet, using as much cloud cover as was available. Two minutes after these eighteen hundred anti-personnel bombs had gone off, the three trained Liberator crews would each drop their four torpedoes, led by Strickland.

The idea received Air Vice-Marshall Nuttall's blessing at Group, the Equipment Section indented for and received the anti-personnel bombs. The armourers got busy on the special bomb-racks. Certain snags to fitting them in the bomb-bay reared their ugly heads and caused a week's delay, as the *Groningen* preyed on stragglers of Murmansk-bound convoys, and had already sent a further three to the bottom. There were other problems over replacement aircraft but suddenly, out of the blue, two new Liberators were diverted to 507 Squadron on the AOC's orders.

And then suddenly, everything was ready. Other operations were reduced to a minimum. The names of nine crews appeared on a special stand-by Mayfly—Strickland and the other two torpedo aircraft, Irvine detailed in the centre of the second vic formation of the parachute-bomb droppers.

Now there was nothing to do but wait for a sighting, and that meant fidgeting round Flights in the morning and hanging round the Mess in the afternoon. It was an almost totally monastic existence.

However, one day towards the end of March, he managed to take Emma Jones to the camp cinema. Whatever they had shared between them on that brief sad excursion to the Mowbray's cottage had not blossomed in the ensuing days. The fault was not entirely hers. Though she had not pushed herself forward in any way. He would have liked her to have been more forthcoming, to have taken the initiative. He shared the average pilot's fear of any real emotional attachment. Mowbray's example was in its own way an awful warning. Even he, not overburdened with understanding of the female, recognized that from now on Madeleine Mowbray's lot in life was like half a pair of scissors. If Emma had approached him, he'd have welcomed her. But she didn't and he didn't.

Then that Saturday he happened to see her eating late tea in the dining room. He felt himself possessed of a vague gnawing ache to be near her. He waited and waylaid her as she left the dining room.

"They tell me," he said, holding the glass doors open for her, "that there's a smashing flick on at the fleapit."

"Oh," she flushed, looked gratified, and asked, "What is it?"

He hadn't a clue of course. He didn't even know if there was a film on at all, though since Ensa Sylvia's reorganization the showings had been fairly constant and usually good. "I think it's *Captain Blood*. But does it matter?"

"Not in the slightest." She smiled. "But I hope it isn't."

"*Blood, Captain*?"

She nodded.

"Seen it?"

"No. And I'd rather not."

"Probably be Errol Flynn."

"Even so."

"But you'll come just the same? Good girl! See you in five minutes then. It'll have to be the early house. I'm on the Mayfly."

Her eyes clouded. But she made no further comment. She appeared punctually in five minutes. They walked briskly to the camp cinema and joined a modest queue waiting for the box office to open. The film was *The Road to Singapore*. Funny at least. That was something. Peter had already seen it. Maybe she had too. Because he had the feeling she was as aware of him as he was of her. They sat, holding hands, but keeping them modestly tucked out of sight, the way officers should, in that same warm companionable silence. That warm companionable silence was something like an escapist film in itself. When the lights went up in the concrete cinema he felt as if he was being wrenched from it like a warm womb.

The night outside was cold and blustery. Wraiths of cloud fled across a swelling moon. "I'd like to buy you a drink," he said, kissing her briefly in dark shadows outside the Officers' Mess, "but," he looked up at the sky, "I have a horrible hunch that tonight's the night."

His hunch was right. The inhabitants of Room 27 were woken at five-thirty, briefing at six-thirty. A Catalina flying boat on anti-U-boat patrol had sighted the *Groningen* at 71 North, 01 030 East. The nine Liberators took off at first light one after the other—no WAAFs, no padre, no Station band—

211

Strickland as usual going first in S Sugar and Irvine last in F Freddie.

The weather was just right. A curtain of cumulus at two thousand feet that would provide cover but sufficiently broken to keep an eye on the sea. The Liberators flew in loose formation at five hundred on top,* glittering white in the sunshine, skimming through the odd puff of cloud that stuck up above the others. As this identical weather continued further and further north, without showing the least tendency to change, the spirits of Irvine's crew brightened.

"Couldn't want anything better than this, Skipper," Henty suggested to Irvine, pouring him a cup of coffee from the big thermos.

"Quite looking forward to seeing the old girl again," said Miggs from the top turret.

Garth interrupted his navigation to interject, "Let's hope it's for the last time!"

In the rear turret, Mosco remained very quiet apart from enquiring whether there was any petrol leak from the tanks "*this* time, Kapitan."

"None, Mosco."

"Good, Kapitan!"

They passed into the Arctic Circle with the cloudscape below looking like an endless plateau of snow and ice. There was no chance really of German fighters, but Irvine could see the turrets moving restlessly in the aircraft around him—left, right, up and down—as the gunners searched the sky. In their own way the nine Liberators, the roundels blazoned on their white sides, flying steadily northwards with the thirty-six propellers cutting up the sunshine into pineapple chunks, had a carnival appearance that was immensely cheering. Everybody was around. Everybody was keeping an eye open for everyone else. Sometimes the Liberators flew so close, people waved to each other from the beam-gun positions. There was not the loneliness of the usual patrol, nor the tension of the last combined attack on the *Groningen* in the Skagerrak, when everyone knew they were being plotted on the radar and that German fighters would be awaiting them.

Thirty miles from the expected position of the *Groningen*,

* Five hundred feet above the tops of the cloud.

Strickland waggled his wings and dipped Sugar's nose. The other eight Liberators followed him through the cloud and towards the sea, levelling off at two thousand feet just below the overcast.

"Christ, Skipper! Look at them!" Jarman called out from the front turret. "That's going to make things difficult!"

The view down here was strange: the sea dark grey, but every now and again, right round the horizon, huge diamonds glinting as the sun through slatted cloud lit up an iceberg. The Radar reported a mass of blips—"too many to count". Sheltering up here, the *Groningen* would have considered herself quite safe from radar. The only hope of finding her was a visual sighting.

Tagged onto each other like a gaggle of white geese, still maintaining radio silence, the Liberators began the usual square search. More than an hour went by. There was still no sign of the ship. Irvine was just eating the last bully-beef sandwich, thinking it looked like another abortive sortie, when suddenly into his ears, very high and sharp, came Strickland's voice on the R/T, "There she is! Starboard! *Starboard!* Twenty degrees starboard!"

Irvine turned his head. Just to the left of a towering mountain of an iceberg was the now familiar grey-green shape, the camouflage spotted with drops of sunlight, a thin wisp of smoke leaking out of her two funnels. There was a glassy calm on the sea, and if the ship was moving, she was doing so extremely slowly, for there was no sign of a wash from her cruiser stern. The whole scene looked as though it was preserved in alcohol: motionless, other-worldly, some weird museum relic of Arctic exploration.

"Get into formation!"

Strickland was leading the two other torpedo bombers right down to the sea. In contrast, Dacres in A Able led the six parachute-bomb aircraft up through the cloud again, levelling off in the sunlight at four thousand feet.

"Sugar to Able." Strickland's voice again on the R/T. "Have you identified her on your radar?"

"Yes."

"So have we. That big iceberg makes things easier. Get into your two vic formations well west. Then make your attack.

With luck, you should get a visual of her through cloud. We'll circle on the deck till I reckon your bombs have done their stuff. Then we'll make our run-in. OK, Able?"

"OK, Sugar."

Back again, just above the cloud layer, Irvine throttled back behind Able and waited for the other two aircraft of the second vic to come up alongside him. Then, formed up tight, the two vics, one behind the other, moved towards the *Groningen*, now clearly identifiable on the radar at five miles. Through torn scraps of cloud could be seen the steely-grey sea, dotted here and there with white.

She hasn't seen us—that was what Irvine was hoping—as nearer and nearer to the ship they came. But a mile away, just as he caught sight of her superstructure through a gap in the cloud, all hell broke loose. Instead of white, the air had become grey and black and brown. He could smell smoke and cordite, and heard the rattle of shrapnel bursting against the Liberator's metal sides. Long red strings of Oerlikon shells like continuous strings of tiny sausages criss-crossed the air ahead. F Freddie began bucking and bouncing, twice nearly sliding into the Liberator on his left.

"Bomb-doors open!"

He heard the hydraulic pump whine. Far below them, a quarter of a mile ahead, was the *Groningen* beam on. Dacres was doing a good job of leading the Liberators, all six with their bomb-doors open now, right over the ship. Now over the R/T came his voice, "Release bombs!"

Irvine saw them begin to fall out of the bomb-bays of the three Liberators ahead like the beginnings of a storm of huge hailstones. And then suddenly, all happening in a fraction of a second, he saw that the parachute of one bomb had opened directly in front of him. Immediately he pulled up hard, and turned to starboard as far as he dared, after his own load had gone.

But the controls had not even begun to take effect on the position of the aircraft when the parachute-bomb, looking like a miniature aerial balloon, the bomb under the canopy swaying to and fro, in agonized slow motion came relentlessly towards F Freddie, bounced twice just beyond the front turret, rolled round the fuselage side, then abruptly stopped as its parachute strings became entangled in the pitot head* that jutted a small dagger into the slipstream outside, just four feet ahead of him.

Mesmerized, he watched it, the parachute fluttering, the strings winding, the small round bomb bouncing against the duralumin side. He could see the detonator, turned outwards at present but all the time rotating as the bomb twisted in the slipstream.

"Craik!" he shouted. Not that he expected his Engineer could do much about it. He had turned away now from the others, was heading for home for all he was worth, all thoughts of the *Groningen* swept clean out of his mind.

The Engineer came up from the catwalk, well pleased with himself and smiling. "All bombs gone and bomb-doors closed, Skipper!"

Then he saw. He saw the bomb doing its little dance, attached by its puppet-strings to the pitot head. The satisfaction left his face, and the gob-stopper eyes bulged.

"What can we do?" Irvine had opened his side window, stretched his left hand into the slipstream but there was not a hope of reaching the bomb from the cockpit. "We need something long. Some long metal tool . . ."

But Craik had no suggestions. Neither had Henty. Nor the others of the crew who came up to look at it. "Christ . . .!"

The fabric on the little parachute had begun to tear. Irvine saw silk threads waving frantically in the wind. The rent was lengthening. Soon the thing would be torn free by the slipstream.

He tried to think straight. If the bomb did go off here, they would all have had it. That would be the end of it. He had to get down to the sea. At any moment, he might have to ditch. Throttling back, he pushed the nose down, his eyes glued to the little swaying bomb.

The rent had increased. It was right against the rim of the parachute now. Then it was torn right across. For a few seconds, the silk strings held. Then they, too, began unravelling.

The next moment, through the open window, Irvine heard a *whoosh* followed by a banging against the side of the aircraft. For a moment, he thought they'd shaken the damned thing free, they'd escaped unscathed.

* The pitot head is a hollow pipe by means of which air pressure is measured and turned into an airspeed indication.

And then from the far rear of the aircraft, he heard an explosion. The Liberator tilted forward, then tried to crab sideways.

The bomb had exploded on the port tail fin. Rudder control had gone. He was having difficulty with the elevators. But at least they were still flying.

He picked up the microphone. "Mosco!"

There was no answer. He told Henty to go down to see if Mosco was all right and sent Craik to inspect the damage.

Garth came up with a course for home and an ETA in five hours' time. At least they were still in one piece, and the Liberator was flying reasonably well. With a bit of luck they'd get home all right.

He felt Henty touch him on the shoulder. "It's Mosco, Skipper."

"What's the matter?"

"He's . . . well, he's pretty bad."

In exasperation, Irvine shouted, "How bad?"

Henty shrugged his shoulders. "The thing . . . it went off on the port tailplane. In the turret, Mosco—"

"Where's the First Aid kit?"

In a fury, he beckoned Henty back into the right-hand seat and clambered out onto the flight deck. Brett produced the First Aid box from the side of the radio, and holding it in his hand, he made his way to the back of the aircraft.

Just stepping up from the cakewalk at the end of the bomb-bay, he bumped into Craik on his way back.

"Well?" he asked the Engineer.

"Port rudder and elevators are in a bit of a mess, Skipper."

"How's Mosco?"

"Mosco?"

Irvine pushed past him. He could feel that hollow feeling in the pit of his stomach. He was back five months in time, struggling down to the rear turret, there just to find those empty leather gauntlets on the breeches of the guns.

The doors of the rear turret were open. And at least he could see the Rear Gunner inside.

"Mosco?"

The great green bundle in its Sidcot flying suit fell heavily backwards into his arms. He saw a thin trickle of blood come out of the mouth. But the eyes were open and moving, and he could hear the stentorian snorts of breathing. At least the Pole was alive.

"Mosco?"

The head flopped sideways onto Irvine's shoulder. The eyes had steadied now, and were looking at him. Grey-green eyes, bloodshot in the corners, watering heavily.

"You all right?"

The lips were trying to say something. Bubbles of saliva began oozing down the grey chin.

"Are you hurt?"

The head started nodding.

"Can you tell me where you're hurt?"

The Pole pressed forward, began holding his side.

"Better get you out of the turret, Mosco."

Irvine took hold of the Pole's shoulders and tried to pull. "Can you push, Mosco?"

The pilot could feel some feeble pressure being applied as from outside the turret he sweated and heaved. "Can't you do a bit better than that?"

He tried again. "Are you in pain?"

"A leedle, Kapitan."

"If I gave you morphine now, I'd never get you out of the turret. Come on, let's have another go!"

Again, he heaved and pulled. The big green bundle moved a little out of the perspex-and-steel prison, then sank back inside again.

"Come on, Mosco! Push!"

There was a little paroxysm of movement and vibration. Then stillness again, except for heavy breathing.

"*Push!* With your feet!"

Again, but weaker, came a shudder and a scrabbling. The tail swung to and fro in sudden uneven air. I've got to get him out quick and see what Henty's up to, Irvine thought. All the pent-up foreboding and irritation and strain exploded inside him, as he shook the green body of the Pole and said, "Mosco, you're not trying! Make an effort!"

The head fell right back now. The mouth opened. Irvine could see the skin was an alabaster colour like on the tops of tombs. Little drops of sweat coursed down the lined cheeks.

The grey-green hound-dog eyes were right up in the corners of their sockets, and the look in them was so strange. Not like any look Irvine had ever seen. Not sardonic, no. Not sad either, because in some odd way, under all that bloodshot watering, it was as though they were also smiling. Affectionate rather than reproachful.

"*Mosco!*"

The eyes had glazed over. The ungainly body rested like a heavy rock against him. The mouth had fallen wide open. But there was no movement, no breathing. Only the whistling of the wind through the beam gun position, the sudden scream of the hydraulic pump, and, far away, the sound of someone thumping down the bomb-bay cakewalk, and a few seconds later there was Craik back again.

"Need a hand, Skipper?"

He shook his head. As gently as he could, he laid Mosco's head and shoulders down on the metal floor of the aircraft—half in, half out of the turret. Then he went up front and took over from Henty.

It was night by the time they landed. All the other aircraft were safely back. Whether the *Groningen* had been hit by the torpedoes was a matter of conjecture. At the last moment, the captain ("wily devil, Leitzen," said Strickland) had turned bow on to face them as they came at him, presenting a minute target. Then there was some argument going on that two torpedoes were defective and whether three had been dropped too high and broken up on touching the water.

The *Groningen* had certainly been afloat when the last aircraft left. But Strickland remained convinced she'd been badly damaged. The parachute-bombs had caused real havoc. "I wouldn't be surprised," Strickland said, "if a couple or more went down her funnel or into her magazine. Even if she does make it back home, she'll be out of action for months. And stuck in a Norwegian fjord, she'll be a sitting duck for us!"

He was sorry when Irvine told him about Flight-Lieutenant Moscovich. "Poor old Mosco! But he had a good, long innings. No chicken, was he? And killed in action against the *Groningen*, Peter . . . what better way to go?"

218

FIFTEEN

IRVINE was given a young Canadian timber-cutter called Connally out of the aircrew pool as replacement Rear Gunner—small, tough, wiry, totally different from Mosco. A week after the Pole's death, his crew was top of the Mayfly again, and just after lunch he was walking over to the Operations Block for briefing when the squadron Hillman van drew up beside him, slowed, stopped, and Strickland's head emerged out of the driver's window.

"Peter . . . could you pop into my office before going out to your aircraft?"

Irvine's heart sank. "Of course."

Christ, he thought, they've found the *Groningen*! I'm going to get a special pep-talk to inspire me before I go! But if that was the case, surely Strickland would be rarin' to go himself? As Irvine manoeuvred his way round the brick-and-concrete blast walls and entered the gloomy corridor behind, he looked out for further portents: the sound of clacking teleprinters, people rushing up and down, telephones ringing.

Nothing! Quiet as the grave! He breathed a sigh of relief.

Are all people like this, he thought, as he pushed open the door and saw Brackenbury's face, pale as gin, sorting through his Intelligence reports, or is it just me? If they had found the bloody ship, because of my role as aircraft captain in charge of eight other lives, I would be required to put a great big smile on my face and rub my hands together and give every appearance of straining at the leash. And now because it's only a stooge patrol off the Skagerrak again, already taped up on the big map, I have room for another worry because I see there's no aircraft against my name, and it'll be my luck to get M Mother, the most temperamental Liberator of the lot. F Freddie was still on the Q Form and in the hangar, awaiting Emma Jones' successful completion of her Griselda trick of weaving a new rear turret and port tailplane out of a lot of old iron.

Nothing much in the briefing. Met were giving a fair amount of cloud. Half way through Brackenbury's sermon on flak and fighters, the WAAF Operations Sergeant chalked up S in the empty aircraft space beside his name: S Sugar, Strickland's aircraft, still the best Liberator on the squadron.

The initial lift at seeing it was almost immediately replaced by suspicion. Why was he getting it? Was this something to do with Strickland wanting him to pop into his office? Why did he want to see him before take-off?

He sat up front with the WAAF driver pondering that same question as she drove round the perimeter track and stopped outside the squadron offices. The crew somersaulted out to get their parachutes from the lockers in the crew room.

"Get mine, would you?" Irvine asked Henty. "Strickland wants a word with me."

Then he knocked on the door of the Wing-Commander's office, went inside and saluted.

"Ah, Peter! Sorry to drag you in before take-off."

"That's all right, sir."

"It's just something I know you'd want to do—" Strickland gave a little nod of his head towards the far left-hand corner of his desk "—for Mosco."

Irvine's eyes followed the direction of the nod and saw sticking up amongst the papers and to one side of the wire in-tray what looked like a small Grecian urn of a pale marble colour with two handles on either side of its tapering shape and a round convoluted top. He stared at it, uncomprehending. So out of place, so alien in its environment.

"As you know, at his own request, Mosco was cremated—"

Now he understood. The look of incomprehension was replaced by one of mesmerized fascination. Inside there, compressed into that tiny incongruous shape, was that barrage-balloon bulk, that big grey face and those hound-dog grey-green eyes. Reduced to miniature-size, contained, the rasping croaky voice silenced.

"And the poor old chap made one other request. Something we can well understand . . . far from home and exiled as he was.

220

Something we'd be only too glad and honoured to do for him. Especially you, Peter, his captain—"

Strickland leaned over his desk, picked up the urn and handed it over to Irvine.

"He asked for his ashes to be spread over Poland."

"Poland!"

"His homeland. The place of his birth. The country whose frontiers we entered the war to defend."

"But I'm on a Skagerrak patrol!"

"Just before you start that, you can slip down the Kattegat to Bornholm. That's where the U-boat training ground is, and you can see what's going on and bomb any likely target and have a go with the 57 millimetres too. We've got them working now. Then you can nip across the few miles to the north Polish coast, and do what Mosco asks."

"But it's daylight!"

"Not daylight, Peter. Dusk."

"There's half a dozen fighter stations—"

"Keep down on the deck and you'll be all right. Climb to a couple of thousand, open up your side-window, and perhaps say a prayer as you empty the urn and scatter his ashes."

"Surely Group—"

"I've telephoned them. The AOC agrees. You'll have brought Mosco back to the land of his fathers, Peter. There'll be plenty of time afterwards to go to the Skagerrak and do your patrol."

His crew were already in the van when he left the squadron offices.

"What's that you're carrying, Skipper?" Henty asked.

A complete silence fell after he told them that lasted, apart from monosyllabic orders and responses to checks and drills, till they were well into the Kattegat, hugging the beaches of the Swedish west coast and trying to look like a neutral puff of cloud in the darkening violet light of early evening.

But the Swedes were not fooled. They started sending up what looked like illuminated balls connected to chains, red, green and yellow, strung out ahead and exploding one after the other like fireworks on Guy Fawkes night. None of it was particularly near the aircraft but there were indignant remarks over the intercom that this hostile behaviour hardly became a country that wasn't even in the war.

221

"Fighters now, Skipper," Miggs reported. "Three of them dead behind us."

"Can you see them, Rear Gunner?"

"I can see the bastards, Skipper," Connally said.

"What are they doing?"

"Following us."

"What are they?"

"Me 109s."

"How much longer before the north Polish coast, Navigator?"

"Thirty minutes, Skipper."

Irvine pushed the throttles forward, and took the Liberator down within inches of the sea. He had instructed his crew to look out for likely targets to drop their bombs on, but if anybody saw anything, nobody reported it to him. He had his hands full simply flying the aircraft, hearing over the intercom an almost continuous stream of sightings of fighters above them coupled with the calling from the front turret of flak bursts ahead. Twice, Me 109s came down and attacked, sprays of silver tracer spreading fanwise above them, answered by inconclusive chattering from Sugar's .5s.

Christ, Irvine thought, I can't fight my way through this lot simply to drop Mosco's ashes over his native country! What's the point of it? At this rate we're not going to get anywhere near Poland, and it wouldn't be any comfort to Mosco, simply coming down in the Kattegat along with the rest of us!

After one particularly close attack when an Me 109 skimmed practically over the top of the fuselage, he had actually begun wrenching the Liberator round to go back—but he stopped himself. He owed it to Mosco. Britain owed it to Mosco. Mosco had never let up in his fight against the Third Reich, he deserved the funeral honour of return to his homeland. RIP, wasn't that what they said? Mosco's spirit would certainly never rest unless his request was carried out.

"Bornholm, Skipper," Garth called out.

They were pretty well there! Only another fifteen minutes, and all the time it was getting darker. Down here, the sea was black as ink. It was only up in the sky that there was light— pale as a butterfly's wing. Darkness falls from the air, he thought —what a load of crap, what a snare to believe in and turn you into German-fighter-fodder! Darkness works its way from the ground upwards, mercifully covering you over with its arms . . .

"Me 109 nine o'clock high! Attacking! Turn left, Skipper! *Left!*"

He slewed the Liberator round, his port wing-tip practically touching the sea. As far as the U-boats down below were concerned, they could carry on training. His eyes were totally occupied with the radio altimeter—the needle flickering at twenty-five feet—and the artificial horizon to keep him from turning upside down and sideways. As he often did, he began counting: one, two, three, four, five . . . fifteen . . . thirty seconds and we're still alive! Still in one piece and a couple of miles closer! One, two, three, four five . . .

"Polish coast ten miles ahead, Skipper!"

"Don't take me anywhere near a town!"

"This course should be all right."

Sixty, seventy, ninety . . . now he thought he could just see a curved line on the horizon ahead. Sweat was forming on his forehead and running down into his eyes. His arms ached with jinking and turning so low down. It was last light now, the dying of the day. Just enough illumination to make quite sure he was well over the fields and hills of Poland, to do the job properly. The right time for a funeral, that sad stillness over everything, and the stars very faintly beginning to come out in the sky.

"Coast, Skipper!"

Through the sides of his eyes, he was aware of the dark shapes of rocks. He pulled back on the stick. S Sugar began a power climb which he eased off at two thousand feet and levelled off.

Then he opened his side window. Looking up, he saw no sign of fighters. No flak was coming up from below. Down there he could just see faint grey ghosts of houses, the black skin of forest covering a hill. He told Craik to get the urn from its place of safety, propped between the radio spares.

"Here you are, Skipper!"

He held the urn in his hands. It felt very cold. Was it marble, he wondered. More likely alabaster. Should he say something, an appreciation of Mosco or a prayer? It seemed so heartless, just dropping the ashes out . . .

He pressed the button of his microphone. "We're flying over

223

Mosco's homeland now. From all of us who knew him and flew with him, I'm saying goodbye."

Telling Henty to fly straight and level, he lifted the urn up towards the open window, and then out into the slipstream. All round the cockpit, the little green phosphorescent numbers on the instruments glowed like candles.

Taking hold of the top of the urn, gently he began raising it.

There was a sudden *whoosh*. It was as though out of the little urn a genie had escaped, inches thin at the bottom, not disappearing downwards but being sucked back into the aircraft, a great, grey, smoke-scented cloud, swollen twice, no, three times life-size, whirling round the cockpit, covering everything with a sort of gritty ectoplasm, ash falling everywhere, covering everything, choking eyes, nose, ears, drowning them in ashes, and above the sound of the engines and the whistling of the wind through the open side window, it was as though there was Mosco's voice as dry as his dust, "Some day I write a book about the RAF . . . a *fonny* book!"

"A *fonny* book, that's what he used to say, old Mosco." Peter Irvine picked up a pebble from the shore and hurled it into the winking glassy waves. They were walking along the shore. The tide had just turned and was running out in a strong, smooth ebb. "He was going to write a fonny book," Peter hurled another pebble, "about the RAF."

"I expect he could have," Emma replied slowly and carefully like someone picking her way on a rocky shore barefoot.

This time, Peter Irvine had most definitely of his own free will and out of his most urgent necessity contacted her. He needed her. Christ, how he needed her. He couldn't see her at breakfast in the Mess, though he'd hung around the dining room for over an hour. Then, giving up any idea of making it look like a casual meeting, he'd telephoned her at her office in the Stores. Somehow without undue persuasion she'd wangled the afternoon off. A fine sunny one too, though that didn't make any difference to Irvine. The fragile sun had insufficient power to warm him. He felt chilled to the marrow, his flesh half dead, his blood congealed. His skin crawled with Mosco's ashes. He could feel them in his eyes, up his nose, in his mouth. God help him, he could *taste* Mosco! He'd bathed three times

224

since the night before. He'd washed his hair, he'd pared his nails, he'd rinsed his eyes, he'd scrubbed his teeth a dozen times. But still they seemed to grit. Probably by now they gritted on too much toothpaste. But now, he knew, shuddering, that it was Mosco. Christ!

"I doubt it. I doubt if anything he wrote would be funny," Irvine went on to Emma irritably. "Mosco had very little sense of humour."

"Perhaps he had a different sense of humour?"

He shook his head. "Mosco never laughed. Never out loud." Irvine strode on ahead. The curve of beach gave out here. A horn of rocky land covered with fir trees emerged from the woods behind and poked thirty yards or so into the sea. The path they were following wound round it, into the woodland itself. There was a small boulder-strewn slope to climb. Irvine stopped and stretched out his hand to help Emma up. He kept hold of her hand as they began to wander along the path. Their steps sounded soft and muffled. The path was mushy with last year's leaves. "Mosco had such a miserable life," he exclaimed indignantly.

"You don't know that."

"I do. *And* I know he had nothing to laugh about. Ever. Except last night. Yes, last night. That was something. I think even Mosco might have laughed about that." He suddenly began to laugh himself, or was it crying? He didn't know. All he knew was that the words came tumbling out.

He was aware that without interrupting him, Emma Jones sat herself on a fallen log, sitting upright as if on a Victorian sofa, hands folded in her lap, staring up at him, her eyes enormous. That at some point, he subsided on the log beside her, and took her hands in his. He squeezed them from time to time to punctuate his account. But when he came to the part where Mosco's ashes blew back all over him he dropped her hands to gesticulate, while tears of laughter and horror and hysteria ran down his cheeks.

She didn't make any comment at all from start to finish. But when the last words dribbled out of his mouth, she threw her arms round him, kissing his lips, his eyes, his nose, his forehead, his hair, wildly, abandonedly, almost as if putting her life-giving lips where the dead ashes had been.

225

He kissed her back, at first gratefully then feeling his body tauten and stiffen with desire as if indeed filled with some life-giving elixir.

"I love you, Emma." He cupped her face in his hands, kissing her passionately. "Oh God, I love you." His voice sounded a little theatrical, a little like a stranger's, but the sentiment was real. The lines his own.

He felt an urge to unbutton the top of her jacket. But it was an urge he recognized as unworthy, unseemly and unlikely to succeed. So he got up and pulled her to her feet. He felt refreshed and purged. He regarded her flushed face affectionately. "I really do love you, Emma. I've never met anyone like you before. D'you feel the same, d'you think?"

She smiled up at him looking tremulous, doubtful, pleased, excited. Slowly she nodded.

"Of course," he said, "we couldn't do anything about it while the war's on. But . . . later . . . when it's over . . . you and me . . ." He put his arm round her shoulders. Her head rested just below his chin. Her hair smelled sweet. Sunlight glittered down between the mesh of unleafed twigs. After a while, the path wound round and back to the shore again. The sea glinted. In a little sheltered hollow just before the beach, there was a small south-facing glade sheltered by hazel trees from the prevailing wind. It was filled with snowdrops. The odd primrose and a few early violets poked through. Their delicate scent mingled with the graveyard smell of the moist earth and dead leaves and the sharp tang of the sea, to give a distant, unharrowing funeral smell. He bent down and picked a couple of the snowdrops. He held them in his hand as they walked by the waves and over the rocks again. It seemed fitting then to toss them into the sea. He watched them half submerge.

"Good type, old Mosco," he said, as miraculously the memory of Mosco, like the flowers, went gently ebbing away to some distant shore.

"Contact . . . fifteen miles." Miggs' voice from the radar. "Forty degrees to starboard."

"Thank you, Radar."

"Only a small one, Skipper."

"Turning starboard! All guns on *fire*!"

"A rock, I reckon."

"All the same, better investigate."

"Or a trawler."

"Are we centred on it?"

"Yes, sir . . . at fourteen miles."

After the iceberg incident, all his Radar Operators were cautious over contacts. The Norwegian coast was littered with rocks and tiny islands, and it was perfectly true that the sudden intense excitement of homing on a blip usually fizzled out into a craggy excrescence.

Today's trip was Irvine's first operation carrying four torpedoes and a Leigh Light. The take-off had been even more excruciating than usual—what with the 600-pound light on the wing that needed almost full right aileron trim to compensate, and the added weight of the seven accumulators and generator to illuminate it.

"Twelve miles, sir."

Instead of a rock, this blip on the radar might be a Norwegian fishing boat. Then the feeling inside the aircraft was totally different. Tiny, defenceless, a *petite amie*—often with the crew's arms outstretched and waving. Christ, what a marvellous feeling of pride! The long shadow of the Liberator's wings on the sea, elongated like a spear towards the enemy coast, the black antennae of the silent guns moving away from the trawler and up into the sky towards anything that dared approach it.

Under the shadow of my wings—curl up, feel safe, be at peace. Irvine would circle the ship, opening his side window, wave furiously. The crew would rush to the beam gun positions and wave.

And that was the strange contradiction of it all—the extraordinary warmth that flowed from being a protector. It was the same when the Liberators were going off in formation on one of Strickland's my-idea-and-I-think-it's-a-very-good-idea efforts to sink the *Groningen*. Flying tight together, prickly with guns, the fuselages white as saints' haloes under the glittering sun, how glorious it was to be with them! Onward, Christian soldiers—onward, *onward*! They moved so beautifully, so effortlessly, their propellers sweetly turning. They flew so purposefully, so confidently, so totally righteously! What a privilege it was to be in their company! All of a sudden you felt ten miles high. Watching them, you couldn't believe that M Mother, whose skin you could practically touch on your left, was ginger-haired Linton, pale and gangling. Or that on your right was not K King but the quiet Dacres or that ahead was really Mason, whom you disliked, not A Able. Only the leader, Strickland, and S Sugar, way out ahead, solid and shining, calling out "Closer, chaps, closer!" were totally fused into one pulsating personality.

"Twelve miles . . . still dead ahead. But it'll be nothing, Skipper, nothing . . ."

"Switch off the radar."

If it was anything, they should be able to see it visually. That was another fly in Strickland's ointment to dispose of the *Groningen*. Since radar sends out a signal and measures the echo's time of going out and return, this can be listened to like any other radio if you know the wavelength. Which now the Germans did from a bomber that had crashed intact. All they had to do was to listen on the ten-centimetre band on their Metox receiver, and they would get all the warning they needed of an aircraft attack. All thirty-six of the *Groningen*'s guns— heavies, Oerlikons, multiple pom-poms—would not only be pointing in their direction if they kept the radar on, the gunners would actually have their fingers on the triggers.

"Keep a sharp lookout, chaps!"

It was one of those dull, grey afternoons, the sky puffy with ragged cloud. They were past the fifth hour of their patrol off the north Norwegian coast. Twenty minutes more, and they would be on their way home. With luck, they should be able to land at Kilcreggan before last light.

Irvine pushed the nose of F Freddie down towards the sea. Down low, you couldn't be seen so far away. Against that was the fact that you couldn't see so far either. He levelled off at three hundred feet. There was a beam wind and it was bumpy. Down below he could see the tongues of the white caps lapping southwards.

There was no particular excitement. Beside him, Henty broke off a piece of plain Bourneville chocolate and put it in his mouth. Craik was filling in his hourly instrument readings. Miggs had left the radar and was standing between the pilots gazing out of the windscreen and humming *Annie Laurie*.

228

And then there was a sudden click as a microphone was switched on.

"Rear Gunner to Captain."

The Canadian Connally was calling him.

"Yes?"

"I can see a ship."

"Trawler?"

"Bigger."

"*How* big?"

"Very big."

"How many funnels?"

"Two."

"Stern?"

"Cruiser."

Oh God, Irvine thought. Sweet Jesus Christ! "Where?"

"Port beam."

"Turning port."

"Going behind us now."

"How far?" He tipped the Liberator up on her port wing. "*How far?*"

"I—"

There was a sudden explosion that almost tipped F Freddie on its back. A dirty blob of brown smudged the nearest white cumulus.

"Too bloody near!" Henty said.

And then, from the rear turret, like an announcement from the sepulchre of a cathedral, "Captain . . . it's the *Groningen*!"

Another brown blob appeared in front of their nose—then another and another. Irvine kicked the Liberator right round. He had seen the long camouflaged shape and the two raked funnels far too distinctly for him to be able to nurse any illusion. It was the *Groningen* all right and less than two miles away. Pursued by brown blobs, he scuttled out of range.

"Trembath!" He pulled at the sleeve of the Radio Officer behind him. "Get an accurate position from the Navigator. Then send a signal. *Groningen* sighted course south, speed twenty-five knots. And give our position."

That part was easy. The next part was easy too: continue shadowing till the latest possible time, giving a succession of position reports.

"Craik," he said. "Bring the boost back to −3, revs to 1700."

The Engineer leaned over and brought the throttle levers gently back, then touched the rpm switches. The speed dropped back. The Liberator hung from its propellers like a bat in a belfry on the afternoon air.

"Where is she, Rear Gunner?"

"Behind us. You're going away!"

The next part—that was the real difficulty. What was he going to do now?

There were no specific instructions issued to 507 crews. Because of the continuously changing nature of their operational work none could be. It was left up to the Captain to do what he thought best—within reason. If he saw the *Tirpitz* for instance, Command would not expect him to do other than report her position. He was not Japanese. He could not be expected to commit hara-kiri. All attacks had to have a reasonable chance of survival. Otherwise it wasn't fair to his crew. Only too well did he remember poor Bertie Maltravers and Guilonard's crew.

The *Groningen* had certainly less armament than the *Tirpitz*. But now the gunners were all alert, what chance had a big fat Liberator with no anti-flak support to get within miles of dropping its four torpedoes?

"Still behind us, Captain . . . four miles now."

"Thank you, Rear Gunner."

"When do we turn to attack?"

Irvine clicked on his microphone but said nothing. Instead he tugged at the Wireless Operator's sleeve again. "Got that position through?"

"Not yet."

"What's the trouble?"

"Static. Can't raise 'em!"

Well, that solved one thing. He turned back to address his microphone. "Trembath hasn't got the sighting report through yet. We can't attack till then. When he does, if we attack in daylight, the chances of us dropping our torpedoes to any effect are small, and of getting away with it nil. Because of that, I think everyone in the crew should have a say in what we do."

The real democratic process, even in war. Would any historian, he wondered, ever give a thought to this possibility? Of having a vote amongst a crew, as though they were in the

230

House of Commons, as to whether they should undertake a suicide attack or not?

"Captain . . . I say go. *Go now!*"

"Thank you, Rear Gunner. Garth?"

"No. Not a chance."

"Thank you. Craik?"

"No."

Now the two Aussies, Brett in the mid-upper turret, Jarman in the front. Two yeses in quick succession.

"Henty?"

"Not yet."

"Trembath?"

"Wait."

It looked a certainty now. Just Miggs left, and he could surely be relied on.

"I say attack before we lose her!"

Irvine paused to take a deep breath. Of course Miggs these days was different—quieter, less extrovert. Altogether more responsible, Irvine had thought—as satisfied with the news as Craik when his Engineer had informed him that Miggs' big romance with Deirdre Winter was off.

So all in all, this vote came as a shock.

"Thank you, Miggs. Thank you very much indeed," Irvine said at last. "That makes it even. Four yeses, four noes." He felt a pull at his sleeve from the Radio. "Got an R, Skipper. Message received and understood."

"Trembath has just told me Base have got our sighting report. So what we do now depends on my vote."

The worst thing that could have happened. He needn't have had a vote at all—except it did show he had all their interests at heart. Well, he had those all right even closer to his heart than they reckoned, and a good deal closer apparently than they had them to their own hearts. Rather crossly, he said into the microphone, "Tactically, I think it would be a mistake to attack now. We've got no anti-flak . . . no cover. They'd just shoot us down and then scarper and disappear. No, we must shadow till our endurance is up. Then, when night falls, we'll make a torpedo attack under cover of darkness with the Leigh Light."

Nobody said anything. The shadowing was resumed in a large

231

circle all round the ship. Every now and again, as if to remind him of her fire-power, the *Groningen*'s gunners planted a blob of brown in front of his nose.

The sun sank into the sea in a blaze of scarlet. The cloud gradually grew greyer, then turned black. One by one, the stars came out. The superstructure of the ship merged with the night, but her wash could still be seen. There was no sign yet of a relieving aeroplane to shadow, though a signal had said that two were on the way.

Twenty minutes before what Garth had told him was the latest time he could turn for home, Irvine said, "Well, now we go in! Everyone . . . action stations!"

He turned the Liberator towards the centre of the circle they had been flying.

"See her, Front Gunner?"

"No, sir."

"Mid-upper?"

"No."

His second pilot pointed. "Isn't that her over there, sir?"

"I can't see anything."

"No, I don't think it is." Irvine paused. "Anyone see her?"

Nobody could.

"Oh well, better have the radar on, Miggs—"

There was two minutes' silence as Miggs settled himself behind the screen.

"Radar?"

"Yes, sir?"

"Got her yet?"

"Don't think the set has warmed up yet."

Another two minutes passed.

"Radar?"

"Nothing, no. The brilliance is down. Nothing to worry about."

Two more minutes passed.

"Radar?"

"The Gain is down. Not to worry! I've got my screwdriver out."

Two minutes later, the radar was in pieces. Back in his old form, Miggs' smiling face popped up front to say, "I'll get it fixed in a jiffy, Skipper!"

232

From the windscreen nothing could be seen except blackness. Ten minutes later, it began to rain.

For the next forty minutes in the darkness, they scurried this way and that. Someone saw "something white", a shadow was reported on the starboard beam, the Front Gunner shouted "There she is!"

Then the rain turned electric. Wriggling phosphorescent snakes crawled down the windscreens. The propellers became four spinning Catherine wheels, sparkling and fizzing with the static of St Elmo's fire. Trapped in the wet cave of the storm, they turned left, right, north, south—the heavy silence that now hung over the aeroplane punctuated by brief bright gasps from Miggs at the radar. "Couple more minutes, Skipper, and she'll be hunky-dory!"

Finally, nose in his fuel charts, Craik proclaimed "We've 'ad it!"

By which was intended that they now had insufficient petrol to reach home.

As Irvine swung F Freddie's nose round to a south-south-westerly course, he declared, "The relieving aircraft will have the *Groningen* on their radars now."

Both he and Craik were wrong. F Freddie landed in Kilcreggan with nothing actually showing on the sight gauges, but thirty gallons still in the tanks. And the relieving aircraft did *not* find the *Groningen*. She had slipped away under the rain-curtain, merging with the myriad islands.

Irvine had expected Strickland to be furious and there he was perfectly right. Why hadn't he attacked straightaway, he asked Irvine in Operations. He carried four torpedoes for the express purpose of sending such as the *Groningen* down to the bottom. Immediately, without batting an eyelid, without a second thought.

"What are you made of?" he demanded. "What *are* you?"

It was a difficult question to answer, and Irvine did not try to answer it.

In the bar that evening, it was answered for him. It had been fairly quiet—just Mason and Carter and one or two others. They were, Irvine thought, fairly cool, fairly guarded. In the circumstances, he would have expected them to ask about the

233

Groningen, what did she look like, the accuracy of her guns.

But nobody made any mention. Only the Doc asked what had happened. Irvine did not feel like giving him anything but a short and clipped account. Then he joined Emma Jones over by the window and they began talking about how to hitch a lift together next day into Blairculloch, the railway terminal.

The place began to fill up. There had been a film show down at the Station cinema. Awful according to Rory Ames and everyone was crowding in for a drink to get the taste of it out of their mouths.

The place became so crowded and the air so thick with cigarette smoke that Irvine did not see Strickland come in. He was just finalizing the plans for the morning with Emma when he heard the piano and looked up.

Crackers was showing off with *In the Mood*, his fingers scurrying like white mice over the keyboard.

Nothing serious. Serious sing-songs only occurred after tragedies. Irvine looked down again.

In the Mood gave way to the *Girl in the Alice Blue Gown*. Singing started softly, sporadically.

And then all of a sudden, halfway through saying to Emma, "Well, that's fixed then, we'll—" Irvine was aware that a group had formed round them.

They were holding their tankards in their hands, standing in a semi-circle, looking at him.

He raised his eyes, Carter on the left, Rory Ames, Mason, even Dacres—he looked from one to the other of them. Just behind one of the younger second pilots was Strickland.

Muffled by the wall of bodies, the piano came through plaintively, quiet as a sigh.

"Goodnight, ladies . . . goodnight, ladies . . ."

They had started singing, beating time up and down with their tankards.

"Goodnight ladies . . ."

Emma had already got up and was moving to the door. Just for a few more seconds, he sat there stunned, hypnotized by the look in their eyes, trying to gauge what it was. Contempt? Disappointment? Fury? Fear?

The *Groningen* was still in the land of the living. Now he had failed, others would be called. Who would be the next to crucify

himself? Could it be Ames? Could it be Mason? Could it be—
Irvine suddenly saw what each one was thinking—. . . *could it
be me?*

"Goodnight, ladies . . ."

He got up, his cheeks burning. Still holding his tankard,
slowly he began to walk behind Emma to the door. Every step
he took, he felt like running. He felt like rushing out of the bar,
out of the Mess, out of the Station—anywhere to get away. He
slowed his step even more. He looked at Ames, turned his head
and looked at Dacres, turned his head and looked at Mason.
Just before he reached the door, he turned his head right round
and looked at Strickland.

There was dead silence. Then he opened the door and said
in a casual matter-of-fact way, "Hang on, Emma! I'm coming
with you."

Together they went into the Ladies' Room as though nothing
had happened. Someone had found some snowdrops and had
put them in a vase on the side table. They went over and sat
side by side on the chintz sofa. Irvine said, "Now where were
we exactly?"

Next door, the silence still continued. It was minutes before
the piano sounded, longer still till the singing of the 507 anthem
started.

"An airman told me before he died . . ."

It came loudly, frenziedly, with the oil-less screech of metal
on metal, the agony of a job still waiting to be done.

". . . round and round went the bloody great wheel,
    In and out went the prick of steel . . ."

235

SIXTEEN

"LMF, Doc! Lack of Moral Fibre! Irvine's got to go!"

Flint sighed. The RAF took these young men (no compulsion, all volunteers), spent time and money training them, excused them discipline, parades, bullshit, turned a blind eye to anything they got up to—drink, women, breaking up the Mess—gave them decorations and honours, made them the spoiled darlings of the nation . . .

On one condition.

But if they broke their contract on that it meant demotion down to the ranks, an experienced operational pilot ending up as an ACH. Would future historians, Flint wondered, continuing writing the quite unnecessary directive on his desk simply to give himself time to think, ever give thought to the three thousand young men every year (that figure was kept a deadly secret) who found they could not keep their side of the contract; they could not continue flying.

"Be with you in a tick, Guy. Just want to finish this off."

The doctor did not want a head-on clash with Strickland. Several times over the past months he had been near it. Farquhar had finished his tour, and Flint had insisted on his going on rest, in spite of Strickland's protests at losing such an experienced captain. A feud between squadron CO and squadron doctor—he had seen several fatal examples—inevitably resulted in squadron morale sinking to rock-bottom. The only solution was the posting of one of them—almost invariably the doctor.

Flint came to the end of the directive. He put down his pen. Reluctantly he looked up.

"I've got a very good opinion of Peter Irvine."

"So *had* I."

"And now he's pretty experienced. Over thirty ops."

"During which he's achieved bugger-all!"

"Tell me, Guy—"

Flint paused. It was like a chess game. One false move and it'll be check-mate.

"—who on the squadron *has* achieved anything?"

The doctor was aware that that one was very, very close. He saw the scar on Strickland's left cheekbone whiten. "Nobody's been given the opportunity."

"But neither has Irvine."

"He was given the *Groningen* on a plate!"

"*On a plate?* The report I read—"

"And he was too scared to go in!"

There was another pause. Then Flint said, "Guilonard went in."

"That was different."

"But nobody knows what *happened* in Guilonard's attack!"

"Irvine," Strickland said, speaking slowly and distinctly, "broke cloud only a couple of miles from the *Groningen*. He was flying low. He hadn't been spotted. All he had to do was to fly towards her for another forty seconds and—"

"During which, like Guilonard, he would certainly have been shot down!"

"—drop his four fish and finish the whole thing off for all of us."

"So LMF is Irvine's punishment for not attacking the *Groningen*?"

"Not only does he not attack her. He loses her!"

"He can't be blamed for his radar going wrong."

"Every bloody trip he's sent on *something* goes wrong!"

"I've read all his intelligence reports and I don't agree with you."

"All Irvine does is think about girls."

"Girls?"

"He and that Jones girl are far too thick."

"So he's to be made an example of."

"I suppose you could call it that."

"You'd squeeze some use even out of his disgrace."

"You could put it like that, too, I suppose."

"But suppose you're wrong?"

"Doc, I *know* I'm right."

237

"Like you know what happened to Guilonard?"

"Like I know what happened to Mowbray!" Strickland snapped back at him. "I told you something would have to be done."

"He was shot down by night-fighters!"

"He wouldn't have been if he'd kept right down on the water." Strickland leaned right across the desk. "But his George was U/S. And Mowbray's instrument flying—"

"You never liked Edward."

"Like? Dislike? This isn't a girls' school!"

"He menaced your leadership."

"How?"

"He was always contradicting you."

"He was my Devil's Advocate. All squadrons should have one."

"Except 507."

"Because it has a Devil already." A ghost of a smile flickered round Strickland's lips. "Me." The gold flecks in the grey eyes seemed to sparkle. "That's what you really mean, isn't it?"

"It isn't what I mean at all. We've had a lot of losses. We haven't achieved *any*thing. I know how you must feel."

The quizzical smile was still on Strickland's face. "You do, Doc?"

"I think so."

"You read us all like books, eh, Doc?" Shrugging his shoulders, Strickland got up to go. "Really I should be grateful to you. I was the first person to say Peter Irvine was all right. I was the one who gave him his chance." Strickland picked up his hat, put it on his head and sauntered towards the door. "Gratifying to us amateurs, Doc . . . us chaps who know nothing about psychology . . . to have our judgement backed up by professionals like you."

What particular shaft of his, Flint wondered, had actually struck home at what served Strickland for a heart? What particular words of his had saved Irvine from the brink?

At any rate, open conflict between them had been avoided, and for that he was grateful. How long that truce would last depended on the amount of success 507 Squadron managed to accumulate.

The *Groningen*, Flint thought, was really like a number in roulette on which Strickland had gambled. Wisby, Guilonard, Wingco Vance, Mowbray, Wilkes, Tallack, Jerningham, Price were the chips he had placed on it and lost. But the number was bound to come up some time—that was what Strickland was betting on—provided he kept his nerve and managed to hang on to that handful of chips, his seven serviceable Liberators.

With the American source practically dried up, spares were the real difficulty. But for the next week things went reasonably brightly. Nobody went missing, nobody was shot up. Things for Strickland, if not on the upturn, at least were pegging level.

And then early in April suddenly the roulette wheel appeared to become weighted in Strickland's favour.

The number he had put his money on showed every likelihood that it would turn up. Strickland had always maintained that the *Groningen* would return to Falstand Fjord to huddle in safety under that huge cliff edge for overhaul and the taking on of fuel, stores and ammunition for a long sea patrol, possibly in the Far East. Once the overhaul and taking on of stores had been completed, the merchant cruiser would have, of course, to steam back up the narrow twenty-six-mile fjord to reach the open sea. This trip Captain Leitzen would choose to do early at night in the worst possible weather and to get as far away as possible before dawn to avoid detection.

That Saturday evening a message was received from the Norwegian underground that the *Groningen* had arrived at her safe berth at the head of the Falstand Fjord. Two days later, oblique photographs from a PRU Mosquito confirmed it.

Flint had never seen Strickland so delighted. All his buoyant self-confidence had returned. The reverses of the last few months were brushed aside. Captain Leitzen of the *Groningen* had done exactly what Strickland had said he would do. It was as though he had fallen into a trap of Strickland's own making. Like the fly, he had come into the spider's parlour. Though safe enough there, as soon as he came out, seven highly trained crews would be waiting for him when he least expected it.

At long last, after so many reverses, the tide appeared to be turning in Strickland's favour. Squadron morale went up sharply. So did Strickland's position as a leader. His cup of joy overflowed when, on Thursday, he had a phone call from Machrannoch.

It was Captain McCleary, the Commanding Officer who had sat next to him at the Dining-In night. At first he thought it was a final demand for the return of all those loaned Liberator spares, but the man's voice sounded diffident, almost apologetic. "We have a problem—"

There was a long pause.

"You see," Captain McCleary went on hesitantly, "we're having a dance here for Easter."

"No problem, Captain." Strickland had grasped the situation immediately. "We'll send you over a Liberator-load of our WAAFs."

Assistant Section Officer Jones was detailed to be in charge of them. "Your last chance, Griselda," Strickland told her. "Here's a list of spares we need."

She had no wish to go. The chauffeur detailed to drive the bevy, Peter Irvine, had no wish to go either.

"It'll be hell," she told him as they walked towards the aircraft, "These things always are. There's too much to drink. And the girls get silly."

"Silly things, girls." Irvine eyed her teasingly. She smiled back but rather doubtfully.

"I suppose you'll dance with Bob Greaves?"

"Is there any reason why I shouldn't?" There was a question in her eyes that was deeper than the one her lips formed.

He answered hastily, "No, of course not." Because she might have taken him a little too seriously that afternoon in the woods. Though he was in his own mind still serious about her, he had not followed up his vague talk of "after the war", "you and me".

"Then I will if he asks me."

"Oh, he will. *He will!*"

She smiled.

"Do you like him?" Irvine asked crossly.

"Yes." She paused with her foot on the shaky catwalk of the Lib, and added softly, because the three-ton truck had just drawn up filled to the gills with airwomen. "But that's all."

"That's what *you* say." He made a derisive sound.

The back flap of the three-tonner was let down, and out they

240

swarmed over the intervening tarmac behind Emma up the steps into the aircraft, followed by just three operating crew—Henty, Miggs and Irvine. Chattering and laughing they pushed forward up onto the bomb-bay cakewalk.

It was a marvel to Irvine how many permutations they could make out of their "one inch off the collar" hair. Some wore it swept up in a pile of curls with the uniform cap perched precariously on top. Some had a lowish page-boy netted so that it didn't quite touch the collar, one or two with it twisted into a bun, some with it brushed and curled round the brim band of the cap itself, like runner-bean tendrils. Henna and tongs and oceans of peroxide had been used. The WAAFs always managed to get hold of perfume. They'd no doubt be hoping to get a whole Champs Elysées of it tonight and the aircraft reeked.

They nearly didn't go. There was a mag drop on Number Four, but Irvine felt he couldn't let down the WAAFs or their hosts.

Holding his breath, he pushed forward all four throttles and prayed the starboard outer wouldn't fail on take-off.

It didn't. With a sigh of relief he levelled off at five thousand feet and set course for Machrannoch.

He couldn't even distinguish Emma's Coty from the rest, though she sat on an upturned box near him and Henty. Occasionally they exchanged smiles but she said nothing. She looked as if she'd had her hair done like the rest of them. Her cap was placed very lightly on top so as not to disturb it. But it disturbed him. It was as if she might be off on the hunt like the rest of them. Wasn't she satisfied with him, Irvine? He'd told her he loved her, hadn't he? And though he was too young to marry, just as he was too young to die, he meant what he said. And on balance he was more afraid of losing her to someone else than he was of marrying and widowing her. It was all very complicated. No wonder there was comparative quiet on the flight deck, though Miggs, who was on the radio, did enough talking for all of them.

He was all spruced up with civvy shoes and a Van Heusen shirt and collar. On landing at the American base, he stayed on his seat while everyone else got moving. As soon as the checks were completed, the pilots shepherded the girls out. Emma Jones went to the back to help them. Still Miggs sat, watching the perfumed and powdered girls go by.

Deirdre Winter was nearly the last. He put out his hand and grabbed her as she passed the W/T set. She didn't say a word. She just stood staring down at him, her eyes smouldering. The last few WAAFs had to push past her in their haste to get to the bomb-bay cakewalk and out.

Looking up into her face, he noticed it had grown thin. Her chocolate-box prettiness had matured.

"Well, Sergeant?" she asked him coldly, her voice hard.

"Why have you come here?" he asked.

"Is it any of your business?"

"Yep."

"Like hell. You and me's all washed up. And don't you forget it, Sergeant."

"Ah, Deirdre Winter. But it isn't just you and me. Like you said. It's you and me and him." He pointed to the region just below the polished buckle of her belt.

"You bloody swine." She tried to jerk her hand away.

"You might be wanting to get him a Yankee Dad."

She brought her free hand up then and was within an inch of his face, when he caught that too.

"Naughty, naughty! I've told you before about a non-commissioned officer. I could put you on a fizzer. Have you up in front of ma'am."

"You're a bloody swine, a bastard . . ." she stopped suddenly at the word.

" 'sall right, Deirdre. I'm only kidding."

"Anyway, you said it wasn't yours."

"Oh, it's mine, love. I know." He let go of her wrists. She stood there, rubbing them, eyeing him suspiciously. "So why did you come tonight?" he asked her.

"For a bit of fun."

"Aren't you getting any?"

"No."

"What about all your other boy friends?"

"I don't go out with them no more. Not since then. That night."

"I was wondering what had happened to you."

"Why?"

He shrugged. "I dunno. I suppose I missed you." He stood up. "Would you like to sit down a bit? We could go up front. I don't suppose you like standing around." His eyes returned to the polished belt region. "Not now."

She nodded, following him to the pilots' seats at the front. Sitting in Mr Irvine's while he settled himself down in the second dickey's. The ground from here looked a long way away. She felt slightly dizzy. He watched her face anxiously. "Are you all right?"

"Of course I am."

"Do they know? That lot? About it?"

"No. And I'm not telling them yet."

"Are you frightened?"

"Yes."

"You don't have to be."

She screwed round her head, her eyes were hard again. He could see them glint even in the darkness, "Oh, yeah? Sez who?"

"Sez me."

"Yeah, Sergeant, well you're not having him, are you?"

"Don't talk like that, Deirdre."

"You just want to drown him, don't you, Sergeant? In a bottle of gin."

"Christ, Deirdre. Not now I don't."

"Well, it's too late."

He almost jumped out of his seat at that. "What d'you mean it's *too late*? You've not got rid of him?"

She looked at him, surprised. Then smiled. "Course I haven't. Too late I meant for you to take an interest, clot." But she spoke more gently. "You've had your chips as far as that's concerned."

There was a long silence. Then Miggs said softly, "Deirdre?"

"Yes?"

"Do you want to go to this lark? This dance?"

"Not specially."

"How about staying with me, then?"

She looked round at him coldly again. "Doing what, eh, Sergeant?"

"Oh, Deirdre, don't get me wrong! Not that, for crying out loud!"

"And I would cry out loud, Sarge, I promise you."

"I didn't mean *that*."

"You'd maybe reckon it's safe. Damage done."

"Deirdre, how could you?"

"How could *you*?"

"Easily." He drew a deep breath. " 'Cos I loved you."

She sat staring ahead, still as a statue, saying nothing.

"Still do."

"Funny way of showing it."

"I came specially to see you."

"You was *detailed*, Sergeant."

"I was detailed, yes. But I came to see you. Got dressed up to see you. Waited to see you. Brought a picnic just for you and me." He hauled out the torch from the seat slot and shone it on a tin ration box just beside the console on the floor. A little further and the small light glinted on bottles. "Cider, beer and a thermos of coffee. Spam sandwiches and meat pies. How about that?"

"What's it all in aid of?"

"I'm glad you asked, Deirdre. It's a party."

"But it's just you and me!"

" 'sright. A celebration. Now it's a bit chilly in here, so wrap this rug round you. There. That better? Here, have a sandwich, while I uncork the wine."

"What're you celebrating, Miggs?"

He just laughed teasingly, but didn't answer.

"Heh?" She asked in a different tone. "You're not posted, are you?"

"No fear."

"Promotion. That's it. You got your crown?"

"Any minute, Deirdre, love! Any minute! But not just now."

"What then?"

"No. I've been shopping."

"Oh." She sounded disappointed.

"I'll show you." He leaned forward and switched on the instrument lights. "Mind, after what I said, all that crap, you may not want 'em."

"*Me?* What's it got to do with me?"

In a quick movement he thrust his clenched left fist in front of her face. Suddenly, he turned it over, and opened up his hand so that the objects on the spread palm caught the lights

244

from the panel. In the centre lay a plain gold wedding ring, and to the side a thin hoop with a single small but glittery diamond.

Leaning forward, his breath held, he watched her face carefully.

"Sergeant," she said in a warning tone, "don't you tease me. Where d'you get these? Out of a cracker? What funny trick are you playing now?"

"So help me! No funny trick! Out of a cracker in-bloody-deed!" He picked the engagement ring up daintily between his finger and thumb and held it under her nose. "That's a real bloody diamond! You could cut the bloody windscreen to shreds with it. And set in real *nine carat gold*." He stabbed his little finger at the wedding ring. "So is that! They're bloody hard to come by! Never mind costing a fortune. Some bloody brides have to make do with fucking curtain rings. And you say out of a cracker! I'll give you crackers, Mrs Miggs!"

But she didn't answer with her usual sauciness. "Brides," she repeated. Tears flowed endlessly down her cheeks. After a while she gulped, "Miggs, are you asking me . . ."

"No, you silly bitch, I'm telling you! We're engaged as from now. Put that diamond on your finger. Don't lose it, for Chrissake! It cost a bomb. It's our capital. We're getting married."

"Married?"

"That's what I said."

"It isn't because you're sorry for me, is it?"

"No. And I'm not. Not a bit. It's me I'm sorry for. And him. Our lad. For having such a silly Mother. Out of a cracker, indeed!"

"Do you really, *really* want to?"

"I do! I do! More than anything, so help me! Cross my heart! All right?" He leaned towards her and turned her face towards him. "Well, aren't you going to give me a kiss?"

She smiled and kissed him chastely, rather decorously.

"Come on. Kiss again. Like you used to. That's better."

"D'you mind getting married in Manchester, Miggs?"

"Manchester? Oh, your Mum, you mean. What'll she say?"

"She'll be pleased. Mind, she won't say so, she never does. She just says when she isn't. It was the other thing that'd have sent her round the twist. But a wedding! She'll like that. They'll

245

have a street party. Everyone'll pool their rations. And I can't go on calling you Miggs." She paused. "What's your real name?"

"It's not like me. Don't ask. Doesn't suit me. Isn't *me*."

"You were christened it, weren't you?"

"Yes."

"Well then. Let's have it. The one beginning with L."

"You won't laugh?"

"Course not."

"It's . . . it's, Lionel." He paused. "It means little lion." He paused. "Go on, laugh."

"Why should I laugh? Nothing wrong with Lionel! But you're right," she put her hand on his knee then stroked his thigh. "It doesn't suit you. You're not a *little* lion. You're a big one! A big brave lion, Miggs, that's what *you* are!"

The enthusiasm of the reception the other WAAFs received at the hands of the Americans had gone to their heads. So had the Scotch, Bourbon, Rye, Malt, Irish, Old Kentucky, Southern Comfort. They had been whisked away into a sea of dark blue. Bob Greaves had come over and claimed Emma. "I guess," intercepting Irvine's scowl, he had smiled, "we've got a lot of business to discuss."

"I bet," Irvine had said.

The Naval Captain came from Missouri and had treated Irvine and Henty with an old-fashioned courtesy that neither of them were used to from senior officers. The food was out of this world—salmon, crab, turkey, pork, whole sides of beef and six flavours of ice cream.

Surrounded by hospitable Americans, Irvine and Henty drank lemonade and ate sparingly. Most of the time, Irvine's attention was preoccupied, looking around the room anxiously for Emma and his charges.

He had one dance with her. She was preoccupied too, constantly looking around, not bothering to talk. Charitably he could have supposed she was keeping an eye on the girls. Uncharitably that she was watching out for Bob.

"He's a good dancer, is he, this Greaves guy?"

"Very."

"I watched you just now. Bit showy, isn't he?"

"A bit," she smiled. "A bit like Strickland."

"You don't like Strickland, do you?"

"No. Do you?"

"I'm not sure." He shrugged. Somehow he felt almost superstitiously afraid to voice his dislike.

"He uses people. That's what I don't like about him. Then when he's used them, he drops them." she said.

"Who's he given the chop to, then?" Then enlightenment dawned. "Oh, I know. Your room-mate, the Ensa girl."

"Yes. According to the grapevine, it was he got her moved back to London. Said she wasn't suitable for this sort of Station."

"I'd have thought she'd have been glad."

"Well, she wasn't. She was keen on him."

"You girls! What was she hoping for? Wedding bells and an announcement in the *Daily Telegraph*? She'd have to be an earlier bird than her to catch Strickland."

Emma Jones' eyes blazed. Her anger seemed deeper and more personal than that for a room-mate. Very clearly, standing on tip-toe to say it in his ear, her voice reached him through the blare of the band. "You make me sick!"

And without giving him the chance to grab her hand, she stalked off.

He didn't see her again for hours. But he saw several girls being sick, or rushing with their hankies to their mouths in the rough direction of the toilets. But the party went on unabated. The band blared out. The drink flowed. Gifts of candy bars and nail varnish, scent, sweets, cigarettes and chewing gum were stuffed into breast pockets and skirt pockets. The noise was fantastic. Everybody seemed to be enjoying themselves except Henty and Irvine.

Then, through a haze of tobacco smoke, they saw a pale figure sway and fall. Running across, they managed to get to the girl, heave her up, and, mumbling that they'd give her some fresh air, half carried, half dragged her back to the Lib.

There they found the place was already like a bloody casualty clearing station.

Full of righteous indigation, Irvine went back hot-foot to find Emma. He had hardly set foot inside the dance hall, when a hand was laid on his arm.

247

"I've looked everywhere for you, Peter!" He looked down to see her face, flushed, brows wrinkled up, eyes sparkling—an odd mixture of anger, appeal, reproach.

"Christ!" He rounded on her. "*You've* been looking for *me*."

"There's no need to shout." Her mouth trembled and then consciously tightened. "You knew I had to . . ."

"I knew bloody nothing! All I know is I've acted as bloody nursemaid and—"

"Shut up!" she hissed furiously. "Damn you! Shut up! We've got to go! They're all half cut. But we've got to do it decently. Make some excuses."

Irvine drew in a long breath. Then he said stonily, "OK, ma'am. We'll find your friend Greaves." He gave her a furious look. "He won't be bloody far away."

"He's just over there," she said jerking her head towards the bar. "Tell him—"

"I know what to tell him."

Pulling her behind him, he shoved his way to Greaves and tapped him on the shoulder. "We've got to get back," he said thickly. "Weather at Kilcreggan's closing in. Terribly sorry. Lovely party."

Greaves was all concern. He told the Captain. All courtesy and efficiency, the American machine went into action. When the difficulty of rounding up the Liberator's passengers was realized, motorcycles arrived with white-helmeted, stone-cold-sober military police, who simply fanned out through the hall, out into the living quarters, flinging open doors, bundling their guests into a trailing bus one after the other as soon as they found them.

Then at the aircraft there was further trouble trying to make absolutely certain that they'd got everybody.

Greaves stayed with them till the end. Irvine said in parting, "Everybody did enjoy themselves. Awfully good of you to have us. Sorry to break it up like this. But you know what the Scottish mist is like."

Irvine didn't waste time on the Auxiliary Power Unit. He started up on the batteries and fled for the end of the runway.

The scene on the flight deck both during and after take-off resembled a Renaissance painting of Sodom and Gomorrah. Bodies were draped everywhere. There was shouting, swearing, kicking, laughing. Lionel Miggs and Deirdre Winter, like an old married couple, coped with them as best they could, all the time shaking their old heads at the behaviour of the younger generation.

Then the weather became bumpy and the passengers quietened down to be sick.

Every now and again, Irvine said the odd word to Henty, but to no one else, not even Emma just behind him.

When they landed in clear moonlight weather, the atmosphere on the flight deck was still frigid. There was still a mag drop on Number Four. Lorries carried the moaning WAAFs into the night.

Strickland heard all about it next day. "What the bloody hell were you playing at, Irvine? Breaking up a bloody good party while everybody was enjoying themselves."

"Some of the girls, sir, were . . . ill."

"A party like that . . . good for the girls, good for the Yanks. And bloody good for the squadron!"

"Things . . . getting a bit out of—"

"Rude, Irvine. Bloody rude! To the Americans of all people, who've been so good to us!" He leaned right back in his seat and glared across his office desk. "Every job you're given, Irvine . . . all you do is to fuck it up!"

SEVENTEEN

DURING the next three days, no action was taken by Captain Leitzen. There in Falstand Fjord lay the *Groningen*, from the PRU photographs to all intents and purposes dormant and unmoving. It was only from Norwegian underground reports that British Intelligence knew of the continuous and feverish activity on board as she took on stores, overhauled her engines, filled up with diesel oil and ammunition and repaired her war and weather damage.

On the other side of the North Sea, 507 Squadron's activities were just as continuous and feverish. Withdrawn completely from all operations, seven crews in seven Liberators trained every night, sometimes in appalling weather conditions, now carrying out concerted practice ballet acts all together with split-second timing, screaming with engines at full bore inside the cup of the mountains to flatten out just above the water, each from a different angle so as to split up the flak and drop their torpedoes on the target wreck in Loch Nairn.

Amongst this company was Irvine in F Freddie for the sole reason, Strickland told him bluntly, that because of the casualties he had twenty-five more operational trips than any of the new and very green captains that had been posted as replacements to the squadron. Furthermore, he had done more Leigh Light torpedo dropping in Loch Nairn than any other 507 captain and—this said very grudgingly—his results hitting the target "weren't all that bad".

Irvine had listened to this lecture in silence, wondering if it was possible to hate anyone more than this calculating fish of a man, wrapped up totally in his one obsession, using everybody quite cold-bloodedly—Emma Jones, the Yanks, Sylvia Talbot, the WAAFs, his own aircrews—to achieve his purpose.

That hate translated itself into a curious steadiness and accuracy in his flying. Never was Strickland going to be allowed the opportunity of ever criticizing him again! Now his crew in the Sergeants' Mess were boasting about his flying. Nobody, they said, could fly a Liberator on a pitch-black night, thirty feet above the water on the radio altimeter, so spot-on as he could. Even Curly Craik could be heard whole-heartedly agreeing with Miggs that as far as their Skipper was concerned they'd been "bloody lucky".

So Mason's A, Carter's B, Irvine's F, Dacres' K, Linton's M, Ames' R and Strickland's S every day became that much more effective and efficient in preparation for the night that the *Groningen* set off for the sea down Falstand Fjord. A code name had been given to that date—Operation Achilles. The service-ability of the aircraft remained miraculously good—the only problem being the constant recurrence of the mag drop on F's Number Four engine that Irvine had first reported to her groundcrew, Race and Heaton, after his hectic jaunt to the American dance at Machrannoch.

Everything then was going fine. Everything was running in Strickland's favour. All the portents pointed to a highly successful operation against the *Groningen*.

Dacres was the last to leave in K King. All seven serviceable Liberators had been carrying out a simultaneous mass night-training exercise on the wreck in Loch Nairn—three aircraft attacking from the port, three from the starboard, with Strickland supervising in S Sugar. Dacres had come in just behind Irvine's F Freddie, switched on his Leigh Light at two miles, and dropped his practice torpedoes from fifty feet exactly.

All four hit.

"Bloody good, Skipper! *Bloody* good!"

His crew were jubilant. Nobody else had got four. Nearest was Irvine with two. Tommy Dacres was too quiet a person vocally to demonstrate exhilaration, but a smile of satisfaction spread across his face and he allowed his crew (and himself) a treat by giving them a beat-up over the dark waters of the Loch coupled with a screaming split-arse turn at full power right against the rock face.

"Skipper . . . terrific!"

Crews always like low flying. Back they go to their fairground days, being whirled round in the Big Wheel or hurtled down on the Big Dipper.

"Give us another one, just like the other one," Vine, his Front Gunner, chanted over the intercom. "Give us another one, *do*!"

But Dacres would not. One was enough. Sedately he straightened up, climbed out of the loch towards the stars. High above the mountains he set off south.

"Estimate Kilcreggan . . . 04.32, Skipper." His Navigator Parkinson came up to the flight deck and stood behind him. Eames, his second pilot, took the paper off a bar of Cadbury's milk chocolate, broke it in pieces, passed them round.

"See for miles, eh?" Parkinson said.

Dacres just nodded. The moon had added a thin silver to all the other lights in the sky.

"We must be top-scoring crew." Fuller in the rear turret chatted to Vine at the front as, at six thousand feet, K King flew serenely homewards.

Parkinson pointed. "Flarepath ahead, Skipper."

Dacres nodded.

"Can't see anybody else's navigation lights," Vine said. "The others must have landed."

"Tired, Skipper?" Eames asked.

"A bit."

Behind them, Parkinson stretched his arms. "Bed! Ah, bed!"

Over his shoulder, Dacres called to his Engineer, "Twenty inches!" and, pushing the Navigator aside, Thrale leaned over and drew back the throttles.

K King's nose dipped.

The gunners got out of their turrets, lugged up their parachutes to the front, preparatory to landing and out.

In total contrast to the sparkling sky, the ground was a sea of darkness.

"Blackout's pretty good, eh Skipper?"

They were slipping lower and lower down into it.

"Give me the wheels," Dacres said.

They came rumbling down.

"Three green lights!"

252

"Not doing a circuit, are you, Skipper?" Eames asked.

Dacres shook his head. "Tell them we're coming straight in."

The second pilot reported to Flying Control.

"Cleared to land, Skipper."

The runway lights were over to port now.

"We're a bit high . . ."

"Fifteen inches! Half flap!"

The runway lights were still over to port, but now they were rapidly rising to meet the aircraft. Looking to the left out of his window, Dacres saw a red light cheerfully winking at him and, pushing the nose down further, turned the control column hard over to the left to line up with the runway. Up went the starboard wing, higher, then higher. He glanced over Eames' head at it, saw the green navigation light strangely out of place amongst the silver stars, swung his head right round to the left again to check the port, saw suddenly not one red light but *two—*

Immediately he slammed the throttles forward. Wrenching the stick hard back, he was just straightening up when the port wing tip caught the red-lighted summit of the hill.

K King slewed right round, turned upside down and crumpled against the cliffs.

Ten minutes passed before Flying Control realized what had happened. They had gone on calling K and getting no answer till finally they sounded the Crash Alert for the fire engines, ambulances and police and telephoned the Officers' Mess.

As soon as he had been told, Andrew Flint flung his battle-dress over his pyjamas, put on his greatcoat and tore down to the hospital where his two senior orderlies, Mullins and Pearce, had already got the Station ambulance started and everything necessary inside it.

The hill at the west end of the east-west runway—that was all the information that Flying Control could give them. Flint drove with his foot hard down on the accelerator—out of the Station, through Kilcreggan village, up the mountainside past the hospital and onto the moor below the line of peaks.

Starlight cast an eerie glaze over the withered heather. The hooded headlights cut a tiny yellow cave out of the darkness, illuminating only the rutted road and the winter grass. There

253

was no sign of where K King might be. If there had been survivors, surely they would have been signalling . . .

Unless of course they were too badly hurt. At least one could cling to that hope. Twice in the summer Flint had flown with Dacres' crew, and had got to know them pretty well. Only yesterday evening, he had sat next to Tommy Dacres at supper. More talkative than usual, the pilot had been telling the doctor of his early days in the pre-war Air Force, describing the rigours of Halton.

"No sign here, sir," Mullins said.

Were they thinking about the ordeal ahead of them, Flint wondered. Were they remembering, as he had been, hacking at the front turret of S Sugar to get Cargill's body out, cleaning out the top turret, taking to the mortuary Oakroyd's blood-stained gauntlets?

This time it would be far worse. He had that feeling as he swung the ambulance round a hair-pin bend, climbing up from the moor onto the rocky ridge.

"Where shall we start looking, sir?" Pearce asked.

"The highest ground." It was usually the peak, the summit, almost like a finger of fate coming up and touching the wings. "Another six inches and they'd have been all right." "A foot to the left, they'd have been safe"—those were the stories you always heard.

"Won't see much before dawn," said Mullins.

From far away across the moor behind them came the mournful sound of a bell, the fire-engine searching in vain.

"No fire," Pearce said. "That's something."

"Bit of luck," said Mullins, "and they'll have got away with it."

At the top of the ridge, just before the slope down again, Flint stopped the ambulance and the three of them got out.

It was still quite dark in spite of the stars. The doctor could just make out the line of the mountain range above them, very slightly darker than the night sky. But there was no detail, no hope of seeing anything. Their torches busily fingered over old heather stumps and rabbit runs.

"You search over there, Mullins," Flint pointed to the left. "And you go right, Pearce. I'll try straight ahead."

He was aware even as he said the words that he would be

the one who would find something. Heavy drops of dew glittered in the torchlight all over the short grass. The air smelled cold and wet and heathery. The path gave out and he found himself pushing through dense bushes of dry bracken.

It was hopeless looking really, he thought, as he struggled upwards, still holding his bag filled with pain-killers and First Aid equipment. I can't see more than a couple of yards ahead. Yet if there *are* survivors, the sooner we find them, the better. Somewhere hidden in this darkness there might be people in pain.

The grass began to give out. Slate and rock took its place. Granite boulders bulged out of a thin, dark soil. He slipped on a steep slide. Panting, he stood for a moment trying to get back his breath, all the time swinging his torch to and fro over the cliff side above him, looking for any signs of metal.

Nothing! Nothing at all! Again he began scrabbling upwards over loose soil.

He had been so sure it would be a piece of the aircraft he would see first, a bit of white or silver from the duralumin fuselage, that when he saw it, he could not believe his eyes.

He stopped dead in his tracks, watching the pattern of light from his torch again sniff round the bracken roots like a hound-dog on the scent.

There it was! He stilled the torch, tried to keep it focused.

Under the cinnamon-coloured bracken, lying on the short grey-green grass, a fringe of black hair. The torchlight trembled away from it, illuminated a pale white forehead, glistened on the moisture of an eye, settled on the bone and flesh of a severed neck lying in a pool of blood.

Abruptly Flint turned the torch off. A head cut from a body was bad enough. But a face you recognized, someone you had been talking to only hours before, a gentle, quiet face that had done no harm to anybody, that was unbearable! He could not be expected to cope with this!

His legs felt suddenly weak. I'll faint in a moment, he thought, something I've never done since watching my first major operation as a medical student. He sat down on a rocky ledge, holding his head in his hands, trying to recover himself, trying to beat back the nausea.

K King must have crashed against the cliff face. In a fraction of a second her duralumin fuselage must have been changed into a hundred cutting sword-edges that had hacked her crew to pieces. Not only Dacres but all of them would have been butchered to bits and their brains, their entrails, their eyes, their arms, their legs, their heads, their hearts scattered all over the mountain.

"Nothing here, sir!" Mullins' voice came echoing up to him. "Have you found anything?"

A wild desire seized Flint to shout back, "Yes, I have! Bring up those mortuary bags we brought and start picking up the pieces, while I go back to the Station in the ambulance to report."

Get away! Don't look! Nobody should ever be allowed to see this!

"You all right, sir?" Pearce calling out to him now.

Mullins and Pearce—they're tough. They're used to this sort of thing. They can take it. More, they didn't know the crew like I do, Flint thought. It isn't so personal. It isn't so obscene.

They must do it. They must collect the remains, sort them as best they can. He must leave it to them.

Far away in the east, the sky was lightening. A shaft of sunshine lit up the rocky summit, set off another shout from Mullins. "There it is, sir! Up there, just above you!"

He did not want to see. He just sat there in silence, listening to the sound of the medical orderlies' feet scurrying through the bracken towards him.

And then suddenly he realized . . . nobody must see this but me. This is my job. It belongs only to me.

And he got up and walked towards the orderlies, stopping them in their tracks, turning them round and leading them back to the ambulance.

There he collected the bags himself. There he told Mullins to drive back with Pearce and tell the Station what had happened.

"Collect me here this afternoon," he said. "No one else is to come."

They protested at first—then seeing the set of his face, they left him. Carrying the bags, he went back to the foot of the cliff. Now he could look up at the crumpled port wing crucified on the crag, the engine embedded in rock, the jagged silver skin glittering in the morning sun. Far below him, down there on the coast, he could see Runway 09 empty and waiting, the rectangles of hangars, the six white Liberators sitting safely on their Dispersals.

I'm just like a carrion crow, he thought, going from piece to piece. Lifting up an arm and trying to decide whether it was Parkinson's or Dacres'. Scraping blood off a face and identifying Eames. Vine was in the top turret when it happened for he was still in it now, fettered in the twisted barrels of the guns.

All morning, pushing away the bracken, picking away at the slate and the rocky ground. Two at least—Thrale and Fuller—had escaped relatively unmutilated.

All sense of nausea had left him. It was as though filling these bags was a duty, some debt that he owed Dacres and his crew. It was as though some pact had been formed between them. No other eyes but mine shall ever see. Nobody else shall know because nobody else could bear it. This is my truth and my secret.

The sun shone all day. Round three o'clock, he saw the ambulance come winding up the hill. He waved to Pearce and Mullins and they came up to the foot of the cliff with the stretchers.

Mullins drove back to the aerodrome. All the time, he kept glancing at Flint concernedly as Pearce did. But neither of them said anything, except to suggest back in Sick Quarters that he should leave evening surgery to them.

But he did not. After a bath, he came back and carried on with his normal routine. He went in to dinner at eight, though he wasn't very hungry and ate hardly anything.

Afterwards he had coffee, read the newspapers, stared at the blackout of the ante-room windows.

Just before ten, he went into the bar.

Strickland was up at the counter with most of 507's senior captains.

"Bitter, Doc?"

"Thank you."

No funeral sing-song tonight. No Crackers to tickle the ivories. Moroseness hung limp over them all.

Except for Strickland. He was furious.

"How bloody stupid can you get? If Dacres had pranged on the exercise, I could have forgiven him! Bloody tricky dropping

257

torpedoes in a Lib at the best of times, never mind with cliffs all round you! But to finish off the training perfectly . . . all his fish hits . . . and then come back to perfect weather, visibility thirty miles, not a cloud in the sky and simply fling himself at a block of granite—" He lifted up his tankard and banged it so hard that the beer sluiced all over the bar counter. "Christ! *Christ* . . . what can you *do*?"

"What's up?"

For one awful moment at his evening surgery next day, Flint thought 507's senior captains were all reporting sick to get off flying. He looked from one to the other of them: Ames, Mason, Carter, Linton, Irvine.

They shrugged their shoulders. "We don't know, Doc. The Wingco told us to come."

At that moment, Strickland came in through the door.

"Hello, Doc." His voice sounded sympathetic. "You must have had a rough time yesterday."

Flint simply said, "I was just enquiring what this was about."

"It has a connection with what you were doing yesterday."

"I don't understand."

"I've held an Enquiry into the accident to K King. Dacres had been cleared to land. He had the field in sight. He must have mistaken the red light on the high ground for his port navigation light and begun to let down." He paused. "Gross carelessness."

Flint felt the anger rise inside him. "You mean he made a mistake . . . like we all do."

"No, Doc." Strickland shook his head vigorously. "He committed a crime. The crime of gross carelessness in handling one of His Majesty's aircraft."

"Are you thinking of court-martialling him then?"

What sympathy there had been on Strickland's face evaporated. Sourly he said, "This isn't a time to be facetious."

"You don't have to tell me that.'

In the small room, the silence actually hummed. Flint could feel Strickland's eyes on him. The squadron pilots looked uncertainly from their Doctor to their Wing-Commander. With an effort, Strickland said rather more quietly, "We're short of aircraft. Short of spares. Short of experienced aircrews." He paused. "Just like the Battle of Britain."

"I don't see what the Battle of Britain's got to do with it."

"Only that Dowding* at the height of that battle sent a telegram to all his Fighter Stations saying that accidents due to gross carelessness were continuing and ordering that those pilots responsible should be subjected to the most degrading and humiliating punishment."

"Poor Dacres is beyond that sort of nonsense."

"Nonsense? I totally sympathize with Dowding." Strickland paused. "Dacres can still serve a useful purpose."

Arms folded across his chest, he stood with his legs apart. The scar under his left eye had gone white.

Suddenly Flint realized what he was going to try to do.

"Look, Guy, let's talk about this in my office."

He led the way out of the waiting room. As soon as they were inside his office, Flint closed the door and turned to face Strickland. But before he could open his mouth the Wing-Commander forestalled him.

"Seven Libs . . . I needed *seven*! Attacking each at their particular angle. I'd have sunk the *Groningen* with seven! Six isn't enough! She'll get away again! Don't you see?" He banged both his fists on the desk. "The best crew gone! The rest have got to be made to realize . . . never do that! Never relax! Never let your flying be less than perfect." The light-flecked eyes swept over Flint's face. "So that's why they've actually got to *see*. They've got to *see* Dacres. They've got to *see* Parkinson, Eames, Fuller . . ."

He's bomb-happy, Flint thought. Ever since that S Sugar business, that's what spurred him on.

Not promotion, not decorations. Revenge, he had once thought: like Guilonard, a relative, a girl-friend killed by enemy action. Or pique, the blind belief that he was always right. Machismo, the need to prove himself a man. Fury at Captain Leitzen's outwitting him. All these he had considered as Strickland's driving force.

". . . Thrale, Vine . . ."

The roll-call had ended.

* C-in-C Fighter Command.

259

"These men were Dacres' crew. The pilots will be shown them as they are now."

Suddenly Flint could control his anger no more. The memory of yesterday came flooding over him. He saw himself again guarding those bags with their pitiful contents. Eyes blazing he shouted at Strickland, "Then why weren't the pilots shown the men you killed in S Sugar?"

There was a deathly silence. Strickland stood as still as stone. All the blood had drained from his face. His skin had become the colour of parchment.

"*That's* what you've reckoned then? You and your psychology!" He spat the words out. "Listen! Yes, you'll listen! On my first squadron when I was a sprog PO,* the CO was a real tough called Ryan. Day after I arrived, we were sent to Malta. We lost five Blenheims ship-busting in four days. Then we lost both Flight-Commanders, and I found myself in charge of 'A' Flight. A week later, we were down on the deck attacking a convoy in the Gulf of Sirte. I was just behind Ryan when he exploded. And when I got back to Malta . . ." he paused, "I was the only pilot of the squadron alive. Two days afterwards, nine more Blenheims arrived from England. And suddenly, I was Acting Wing-Commander. Surrounded by a lot of babies. Christ, I felt as old as Methuselah!"

He walked over to the window and stood there staring out at the playing fields beyond.

"I was landed with them. Caught, they say about a girl who's pregnant. Well, that's what happened to me."

He turned round and again came back to Flint's desk. "You've *got* to get the boys to attack. But the Jerries have done nothing personal against them. 507 fights a uniformed Navy which has fought bravely and skilfully and on the whole humanely. These boys like the idea of learning to fly, wearing an RAF uniform, having a much better time than they would have done in civvy street. They haven't a clue why this war started. All they know is the politicians made a balls-up and look to youth as usual to get them out of it. Hoodwink them, manipulate them . . ."

"*You* manipulate them."

"Sure. I beg, borrow, lie, flannel, steal—"

* New Pilot Officer.

260

"And put the bodies of your friends on show?"

"To make sure no one would ever do the same as Dacres. We've lost nine aircraft against the *Groningen*. But if we lost a couple of squadrons and sank her, it'd be worth it. That bloody ship is building up a legend. They don't want to attack her."

"Who can blame them?"

"I can. Because if we'd attacked with seven we'd have sunk her and got away with it. Now with six, we'll have casualties. One more effort like Dacres' and it won't be the *Groningen* but us that are goners. That's why they've got to see for themselves."

Now Flint's fury reached its crescendo. He flung open the door. "Right, Wing-Commander! You shall see! But I warn you—"

Walking towards him, Strickland said coldly, "Yes?"

"You'll never fly again!"

Strickland was just saying. "We're tougher than—" when the telephone rang out.

Like a hunting-horn, Flint thought, sounding the view-halloo. Strickland must have thought much the same because he bounded across the room and grabbed the receiver.

"Strickland here . . . Operation Achilles." His eyes flicked across the room meaningfully at Flint. "So soon?"

Then he put down the receiver. For a few seconds, he stood in silence looking down on it. In a strange kind of way, like Flint had done up on the mountain yesterday, Strickland had come to his own watershed. In quite a different tone of voice, he said, "It's tomorrow, Doc."

261

EIGHTEEN

ALL morning, excitement mounted. No visible signs, no panoply, no bugles blowing. Small things, sounds mainly: the hiss of bicycles as swarms of fitters and riggers left their barrack blocks for Flights: stores lorries moving equipment: the chug of the pumps at the underground petrol tanks filling up a queue of bowsers.

Nobody running. No rushing around. No shouted orders. No marching. No human noise at all. In the Mess, the Tannoy blaring incessantly for Wing-Commander Strickland. A studied normality otherwise. Routine things: breakfast, reading the newspapers, strolling to Flights. Everyone moving in painful slow motion. A studied calm. Quiet shadows, a stillness broken by footsteps as measured as in a cloister.

And yet the excitement could be grasped, held in everybody's hands. Heartbeats quicker than seconds, but everybody heard only their own. Everybody suddenly terribly kind, studiedly thoughtful. Speaking of inconsequential things, now and then only and softly, lest the fragile silence shatter.

And then in the late morning, at last the overture. A symphony for Pratt and Whitney engines from all over the airfield: *pianissimo* on starting, slow and soft, *andante* at two thousand revs as the magneto switches were tested, then a passionate *fortissimo* at full power, a frenzy of three hundred and thirty-six pounding pistons in three hundred and thirty-six cylinders, the high fluting of twenty-four propellers whirring.

"The *Groningen*'s coming out tonight!"

All over the Station, telephones ringing—in Admin, the armoury, Control Tower, cookhouses, Intelligence, even Sick Quarters where Flint was holding his morning parade.

Staccato from Strickland: "Any aircrew sick?"

262

"Three."

"They'd better be fit by tonight!"

Flint would have liked to have said they wouldn't be. He would have liked to have gathered that little trio into the safety of his hands. But they had all shuffled in sheepishly—a cold, a bad sore throat, a cut on the hand—just saying, "Just give me something to keep me going, Doc."

They wouldn't hear of being taken off flying. Why not?

Last-minute crew changes were unlucky, that was one reason. Then they wouldn't want to let their captains down. Not wanting to miss it was another reason. Last and biggest reason was Strickland.

"They say they'll fly, Wing-Commander."

Through the open window beside him came the *krk* of a tractor coming up the slope by Sick Quarters, and looking out Flint saw the trailers it was towing, on each of which were two torpedoes with shiny blue heads.

And five hundred miles away, he thought, in Falstand Fjord there would be the same hectic exhilarating rush to get moving—the *Groningen* refuelled, the guns checked and loaded. They would be making preparations to take away the torpedo nets, the engines would soon be started, the last leave-man checked on board. There would be a flashing of signal lamps between the destroyers, the fighter squadrons at Almo and Malstrom put on readiness, the gunners on the banks of the fjord alerted. Holding his last conference with his officers, Captain Leitzen would be discussing routes, tactics, anti-aircraft firing patterns, studying the minefields, pressing the meteorologists to guarantee for him that the fog and wind would continue before opening up the sealed and secret orders for his patrol.

Would it cross his mind, would his Intelligence tell him that those phantom white Liberators that had shadowed him for months—Mason's A, Carter's B, Irvine's F, Linton's M, Ames' R, Strickland's S—would be waiting?

The tractor disappeared round the corner to Dispersal. Flint asked, "What about the weather?"

"I'm speaking from the Met Office now." In the background, Flint could just catch a murmuring of low cloud, sleet, gale-force winds. "It's perfect!"

The receiver clicked back in its cradle. Crews OK, weather

263

OK, load OK, Intelligence reports coming smoothly from Group, Air Vice-Marshal Nuttall delighted.

One by one, Strickland was ticking the items off as though on some gigantic check-list. As he left Met and walked across to Squadron Headquarters, he sent his eyes over to the six Liberators, Pratt and Whitneys still blaring, watched the propellers slow down and stop in turn as each one was shut down.

Briefing would be at 1700 hours—that had to be announced. That would give time for the crews to make a last check of everything. Then they would sit in their aircraft until Intelligence confirmation that the *Groningen* had left her berth and was proceeding up Falstand Fjord towards the open sea.

On the gravel path by the door of the crew room, he was met by the Maintenance Flight Sergeant accompanied by the rigger and fitter of F Freddie.

"Hello, Chiefie—" He nodded to the airmen. "Race . . . Heaton."

"Morning, sir."

"Everything top line?"

"Everything, sir—" The Flight Sergeant hesitated. "Except F."

"What's the matter with F?"

"Well, sir, Mr Irvine's been having trouble with Number Four."

"What sort of trouble?"

"Mag drops, sir."

"That's nothing!"

"Sir, it's three hundred."

"Plugs."

"No, sir. The magneto. We're getting a complete cut-out now on number one switch. And the other's shaky. Engine's giving nowhere near full power."

"Why wasn't this discovered earlier?"

"We knew there was trouble, sir. We put an indent into Stores two days ago. No magnetos. No hope of magnetos. We were keeping our fingers crossed but now—"

"Fingers in more like!"

It was unlike Strickland to roar but he did this time. "If we're going to sink the *Groningen*, we need all six aircraft!"

264

"I realize that, sir."

"I promised Air Vice-Marshal Nuttall a full turn out!"

"Five's the most we can do, sir."

"*Six*, Flight."

"No, sir, I'm sorry, but—"

"Can't you patch it up?"

"Not a hope."

"Can't you try?"

"It's gone, sir. *Gone*."

"Then get another magneto."

"From where, sir?"

"From Stores."

"Sir, for two days we've been trying but—"

"I'll get one myself!" His voice had risen. "I'll go over to Stores myself!"

Five minutes later he was in a face-to-face confrontation with Wilkinson in his office.

"We've done all we can, sir."

Wilkinson regarded the Wing-Commander warily. In his time he had seen many commanding officers beating their breasts complaining about the inefficiency of Stores and the impossibility of getting replacements. But Strickland was different. Strickland normally took things coldly, inscrutably, showing no feelings.

"I have enough to do planning this attack, organizing it, flying in it. All you have to do is get your fingers out. Get the spares. Keep the aircraft serviceable. It's not much to ask. A magneto. Something all Stores should have loads of."

"Not just a magneto, Wing-Commander," said Wilkinson. "An *American* magneto."

"So what's so different about an American magneto? We are given American aircraft to fly. It's your job to see we get the spares to back them up. But do we? Do we hell!"

"We've done our best."

"And *what* have you done?"

"We've rung every MU in the country. We've tried Group and even Maintenance Command."

"And you can't even get a magneto!"

"We've tried everywhere."

"Have you tried the Americans?" He looked from one to the

other of them. "The Americans at Machrannoch? Well, *have* you?" He looked at them both. "No. I can see you haven't."

"I did," said Assistant Section Officer Jones.

"Who did you ring?"

"Lieutenant Greaves."

"And he said he hadn't got one?" And when the girl nodded her head, "And who can bloody blame him?"

"Assistant Section Officer Jones did very well, sir," put in Wilkinson.

"All she had to do was look nice and pretty and co-operative. Look at that shambles with the WAAFs!"

"That wasn't her fault."

"And what about repaying the spares?"

"We've said we'll return them as soon as we can."

"They're stock-taking," Assistant Section Officer Jones said.

"That's their polite way of saying no more!"

"Sir, can't you wait?"

Even before he had the words out of his mouth, Wilkinson realized they were a mistake.

Strickland blazed back at him, "Wait? *Wait?* This is the last chance we'll get . . . and you say wait! Seven trained crews in seven Liberators were going to do this job. Then we lose K. Now you're suggesting we cancel!"

"Sir—"

"Or go without F."

"I can understand your disappointment, sir."

"F goes! Make no mistake about that!"

He glared at the pair of them. "So what are you going to do about it?"

There was a silence. Then the girl said, "I'll telephone Lieutenant Greaves again."

"No, you don't!" He strode over to the desk. "You'd balls it up. I'll phone myself." He picked up the receiver. "Get me Machrannoch! All lines engaged? Then break in on one! Top priority. I want the Commanding Officer . . . Captain McCleary! Now! Immediately!"

"There's some difficulty getting you off tonight."

"So I've heard."

Irvine looked up from stirring his coffee into the eyes of

266

Wing-Commander Strickland. The eyes were still the same bland grey, the manner was still insouciant, almost throw-away, the white high-necked sweater was just as immaculate, but the voice was higher, louder and harder.

He hates me, Irvine thought. But not half as much as I hate him.

Around them as they stood to one side of the ante-room, the normal after-lunch somnolence had spread. Emma Jones sitting in her usual place on the sofa with Doc Flint beside her reading *The Times*. Same Wednesday mince and rice pudding on the menu. No one could have possibly perceived the under-currents. No one would have guessed at tonight's Maximum Effort.

"Bit of a jinx, eh?"

"Jinx?"

"When it comes to the *Groningen*, everything you touch goes wrong."

"I've reported F's mag drop on my last three trips."

"Always you, Irvine. *You*."

"I wouldn't say that."

Strickland shrugged his shoulders. "Everybody else does. You come back with a petrol leak. You attack an iceberg. Then you're actually given the *Groningen* on a plate. Not only don't you even try to attack, you manage to lose her!"

"The radar—"

"Then Christ Almighty, you lose poor old Mosco!"

"It wasn't my good idea to use parachute-bombs."

"Can't even manage to deposit his ashes safely back on the land of his fathers. Then there's a real how d'you do when you take the WAAFs over to Machrannoch that must have done the Yanks' party and our reputation a hell of a lot of no good." Strickland drained his cup and put it back in the saucer. "Born loser, Irvine . . . that's you!"

Hate does wonderful things, Irvine thought. It stirs the blood, tenses your muscles, brings you to the sticking point. Normally before a trip I wouldn't have been able to manage much of that fatty mince and none of that damned rice pudding—but today I had two helpings. Normally I'd have been watching the rain on the window and listening to the wind. My mouth would have been a bit sticky and I'd have been aching for a smoke.

Strickland put down his cup on the table beside Emma Jones. "I should have realized. Others did. There was a lot of fuss over giving you a command. But I trusted you." He gave a slight shrug. "And you let me down."

"I let no one down."

"On tonight's trip, I nearly fielded a relief crew. Carruthers or Drake. Then I thought I'd give you one last chance . . . if that's possible."

"Kind of you."

"Besides, you've done all your training." He ran his cold grey eyes over Irvine's face. "You don't seem particuarly upset about F being unserviceable."

"What's the point?"

"Even rather glad."

"Glad?" His crew had been glad. The *Groningen* burned no holes in their hearts. But he had been aware only of an acute disappointment, a furious resentment that he had already unloaded on Maintenance. Knowing then what Strickland would say, ever since this morning he had been almost in a panic to go. "Glad?" Irvine repeated. "I told Flight I'd take her . . . duff magneto and all. I told him I'd—"

"I really do believe, Peter," Strickland drew his top lip into his mouth and sucked it appreciatively, "that I've managed to inject some fighting spirit into you at last!" He lifted up his head and smiled. "So you'll be glad to know that you won't be missing the trip after all."

He appeared to be studying Irvine's face for dismay. The smile of pure pleasure seemed rather to disconcert him.

"Good!"

"I managed to fix it. Equipment here are bloody useless."

Out of the corner of his left eye, Irvine was aware of a bright red flush spreading over Emma's face. He opened his mouth to say something, but Strickland was already in full spate. "I rang Machrannoch myself. Went to the top. Spoke to the Captain. He's diverting a training flight and dropping a magneto this afternoon."

"Good," said Irvine again.

"Decent of the Yanks, considering. Well," Strickland looked at his watch. "*Tempus fugit.*" He was smiling now, perhaps

268

because his plan was proceeding one hundred per cent after all. Every little detail correct and organized. A Maximum Effort. "See you at Briefing." He began to walk briskly over to have a word with Ames and Mason, throwing over his shoulder his final benediction, "And don't be late!"

As Strickland moved away, Irvine was aware of Emma's furious face looking at him, but he pretended not to see. As though suddenly galvanized into action, he strode through the open glass ante-room doors, down the corridor into the cloakroom for his coat and hat, and then went out onto the steps of the main entrance.

It had begun to sleet, that cold, hard variety that stings like nettles against the face, but Irvine felt nothing. He was exhilarated by his hate of Strickland. He was uplifted by the thought that he would soon be airborne, that he would be flying against the *Groningen*, that it would be he—not Ames, not Mason, not even Strickland—who put his torpedoes into her side. The weather meant nothing. The mountains meant nothing. The *Groningen*'s guns meant nothing. All he had on his mind was to crucify Strickland on his own flying performance in F. He would show the bastard . . .

His crew received the news that they would be going after all at first with dismay, then with a resigned stoicism. He kept them at it all afternoon, getting the turrets greased, the long lines of .5 ammunition running smoothly over their runways, the guns checked, the wireless and the radar meticulously inspected. Garth laid out his Mercator chart, plotted the track to Falstand, actually began filling in the preliminaries of his log.

Burning with determination that nothing should go wrong, Irvine actually supervised everything. At five past four he and Henty went off to have a look at the latest weather charts in the Met Office and then spent the rest of the time before Briefing genning up on the latest reports in Intelligence.

Aircrew began pouring into Operations at ten to five. On the stroke of the hour, Strickland rose to address them.

"Gentlemen . . ."

Fifty-three young men sat in front of him, all in blue battle-dress, whistles incongruously hanging from a hook on their collars. Fifty-three pairs of vari-coloured eyes looked at the scale model of Falstand Fjord and all the photographs of the

269

Groningen, her crew, her captain, arranged around the Operations Room.

"... I don't really have to tell you anything. You've practised what we're now going to do to the *Groningen* till you can do it in your sleep. According to the Norwegian Resistance, she slips her moorings at 1909 hours, that's in just over two hours. Set your watches, please." He looked down at his own. "1705 exactly . . . *now!*"

The shuffling as the exercise was completed died down.

"Everyone will wait in their aircraft till we get the radio message from Norway that the *Groningen* is definitely on her way. Her speed in the fjord will be twelve knots. It will take us two hours and fifty minutes to reach the Norwegian coast. By that time she will be in the widest part of Falstand Fjord, her look-outs peering out into heavy rain and getting their oilskins drenched. They won't be expecting seagulls, let alone 507's torpedoes."

He nodded to the Met Officer, who indicated the tight concentric rings of isobars round the coast of Norway, spoke of low cloud and gale-force southerly winds.

"Except in the fjord itself, which is protected by the mountains."

Brackenbury was next on the stand, pointing at Stavanger airfield with the tip of a billiard cue. "I don't have to tell you that Jagdgeschwader 112 and Jagdgeschwader 105 . . . Me 110 night-fighters . . . are stationed here. They shouldn't trouble you. By the time they know you're in the fjord, you'll be away. All the same, keep on the deck coming home and tell your crews to keep their eyes skinned. Some of the guns around Falstand Fjord are actually up on the mountains. But with luck the weather will be so bad they won't be able to see you."

"They'll see our Leigh Lights."

"Which will only be on when you're actually on the attack. If they fire then, with luck they'll hit the *Groningen*."

The Armament Officer next—dapper little man with a handlebar moustache. "Your load is four torpedoes, except of course for S"— he looked reverently towards Strickland —"which carries the two 57 millimetres firing forty six-pounder shrapnel anti-personnel shells a minute through the nose and six rockets on each wing. The Wingco is now satisfied with the trials, and he is going in first to blast the flak to Kingdom Come!"

The whole atmosphere was like a relaxed conversation, jolly round the bar, a necessary preliminary to the sing-song afterwards. The Navigation Officer could always be relied on to sail close to the wind with a couple of dirty jokes, and even the Signals Officer—usually such a serious bod—managed tonight actually to raise a smile on the issue of call signs and frequencies.

But it was Strickland who raised the biggest laugh when he came back on the platform again to give them a final run-through and said, "Maximum effort tonight, chaps. Every serviceable aircraft on the squadron flying. We've even managed—" he paused just that right amount—his timing was always superb, "to get Peter Irvine airborne."

I hate him, Irvine thought, listening to the roar of laughter. Christ, how I hate him! For giving me the image. For keeping it up with lies and innuendo. The squadron kick-it, Peter Pan, the boy who didn't want to grow up. Blaming me for everything, the losses, the lack of success, for the fact that the *Groningen* is still afloat, for petrol leaks, for the fiasco with the WAAFs, even now for F's unserviceable magneto.

He stared at the man standing there on the dais above them.

"I'll taxi out first in S . . . Radio silence . . . nothing on the R/T please, we know the Germans are listening. A green rocket from the Control Tower will tell us that the *Groningen*'s on her way. Each aircraft will follow me and join the procession in this order. F"— momentarily his eyes caught Irvine's stare, then shifted away —"B, A, R and M." He paused. "Any questions so far?"

"Take-off clearance?" Linton asked.

"Green Aldis from Control at one-minute intervals. Once airborne, circle the field as usual till everyone's up. Yes, I know the weather's bloody, but you'll be quite safe flying clockwise at five hundred feet with navigation, ident and landing lights full on."

"All lit up like Christmas trees," Carter put in.

"Why not the Leigh Light, too?" asked Ames.

"Why not indeed?" said Strickland. "And now, gentlemen, to the serious business. Once we're all up, we set course for Falstand in the same order we took off, lights still on. All each of you has to do is to follow the man just in front. In case you lose his lights, you can pick him up again on your radar."

"What height?"

"Five hundred feet . . . going down to fifty on the radio altimeter thirty miles from the fjord entrance."

"Lights still on?"

"Downward idents only then. Switch off everything else five miles from the coast." He ran his fingers through his hair and smiled. "Don't worry . . . in that weather they'll never see us."

"I'm not worrying about *them*," Ames said. "I'm worrying about Linton just behind me."

"No need to, boy!" Linton promised. "I'll keep my beady eye on you!"

"Once we're in the fjord, everything will be easy. The Norwegian underground will have a light every mile along both banks shining upwards. I will take the south bank followed by A and B. Irvine will take the north bank followed by M and R."

Someone started humming. *I'll take the high road and you take the low road. And I'll be in heaven before you*, sang someone else, but very softly.

"All lights off then. Listen out on the R/T. As soon as I've got the *Groningen* on the radar, I'll tell you. I'll give you a running commentary of exactly what I'm doing and call you up each in turn to do your stuff. I'll make my run in from the south bank against her port side. I'll put my Leigh Light on at three miles and open fire with the 57 millimetres, followed by the rockets. That should draw their fire away from A and B dropping their torpedoes behind me. Meanwhile F, M and R will be attacking from the north bank against the *Groningen*'s starboard side. Everyone must wear their dark goggles against searchlight glare. As soon as you've dropped your fish, F, M and R will do a steep turn to starboard. A and B will also do a steep turn to starboard. That'll keep you nicely out of each other's way and you can scarper home independently back to the bar."

"What about you, sir?"

"Oh I'll just hang around for a few minutes watching the fun. Then I'll be joining you."

He stopped. He looked down at them. He smiled that

curiously winning smile of complete confidence. He gave no stirring speeches, no I-know-I-can-rely-on-yous.

"Just another job of work," he said, the understatement exactly fitting their mood. "Just another sinking. What we're paid to do."

"Not enough!" called Carter.

"But we'll have the *hell* of a party. And this time, Ken, the drinks are on me!"

They began to leave then, the Navigators picking up the colour of the day cartridges to stuff in their green canvas bags, the Radio Officers writing down the frequencies, before stamping down the corridor to the waiting ten-ton lorries, their hooded headlights blurred by mist.

Now it was bucketing down—rain, sleet, the lot. But Irvine was conscious of none of it. His mind was already in Falstand Fjord. Cold it might be outside, but he was warm. He saw himself making his run-up, seconds behind Strickland. He heard the bomb-doors open, saw the *Groningen*—the sharp bows, the cruiser stern—brilliant under the Leigh Light, felt the Liberator lighter as he dropped the torpedoes, heard the Rear Gunner's shout of triumph . . .

"We're here, sir," said Miggs.

The ten-tonner had stopped beside the white flanks of F and the first thing Irvine saw through the mist and the rain were the cowlings still off Number Four.

He yelled to Heaton and Race in their oilskins sheltering under the wing. "What the hell's the matter *now*? Haven't you got that damned magneto on *yet*?"

"We haven't got it yet to put on, sir."

"Haven't got it? *Haven't got it?*" An icy waterfall had started running down his neck under his collar and down his back. Cold reality cracked his warm dream. "One was brought over from Machrannoch."

"When, sir?"

"When? *When?*" he shouted at them, the louder for not knowing the answer. "It was all arranged! Wing-Commander Strickland arranged it!" That vision of Falstand Fjord had been completely replaced by Strickland's face and his cold grey eyes. "The magneto? Where is it?"

"Search us."

273

"What about Stores?"

"Chiefie's been trying Stores. No magneto in Stores."

"But a magneto can't just vanish!"

"Did it ever arrive, sir?"

"Arrive? That B-24—"

"What B-24?"

"The B-24 from Machrannoch."

"We never saw no B-24, sir. When did you see the B-24?"

"Me?" He had seen no B-24 either, but he had had other things to do. Other things on his mind. It was not his job, maintenance. "Your job," he shouted. "It's your bloody job to keep this aeroplane serviceable!"

Irvine was aware even as he yelled and swore at them that he was committing the unforgiveable sin in dealing with RAF groundcrew. They would work their fingers to the bone in all hours and in all weathers. But you had to show that such selflessness was appreciated. You must never ever rail against them, because you would invariably find that it wasn't their fault, and you'd find yourself in the undignified position for an officer of having to apologize.

"Bloody Maintenance!" Irvine shouted at Strickland's face caught in a cartoonist's balloon perpetually in front of his eyes. "Bloody Stores! Christ, what a bloody cock-up!"

The lorry had already lurched off into the night. Leaving his crew to get settled in the aircraft, he walked to the Dispersal Hut, mud sucking at his flying boots.

"Chiefie," he roared at that harassed individual through a fug of coke fumes. "F's magneto! What the bloody hell's been happening?"

The Flight Sergeant didn't know. That was exactly what he'd been trying to discover for the last hour, at the same time having to cope with getting five other Liberators serviceable in weather fit to drown a pig.

Irvine strode across to the table and picked up the receiver.

Yes, Flying Control had clocked in the B-24. Landed 15.39, took off 16.12. The Controller hadn't been on duty then. He knew nothing at all about a magneto. Certainly one had not been left in the Tower.

Irvine tried Stores. Only a corporal on duty. He knew nothing about a magneto. He tried the Mess. No Wilkinson.

No Equipment Officer. No Duty Officer. No Squadron-Leader Maintenance. But he managed to get the Duty Commander— the Group-Captain himself.

"All I can say is we've got to find that magneto. No, of course take-off can't be postponed! The show must go on. Of course it must. And to the split second!"

It was all like some extraordinary mystery story. The phantom B-24 that nobody saw. Or did they? Was it camouflaged in the fog? Was it a ghost already? Find the murderer before you yourself get murdered. A riddle to solve or off with your head!

"How long will it take to fit, Flight?"

"Once we've got it . . . an hour, sir."

Irvine looked at his watch. 17.39 already. If things went according to plan and the *Groningen* left at the expected time, he had an hour and a half before take off.

Half an hour to get the magneto.

He dashed out into the rain. There was a van outside and he took it. The rain was beginning to thin now, just as Met had said, but he didn't notice it. He drove furiously, his foot hard down on the accelerator, up to Stores—it *must* be in Stores, he had already worked that one out, because the B-24 wouldn't have come without it and the forms procedure would all have to be filled in—yes, even in an operational emergency!—and they'd have got all tied up with paperwork and the bloody inefficient Stores Officer.

Outside, he braked, switched off, got out and dashed to the doors and opened them.

An SP's voice, disembodied in the darkness, called out, "Mind that blackout!"

"Christ!" he yelled at an astonished Stores corporal as he slammed the doors behind him. "*Christ!*" And then, "That magneto the Yanks brought in two hours ago. Give it to me!"

The stores corporal only became even more astonished. Magneto? Yanks? Two hours ago? Well, two hours ago he was having his char in the airmen's dining room—

"It's here!" He brushed the Corporal aside, made for the dark caverns behind the offices. "It's got to be here!"

He switched on the light. Rows and rows of shelves: battle-dresses, that gluey anti-gas clothing that smelled like Japanese lanterns, WAAF caps, grey issue blankets, groundsheets.

275

He raced past the lot of them, turning to the left. Furniture: chairs, tables, rugs. Sandbag cases now, a row of grey-white tombstones, coffins. Crockery: cups, saucers, plates, brown tin tea-pots.

He dashed towards the gloom at the far end. Phosphorescent numbers and needles glistened like fireflies in the darkness. Aircraft instruments—this was more like it!

"Where's the light switch down here, Corporal?"

"Here, sir."

Light flooded over cylinders, brake drums, hydraulic fluid, mainwheel tyres, wiring.

"You're right, sir. A magneto did come in. I've been studying the paperwork."

"Then where is it now?"

He pushed aside plugs, valves, bulbs. Nothing, no sign!

"I don't know, sir."

"Surely there's some order in this chaos?"

"These are the shelves for ignition spares, sir. *Should* be here."

"Can you see it?"

"No, sir."

"Surely they wouldn't just shove it on the shelves?"

"Why not, sir?"

"*Why not?*" Irvine almost doubled up with fury and frustration. "Because my aeroplane is unserviceable! The Yanks flew in a magneto specially. I'm taking off on a most important operation in," he looked at his watch, "Christ, in fifty minutes!"

"The Assistant Section Officer might not have known where to put it." The conspiratorial grin said *you-know-what-women-are*.

Irvine's right arm suddenly stopped in the act of reaching up to the top shelf. "Assistant Section Officer?"

"Assistant Section Officer Jones, sir. She signed the incoming indent."

"Incoming indent?"

"For the magneto, sir. You were quite right. From the American Navy at Machrannoch." He gave a hollow laugh to show he'd heard it all before. "On loan."

"But she knew it was wanted immediately for my aircraft!"

"Did she, sir?" The corporal shook his head. "Tck-tck-tck!"

"So why didn't she give it to Maintenance?"

"Tck-tck-tck!" There is nothing nicer for a corporal to hear than that an officer has done wrong, especially a female officer. "Naughty!"

"Flights have been ringing Stores for *hours*!"

"It does seem, sir, that wires became crossed."

"Wires crossed, hell! Finger trouble."

"Assistant Section Officer Jones is young, sir," purred the corporal. "New, inexperienced . . ."

"Give me your bloody phone," Irvine cut his catalogue short. He grabbed the instrument as it was slid across the counter to him and asked for the Officers' Mess.

To the Mess clerk who answered him, he said tersely, "Assistant Section Officer Jones. Tannoy for her again, will you. See if she's surfaced yet."

"Most likely gone into Kilcreggan on the Liberty bus, sir," the corporal suggested, as fruitlessly in the earpiece echoed the Tannoy from the Mess, "Assistant Section Officer Jones, phone call corridor." On and on it went like some blasted R/T call, obviously no one answering.

Impatiently he slammed the receiver down. A thought had just struck him. A crazy irrational thought. Never would he have conceived of it with a man. But with a woman you never quite knew.

"Where's the office, corporal?"

"Up the ramp, sir. Turn left. Second door from the end. But I've buzzed her. No joy. They've all gone . . ."

But Irvine was already springing up the concrete ramp. Turning left he ran down the corridor. He found the green painted door. No rim of light edged it. The corporal was right. She'd gone. He threw the door open without knocking and felt for the switch.

As it clicked on, he heard a faint indrawn breath. Quite what he had expected to see he didn't know. But certainly not Emma herself, sitting behind the big square desk. What he *had* hoped to find was there, though. On the desk in front of her reposed the magneto. She was staring at it as if it were a cobra. While, as if caught in the act of summoning aid, her right hand rested uncertainly on the receiver of the telephone.

"Emma!" he shouted. "What the bloody hell? I've been looking all over . . ."

"Peter, I didn't know what . . ." she looked at him, licked her lips, then shrugged as if giving up some impossible task of explanation ". . . to do." She finished lamely.

"Didn't know what to do? Christ! You stupid girl! Didn't know what to do with it? Send it round to Flights, of course." He reached forward and lifted the magneto in both his hands, cradling it. "Don't they teach you bloody anything?"

He turned towards the door.

"I didn't mean that," she said.

"I've raised bloody Cain looking everywhere for this damned magneto. And all the time, you . . ."

He broke off at the sight of her face. Its nakedness unnerved him. It was as if he could see it all. The workings of her mind, her fears, her absurd desire to protect him, with awful indecent clarity. The sight shocked him, as if he had been staring at the innermost complexities of her secret female being.

Furiously, he tucked the magneto under his left arm and wrenched open the door. He avoided her eyes.

"I'm sorry," she said.

"So you should be." He let the door slam shut. Out in the corridor sweating with anger and outrage he was suddenly ashamed of having left her like that. If he'd got time, he'd have gone back.

But time was just what he hadn't got.

The forlorn white shape of F Freddie emerged out of the wet night. The groundcrew were still sheltering under the starboard wing.

He pushed the magneto into their hands. He could not waste time on any explanation.

"And now get cracking!"

They worked by the light of torches. From the second pilot's position, Henty directed the beam of the Aldis lamp on Number Four till they told him to stop. Then the Flight Sergeant came round to help. So did the Station Engineering Officer. The starboard wing was swarming with bodies.

Already strapped in, Irvine sat in his seat, fidgeting with the gyro knob, the throttle nut, the lights, the VHF. F was still connected to the trolley acc and the motor could be heard puttering away together with swearing from the wing and the soft sound of rain on the windscreen.

"Christ!" Irvine looked at his watch. "Five to!" Leaning across his second pilot he shouted to the men on the wing, "Isn't it ready *yet*?"

Out of the darkness, an anonymous voice shouted back, "Give us a chance!"

"Soon be all right, Skipper," Miggs whispered to him soothingly from the radio. "Be ready in two flicks of a cow's tail."

Through the rain, he could just make out the white smudges of the other Liberators. Nearest him was Mason's A, then Rory Ames' R. Furthest away, up the slight rise, was Strickland's S.

"Seven minutes past." He muttered it to himself, he said it to Henty, he yelled it at the men on the wing.

"We're being as fast as we can!"

"Hurry up! Get a move on *please*!"

"We're doing our damnedest!"

"I'll miss take-off if you're not careful!"

Holding his breath, he watched the sweep second hand go round and round the electric clock on the instrument panel.

"Nineteen ten, Skipper," Henty said. "The *Groningen*'ll have left."

"We've 'ad it," said Craik from behind his seat.

An expectant hush had descended over the airfield, electric and waiting. "There'll be a delay," Irvine was saying, "there always is," when suddenly the blackness was shot through with a green flash, and seconds later from over the rise came the sound of starting engines.

"We've 'ad it," said Craik again. "Our cowlings are still off. We'll never make it now."

"They're starting up!" Irvine yelled at the men on the wing out of the second pilot's window.

"We can hear."

Now there was a chorus roaring heavenwards. Lights came sparking up, little red and green pimples of navigation lights, the white of identification lights.

And now from over the rise came a long pencil of a landing

light moving slowly down from Dispersal to the perimeter track—Strickland in S.

"They're moving!" Irvine yelled through the window.

"We can see."

Hypnotized, Irvine watched the slow progression of that leading Liberator. Others were following now, leisurely nodding their noses, brakes squealing, on the way to Runway 09.

S got larger. Irvine could actually see Strickland's face through the open side window. The Wing-Commander had the instrument lights turned up so there was a greenish tinge on his skin.

Twenty yards away from F, he slowed and stopped. He put his head right out and above the sound of the throttled-back engines, he shouted, "Irvine! What the hell's the matter *now*?"

"The magneto. They're fixing it! Won't be long!"

"True to form right till the last, eh?"

"We'll catch you up! We'll be there!"

"Don't hurry!" That slow sardonic drawl came loud and clear through the hissing rain. "We'll do better without you!"

Slowly S began moving again. And, behind Strickland, the others were following in procession one after the other just as the Wing-Commander had ordered—Carter's B, Mason's A, Ames' R, and Linton's M. They had simply closed their ranks, Carter's B filling up the vacant position behind Strickland that F had left.

"When will you be ready?" he shouted at the men on the wing.

"Not long now."

They would be taking off in a moment. S was poised in the centre of the runway—four whirring propellers turned into four rainbow-filled bubbles under the glitter of the landing lights.

Irvine heard the roar. He watched the Liberator moving, shaking on her oleo legs, pounding on and on till the very end of the runway, till the wheels lifted and she was airborne.

One by one, he watched the other four go, climb up, join Strickland in the sky, make one circuit of Kilcreggan and then one behind the other fly off eastwards into the night.

"They've gone!" he called out to the men on the wing.

"We're just putting the cowlings back now."

A hush had descended on the field. The sweep second hand of the electric clock went round and round. Irvine kept shifting in his seat, moving his body against the encircling straps, every now and then calling out to Heaton and Race on the starboard wing.

At last! "Cowlings back on again!"

But then there was a run up—the Engineeering Officer insisted on that. When finally Irvine got the 700* signed and all four engines were running, Irvine did not wait for a green. At breakneck speed he taxied round the perimeter track, doing the Before Take-off check as he went, never pausing at the head of the runway but simply opening up to full power.

Finally airborne, he made no circuit but simply carried on eastwards with the engines at almost full power.

When Craik objected, pointing to the engine temperatures which were all in the red on the gauges, Irvine said grimly, "I don't give a damn if they go off the clock! We've *got* to catch the others up!"

* Maintenance Log.

NINETEEN

THE Liberator rattled like a goods train. From the rear turret, Connally reported exhaust flames like streamers and, looking through his open side window, Irvine could actually see the cylinder heads glowing like red-hot coals.

The engines were running rough, too—the propellers continually going out of phase. Every now and again there was a hiccup like a missed heartbeat, and Craik, practically prostrate in front of the throttle box, would beg for a reduction of power.

"No."

"But sir, they'll seize!"

"We're doing 165 knots. That'll cool them."

Cold rushing air round their fins—and Christ, it *was* cold, Irvine thought looking down at the air temperature gauge—would have to do them. Plus the wetness and the wind and his own prayers. Good Pratt, dear Whitney, keep them turning! Engine temperatures, oil pressures, oil temperatures, I know they're well outside limits but don't let it worry them.

The only thing that mattered was that F was going twenty knots faster than the others.

"We're eating petrol," said Henty.

"We'll be nice and light coming home."

His second pilot just shrugged his shoulders, and, since Irvine was clearly so determined, no one else said anything. They sat in their allotted places throughout the aircraft, suffering the continuous vibration and the jolts and jars of the turbulent air in silence.

"Estimate the Norwegian coast . . . twenty-two thirty, Skipper."

"Thank you, Navigator." To give his crew a boost, Irvine added, "We're really moving, chaps!"

The cloud was lifting. Flying at five hundred feet, Irvine could just make out the horizon. Every now and again, there was a spark ahead and Irvine's heart would give a jump, and he would crane forward, sure it was a Lib's light till he saw it was only a star.

Radar reported the coast at ninety miles. There was still no sign of the others. He switched off all his lights except for the ident.

"Can you make out Falstand Fjord?"

"Not yet, Skipper."

He was assailed by doubts on Garth's navigation. "Sure we're on track, John?"

"Sure, Skipper. Just got a Gee fix."

At fifty miles from the coast, he went right down to the sea, every now and then catching sight of the whitecaps below. Still nobody said anything. On the intercom, it had been the quietest trip he could remember.

"I can see the entrance to Falstand Fjord now, Skipper," Miggs reported from the radar.

"Good." He strained forward against his straps, put his forehead flat against the perspex staring ahead. "Can anyone see the others?"

Nobody could.

"Can't be far ahead of us."

There was nothing on the VHF. The attack couldn't have begun yet. A drizzle pockmarked the windscreen: not much, just little beads of water forming themselves into necklaces and sliding down the perspex.

Suddenly from Jarman in the front turret: "I can see the coast, Skipper!"

So could he—a black line darker than the sea beneath them. "Steer to Aalstrom lighthouse, Radar."

"Five degrees port . . . steady . . . that's it!" And seconds later, again from Jarman in the front turret: "Christ, Skipper, did you see the flash?"

"Guns?"

"No, it's the beam. The lighthouse beam. There it is again!"

Hooded, of course, and alight. But specially lit, no doubt, for the *Groningen*'s benefit, last pinpoint before her long trip . . .

where? Purposely Irvine kept away from it, steering well south into the mouth of the fjord.

Still nothing on the VHF. And the fjord was as dark as the inside of a tunnel. If the attack had started, all hell would have been loosed.

Cautiously he edged round to the left, looking for the promised Resistance's lights on the northern shore. He was down on the water now, his attention flickering between the night outside and the radio altimeter, now reading thirty feet.

"Pull up if it goes any lower," he said to Henty.

At least in the fjord it was calmer. Abruptly the wind had dropped.

And then suddenly over the VHF, Strickland's voice coming out, it seemed, of a disembodied nowhere. "Here we are then! Everyone inside the fjord? Able?"

"Mason mobile."

"Baker?"

"Here."

"Mother?"

"Yep."

He went through the roll-call like a schoolmaster.

"Roger?"

"Present."

"And Freddie!" Irvine shouted into his microphone. "I'm just behind you!"

But nobody heard him. He'd be too far away, too low, the fjord curved here and high ground would be in the way. Strickland's voice interrupting anyway, loud and clear and calm. "So far, so good. They haven't spotted us yet. Has everybody got the *Groningen* on their radar?"

Back came four quick affirmatives.

"Seven miles ahead of me now. Exactly where we'd been told. Bloody big blip! Tim and Rory . . . you in position to attack from the north?"

"Yep."

"Affirmative."

"Able and Baker?"

"Just behind you, sir."

"I can see your exhausts."

284

"Fine!"

His side-window was wide open. As always came a soft puttering, like a motor-boat along a river, from a combination of engines and sliced slipstream. The scent of salt-water, too, and a breeze over his hot face. All at once it was as though he was back in the Norfolk marshes that gave out to the sea, chugging through the evening to Great Yarmouth where as a boy he always went for holidays. Down below there a fringe of grey spume, a dark bank—and then suddenly from far ahead the memory dissolved back into reality, pierced by an illuminated spear that was certainly a Leigh Light.

The spear moved. A minute ship glowed white under its rays. Seconds later, the yellow flashes from Sugar's 57 millimetres, followed by streams of red and white tracer from all over the fjord.

"The Wingco going in," Henty said, and, as though to confirm him, over the VHF Strickland's voice, "There she is then! That's woken them up. Christ, but they're being unfriendly! They're not liking the 57 millimetres one little bit!"

Searchlights now from the *Groningen* and the banks of the fjord—flat across the water, swinging horizontally.

"Careful, Jack . . . Ken! Come in just behind me!"

"Following you, sir."

"Don't put your searchlights on till I let my rockets go! M and R?"

"M can see you, sir."

"R has you in sight."

"So has everybody else. Christ, these bloody pom-poms. Rockets gone!" The night was suddenly streaked with scarlet flashes. "That's quietened them down!"

"Carter running up to drop."

"Mason ditto."

Irvine slammed the throttles hard against the stops. Seeing another Resistance light to the right, he kicked the Liberator to starboard. A kind of frenzy had taken hold of him. First the sound, now the sight of the attack had injected a mixture of fury and panic into him. He felt sick with excitement and at the same time in an agony of frustration. He wasn't going to make it! He was going to miss it! He'd be too late! Under his fidgeting fingers, he felt the control column trembling from the vibration

285

of the roaring engines as he pulled it and shook it as though trying to drag F bodily forward.

"Come on, you old cow!" Inside his mouth, his tongue felt big and thick and dry. "Faster! *Faster!*"

Ahead of him, the two lights were getting steadily bigger, the bursts of the gunfire brighter, the dark night now pocked with tracer.

"Tim and Rory . . . go on in from the north now! *Now* while the flak's occupied with Jack and Ken!"

Strickland was standing off, masterminding the whole operation. Sugar's searchlight had gone off, but in its place came the two beams from Able and Baker. But the whole sky now was a criss-cross of searchlights, and the Leigh Lights looked tiny and pitiful, white pin-stripes by comparison.

Ahead now was a red and white rainstorm, spattered with the big orange bursts of the 88 millimetres. A Liberator caught in criss-cross beams, a phosphorescent ghost, coming up from the south bank . . . Able—he could actually see the letter A on her side . . . blotted out by yellow daubs of explosions . . . now burning from nose to tail, a flaming arrow.

"Poor old Mason," Irvine said, swinging away from high ground streaked with snow, flattening out even lower on the water.

"Baker's torpedoes went astern." Strickland's unemotional commentary continued. "Ames . . . Linton . . . it's up to you now!"

"R running up now."

Then Tim Linton's voice: "I'm just behind you, Rory."

The whole of F Freddie was vibrating now—trembling, shaking, juddering, propellers unsynchronized and screaming their heads off.

"We'll make it, sir." Henty trying to be soothing. "Can't be more than a couple of miles away now."

More like six, but Irvine said nothing. He sent Craik to open the bomb-doors and to hold them open on the catwalk to stop them creeping. At least he could get everything ready for the attack. He'd come in as quietly as he could from the north after Linton's M.

On went another Leigh Light like a candle flame—Linton? Ames?—flickered bravely against all those carnival colours, then all at once snuffed out. A bronze bonfire began burning on the water.

Strickland made no mention. Imperturbably, uninterrupted, on went his voice, slowly, quietly. "Up to you now, Rory! Take your time . . ."

F was getting closer now. Every now and then Irvine could see bits of the ship come up out of the darkness behind her gunfire bursts: her two funnels, her bow, the six 5.9 inch guns—they were actually using those now—brought up from behind the bulkheads.

Irvine picked up his microphone, switched it on, was calling out "F Freddie here. I'm—" when suddenly Strickland's voice on the VHF—no longer calm, no longer quiet. "The bastard turned inside you, Rory! Got his bows head on to the torpedo tracks. Inches, they missed by inches!"

And now he could actually see S on the other side of the *Groningen*, her white battle-scarred sides momentarily glimmering as a searchlight slid over her. The same searchlight stopped, came back, started waving—but Sugar had gone.

Henty looked across at Irvine. "They won't get the Wingco! They can't shoot him down!"

As though to confirm it, back came Strickland's voice on the VHF, high and furious, in an agony of frustration and disappointment at no hits on the *Groningen*.

"You won't get away! Christ no, if I have to—"

Into that short pause, Irvine shouted, "F coming up now, three miles west."

Just for a moment, silence. Then Strickland's voice, "Irvine? Irvine . . . that you?"

"Irvine in F Freddie . . . positioning to attack."

"Peter . . . Christ, Peter!" Suddenly he had been presented with a windfall of four more torpedoes. The anger disappeared from his voice. Excitement, hope, confidence now inflamed his words. Quicker certainly, but quieter, calmly, immediately, he rearranged his battle plans.

"Peter . . . we'll do this. I'll come in from the south, put my Leigh Light on at three miles. He'll think I'm another torpedo dropper and turn bow on towards me to minimize his target. You keep on coming in from the west, boy. *Don't* put on your Leigh Light unless you have to. She should be nicely silhouetted for you in the light of mine, placed beautifully beam on to receive your fish. Got that?"

"Roger."

"Straightaway! We do it *straightaway*!"

"Freddie all set."

"Here we go then!"

Irvine only had time to check the crew had been listening on the VHF and were all briefed.

"*Groningen* . . . two miles dead ahead." Miggs from the radar.

"Everybody ready?" he was asking over the intercom when again that white shaft from the black sky penetrated down, fingered the surface of the water, lodged into the ship's superstructure.

"Wingco's Leigh Light," said Jarman from the front turret.

The *Groningen* had been turned half into one of those transparent fish you see in aquariums, half into black shadow. As he adjusted Strickland's torpedo sight up on the windscreen in front of him, Irvine could see she was turning just as Strickland said she would. A vast white feather of waving wake streamed in a burgeoning curve from her stern.

"*Groningen* . . . one and a half miles. Blip's getting bigger and bigger!"

Inside his black cave, Irvine pushed the Liberator lower, brought the throttles back, slowed her down, guided by the tiny little phosphorescent pinpricks of light from the instruments.

"*Groningen* one mile."

She looked huge. Beam on now, all bright green and grey camouflage varnished and shiny under S's Leigh Light, her guns sent a staccato of red and green dots and dashes southwards at Strickland, punctuated by big yellow blots from the 88s on the shore.

"Three-quarters now."

She was filling the torpedo sight beautifully, swelling bigger and bigger every second. Irvine felt the port wing tip drop, straightened it, kept the ship in the centre.

This was the place they usually dropped from. But he could not afford to miss. She was going fast, twenty-five knots he had put as deflection on the torpedo sight.

"Half a mile."

He kicked her round slightly to starboard, aiming ahead of

the bow. They must have heard him now, for the guns came swinging away from S. Long tracks of tracer came pouring towards him.

He still hung on. He hadn't to get too close, that was his worry now. The torpedo driving motor had to start, the gyros come into operation, the weapon had to adjust itself to this sudden new element. Five hundred yards, the Armament Officer had said, was the absolute minimum.

He could see the bow wave now, the upward lift of steel to that sharp cutting edge.

Putting his thumb on the release button on the control column, he pressed.

He felt the Liberator go suddenly lighter, pushed forward the throttles, heard Jarman opening up in the front turret, the ping of shrapnel on the aircraft's skin, smelled the scent of cordite from the bursting shells. Right down on the water he went now, inches away, just in front of the bow, hugging the surface of the fjord, pursued by those lethal green and white fireflies, feeling F judder and shake under the blast of exploding 88 shells, counting all the time one-two-three-four-five. Every second we'll be safer. Ten more seconds, we'll be safe. Five more seconds—

"Peter." Strickland's voice again. "Dead on . . . all four. Running beautifully, they're—"

The night erupted. Suddenly it was like being in the crater of a volcano. Visible all round were the steep walls of the high mountains, streaked with snow and ice.

"Christ, Skipper!" Connally's awestruck voice from the rear turret. "Smithereens . . . she's been blown to bloody smithereens!"

And over the VHF, Strickland's voice, sounding far away, "Good *man* . . ."

Irvine began turning, slowly, carefully. He had lost all rudder control, the pedals were slack and useless. The ailerons were sluggish, not much of them left, and the elevators were worse. Painfully F Freddie edged round to port onto a westerly heading to the mouth of the fjord and home.

"All four, Skipper," Connally said excitedly. "Christ, every fucking one! Can you see her now?"

Only flames. Bright yellow oil flames, streaked with black

289

oily smoke reaching up to the low cloud ceiling. Nothing left above the surface except fire.

Henty leaned over the throttle box towards him. "We did it then."

"Eventually," said Irvine.

"Bloody marvellous, Skipper!" Miggs off the radar and dancing a jig on the flight deck. Garth coming up with a course for home, an unaccustomed smile on his usually grave face. Trembath declaring he'd always known theirs was a lucky crew, and the Australian Jarman growling from the front turret, "Best fucking crew in the business!"

"And now," Curly Craik said, handing in his damp squib as usual, "we've got to get home."

The shadow of that trip of months ago crossed Irvine's mind, so like this one, same place, same ship, same—

"Is everybody all right?"

Everybody was. Irvine could breathe again.

"Check the damage," he said to Craik. And to Miggs, "Report *Groningen* sunk to base on the W/T. And I'll call the Wingco on the VHF."

But there was no reply on the VHF. Nothing on the W/T either. "Both got the bullet . . . and how!" reported Miggs. "Output valve gone. Aerial lead in the set severed. But give me a minute, Skipper . . . and I'll fix 'em."

At least there was no opposition. As delicately as playing with eggshells, Irvine flew F along the north coast of the fjord, following the Resistance lights. Not a gun fired at them. Everywhere seemed stunned into silence. Only there in the centre, as they crept round the corner at Aalstrom lighthouse back into the buffeting winds of the North Sea, was an angry red furnace burning a hole in the blackness behind them.

Garth sent a note up giving the ETA Kilcreggan as 01.22. Craik returned from inspecting the damage. "No port elevator, rudder control wires gone, ailerons mostly shot away. Counted three hundred holes, Skipper, and then gave up."

Irvine looked into the big gob-stopper eyes, expecting to hear the eternal "We've 'ad it!" Instead he actually saw a smile on his Engineer's face and both thumbs held up. "We're doing fine!"

The winds were bad on the return trip, a head component

against them and slewing the Liberator this way and that in heavy turbulence. It was difficult flying, but at least they had all engines turning, the aircraft was light enough and the speed was high.

The human jubilation more than any aerodynamic efficiency kept F Freddie airborne. She ground her way back to Scotland, a little world all on her own—totally cut off, no messages in or out—left wing badly low, oil pressures dropping right down on two engines and oil temperatures off the clock, skidding and sliding in the uneven air till half an hour out, totally unexpectedly, Miggs announced to Irvine that he had replaced the valve and aerial lead on the W/T and he was in touch with Control. So the news that they had sunk the *Groningen* preceded them, and they arrived at Kilcreggan to find a royal welcome and the red carpet waiting.

F's fitter and rigger had already a bucket of yellow dope and had started to paint a sinking ship on her side even before the propellers had stopped turning. The crews of the ambulance and the fire engine that accompanied them down the runway as they landed, finding she required none of their services, gawped at her holes, her crumpled plates and her bent stanchions instead.

No ten-tonner took Irvine down to Operations but the Group-Captain's own car. In Intelligence, the cocoa was all ready. Brackenbury was all smiles and congratulations. Messages hinting broadly at promotion and decorations had been received from Air Vice-Marshal Nuttall and Coastal Command.

Listened to by what appeared to be half the Station, surrounded by his crew, Irvine told the story, the attack, the flak, the crafty tactics of the Wingco.

". . . Jacko went down in A. They got Tim Linton, too. But the others are all right. They'll be here any moment now. Rory Ames in R. Carter in B. And of course the Wingco in S, but he'll be later because as always he'll hang around to the bitter end . . ."

They heard the news of A and M in silence. But two Liberators for the sinking of the *Groningen*, that was still a very small price to pay. No longer would that ship brood over Kilcreggan like the Giant in the fairy story, every so often being fed young men like some primeval maiden tribute. She was gone, her legend of invincibility exploded, reduced to nothing but good for a party.

And a hell of a party at that! It had already started by the time Peter Irvine arrived in the Mess, again driven there by the Group-Captain himself in his car. The bar was crowded. The bar officer (not Garfield, he was on rest) had released his entire stock of the carefully hoarded spirit ration. Whisky flowed—Black Label at that.

"Don't let's hog the lot," Peter Irvine said as everyone shoved glasses of whisky into his hand. "Save some for Rory and Ken and the Wingco! They'll be along soon, and Christ, will they be thirsty!"

High Cockalorum began. Standing right back, running the full length of the room, Irvine vaulted to the top of the struggling packed mass of humanity beneath him, lifted his clenched hands high above his head in the victory sign as Strickland had done, while those round the bar sang and thumped their tankards.

"For God's sake," he said as they thrust another whisky into his hand, "save some for the others! Save some for the Wingco!"

They were all pretty new, that was the trouble. Not one who had been on the Station more than a month. Kids really, all on their first tour. He could hear them talking amongst themselves, talking about the *Groningen*, talking about F Freddie, talking about his crew.

". . . couple of mad Australians . . ."

". . . Wireless Operator called Miggs. Doesn't give a bugger for anything. Real lion . . ."

". . . goes in cool as a cucumber and takes a photograph of the *Groningen* at nought feet. The actual *name*, man! . . ."

". . . can't keep him off ops. Meat and drink to him . . ."

". . . took off half an hour after the others. Caught them up at full bore. Everything off the clock. Engineer didn't give a damn . . ."

". . . you've got to feel sorry for the Jerries when they've got fuckers like Irvine against them . . ."

Thick, grey cigarette smoke filled the room. Behind the bar, the bottles glinted in the lights like sparks of tracer.

"Save the whisky!" Irvine called out. "Remember the others! The Wingco . . ."

He turned to the Signals Officer. "Any news?"

292

"We're still calling them."

"Shot up . . . engine gone . . . slow . . . head-winds," Irvine said. "They'll be along. B and R and S. They'll be along soon."

But there was nothing from them when Crackers, the old Gas Officer, opened the piano, began tickling the ivories, softly began crooning.

". . . the bells of Hell go ting-a-ling-a-ling
For you but not for me . . ."

And then there were more drinks, Irvine was calling out it was his round and everyone was laughing and shouting. The WAAF officers were there, old Mother Beauchamp, the pale-haired Cypher Queen. He saw Emma Jones and went over to her and said, "Well, I'm back all right, you see!"

But was he? Was this the same Peter Irvine? Was Peter Irvine here at all? He listened to her congratulations, saw her eyes bright, bought her a gin and orange, while from the piano in the corner came the old yearning RAF songs.

"No one can raise any of them." The news came from the Group-Captain, holding his drink close to his chest, shaking his head. "Missing."

Missing? Ames, Carter, above all Strickland. Strickland the invincible, the man with the legend, the pilot they couldn't shoot down. It was preposterous, a lie! The truth would out in the end.

There had been so many, these additions were insupportable. Wisby, Guilonard, Maltravers, Vance, Mowbray, Wilkes, Tallack, Jerningham, Price, Dacres, Mason, Linton. Now Ames, Carter—

And Strickland.

Suddenly Irvine realized he was alone. Of all the crews who had been in this bar that night he and Strickland had returned shot up, only he remained. His eyes swept the others—strangers, babies, all looking towards him.

". . . the man who sank the *Groningen* . . ."

Two of them had actually called him "Sir".

There was no one else. He was left holding them here in his hands. Caught! He was caught! Standing over by the window, he felt a cold draught blowing on his face, and turning saw a rent in the blackout, the window open behind it and the north wind blowing in.

293

". . . an airman told me before he died
I do not think the bastard lied . . ."

Irvine shivered. Suddenly he felt as old as Methuselah.

"What does it feel like," Doc Flint beside him now, congratulating him, "to be in Guy Strickland's shoes?"

He looked down at the doctor, not answering. There was no answer to give. There was nothing else to do. Except to jump on a chair and shout, "They're not sending us any more beer!"

"Boo!" they yelled happily back at him.

"They're sending us champagne instead."

"Hurrah!"

"They're stopping bacon and eggs in the Aircrew Mess!"

"Boo!"

"They're giving us steak instead!"

"Hurrah!"

"They're taking away the WAAFs!"

"Boo!"

"They're sending us Windmill chorus-girls instead!"

"Hurrah!"

And from the group round the piano in the corner, softly at first, "Goodnight, ladies! Goodnight, ladies."

Peter Irvine saw Emma Jones still looking at him from over by the bar. As the singing grew louder, he walked over to her and as Strickland had done that night, he bent down and kissed her, while everyone cheered and banged their beer mugs.

"Goodnight, ladies." He sang it himself now, hoping she would understand.

"Goodnight, ladies! Goodnight, ladies! It's time to say goodnight . . ."